Wake up to a Nigh

He lay waiting.

His mother had t

The boogeyman

He was nearly as
opening. He never heard the boogeyman speak – only
felt him as the whirled vortex of disturbed air or a pair
of hands, and he saw him, of course, usually through
squinted eyes. And, yes, he smelled him. The boogeyman stunk.

He tried to lie still, but couldn't help tightening up,
closing his eyes a little harder, pulling the covers
against his chin.

The bed jiggled as a knee brushed the mattress.

Next would come the hands.

They patted his small shoulders and bunched the
covers even tighter against his throat.

He held his breath against the stench of the boogeyman's breath.

Next, the closet door would open.

And the boogeyman would go in and take a nap too.

By the same author

Beastmaker
Beaststalker

JAMES V. SMITH, JR

The Lurker

Grafton Books
A Division of HarperCollins*Publishers*

Grafton Books
A Division of HarperCollins*Publishers*
77–85 Fulham Palace Road,
Hammersmith, London W6 8JB

A Grafton UK Paperback Original 1991
9 8 7 6 5 4 3 2 1

Copyright © James V. Smith, Jr 1988

ISBN 0-586-20903-4

Printed and bound in Great Britain by
Collins, Glasgow

Set in Century Schoolbook

For my darling Lynette.

BOOK I
Harmless Lurkings

1

'Sherman and Darwin, come back here,' Sherman's mother called after them.

They ignored her and kept running, slamming the screen door in her face.

'You smart-ass kids!' she screamed after them. 'Come *back* here!'

They didn't.

'Don't listen to her,' said Darwin. 'She's drunk.'

'Again,' said Sherman. 'I wish she wasn't my mother.'

'Nobody is *my* mother,' Darwin crowed. 'I don't have a mother.'

They ran into the dusk, two fifteen-year-old would-be toughs determined to define their own limits without meddling from adults.

An hour later, though, Darwin wasn't really feeling so tough, certainly not brave. He lay beside Sherman in the cool grass, lay shivering in the dark. He trembled, not from the chill but from fear. His scrotum had drawn up so tightly between his legs, it felt as if somebody were trying to cram a golf ball up a place where there was no hole. He tried to reach down and soften the hard itch of fear but only aggravated the hurt.

The house stood dark, looming before them.

'Sherman,' he said, 'let's not go in. Let's throw a couple rocks at it and run.'

'Quit playing with your nuts.'

'I ain't playing, asswipe, I'm only scratching.'

'You don't scratch a itch like that for half a hour and you don't see if a house is haunted by throwing rocks at it.'

'Dammit, Sherman.'

'We been through this a million times. We're going in.'

'I don't have to, ya know.'

'Then leave, Darwin. I can do it by myself. I ain't a chickenshit, ya know.'

'I ain't a chickenshit, neither.'

'Then get your ass moving.'

'What if the Slime comes back tonight?'

'We kill him.'

'Kill him? Are you frigging nuts?'

'Jeez, listen to you – the guy who's always messing with people's minds . . . sassing my mom and all – and now you can't take it when your little old mind is messed with. I'm kidding, Darwin, now stop whining out your ass.'

'You're a million laughs, Sherman. What if he *does* come back?'

'We run.'

'What if he catches us? All I got is an old rusty pocketknife.'

'Quitcher worryin', willya? You sound like my old lady or something. This ain't even much of a haunted house.'

Sherman was right.

As haunted houses went, this wasn't much of one once they got up close. Even at Halloween. If anything, the yard was more haunted than the house. The tangle began at the fence. Tall grass and weeds seemed to prop up the randomly leaning pickets, weathered gray

10

with remnants of white paint wedged in the splits of the wood grain. By day Sherman had selected a scouting path they would take to the house at night. By no means did he choose the path of least resistance. In fact, Sherman designed it to be an extremely troublesome approach.

'First place, it makes it a challenge,' he told Darwin. 'Second, anybody chasing us would have a hell of a time, while we would be taking a path out we already scouted on the way in.'

'Great,' said Darwin. 'That's just peachy fucking great.'

An hour after sunset, they had walked boldly up to the spot Sherman picked and tugged on two pickets. The nails gave – they'd already been loosened – but the vines woven into the slats clung tenaciously. Finally, they each pivoted their slat away to make a V-shaped opening.

Sherman vanished into the weeds and darkness. Darwin looked around. There in the distance was a streetlight on a utility pole where the development's edge began – where hundreds of kids prowled around in spook suits begging for candy. Back there were relatively clean yards and unhaunted houses. All he had to do was walk away. Sherman might cuss him out, but no harm would come of it. It was all he needed to do. Just walk away.

A hand came out of the darkness and grabbed his crotch.

'ShermAANNNNN,' he hissed at the hand.

'Come *on*, you chickenshit.'

Darwin felt a swatch of his hair catch in a sliver of the fence as he bent into the fuzzy gloom and musty stench of the yard.

They crawled.

They had detoured around a trash pile and negoti-
ated a thorny hedge at a natural hole in the spiny
foliage. They had to stop and pick stinging nettles from
their pants and palms. The whole idea of a haunted
house had lost its spooky aura by the time Darwin lay
soaked and itching in the unkempt grass ten yards
from the place. From there it looked like any other
abandoned two-story farmhouse.

Clapboard siding hung off in a couple of places. One
window before them had a broken pane with the paper
cover from a school tablet taped over it. In the dimmest
of light from the moon, Darwin could barely make out
the outline of the Indian chief hung upside down over
the hole.

They lay for a long time in the grass, not speaking.
Darwin grew a little more confident. He even smiled
to himself. This delay could mean Sherman was
searching for a way to back out while saving face. But
as he drew breath to make that very suggestion,
Sherman stood up and padded through the grass to the
house. He pressed his back against the wall and
waited. Darwin craned his neck back as far as it would
go and looked up toward the second floor.

Nothing. He couldn't see a thing. Damn. He lowered
his head, closed his eyes, and pressed his forehead into
the grass to relieve a neck cramp. The grass felt cold.
A chill gripped his body and shook him. He clutched
two fistfuls of grass and clung to them, unable to make
himself go on. He could stay there, he knew, until the
sun came up. Or he could just stand up and go to the
front walk and leave the yard. That would be the end
of this nightmare in his imagination. Even if Slime, or
whatever his name was, were to come, he could say
they were selling candy bars for the band or collecting
them for Halloween or some dumb thing. He knew,

12

just *knew*, nothing could be as bad as going into that house.

What in the hell Sherman even wanted to go in there for, he couldn't even remember. It wasn't to steal. Criminy sakes, they wouldn't go to the biggest, dumpiest house for miles to steal, would they? What was his reason again? The reason they were here?

Some kind of bug with prickly feet walked across his arm.

And seconds later Darwin stood beside Sherman.

'Who *is* this Slime guy, anyhow?' he whined.

In his ghost-story whisper, Sherman said, 'He's the guy the cops are looking for. I seen them talking on TV. I bet he's the one been creeping around people's houses and stealing kids.'

'What? You're lying, Sherman.'

'And then he eats them,' growled Sherman. His eyes lit up in the moonlight.

Darwin was frozen.

Sherman laughed under his breath to let him know it was just a joke. 'You're such a brave back-sasser to my mom during the day, but when the sun goes down, you get chicken awful fast.'

Darwin cursed him again.

Then, backs against the wall, they looked left, right, and up toward the second floor. Sherman, as usual, decided they would find a way inside. Darwin, as usual, regretted he never had the balls to say no to Sherman.

The window with the broken pane wouldn't budge, even with both of them crouching and shoving upward, even after Sherman pushed his hand through the paper and made sure the brass turtle latch was undone.

Sherman studied the thick coats of paint. He saw

13

that the enamel had chipped and blistered off the frame but not from the sliding track.

'Been glued shut,' he announced.

Two more windows on the side. They tried them with the same result. Sherman was devastated by the predicament. It cheered Darwin. He began to breathe normally. Maybe they could just leave after all.

Then, in back, Sherman found the basement window.

It was a storm window held in place with rusted, bent nails. Sherman worked them back and forth with his fingers as if turning an ignition key. On and off. On and off. One by one the nails came out. He peeled the window away and found nothing behind it. The original pane was gone. Nothing remained but a rectangular passage into blackness.

Sherman leaned down and recoiled.

Darwin whined and would have bolted, but Sherman grabbed his shirt front and pushed him toward the blackness.

Before he got close, Darwin smelled it. Like a dead animal beside the road puffed up to twice its size came the odor. It was as if the smell were full of pins, so much did it sting his nostrils. He snuffed like a dog sneezing and leaped to his feet.

'Fuck this,' he blurted.

He no longer bothered to whisper.

Sherman stood up beside him and held him.

Darwin knew it was time to call it quits, chickenshit or no. He'd be glad to argue about it later – in the daylight.

Sherman put his palms on his chest and patted him gently.

'Okay, Darwin,' he said. 'You asshole. I'll go in alone. You stand guard out here. Asshole.'

He stepped around the corner and returned an eternity later with an eight-foot board from the woodpile out front.

He fed the board into the darkness until only a foot of it stuck out. Then he eased one leg into the hole and inched his way down, his body disappearing bit by bit.

Darwin couldn't get over the feeling that his buddy was being swallowed by the house, sucked down into the blackness and stench. And why?

'What the fuck are you doing? Why the fuck – '

The end of the board bucked upward.

Darwin heard the snap, saw the back of Sherman's right hand momentarily pinned between the board and the top of the window frame. Then the hand and board slipped into the blackness.

Darwin dropped to his knees. But no way would he put his face near the hole.

He heard coughing.

Or was it laughing?

Then Sherman cursing.

A spot of light played out of the darkness. Sherman's penlight. Darwin leaned closer and waved the light away from his eyes. He saw it play onto the bloody back of Sherman's hand where he had scraped it in the fall. Then Sherman looked up, the light coming from under his chin casting an eerie mask. Darwin could see Sherman was afraid. Finally. Darwin felt relieved. Now they could get the hell out of here.

'Come on, Sherman, give me your hand.'

Their hands strained toward each other, but they could only touch fingertips.

'I'll get a box or something,' Sherman said, his voice quavering, gagging.

Finally. Finally, Darwin realized, Sherman had reached his own level of fear. Now they could go.

15

The light played around, flitting from wall to wall as Sherman searched, lighting up a dirt floor and concrete walls. There was no furniture or junk that Darwin could see in the small room where Sherman had landed. There was an open doorway to more darkness, a larger darkness. Sherman and his light moved toward the darkest of it and disappeared with the light.

Darwin lay beside the rectangular hole.

'Goddammit, Sherman, get your ass out of there,' he commanded in a shouted whisper.

Darwin held his breath and stuck his head into the darkness. Even without breathing, the terrible odor penetrated his head, somehow leaking in. How could Sherman stand it in there? There must be a million dead rats or something laying around, he thought.

Suddenly, the penlight flitted back into the smaller room. Behind its beam Sherman came racing.

Startled, Darwin ducked back into the night, catching the top of his head on the window frame, sucking in a breath that made his stomach lurch.

'Darwin, help me, there's . . . there's . . .'

The words ended in a frantic gurgle. Sherman's bloody hand jumped up a couple of times and slapped on the bottom of the window frame.

Darwin felt numbed by the infectious fear of his friend.

'Help me, Darwin, get me the fuck out of here.'

This was no joke.

'Darwin, please, God . . . please, Darwin, get me out. . . . There's . . . dead people, for chrissakes, dead people . . .'

Darwin was trying to help. He rolled over on an elbow and stuck in his hand, a shoulder, his head.

16

A wet hand closed on his collar, another on his sleeve. Suddenly, all of Sherman's weight was on him.

'Dead people, Darwin . . . dead . . .'

Sherman's voice ended in a shriek.

And now Darwin felt like screaming himself, although he'd not even seen the sights that had made his friend hysterical.

He heard feet trying to scale the concrete. He felt himself sliding inside. His left shoulder caught on the frame. He held on. But Sherman kept dragging him under, pulling him into the dark sea of stench. Sherman's panic became his own.

He began slipping farther, cursing louder.

He brought a leg around and braced a thigh on the outside of the foundation. It was enough to stop his sliding.

Darwin was able to roll an inch away from the ghastly smell inside the room. They were going to make it.

Then all he gained was suddenly lost. As he fell into the room with Sherman.

The pair of them lay tangled, cursing on the floor. Darwin had hit his ribs and shoulder, emptying the breath from his lungs. He swooned on the stench he gulped in with every chestful of air. God, how horrible a smell. Too big a smell for dead rats. He knew Sherman hadn't been lying. Although he'd never smelled a dead human, he knew Sherman had seen some down here. He felt himself barely holding back a scream, felt himself nearly bawling, felt himself wrestling with Sherman even as he wrestled with his own self-control.

Finally, they stopped struggling with each other.

Darwin realized Sherman was hugging him, no, clutching him.

He patted Sherman on the chest and found the penlight. When the light came on, he saw the terror in his eyes.

Sherman didn't speak, didn't need to.

The eyes said it all.

Neither did Darwin say a word. He was still trying to remember the seconds before his grip had failed. Had there been hands on him? Had he been pushed into the basement?

There *had* been a shove in the back.

Hadn't there?

There had been a grip on his ankle, pivoting his body's grip away from the foundation.

Hadn't there?

He looked up and saw the rectangle of midnight blue outside where the air was fresh. He forced his mind to remember those last few seconds outside the window. His body's memory of the sensations resisted his mind's insistence that there could not have been somebody up there.

Darwin got to his feet. His chest hurt terribly every time he moved or took a breath. He couldn't quite stand straight. He shone the light around looking for a box or something to stand on, maybe another board to replace the splintered one on the floor. He stepped toward the doorway into the other room. Sherman held him back.

'Dead people can't hurt you,' he said. But Sherman held him fast.

He looked into the terrified face, the eyes screaming at him not to go in there. The tiny beam was like a spotlight focusing on the terror in the eyes.

18

'Okay,' he said, 'I'll hoist you up and you pull me out the window.'

The window.

There really wasn't anybody up there, was there? There couldn't be. Honest to . . .

He looked up at the opening . . .

. . . just as a silent curtain of darkness with the form of a man moved across the rectangle, a shadow shutting out the midnight blue with utter blackness.

2

Laren shuddered suddenly and violently, a spasmic, clonic jerk of every muscle in her body.

The eyes had come back to stare at her.

Her heart crashed against the insides of her rib cage.

She felt the stare, the touch of an oily, slimy gaze, the menace boring into her. She turned, looking in every corner of the bedroom.

And there they were. In the darkest corner.

They sent her reeling across her room. She fell back across the bed. The eyes advanced toward her, glowing as if lighted by dim, yellow bulbs. She writhed on the mattress, pressing herself into the covers as if they could protect her. Her arms and legs felt leaden, immobilized by terror, even as she kicked out, generally at where the intruder's body must be, specifically at his groin. Her feet flailed the dark air, hitting nothing. When the eyes came close enough for her to scratch and claw at the red veins, she tried that. But a pair of hands caught her by the wrists and held her. She whined, tried to scream, but even her mouth was numb. She kicked more, feebly, ineffectually, never making contact. He could touch her, but she couldn't lay a finger – or a fingernail – on him ... it ... whatever it was. Then the hands released her wrists and closed coldly on her throat. Then ...

She awakened, still feeling the hands tightening on her throat, cutting off first the circulation, then the breath, then the consciousness within her unconsciousness.

She struggled to keep her consciousness, not to fall back into that sleep, although she realized she'd practically been choking herself, so tightly had she clutched the blanket to her throat.

Her sharp intake of air restored her breath. Then the realization that she'd been dreaming relaxed her pulse.

But not much.

The dream had come back, and if anything, the feeling of the eyes had been even more intense. When Terry had moved in, the feeling had left. And she hadn't had the dream either.

But now the dream was back.

She lay sweeping her eyes around the utter darkness of her bedroom, still clutching the covers to her neck . . . her aching neck. Nothing. She could see nothing. And she couldn't even feel the creepy stare of those eyes that did not belong.

She sidled closer to Terry, felt his warm hip against hers — she hoped her hip wasn't chilly, clammy like the rest of her skin.

He stirred in his sleep.

Crazy. Cripes, she *must* be crazy, she told herself. She was no psychic, no seer . . . nor even a feeler of extrasensory phenomena. She was Laren Hodges, realist, pragmatist, analyst, purveyor of facts and all things concrete. She clenched her jaws as if to reassure herself. No theorist, she. No abstractionist was Laren Hodges.

Goddammit.

So why did she sometimes have this feeling of being watched? Why the fear of the damned dream?

She stiffened her body with resolve not to let those fantasy feelings bother her by day again, not to dream

21

that damned dream again, either. She could control herself, dammit. Even her dreams, she decided.

Dammit.

Couldn't she?

Before she could answer, she felt Terry's hand on her thigh. In answer to him and just to prove she could not be cowed by a stupid, irrational, goddamned feeling only a crazy woman would feel, she rolled to Terry and took him, used him up completely.

The radio alarm went off right at her climax, which came frantically after his and before he became useless to her.

'The Star-Spangled Banner' announced the beginning of her day and the finish of her orgasm.

They lay laughing at the timing of the music.

And finally, she felt relaxed.

She climbed over him to touch the base of the lamp, which answered with a dim glow. She touched it twice more to brighten the room.

She bounded out of the bed and headed toward the bathroom.

That's when she felt it again.

The touch of extra eyes, the relentless gaze.

She whirled, flinging her breasts and arms with the centrifugal force. She glared at Terry, her lover of a week. True, he was staring. He lay grinning, drooling from the corner of his just-awakened mouth.

But his weren't the eyes. She had felt an extra presence. Gooseflesh crept from her neck over her buttocks and down the backs of her legs.

Her own eyes swept a visual arc, searching the room.

He saw her expression of fear and mistook it for passion.

'Not again, babe. I gotta get to work.'

'No,' she said. 'That's not what was on my mind.'

'Yeah. Right. So stop looking at me like that and hurry up with your shower before Max here gets hardheaded again.'

'Terry . . .' she said tentatively.

'Laren, get your butt into the shower before we both get fired.'

Laren cocked her head toward the bathroom and squinted before she dared stick her hand into the darkness to snap on the switch.

He watched her, seeing not the fear but the trim, spare figure of a runner, her muscles toned, her skin smooth. She was a brunette – a natural brunette, he noted to himself with satisfaction.

She began showering in a hurry, unable to rid her mind of those eyes. And before she'd finished, she saw the flash of a Norman Bates shadow through the plastic and flung the curtain aside, startling Terry, who stood straddled before the toilet. Now having fully embarrassed herself and feeling thoroughly sheepish, she slid the curtain back and finished rinsing her conditioner, trying all the while to keep her eyes open, for it was too scary to shut them even for a few seconds.

What had happened to her? she wondered. And how could that dream have come back? And that extrasensory feeling?

When she had finished her shower, Terry stepped into the spray she left for him and sprinkled off. When he was done, he tried to kiss her wetly, but she fought him off. He didn't notice her fear because he was himself afraid. He didn't dare be late. Not again. Not like a couple of times already since he'd met Laren. She was some woman. This might be the one he'd surrender his freedom to. Who could tell? Wait and see whether they shacked up for good. Maybe she'd get over her bitch streak . . . well, maybe in time.

Meantime, he would enjoy her company, her body, her face. She was a looker – not in the beauty queen category, not that exaggerated perfection – but a striking woman, one with character to her looks. She had piercing gray eyes and a mouth he found himself staring at as she talked, for it was a mouth capable of tenderness and toughness, mostly the latter, but a mouth with character.

When he was dressed, he shook his head to clear his thoughts of her sensuality. He bade her good-bye, looked at his watch, and was already out the bedroom door when she called.

'Terry, would you get my shoes before you go?' The voice brought him up short.

'What the hell . . . where are they?'

'Beside the bed. Throw them to me, will you?' Her words were muffled by toothpaste suds, but had he been paying attention, he might have heard her muffled panic. He might have realized she was stalling to keep him in the bedroom a minute longer.

'Shit.' He saw nothing on the near side and marched to the far side. 'Which side did you take them off on? I'm in a hurry too, babe.'

'Oh.' She was wiping a frothy goatee from her chin as she padded from the bathroom. 'Never mind, dear,' she said, extra sarcasm on *dear*. 'Here they are right in front of your eyes.'

He strode around the bed and looked where she was pointing. Right where he'd looked just seconds ago.

'I . . . was sure . . . shit, I must have looked right at them. I've heard of screwing yourself blind. This could be the onset.'

24

She sat on the bed and raised half her upper lip at him.

'Don't be so crude.'

He kissed her head.

'Whatawaytogoblind.'

She slipped into the shoes.

He strode out the bedroom door, and she was close behind.

In less than a minute, she'd locked the door and they were on their way in separate cars to separate jobs in separate parts of the city.

In another minute, Laren Hodges noticed the cold oozing from her shoe. She jerked her car out of traffic, nearly taking two other cars with her. She tore off the shoe in disgust and told herself she was trembling in righteous anger rather than unmitigated fear.

About the same time, in her apartment, her bed moved.

It had lurched and bucked for most of the night.

Now it was jiggling.

It was as if somebody lay beneath it.

Giggling.

Laren endured the hours by making it a day of fury. She spent it stewing alternately in anger and fear. She labored through her troubled mind, searching for the answer to when all this madness had begun.

Was it Terry? Was she really so bad a judge of character? Was he that weird?

No.

In fact, the feelings of not being alone had been the reason she let him invite himself over for that first night, then the next, until on the third night he showed up with light luggage. Now he had begun talking about not renewing his own lease when it ran out next month. She hated the idea of giving up even a fragment of her independence. But she hated it less than the idea of being alone with the feeling of those eyes.

It had been a couple of weeks before Terry that the feelings of extra eyes had begun. She'd begun feeling as if she weren't alone. And now . . . even though Terry had proven himself a fair companion, good roommate, great lover . . . they *still* weren't alone together.

There had been all those occurrences, possibly real, possibly imagined. There had been the pieces of toast she'd brought to the bedroom dresser . . . well, it hadn't been the toast as much as the bites she couldn't remember taking. Terry, when he moved in, denied leaving food out overnight. He shrugged off the 'great toast capers', as he called them. And he vehemently denied leaving the toilet unflushed.

'My mother drummed that into my head from the minute I was potty-trained,' he insisted.

'Well, I *never* leave it unflushed,' she would snap. 'So who the hell did it?'

'First the toast, now the great turd caper,' he muttered impatiently.

Then came the coitus interruptus, when she sometimes would clutch him prematurely and demand to know if he heard anything besides the wet slapping of their bodies together. And his answer was always the same one-word obscenity.

She'd had roommates before. In fact, she'd never had an apartment to herself until moving here from Tennessee. So it wasn't that.

Mostly it was the feeling of the extra presence, mostly when she was alone. So she arranged not to be alone. She waited for him to arrive home before her — easy enough, since he was a broker who could afford to leave after the market closed. And if she didn't see his

26

car in the usual parking space, she waited for him to arrive and then faked that she'd only just gotten there herself.

But now there was that perverse prank this morning.

It had to be Terry.

It just *had* to be, dammit.

After work, she decided she would start a fight to see if she could get the story to be blurted out in anger.

She bashed through the door of her apartment, looking disheveled and bedraggled, her hair mussed, her blouse untucked, her belt uncentered, her shoes in her hand.

Astonished, Terry gaped from his seat at the table, where he'd been digging into *The Wall Street Journal*'s fine print.

She threw the shoes at him, the sneer pulling at her lips and narrowing her eyes to indicate she meant to hit him.

He ducked below the level of the tabletop and the arc of the shoes and came up slowly, a wry grin creeping across his face.

'Bad day at the office, my dear?'

And the fight was on.

Laren's strategy backfired. He didn't blurt out any confessions to pranks of any kind.

The evening marked its time in stiff silence. She refused to talk, let alone engage in sex, until he apologized.

'Until what?' he demanded.

'Until you apologize.'

'For what?'

'For . . . messing in my shoe.'

'What messing?' he whined.

'Why can't you just admit it?'

'What's this with the shoe?' he whimpered. 'Would you get off the shoe for a while? I didn't put anything in your goddamned shoe. Put *what* in your shoe, anyway?'

'Don't play dumb with me, Terry.'

'Just tell me what I'm supposed to be apologizing for.'

'You . . . masturbated in my . . .'

'Jerk off in your shoe? Are you nuts? Whatya think I am? Some kind of weirdo? Or Superman? Remember how many times we did it last night? And again this morning? I ran outta gas, babe. I wouldn'ta scraped together enough . . . I couldn'ta no more jerked off in your shoe than take a flying leap at the moon.'

She refused to talk at all if he was going to talk to her like that. 'By God,' she spat at him, 'I know what semen looks like.'

'Up yours,' he muttered to himself. 'We aren't married, ya know.'

'Bet your ass, sicko,' came the muttered reply.

'Huh? What'd you say? What'd you call me?'

'Nothing.'

'Nothing.'

He drank half a dozen beers.

They went to bed early, exhausted from a week of intense sexual exercise and the crashing letdown of the argument.

'Terry?' she murmured into the darkness of their bedroom.

'Hmmmph?' He was near passing out.

'Just say you did it and that you're sorry and I'll never say another word about it to you.'

'I'm sorry,' he slurred.

'Sorry for what?'

'I'm sorry you got all upset.'

'Just say you did it.'

'Laren . . .' With his teeth he scraped a thick coating off his tongue. His words were precisely articulated. '. . . I – did – *not* – fuck – your – shoe. Good – night – Laren.'

Not good night. But good-bye. She knew it was over. Nothing more need be said, would be said. It would be over. She felt like crying. So this was insanity – crazy bored at work, phantom eyes at home. She practically *ached* to cry.

But she wouldn't. Never. Crying was for vulnerable bitches, and she was anything but vulnerable.

His breathing came, slow, deep, regular.

She lay paralyzed, hardly breathing at all.

Her eyes gazed at the digital clock for the dozenth time. Only a minute had elapsed since the last time she looked. 3:24. Hours since she'd lain there. Worst of all, there were still hours till the alarm.

Her eyes flitted back and forth into darkness so black the room seemed brighter when she closed her eyelids.

Goddamn him. Why did he have to have shades down? Why did he insist on turning the clock so dim? Why couldn't he sleep with just a little light? She needed a peek at the sky to help her get a feel for time as she turned over during the night and when she awakened in the morning. And why couldn't he just say he'd messed in her shoe as a little sick joke? There was still time to recover their romantic balance – if only he'd confess.

But . . .

Why did she keep hearing sounds she'd never heard before? Were they always there?

29

Yes, just the normal sounds of a silent apartment.
Right?
No.
There.
A piece of the darkness shifted.
There, at the foot of the bed, was a form.
Wasn't there?
Her eyes flitted from side to side trying to pick up a confirmation. Her skin prickled all over. She stopped breathing altogether.

There, a sound, a scuff on the carpet – or a snort – shut up, Terry, you drunken bastard. Stop breathing for a second so I can hear, she bellowed inside her head.

She closed her eyes to concentrate, but her eyelids wouldn't settle down. Little flashes of red, little galaxies of stars kept forming and reforming into shapes. Christ, there were more ghosts inside her eyes than out.

And inside her chest she was screaming.

She was losing it. This was panic. This was insane, irrational panic. She *was* crazy. She felt her breath coming faster, more agitated, heating up her bursting lungs.

She had to get to the light switch, to see some light, to reorient her senses, to . . .

She was reaching over Terry when . . .

A hand grasped her wrist. By God! A hand! There it *was!* Proof! A hand . . . proof . . . a . . . a . . . ah . . . AH . . .!

She lost it, the last of her composure, in a screaming fit.

More than five hours of pent-up fear lost in a shrill scream impossibly long, high-pitched yelping, a sudden dump of her strictly rational, rigidly controlled demeanor, a momentary loss of her very sanity.

Terry Carter sobered up in an instant as he felt his scalp crawling off his head, his body being torn, clawed. He found himself in a wrestling match with a banshee wildcat, fingernails and toenails digging into his flesh for purchase in the dark. And then she was wailing incoherently, crying for help, for God, for cops, for obscenely named people and things.

Somehow he fought her off and found the light. Otherwise this crazy bitch might have torn him apart, at least disfigured him too much to go to work – shit, how would he ever live *that* down, the appearance of a woman's scratch marks? On his back, fine, but on his face would give the impression he'd raped somebody. He clutched her by the wrists and shook her back to her senses. He might have even slugged her if he would have dared to release a wrist long enough.

When he stopped shaking her, her eyeballs settled down and stared at him, finally narrowing down with recognition. But then she twisted violently to look over one shoulder, then the other.

'What the hell is . . .'

'Somebody was in here,' she panted.

'Laren, come *on*. This isn't another turd caper, is it?'

'Come on yourself. Somebody grabbed me.'

'Bullshit.'

'Bullshit yourself.'

'Come on, that was probably me grabbing you in my sleep. Grabbed you where? Where was I supposed to have grabbed you?'

She looked down at his hands, clutching her wrists. 'He . . . grabbed . . . my wrists . . . just like you're grabbing them now.'

'Exactly. I'm grabbing you. I *did* grab you. Maybe I

was dreaming. Maybe you were dreaming you were awake when . . .'

'No.'

'Yes.'

'Bullshit, Terry.'

'Here,' he said, 'I'll prove it. This place is safe.'

He still held her by the wrists. He stood up and yanked on her until she slid off the bed. Then he let her go finally and went to the bathroom, turned on the lights, and threw out his arms in a display of the harmlessness of the situation. He reached behind the door, waving first to show nobody was there then to pull down her robe from the hook, and he tossed it to her. She put it on, her shoulders sagging, her head bowed. But Terry was not through. He took her by the full sleeve of the robe and pulled on her. She followed. Into the hallway he led her, pointing toward the kitchen, toward the living room, and then he led her on a tour of the house, pulling, pointing, jabbing into the darkness, slapping each light switch until every light in the house broadcast its glow. There was nothing. There was nobody.

He led her back to the hallway and stood, his arms outstretched, his palms up. She looked down at the floor. He took it as a sign of defeat.

'Now do you see? Nobody. Right?'

She shook her head.

'Finally,' he said. 'Now do you feel better?'

She would not be calmed. 'Somebody was here,' she said quietly, insistently.

'Shee-it,' he muttered, and threw up his hands in desperation. He left her standing and ran back through the house reviewing his tour, yelling at her from the kitchen, from the den, from the living room. He came back to her and touched her shoulders. 'Why won't you believe me?' he yelled.

'I do believe you. There's nobody here. Now. But there *was*.'

'Christ,' he whispered.

'I even heard a little laugh,' she said, 'a wheezing laugh.'

And she was so utterly convinced, he almost believed it. But no, it was impossible. He'd been through the house.

'I *think* I heard a laugh,' she whispered.

He snorted derisively down his nose at her and recovered a bit of his own certainty.

Fact was, he'd been laying over with a nut. Certifiable. Afraid of the dark. Fuck me, he sighed to himself. Too bad. But why do I always latch on to the flaky ones, the ones whose elevators skip floors?

They sat up until the sky lightened. He occupied himself by dabbing disinfectant into his wounds. God, what if he got lockjaw or something? No telling with a bitch like this. Next, she'd be telling him she carried the AIDS virus.

She picked bits of his skin from beneath her nails. The tension in the room kept their eyes from meeting.

When she was done removing every particle of his skin, she apologized for the third time, this time as calmly as she could manage. And firmly. For she had regained her usual toughness. If anything – like scar tissue – her exterior had grown tougher.

He ignored it. 'You'd better call in sick, get some sleep.'

'No,' she snapped. 'I can't ... I won't stay in this house alone all day.'

'Why do you have to be so damned ... macho?'

She glared at him. 'What the *hell* do you mean?'

33

But his question was rhetorical. For she could see he had already given up on her. Then he shut up.

No way would he be staying in the bed of a homicidal bitch with shit for brains, she knew. And if he ever wanted to be sliced to ribbons as he slept, he'd invite a werewolf home and try to knock off a piece of that. She'd proven herself an idiot. And Terry would be gone by the end of the day. Forever.

They dressed for work, he sullenly, she resignedly. It was going to be over. That made her as sad-mad as the other made her afraid. Maybe she *was* crazy.

She was ogling the image in the bathroom mirror, half trying to decide if she was sane, half wondering how she'd ever repair her face for work when she heard him curse.

She twisted her body to look into the bedroom.

He was sitting on the bed, his mouth open, his right ankle across his left knee. He held his right loafer over the foot.

A string of slime hung between his sock and the shoe.

'Some joke,' he said.

'It's not a joke . . .'

'Well, some way to get revenge then. What is it? Rubber cement? Corn syrup? Raw egg white?'

'No . . .'

'Snot, then. That'd be your speed, bitch.'

'Terry . . .'

'You are one sick bitch.'

34

3

She strode from the elevator car as if she knew her destination. She didn't have an inkling, but she knew how to walk so nobody would dare challenge her. She'd made her way with that kind of style ever since college. A receptionist stood up behind her desk and its sign, Burglary Division, but Laren ignored her.

A chunky detective in loose-weave polyester made the mistake of eye contact. Laren locked onto his eyes, made an imperceptible course correction, and demanded, 'Where the hell is Hanover?'

The chunk gladly obliged, delighted to be directing her fury elsewhere, nodded, and pointed the eraser end of a pencil at a crew-cut figure with a rigging of suspenders and shoulder holster three desks away.

Course correction again.

She saw him see her coming and saw him act as if he didn't. He started to rise, to flee perhaps. She nailed his ass to the chair with his name.

'Yes, ma'am, I'm Hanover,' he said with a deep, disappointed sigh as he slumped back down.

'We . . . spoke? Earlier? Over the phone? Remember?'

Remember, *asshole?* said the tone of voice.

He squinted at her, unused to such sarcastic manners since his tour with vice and the unsavory bitches he'd found there. He gave her the cop's instinctive, instant appraisal. This was no whore, at least not the stabled type. For one thing, her makeup wasn't put on with a bricklayer's trowel. Maybe she should have slapped some more on, though; she looked a little

35

rough around the edges, as if she needed some sleep. Pretty though. And nice eyes. Class bitch.

'How'd you get up here without an escort or pass?' Pause. 'Ma'am.'

She planted her firm butt in the chair beside his desk.

He noticed it didn't jiggle. Even as she hit the rock-hard maple slab. One firm ass. Rock-hard ass. He closed his eyes for a second-long blink and shuddered inwardly at what his imagination showed him.

She noticed him notice. If he was going to be distracted by her body, she knew she'd have him for lunch.

He opened his eyes and gazed at her butt, wondering if it was naturally firm or if her ass was just puckered up because he'd laughed at her on the phone.

'Detective Hanover?' she said sweetly, the corner of her lip lifting into a sneer.

'Miss Hodges?'

She went for the gonads. 'Hanover, it is made with an opaque fabric. You cannot stare through the dress, no matter how hard you try.' She crossed her legs. 'And I do wear panties and panty hose – pink and buff, to be precise. So save yourself the trouble of trying to look up my dress.'

Snickers rose up from the nearest desks, and Hanover darkened a shade, an evil mask falling over his features. He peered into her eyes, penetrating, gray, bright, metallic as car paint with lacquer finish, hard, angry. He sent the 'class bitch' evaluation to the back of his mind for reconsideration.

'What can I do for you? Ma'am?' A touch of irony tinged his voice on the *Ma'am*.

'Let's start where we began on the phone before we were interrupted by your sudden case of the giggles.'

36

She could see him biting the inside of his mouth. But he adjusted a legal pad on his desktop and poised a ballpoint pen.

She told the story again from start to finish. She avoided emotions and embellishment. Control over such reports came easy to her. She used the details she knew would strike him as most significant. She didn't want to overstate, didn't need to overdescribe. She knew how to talk, to communicate the essentials. Hanover's mask dissolved into intensity at copying her remarks. She adjusted her speed so he could keep up. She had enough experience to know how fast to go.

As she spoke, she saw a couple of men pass by on one pretense or another to eavesdrop. The first she dismissed with a glance. The second with a pause and a long stare. As she was nearing the end of the narrative, a third man, maybe in his forties, stopped boldly next to her. He actually leaned over to catch her words. Then he sat on the adjoining desk without a pretense.

Laren knew neither the pause nor the look would send him away. She used them anyhow, before escalating to a glare. No good.

'Is this any of your fucking business, Dumbo-ears?' she said right into his smirking face a couple of feet away.

'It's Dewey, not Dumbo. Thomas E. Dewey. No relation. Aren't you Hodges?' He wiggled his protruding ears, a lightly defiant gesture.

She refused to flinch at the recognition in his deep brown, almost black eyes. She refused his attempt to disarm her.

'But is this any of your business? Dewey?'

His smirk rounded off at the edges. 'In a manner of speaking, yes.' An amused smile.

This time, his smile disarmed her a touch. It was a friendly smile showing plenty of straight teeth. But immediately she took control of the situation again. Dammit, she was in charge here.

'You're not a cop.'

'Nope.'

Who *was* this guy? Her mind raced. There was a dim spot of recollection. She knew that name from somewhere ... It was on the tip of her mind, but that damned connection to Harry S. Truman kept getting in the way, so she couldn't spring the recollection from her memory banks.

She looked helplessly at Hanover, asking with her eyes that he dismiss this arrogant bastard with the dimpled chin or at least tell her who he was. But she'd already alienated Hanover. No way would he offer to help in word or manner.

Hanover said, 'Ma'am, where did this Mr Carter go when he left your house this morning?'

She huffed at him. 'Stop calling me ma'am, and I won't call you Sergeant Friday. He went to work. He's an account executive with Hammond-Wilson, a stockbroker. I ... don't know where he lives. I've never been there.'

She glared at Dewey. A who-the-hell-*are*-you? look.

'Ma'am ... Miss Hodges, was anything stolen?'

'No.' She saw the detective's eyes flickering savagely with spite. If it was going to piss her off, he'd call her ma'am for sure.

'Did you check?'

'Yes, I checked. Nothing was missing, nothing broken.'

'Was there any sign of forced entry?'

'No.'

'No broken glass, jimmied doors ...'

38

'I know what forced entry means, detective.'

'Yes, ma'am.'

Dewey chuckled.

She studied him, looking for a weakness to exploit, since the insult about the ears didn't faze him. He was capable of a nice smile under that whitening mustache. Probably he wasn't as old as he looked with that whitening hair combed back to hide the overgrown ears. He'd probably been a lady-killer in his day. If, *if*, she were ever to like middle-aged men, that's the kind of hair-aging she'd rather see than bald spots with temple hair grown a foot long and combed over.

But this one was married. No ring, but all the other signs were there. For one thing, his gut had grown into a modest paunch. Middle-aged bachelors didn't let that happen when they were on the make. Maybe he was, at that. Separated probably. If this stud weren't married, he'd be on the make.

He smiled at her, refusing to confirm or deny her opinions of him. The black eyes reflected the smile. Kind of sexy . . . but . . .

'What can you do to help get this guy out of my apartment, detective?'

'Ma'am, one more time . . . did you see the . . .'

'Don't say *alleged*.'

He hesitated, searching for a different word. 'Did you see the subject? Have you ever seen him?'

'No.' Her eyes flinched for the first time in the interview. She didn't have a damned ounce of evidence and she knew it. And no amount of bravado would get this jerk out of his chair to take a look. Next words out of his mouth would be to tell her how he had real criminals, not imagined ones, to track down.

'Ma'am, I'm afraid we're going to need something a little more concrete before we can open a case. I mean, what do we have in the way of . . . concrete proof a person was in your apartment? I mean other than this . . . Terry Carter. He spend the night often?'

She answered with hard silence.

'You two . . . engaged?'

Silence.

'Maybe it was him . . . Carter playing a joke . . .'

Her silence softened a little.

'I mean, really. What proof do we have? I mean, concrete?'

She stared at him still, no answer at the ready.

Somewhat triumphantly, he continued, 'Now if you want, I could ask a uniformed officer to go by . . . to look around your . . .'

'Never mind, Hanover.' She stood up.

'If . . . you know, if I can be of assistance, Miss Hodges, I want you to know you can just call.'

'Yeah. Have a nice day to you too,' she said, a sneer tugging upward as if a string were tied to the corner of that upper lip. The sneer said, Nice day to you too, bastard.

Dewey followed her into the elevator.

She punched the button for the ground floor and stepped back. She'd be damned if she'd let him ask her to do anything nice for him, even something as simple as pushing a button for a different floor. He didn't ask. That miffed her.

She marched out of the elevator toward the building's Agnew Street exit.

He followed, just a step behind.

That pissed her off.

She whirled on him.

'You've got a really vicious air about you today, Miss Hodges.'

'Who the hell are you?'

40

'Thomas E. . . .'

'Why are you following me?'

'Could it be that we're going to the same place?'

'I'm going to work.'

'Me, too. Well, I don't spend a lot of time in the office, but we both work for the same company.'

Her face softened as much as a wearied yet sleepless night would allow it to soften. The image of Truman holding up the *Chicago Daily Tribune* headline dissolved. A tired smile crossed her lips.

'Dewey. You work at the *Post-Herald?* Oh . . . Ted Dewey is your byline. You're the police reporter. Of course' – she pointed back at the police department – 'the cop shop.'

'That's true,' he said, 'and you're fairly new on cityside. Pretty good reputation as a general assignments reporter in Memphis before coming here too. I read your series on rape victims and prevention.'

'You saw the clips I sent in with my application?'

'No. I saw the whole series on the wires. You know . . . rape . . . crime . . . cop shop? It's my beat.'

The remnants of the hard-nosed facade vanished entirely.

'Sure. Of course. I'm sorry for the way I acted. You won't believe this, but I'm not really like that. I . . .'

'You seemed awfully afraid, I mean really shaken by what happened to you.'

'Yes,' she said. 'I was shaken. And angry and tired. I . . . You won't believe this either, but all of a sudden, I feel so relieved to meet somebody from the *Post* like this. It's like running into a traveling companion from the same hometown. I – uh – haven't exactly made a lot of friends in the six months I've been here.'

'Outsider syndrome. Make that competent outsider

41

syndrome. People are a little jealous, a little intimidated even.'

When he smiled now, she noticed how much more warmly she received the expression. No longer was it a wiseacre grin. And he didn't seem to be leering, undressing her with the eyes as men usually did. His big ears were no longer the dominant impression. He'd become a normal person. A man who did the same job as she – probably not as well, of course – hell, certainly *not* as well, that is. But a reporter like her. She dropped her defenses fully, feeling a sudden kinship.

'Do you have to go back to work right away?' he asked.

Instantly her guard was up again, and his smile had seemingly turned into a half-leer.

She cocked her head. Was he simply the same as all the other men she'd met?

'Why?'

'You're more suspicious than the average reporter, Hodges. I'm interested in this sort of thing. I have some theories I'd like to check out. For a story, a long-term thing I've been putting together for years. It's up to you. I don't have to go out to your place.'

'No,' she said. 'I mean yes, come on out and look around. I'm going to move out awhile; I'm going to see if Cindy Lee will put me up until I get over being afraid. I need to pick up some things and I'm ... I won't go back alone. I would even have taken the offer of a uniformed cop ... if it hadn't come from Hanover. The prick.'

4

Laren inserted her key in the door.

'It's locked,' she said.

Dewey gave her a why-shouldn't-it-be? look, all the while thinking how pretty she was. For a snotty, shovy broad.

'I mean, it's *still* locked.'

He kept his expression flat.

'Oh, piss on you, Dewey.'

'Call me Ted, Miss Hodges?'

She squinted at him, seemingly unable to determine whether she was being put on. Dewey enjoyed seeing her on the spot, undecided. Her type always seemed to be so sure. About everything. Aardvark to Zygote. Every damned thing.

'It's Laren. So stop with the Miss Hodges stuff. And get rid of that look that says I'm a silly bitch.'

'Really?' He tried not to smile but had to fight off the feeling of looking like he was trying not to. Besides, he couldn't exactly deny that she *was* a silly bitch.

She looked at him again, studying him. She narrowed her eyes. Finally, she gave up and sputtered, 'Now I don't know whether your look says I'm a silly bitch or I'm feeling it for myself.'

He struggled to keep a flat look. Let her be the confused one.

She pushed the door open. They stepped inside, and she shuddered.

'It's cold,' he said, as if to reassure her.

'You don't have to say that, Ted.' Just the same, her

43

tone of voice thanked him for the reassurance. 'It's more than cold. I'm . . .'

'Afraid.' He finished the sentence with the word her type would never admit to.

'Ted?'

'Mmmmm?' He was looking around, his feet planted but his body bobbing and weaving so he could look around corners.

'I know this sounds crazy but I usually feel him. It's like somebody looking at me.' She stepped deeper into the apartment, glancing back imperceptibly to see if he would follow. He did. 'Crazy, huh?'

He didn't answer. Let *her* be the one to say it. He knew if he assented, it wouldn't be long before he'd be accused of calling her crazy.

She took him around the house to clear it, acting on the surface as if she were touring him through the cluttered kitchen, through the dining area that had been set up and used as an office – though the dust indicated to him it hadn't been used for much writing. And the stacks of paper. All blank. Writing. Was there a reporter in the world who *wasn't* writing a damned book? That is, *thinking* about writing one and never getting around to it? He felt a moment's guilt because his own writing projects had been shelved since . . .

'That's about it,' she said. 'Nothing is out of the ordinary. I've never seen any sign . . . any absolutely beyond-a-shadow-of-a-doubt proof. There was just that hand in the night, which . . . I guess it *could* have been Terry's. And there were the sounds, the movement in the dark . . .'

'Where's the bedroom?' he asked, pointing at the closet door, his raised eyebrows emphasizing the question.

She realized she had been stalling. She shook her

head and pointed at the door off the living room. She wanted him to open it.

He obliged. She heard his heels and soles scuffing a clip-clop on the hardwood, then go silent as he walked on some article of clothing, then continue rapping along. She went to the hall closet door and opened it, stepping back as she did so. She heard the bathroom exhaust fan go on, then off. She looked over each shoulder – God, what was happening to her? This damned business was shaking her self-image. This was making her seem not as tough as everybody gave her credit for when she left a rural Arkansas weekly for the big-city Memphis daily, then to a major metropolitan newspaper.

Criminy, she was about to move out of her first unshared apartment ever. Before the lease was up. On account of what? A feeling was all she had to go on. A goddamned feeling.

She took a deep breath and went into the room with Ted Dewey, her new-found protector.

It was warm and stale-smelling in the bedroom. She might have been embarrassed by what she knew was the unmistakable odor of lovemaking, hers and Terry's individual and mixed musks.

But her nostrils were stung by the smell of the unwashed. She knew what it was – she had interviewed white trash, black trash, trash trash – sometimes trashy people made the best damned feature stories. So she knew trash. And this was its smell, of the unwashed, the scent of stale, cold soil. Trash.

She convulsed. Not because of the smell, but because of the feeling. He was in here. She could feel his – maybe it was an *it* – presence. She could feel its eyes.

'I checked,' he said, as if reading her mind. 'There's nobody in here.'

45

She looked at Dewey and caught him staring at her. Nothing unusual about that. Men stared at her all the time. But Dewey wasn't leering, wasn't undressing her with his eyes. He stood there smiling that stupid little grin, half-amused at this nut case she'd become.

She closed her eyes. God, she was coming apart right under the eyes of this over-the-hill bastard.

He thought about offering her another chance to grasp an excuse for the shuddering. But it was definitely not cold in this room. So that would be too transparent to repeat.

Finally, he simply asked, 'Are you sure you want to move out?' He already knew the answer. This woman, this Laren, this tough-talking, tough-skinned, flinty little self-styled bitch – and proud of it – was afraid. Or maybe she *was* a little crazy.

She opened her eyes and answered with another jerking of her shoulders.

'You ever hear of a haunted apartment?' she asked with a nervous giggle.

'Yeah,' he said. Dryly. Flatly. 'The Amityville Condo.'

She smiled weakly.

'You're shivering. Is it a feeling left over from last night or is it from now?' he asked.

She sighed, half in relief. She smiled, finally trusting that he was not making light of her. Maybe he'd turn out to be decent. Maybe this Dewey would be her friend. Welcome thought, that. Friend. Not many of those in her present life. Or past.

'I can't tell anymore why I'm shaking. But thanks for asking. Do you think I'm crazy?'

He shrugged. 'You wouldn't be the first person who didn't like living alone. I don't like it myself.'

Instantly, he regretted adding the last. He didn't

46

want to give away information about himself like that, especially to a reporter. He knew how they thought. And he didn't want to seem as if he were offering anything, making a move, tossing out a baited line. Then again, he wondered, was that what he'd intended all along? Cripes, what was this woman doing to him anyhow? What was the age difference between them anyhow? Hell, what was he doing even wondering about *that*? Anyhow?

'Mind getting my suitcases down from the top of the closet?' She pointed. She was not looking at him but into the darkness of the walk-in. She did lean close enough with her pointer to flip on the light. Then she stepped back.

He noticed the clutter, snorted the mustiness from his nose. She was full of contradictions, this Laren Hodges, this woman he'd seen at the paper but never spoken to before today. She missed nothing of the details in a story, yet she'd been completely blind to his existence. She acted tough as a street gang leader when he'd seen her at one or two of the evening pub gatherings after the last deadline. She'd ignored him as if he'd been just another pressman or paper handler whose skin was daily spray-painted with ink. Tough-broad act. Too good for noticing scum like him. Yet here she was in broad daylight, afraid to step into her own closet. There was the immaculate living room, the neatly arranged bedroom – not counting the unmade bed and the towel he'd walked over. Yet this closet was a mess, mountains of boxes on the floor, clothes hanging on and over hangers, the pile of luggage precariously balanced on shelves.

She started throwing clothes into the opened suitcases on the bed. As she got to the lingerie drawers, he moved toward the door. She held up a bra to fold it, saw him sidling away. She snapped at him.

'Don't you dare. Don't leave me alone – not for a second.'

He shrugged helplessly, telling her in body language he was just trying to be discreet.

She snickered in reply. 'I can't believe there's still a man alive who would avert his eyes at the sight of women's underwear. With today's television commercials?'

He smiled, raising one eyebrow. 'Just trying to be . . . delicate. I try not to be one of those who stare up women's dresses,' he said, referring to her encounter with Hanover.

She noticed again how his eyebrows had a sign language of their own. Too bad she couldn't write about him. Those eyebrows would make a telling detail in some story.

'You ever married, then?' she asked, letting him off the hook of embarrassed silence.

'Yes.'

'Children?'

The question bothered him. She didn't notice because she was all wrapped up in packing.

'I . . . have a son,' he said. 'But I . . . we're divorced.'

The lie came so easily. Why did he say that he was divorced? Well, separation was *almost* divorce, wasn't it? And they *had* already placed the matter into the hands of lawyers. Still, why did he lie? What advantage did he expect to gain?

Giving another lie to his disclaimer of just seconds ago, he watched her lean over the bed to pack a jogging suit into the corner of a suitcase, exposing her legs halfway up the thighs, emphasizing the tone of her body, a rippling in her buttocks and continuous curves

48

up her back as she crammed clothes into a Pullman piece of luggage.

Enough reasons to lie about marital status, even if she weren't so damned pretty, especially around the eyes and mouth. And she was so full of life, whereas his own existence . . .

'I know about failed marriages. I've been there, pal.'

'Oh? You've been divorced?'

'Not exactly. I was married young. Had it annulled after four weeks of glorious sex.'

She spun on him, swapping her front for the backside he'd been staring at.

Quickly, his gaze swept up, past her breasts.

She nailed him with those metallic irises, daring him to make a wisecrack about glorious sex. He didn't take the dare.

'Uh, why the annulment?'

'I decided I'd rather go to college and make a career. So I got my dad to get me into J-school at Texas. He did it on condition I get an annulment. And I only got married to spite him for not getting me into the goddamned school in the first place. Pretty ruthless family, huh?'

He dodged the issue, though his face probably gave him away. He pointed into the closet at the racks of dresses and suits and sports clothes lining the walls.

'You want anything else?'

She remembered what she'd forgotten in the moments of being a smart aleck. And she shuddered yet again.

Dewey hiked up one trouser crease and knelt beside the bed. Then he hiked the dust ruffle gingerly, as if lifting the hem of a skirt.

She watched him.

'You a good housekeeper?' he said to the polished

area beneath the springs, to the dust devils that had been herded to the wall.

She snickered. 'Not particularly. Now it's your turn to interview me, right?'

He looked into the gray eyes. Avoid the argumentative retort, he told himself. In word and deed. 'You ever dust under here?'

'Are you kidding?'

A side light from the windows was catching her eyes, rimming the irises in polished pewter. It took his breath away to see how penetrating those eyes were. No wonder her sources told her so much. If she were to ask, he'd tell her anything.

'No, I'm not kidding,' he told her. 'You, uh, coming back here later?'

'To live? Never. I'm leaving for good. I'll bring Cindy back to help me pick up my other things. I'll never spend another night in here – alone or otherwise.' She spoke the information loudly, as if whistling while passing through a cemetery, as much to tell the owner of the figmented extra eyes as to answer Dewey's question.

He stood up. She latched on to two of the smaller suitcases, leaving him either to hug the bundle of clothes on hangers or to lug the Pullman. She started out. He followed, staggering under the weight of the both. Godamighty. What was this woman doing to him?

On the second trip she did venture into the closet to hand him a few boxes of shoes from the floor. But the closet seemed too confining for her. She moved outside the door and pointed to the boxes he should carry to the car.

Outside the second time, by the open trunk of the car stood a woman even more striking than Laren.

Was that possible? Dewey thought. She demanded to know from Laren where she was going and why she was deserting her, anyhow.

Laren answered the rapid-fire questions, stopping only to order the embarrassed Dewey back upstairs for the final load. Then she remembered her manners and introduced Marguerite, giving a bit of her background.

All Dewey caught was the Marguerite part. He was too awed by her Amazonian proportions to hear any more. If her name had been something ordinary like Joan, instead of Marguerite, he would have missed that too.

She was a Latina of some persuasion. South American, did Laren say? Brazilian? Hair so black, the highlights were blue. Sapphires for eyes, the light coming from deep inside as if lit by stars from a distant galaxy inside her head. Lips. He stared at her lips as she spoke the obligatory pleasantries. Her mouth became a cosmetics commercial on a giant screen television. Her sultry beauty diminished the – prettiness, it was now – of Laren.

He became aware that the mouth was no longer moving, although he heard a voice. He shook his head at the incongruity.

'Ted,' said the voice, although the mouth was pursed, 'would you puh-leeze get the last load from on the bed?'

It had been the voice of Laren Hodges.

'Oh, sure.'

He still burned, was hot with embarrassment, as he entered the apartment. He cursed himself half-aloud as he leaned over the bed. He kicked the door shut on the way out, mentally kicking his own butt for acting the fool.

He'd been so embarrassed, so wrapped up in himself, he missed the tiny movement from among the shoe

51

boxes on the floor of the walk-in closet. He missed the red-rimmed eye, opening, blinking, shutting, opening, staring, narrowing. Angry.

As he returned to the car, Marguerite was oohing.

'No wonder you're leaving. That's so spooky.' Even though the sun was hot, she hugged her arms. 'I'm going to start sleeping with a gun.'

Dewey gulped, wishing he could be a .357 Magnum.

He stood beside the passenger door of her car as Laren and Marguerite exchanged hugs and empty promises to get together again. He just stared at the hugging, no, really at the pressing of breasts in that special sisterhood only women shared, envious of Laren – well, envious of both of them, but more so of Laren – he could almost feel the swelling of Marguerite's chest against his own. He rubbed the feeling off his pectorals and shook the craziness from his head by looking skyward.

There.

A glimpse from the corner of his eye caught a movement.

He faked as if he were looking at Marguerite but slanted his eyes at the window shade of Laren's apartment.

It did not move again – if it moved at all in the first place.

Laren started the car and slipped it into a space in traffic. He craned his neck to see back at the window, to see if the curtain would move again.

'Awesome, isn't she?'

'Oh . . .' He started to tell the truth: that he wasn't looking back at her, that he was staring to see if there actually was a movement of the window shade. But he thought better of it. She . . . nobody would ever believe he wasn't looking at Marguerite. He wasn't so sure he believed it himself. Was he so dumb as to overlook her in favor of a goddamned window shade? Was he really *that* stupid?

'She's ... beautiful,' he said, mastering the understatement.

'You think I'm crazy, don't you?' she said, her own beauty dimmed by the recent proximity of the Latina. 'I mean about feeling the eyes and all? You know, I even shivered back there in the street. Broad daylight. I mean, I *must* be crazy, right?'

He smiled at her.

She took that as his answer and looked away.

Now *he* shuddered.

Detective Bret Hanover searched Dewey's face for clues.

'You got a date with her yet?'

Dewey snorted. 'I'm married, remember?'

'You're separated, asshole. Save the snow job for somebody who's gonna fall for it.'

'No, I'm not dating her. And I don't plan to.'

'You're sweet on her. I saw you eyeing her ass when you walked out together.'

'Hanover, you're hallucinating,' said Dewey, embarking upon another of his lies. He realized he'd been telling them a lot lately. Since Laren, in fact. 'Look, I don't have anything reserved with her for the next calendar or so. Why don't you ask her out? If she says no, it won't be because I've got any hold on her.'

Hanover narrowed his eyes and said, 'I don't know whether to believe you or not, Dewey. Are you saying she's not good-looking enough for your high and mighty tastes?'

'Hardly,' said Dewey, seeing a chance to get Hanover off his back by telling the truth. *Finally* the truth.

'She's a knockout. If I had half a chance with a woman ten years younger, I'd pray my knees bloody that it would be her.' Or Marguerite, he thought, smiling to himself. Yes, Marguerite. Then Laren. He'd pray his knees bloody over either of them.

Reassured, Hanover said, 'She *is* a looker, ain't she? Think she'd go out with a cop? What're you smiling about? Damn you, Dewey. I never know what you're up to. You're pulling my pecker, right?'

'Nothing. You damned cops are so damned insecure. You're always worried somebody won't like you because of your flat feet, gum soles, penis fascination, gun mania, and general all-round propensity to be Nazi fascist, anal-retentive pricks.'

'Fuck you.'

'And your mastery of the *Oxford English Dictionary*.'

'Go fuck yourself.'

'Look Hanover – seriously – if you want to know if she'd go out with a cop, just ask her out.'

'I might do that.'

'I need a favor, Hanover.'

'Where do reporters like to go?'

'Opera. I need a favor.'

Hanover's face fell. 'Opera?'

'Chrissake, take her to a ball game, a movie, a dinner. She's human – well, you know – almost. And quit dodging me. I need a favor.'

'What?'

Dewey withdrew the lump from the jacket of his sports coat. He pointed to the stain inside.

'A shoe?' said Hanover, his face contorted. 'You some kinda preevert or some . . . Hey, this is her shoe, isn't it? This is the shoe she said somebody jerked off in?'

Dewey smirked. 'No, I've got a new fetish. Of course

it's her shoe, Bret. How about seeing if the lab can get a reading on that stain.'

'Okay,' said Hanover, growing serious. 'You think it's come?'

Dewey grimaced. 'You tell me. That's why I'm asking for a test. I have to . . . be out of touch for a while. If the paper calls, cover for me, will you? Tell them I'm out on a crime or something . . . tell them . . .'

Hanover nodded sympathetically and spoke dryly, 'I know how to cover for somebody, Dewey.' He took a hitch in his breath as if to say something more. But he clenched his teeth against the words and nodded sympathetically again.

The slight young woman pulled out another set of steel drawers, riffled through the papers in them, and slammed them back. Laren paced in a tiny circle between the rows of metal cabinets in the newspaper's library as the wisp of a woman worked.

The woman turned, shrugged in despair, and slumped in defeat. 'I'm sorry, Laren. We don't have anything in the files about sightings of prowlers. It's not under any kind of heading or anything.'

'It's okay, Sandra. I didn't really think we'd come up with anything in the active files. Could you check the microfilm files for me?'

'Sure,' said Sandra, just one of several newspaper librarians eager to please one of the paper's top reporters. 'I'll get right back to you.'

Laren took the eagerness as her due in voluntary servitude. It was the nature of things. The drones and the worker bees had to serve somebody – had to serve the queen. Might as well be her.

5

It was about noon when Dewey drove up to the house, a white three-bedroom in the north suburban sprawl named Cameron Hills, where there really were no hills. Streets scratched into the flat soybean fields were supplanting the corn rotation with one- and two-stories, where the established clapboard farmhouses that didn't fit were bulldozed and those that did fit the grids were tolerated until the town council decided whether a convenience store or car wash could go in.

The sight of the house, the knowledge of its interior, the emptiness of its third bedroom, the fullness of terrible memories – they gave him a rap in the chest. It was as if some mischievous hand inside his rib cage had flicked a finger against his heart, making it switch pace. When he had been away for a while, he wondered how he could have left this symbol, this reality of the Great American Dream. But every time he saw the house – their house, the house that Dewey and Theresa had ordered built, lovingly built – he remembered why he couldn't stand the sight of the goddamned thing.

A Mercedes-Benz in the driveway soaked up the brilliance of the sun and reflected only the deepest-blue metallic rays back into Dewey's eyes. He felt like ramming the damned thing. He might have if he knew it would hurt the sedan more than his own Ford imitation of the Mercedes.

She met him at the door before he could even knock. Their eyes passed the pain back and forth.

'Theresa,' he said.

'It's a bad time, Ted.'

'He's taking a nap?'

'No . . . we . . . I'm having Jesse over for lunch.'

The flame flickered up in his black eyes, but she doused it before they could cover ground that had been worn hard with previous travel.

'I said lunch, Ted. We're having lunch. And even if it were . . . more than that . . .' She shook her head.

'What?' he snapped.

The head came up. 'It'd be none of your business.' She set her jaw, determined to be determined. 'We're getting a divorce, Ted. And you know perfectly well it isn't Jesse's fault.' Pause. 'And it isn't mine. It's . . .' She left the rest unsaid, left *your fault* unspoken.

His eyes dropped. She was giving him the chance to reverse his insane obsession. He knew all he'd have to say would be something like, Let's get out of this town and try a fresh start. She'd probably throw Jesse's lunch into a doggie bag and run him off. Then she'd throw herself into his arms. All he had to say was he'd get help in giving up his madness . . .

He shook the idea from his head. His eyes focused again. On her open, pleading face, the expression pleading for him to become what he had been. He knew if he would just say her name. Just one word. *Theresa.* Try it with a soft tone, a penitent tone. Theresa. *Say it*, he told himself.

'Can I take Matt out this Sunday?' he said instead.

Her shoulders sagged imperceptibly. Disappointed again, she nodded. Tears seeped into her eyes, blurring the green there.

Dewey saw the wetness welling up. And he grew angry with himself. Why was he such a bastard?

'Thanks,' he said curtly, and stalked back to his car.

He could have called to ask that. So why drive all

the way to the north edge of town? What might he have said if she could have invited him in? He didn't know, he told himself. Yes he did, he countered with the next thought. It would have ended the same as it had ended for the last two years – she crying, he shouting. He should be thankful Jesse was there to save them all that went between the beginnings and the endings of that scenario.

He drove past the crumbling two-story 1880s farmhouse that once had been isolated by a day's horseback journey to town. He saw it sitting there waiting, its lot defined by a battered gray picket fence and weed-choked yard, waiting until the encroaching edge of civilization's suburban developments pushed its creaking timbers aside and filled its basement with the very soil that had been the farm's lifeblood.

He remembered the house from when he lived out here. He remembered that it had been isolated by the fields, by the tall grasses growing up, by the weeds. He remembered watching the house year to year as the weather, the winds, the sun, had started to erode it even before the bulldozers could get to it. He noticed now that the roads of the development had been scratched into the earth in a pattern around the house, that curbs and street gutters were forming, linking together chains of concrete stretching out toward the house. He realized it wouldn't be long now before the house would be torn down and in its place would be more developments, more houses like his.

He had been fascinated by that house, he remembered. For a while, it had been thought haunted. His kids thought so. Kids . . . kids . . . 'kids.' He said the word aloud and it died in his throat. The word sounded like a choking noise.

He muttered a curse and crammed the Taurus's

accelerator to the floor. The car gasped, it too choking
... on its fuel, and he had to back off his tantrum,
which made him all the angrier. 'Fuck.' Another choking noise in his throat.

At the picnic table out back, Jesse waved the flies off
from their intended landings on Theresa's plate.
Finally she pushed her untouched salad away, leaving
it to draw flies away from his plate. She gazed at the
three-year-old in the sandbox showering his toys and
himself with grit. She heard a little screech of tires
and looked up at the man across the table.

'I'd better go, Theresa.'

She smiled weakly into the face of Jesse Lewis, a
face her own age but one that looked younger than her
own of thirty-eight, a face a lot less troubled. He wore
a crewcut, a throwback to the fifties that made him
seem even younger. Perhaps in him she remembered
earlier, less troubled times.

'Maybe I shouldn't come out tonight,' he said
tentatively.

'No,' she said. 'I mean yes. I have to start living my
life as it will be without ... him in it. You come out.
You ... must. And I'll be over this ... I ...'

He stood and kissed her on the head, inhaled the
sweet scent from her sun-hot, brunette hair, and a few
seconds later, wheeled the Mercedes into the street.

She brushed off Matt and carried him upstairs for
his nap. She shut the closet door and pulled off his
shoes. They were full of sand and he smelled dirty –
literally of dirt. He'd need a bath first.

The doorbell.

Downstairs, she found a package inside the door and
saw the delivery truck driving away. She locked the
door and reprimanded herself for leaving it unlocked

in the first place. She went to the back door and cursed herself for leaving that one open too.

Then, distracted by her thoughts of Ted and Jesse and marriage and divorce, and forgetting about the bath for Matt, she went about cleaning up the mess from lunch. When she remembered the nap again, she listened intently at the bottom of the stairs, and hearing nothing but the hiss of air through the intake vent in the stairwell, she decided it would be dumb to awaken the boy for a bath.

Upstairs, the closet door opened. A shadow crept across the carpet, up the bedspread, and over the form of the child.

'Nothing in the microfilm either, Laren.' Sandra, the librarian, looked defeated.

'Hey, it's no big deal.'

Still apologizing, Sandra said, 'A prowler wouldn't usually find his way into the paper unless there was a crime committed in connection, you know. Or unless there was such a widespread series of disturbances, that, you know, it was a major problem.'

'Sandy. It's okay.'

'Why not try Ruthey? She does the police and fire runs for the Monday and Friday editions. You know, it's mostly just petty stuff. But maybe you can find a pattern in a few back issues.'

'I'll try Ruth then,' said Laren.

Ruth Minton and her hissing nasal speech defect had been taken off a regular beat. She'd been stuck in front of a video terminal, keyboard, and telephone. She was not allowed to meet the public unless you could call talking to surly police and fire dispatchers the public. It took only a single word of conversation for Laren to understand why.

'Whaaaat?' – the sound came out of the tight-lipped, downturned, receding mouth like the squawk of a choking parrot – 'You want whaaaat?'

Laren, repelled, leaned away and repeated her request. Instead of answering, Ruth Minton snapped two sets of gray teeth down on a potato chip big as a crepe. The chip seemed to explode. Ruth began crunching the few shards that flew into her mouth. She chewed with her mouth open.

'Never mind,' said the astonished Laren. She wheeled away before she could either burst out laughing or become ill.

'Why not try Ted Dewey down at the cop shaaaap?' came the caterwauling, perpetual-frog-in-the-throat voice behind her.

Theresa bounded up the stairs. She didn't want Matt sleeping too long. She wanted him to get to bed early so she and Jesse could spend the evening peacefully.

Her son, all the importance left in her life, was a lump under his bedspread. She grasped the cover's edge and pulled gently back. The bedspread, clutched in determined little fists, resisted. The tiny face looked pained, even in sleep. Funny, when it looked like that – the pained look – he had the expression of his father. She saw the eyes were being squinched shut, either against the light or . . .

'You can stop faking it,' she trilled.

The eyelids fluttered open, revealing those beautifully giant black eyes that were his father's. She saw relief in the eyes.

'Mommy, I'm scared,' he said quite matter-of-factly.

He smelled sweaty, felt clammy, as she picked him up.

'You have a bad dream?' she asked, burying her

mouth into the fine, gritty hollow between his head and shoulder, the hollow that would someday become a neck.

'I didn't have a dream,' he said.

'Oh?'

'No. I didn't go to sleep.'

'And you just lay up here all this time being quiet, I suppose.'

'Uh-huh.'

'And if you didn't sleep, why were you afraid?'

'The boogeyman in the closet,' he said.

She hugged him tightly and pushed the closet door closed.

He clung to her neck until she had undressed him and pried him off to lower him into the already sandy-bottomed bath water.

'Don't leave me, Mommy. Don't leave me alone.'

'I won't, honey. I'm sorting clothes. I'll . . . sing here in the hallway.'

'I saw him, Mommy. I saw the boogeyman.'

She, singing brightly that he was her sunshine, did not hear this eyewitness report.

Hanover was talking into the stained shoe, explaining how the tests had to be done on the stain, apologizing that a piece of the lining had to be cut out.

'The shoe is ruined,' he said.

'I don't care,' said Laren. She shrugged. 'I never intended to wear it again.'

'It's . . . human sperm stain,' said Hanover with a blush.

'I know,' she said. 'Remember, I told you that in the first place.'

Oh, and how did you get such expertise in human sperm? said the question forming on the detective's

62

face. Hm? Huh? Hunhhh? he seemed to be shouting with his expression.

'Blood type O-positive,' said his voice instead. Evenly restrained.

A third voice butted into the conversation. 'That oughta narrow it down to a few million,' said Dewey.

'So,' she said to Dewey, shifting into attack demeanor, 'when did you steal my shoe?'

'You wanted to keep the shoe?' he asked, deflecting her attack.

She glared.

He wouldn't give her the satisfaction of glaring back. Instead his mild expression soaked up the heat of her glare as if he didn't give a shit about what she thought of him.

'What we need next,' said Hanover, breaking the silent deadlock, 'is a sperm sample from your ... Mr Carter – uh, to eliminate him as a suspect.' He left the begged question hanging ridiculously in the air.

She blinked, severing Dewey from her glare with two guillotine chops of her eyelids, and whirled on Hanover.

'He isn't *my* Mr Carter, Hanover.'

She stomped away, her behind view snagging the gaze of every man in the division.

'Then how we gonna ...'

She flung the answer back over her shoulder before he could finish the question. Her eyes caught Hanover roaming her body with his eyes.

'Why don't you go ask *your* Mr Carter for a contribution to the policeman's ball?' A flip of her hair and instant dismissal.

'Balls,' whispered Hanover as her butt swung out the door and around the corner. He looked helplessly at Dewey. 'I don't mind if you wanna fight with her, but do you mind not screwing up my chances to eat crackers in bed with her?'

Dewey didn't bite. Didn't speak. Didn't show any emotion in his expression, unless boredom was an emotion.

'Well,' said Hanover, 'if you're not going to be making a move on her, you sure won't mind if I do.'

'Hardly. I've already told you that. You don't need my permission, Hanover. Make your move.'

'Doesn't anything bother you?' asked the detective rhetorically. 'Doesn't she even *interest* you? A little?'

Dewey smirked. 'My last deadline is past. I get any calls from the city desk?'

Hanover wagged his head.

'Then I'm gone. Tomorrow I'd better file something – just for appearances. Get any crimes solved today?'

Hanover shook his head. 'Tomorrow I got to solve a couple – for appearances. Wanna go for a beer?'

'Naw. I got some things to deal with in my apartment.'

Hanover looked pleased that Dewey refused the offer for a drink.

The evening began creeping over the horizon as soon as the sun turned its back.

Laren let the whirling door spit her out of the *Post-Herald* building. She inhaled the warm air and coughed on auto exhaust. She didn't see the ambush coming until he was beside her.

'Going my way?'

She sneered without even deigning to look at him or even to slow down. 'Very original, Deputy Dawg.'

Hanover said, 'Let me buy you a drink. We can bury the hatchet.'

'You mean, like ... we can be *friends?*' Her lip raised.

'You're mocking me, Miss Hodges. Ma'am.' That sneering lip, he observed. A bad sign.

'And now you're mocking me. And you know what, detective? I kinda like it that way. Tell you what. Let's be enemies, okay?'

'Just let me walk you to your car then. That will be enough for now. We don't have to push it too fast. We can take our time ... you know ... like ... be gentle with each other.'

She smiled, enjoying the joust.

'You *are* walking me to my car – whether I like it or not.'

'What's a public servant for?'

It brought another smile to her face.

'Hanover, don't we have this backward? Isn't the reporter supposed to be ambushing you? Yammering all the stupid questions? Acting the cur, the cad, the bitch, the idiot. Whatever. Begging for information?'

'Ah, information.' He waved his hand before him, plastering the invisible word *information* across the marquee of the blackening horizon. 'Information about the guy who was lurking around your apartment, for instance. Suppose I was to leak some *information* to a certain member of the press? You know, a tip every time we developed a new lead on this ... lurker perp. Now that would be a public service, wouldn't it?'

'The cop shop belongs to Dewey.'

Totally unimpressed, he belched a sarcastic laugh in self-defense. 'As if you wouldn't plant your little ...'

She unsheathed a glare from her metallic eyes and stabbed it into his own plain hazels. 'Ass?'

'... foot. I was gonna say foot – plant your little foot on his turf.'

65

'And in return?'

'You know . . . a little . . .'

'Ass? A little stray piece of ass now and then?' She lifted the corner of her mouth in the savage facsimile of a smile.

'Gawd,' he muttered under his breath. 'You're cold, Hodges. Mean as hell, ya know? That isn't what I was gonna say. You're a real . . .'

'Bitch?'

He bridled at that, but held his tongue, though a silent 'bitch' leaked from his lips.

'I wasn't gonna say that,' he said weakly. 'But you're not really so bad, Miss Hodges.'

'And you're such a sweetheart yourself. You know . . . for an asshole.'

The obscenity – *the* obscenity – actually formed, his front teeth resting on his bottom lip, the air beginning to hiss out, the *F* actually beginning to sound. But he held it, sucking in his lips and clamping down on them with his teeth.

'No wonder,' he muttered as she bent down to unlock her fiery red Fiero, 'no wonder cops and reporters hate each other. First my buddy Dewey turns batshit and throws away one of his best friends, namely me, and now you're passing up the chance for an everlasting . . .'

'Dewey?' She whirled and caught him ogling her from behind.

He cocked his head at her, blinking as if something besides the vision of her butt was in his eye.

'Okay,' she said. 'You can buy me a drink.' She sat down and drew her long, athletic legs into the cockpit. They snaked into the car.

His head fell over to the side to watch the legs disappear, his ear touching his shoulder, his eyes crossed, his tongue pointing at the sky. She was messing with his mind, driving him nuts on purpose, he knew. God, he loved it when women did that to him.

'Detective?' said the voice from inside the Fiero.

He regained his sanity. 'Let's go before you change your mind.'

The evening was smooth for Theresa and Matt Dewey and Jesse Lewis. They stayed within touching distance, the adults brushing shoulders, pressing hips when they passed each other in the kitchen or sat beside each other, the child moving in the wake of his mother, sitting in her shadow cast by the lamp. But as darkness grew toward bedtime, Matt became tentative, even whiney. She pressed her lips to his forehead in the mother's secret way of testing for fever.

'Is it my bedtime?' he asked.

'He okay to take up?' asked Lewis.

She nodded and picked up his thirty-four pounds in answer to both. Matt whimpered.

She tucked him in as Lewis watched, leaning in the doorway.

'Are you going to stay upstairs?' asked the child.

She turned to the doorway. Lewis straightened expectantly, the same question in his expression.

'Yes,' she said to both of them.

They walked to her bedroom.

Matt Dewey drew the blanket over his head and hunkered down in terror.

For the detective and the reporter, one drink had become several, then many, as night fell. The conversation, by mutual, unspoken consent, was about her. She told about her ambition to move up journalism's ladder but asked him to avoid the mention of that to anybody at the *Post-Herald*. He of-coursed her request solemnly and mentioned how obvious it was that she liked to be in control of things and people, that he himself, tough and professional as he was, didn't mind being controlled by the right woman. His eyebrows raised as his suggestion hung in the smoky haze of the cocktail lounge.

At which point she turned the conversation to Dewey.

Hanover drained half a bottle of beer and set it down, with a rap on the tabletop, even through the napkin. 'Shame about Dewey being so screwed up – his kid being killed and all.'

She perked up then and immediately dropped back into the impassive so Hanover wouldn't know she was interested. 'He mentioned his son this very afternoon,' she said carelessly over the crusted rim of a salty dog. 'He didn't talk as if anything was wrong with his child.'

Hanover hadn't missed her sudden shift of attention and the effort to disguise it. He made his living on recognizing such things.

'Thu-errs not nothing wrong with his kid,' he burped. 'I mean, not the son. But the other one, the daughter.'

'Daughter,' she whispered at the discovery. 'Something wrong with his daughter?'

'You could say that. She's dead.'

'Dead?'

'Or kidnapped. I dunno which. She's been gone for years.'

The darkness parted into a vertical split as the door opened. The stuffy closet inhaled a breath of cooler air. The eyes sampled the light until they were comfortable. Then the door widened the vertical split of light.

The eyes adjusted again. The ears filtered every sound, cataloguing the whisper of forced-air ventilation, the distant murmur of a television. An animal in the forest had no sharper ears than these, attuned by years of deadly silent listening from the darkness of closets and basements, attics and spare rooms. The ears could even hear the rapid, panicked breathing from the lump on the bed, the boy huddled in fear under the blankets.

The ears could especially hear the roiling in the intestines below. The intestines had become unsynchronized. They said it was time to move, even before the utter silence of wee morning fell.

The feet had already mapped the floor. They knew where the creaking spots were, knew how to avoid them. The eyes were adjusted, the door open wide enough.

The feet waited until the air conditioning went silent, the air in the vents expiring a last gasp.

The ears tested the list of remaining sounds.

The feet moved, negotiating the surface of the carpet as a ship with bottom-sounding sonar navigates an unmarked channel.

They were patient feet. They waited in the hallway as the ears filtered through the television sounds, as the eyes watched the flickering slit of blue light for a shadow to fall across it. The ears picked up the urgent whispers, the complaining springs of an undulating mattress.

The nose picked up the musky scents of passion.

The stomach loosed a high-pitched gurgle.

The feet moved into the dark hallway bathroom, glided over bathtub toys and backed up to the toilet. A yard of toilet paper uncoiled silently into the water to muffle it.

* * *

Theresa was allowing her guilt to consume her. She blamed herself for not being able to keep her husband, for wanting him in bed instead of Jesse, for treating Jesse like this – to be loving him and thinking of somebody else – to have her son only a few feet down the hall sleeping while she . . .

The scream hit her like a jolt of electricity, a scream of terror that she could discern from a child's complaint of simple pain or petulance.

She leapt from the bed and ran from the room.

Jesse called after her as he tried to unfurl the knot of his pants.

He found them on the bed clinging to each other for comfort. Matt was sobbing.

As Jesse crashed from his adrenaline high, he slumped against the wall. 'What's wrong?'

'Boogeyman,' said Theresa, as matter-of-factly as if there were one.

'There's a boogeyman in my closet,' said Matt.

'Listen, you two. There's no boogeyman.'

'Yes, there is,' the child insisted.

'You see him?' demanded Jesse, ever the accountant whose life was constructed of fact and figures, the only fictions occasional ones with enough documentation to at least make a decent argument with the IRS.

Finally Matt answered, 'No, I didn't see him.'

'See?'

'He touched me.'

Jesse narrowed his eyes. 'Touched you?'

'What do you mean, he touched you?' asked Theresa. 'How did he touch you?' She held the small shoulders so she could look into the black, teary eyes, barely masking the panic in her own eyes.

'Like this.' He patted himself gently on the head. 'I was under the covers.'

She hugged him.

'He lives in my closet.'

Jesse shoved away from the wall and walked to the closet. He tossed out a few toys from the closet floor.

'Smells like dog crap, but there ain't no boogeyman in here, Matt.'

'Under the bed. He's under the bed,' insisted Matt.

'Theresa. I'm exhausted with this boogeyman stuff. Matt, I gotta work, pal. See you in the morning. You need to air out this room, honey.' He stood expectantly with his hands on his hips waiting for her to come.

Theresa peeked down toward her feet to humor the child. But to humor the man, she did not do what she wanted to do. She did not drop to her knees to look under the bed. 'Matt, there's nothing under the bed. See?'

He nodded, unconvinced, knowing he was being humored, patronized.

She peeled his arms off her and tucked him in. He burrowed under, becoming a lump under the covers. She patted his back, trying to loosen the knot of his little body. Jesse cleared his throat. Matt tightened up even more. Theresa sighed, finally giving in, making the concession.

'Boogeyman,' said the accountant as he reached for the naked body joining him in bed. She hugged him but would not allow anything more intimate than that.

'Did you . . . open the closet door?' she asked.

'Huh? Yes, when I looked in.'

'But was the door completely shut? I mean, did you have to turn the handle to open the door?'

'No. Yes. Oh, I don't remember. I was just thinking of boogeymen and you, not closet doors.'

* * *

There was an irregular fold in the dust ruffle around the bed. Long after the mother had left and the boy's breathing had evened out, the fold was pulled straight from beneath.

BOOK II
Menacing Lurkings

6

The sight of the figure outside the window paralyzed the two boys in shock. They were no longer tough street punks. They'd become a couple of scared kids. Sherman hugged Darwin with the penlight between them. Darwin fumbled for the switch and finally doused the beam. In total darkness they shuffled along the uneven floor to the wall and flattened against the concrete, trying to hide, hoping they hadn't been seen.

Darwin knew they'd now have to hide until the figure outside left. Then maybe they could climb out. Maybe they could run away and not be seen here. Ever. He would never be back to this damned house. He . . .

A scraping sound, then a clunk, stopped his heart and his thoughts. The storm window was back in place. An arm waved at them. No, Darwin realized, the arm was not waving but dusting off the glass. Then the outline of a face pressed against it as if looking in.

Sherman hugged him tighter, pulling him deeper into the basement. Darwin fought back. From being out there, he knew it was impossible to see in. Small comfort.

The figure vanished silently.

Sherman relaxed his grip a little.

The pair leaned toward the window, then jerked away . . . as the foggy rectangle of light was darkened with a shadow again. A heavy thud outside traveled through the earth and the wall. To Darwin it meant something heavy had been put in place by the window.

Not only was their break-in discovered, but they were too. And trapped inside. There could be no other explanation.

Darwin knew they'd have to find another way out, perhaps through the other rooms of the basement. He flicked the light on and led the way to the door. Behind him Sherman whined.

They had changed roles completely. Darwin was leading, and Sherman tagged along behind like a sick, frightened kitten, mewing and staggering.

Darwin muttered a curse, beckoning to Sherman, backing out of the tiny room into the larger darkness.

Something tapped him on the shoulder; startled him breathless; brought a shriek to his lips.

He spun with the light and found himself tangled with a pair of legs dangling. As he recoiled, the light splashed around the room revealing a chamber of horrors. His breath escaped as a groan.

Two other bodies hung from ropes. A hole was dug into the earthen floor, a pile of dirt off to the side. It was a grave. They were dead. And this was . . . *no* . . .

It couldn't be real. It just couldn't be. His skin prickled. He'd been in a haunted house at Halloween before, and he'd seen pictures of wax museums of horror. This was one of those, he just *knew*.

He shone the light up into the face of the figure above him. It was that of a little girl. The rope had bent her head to the side. Her tongue stuck out dryly at him. The eyes had dried to black blood blisters. It looked like a poor fake. Her body had swollen like . . . like one of those dogs beside the highway. She was a child who had rotted into the picture of a witch.

He gagged, choking off a little scream, swallowing his bile. No wonder Sherman had fallen apart.

Sherman.

Darwin heard him crying in the other room.

There was a rattling and screeching from inside the other room. Shivering uncontrollably, he stepped back inside the smaller room. His shoulder still remembered the touch of that dead girl's legs. In the tiny light he saw Sherman pushing the splintered two-by-four board against the window frame. It didn't give. Whatever was up there was heavy. He shone the pitifully weak beam up the board to where wood met the window.

What he saw electrified him.

A pair of eyes blinked rapidly through the dirty, streaked glass.

Sherman recoiled, stumbling backward with the board. But Darwin caught him from behind and wrested the two-by-four from him. He tossed the splintered javelin through the pane of glass.

He thought he heard a cry.

'Let's get the fuck out of here!' he yelled at Sherman.

Sherman needed no prodding. He'd seen the face. They ran out together, both hitting the dangling girl, Darwin with his face. As he did, her skin crackled like cellophane, releasing a stench. They both began gagging.

As they went by the grave, Darwin – against every instinct in him – flashed his light at the darkest of the darkness and saw the hole had been partially filled. An arm stuck up through the loose dirt. The wrist was bent backward, the relaxed fingers beckoning them.

They cursed at each other and everything and nothing and found a rickety stairway. They ran up the steps, trying to leave the horror and shock behind them.

Together they hit the door, and it flew open, letting them sprawl on the floor. They were free of the basement. Now, if only they could get out the door before them.

On their hands and knees, they made a move toward the door.

But the door made a move back – toward them – as it opened. But not to let them escape.

In the doorway stood a figure with a ball peen hammer. They knew him only as Slime, the name they'd coined for him because of the way he walked and looked, although they'd only seen him from a distance. Slime's face was wet. That meant blood. Darwin knew he'd stabbed him with the splintered glass and wood. And that hammer meant . . . Sherman was right about Slime creeping, stealing, killing . . . eating. The blood and the hammer meant he was mad enough to kill them.

They were up and running to the right because that was the only way to go. They took the stairs up because that was all they found in the way of escape.

Darwin never heard Slime coming behind. All he heard was his own cursing, Sherman's whimpering, the pounding of their feet on the wooden steps.

At the top, a hallway turned back on the stairs. There were three doors. Sherman grabbed the first. It was a closet partially filled with unrolled toilet paper and trash. Darwin tried a second door. It was locked. The third door was at the end of the hallway.

They ran and threw their combined weights at it. They bounced off. Darwin grabbed the handle, turned and pushed. Nothing.

'Fucking locked,' he screamed.

Sherman cried out unintelligibly.

They heard footfalls on the stairs. Plodding, heavy steps. Now and then an irregular crash punctuated the steps. Slime was bashing his hammer against the banister or walls. Maybe he'd been blinded, Darwin

78

thought. Maybe he was feeling his way along with the hammer, maybe . . .

'Shit!' he cried. 'Open the door.'

'It's fucking locked,' yelped Sherman.

'Pull, you bastard, pull! It opens out.'

The door came open, releasing a stale cloud of trapped stink.

A window allowed enough moonlight for them to see it was nearly empty in the room. There was only a mattress on the floor. No furniture. A closet door. The room stunk, God, it stunk like piss and shit. This was Slime's bedroom. And his bathroom, Darwin knew.

The footsteps now clunked toward them from the top of the stairs.

Darwin saw Slime's shadow creep up the wall. Slime's figure followed, turning the corner. He stopped and staggered a step toward them, his free hand wiping his brow of the wetness, as if to see better.

Sherman screamed yet again, his voice gone hoarse.

Darwin would have screamed, but he couldn't. His throat was locked shut. To him, this was a horror movie of the first order, something that fascinated as well as horrified. He could just walk out any second on the pretense he needed to piss or get some popcorn. Couldn't he?

Slime staggered toward them, leading the way with the hammer, banging along the wall. Muttering threats. Cursing. He cursed threats of murder, and Darwin believed the threats.

Sherman dragged Darwin into the room and they pulled the door shut. Darwin regained his voice enough to scream instructions. He said to lock the door while he got the window open.

'There's no lock on the door,' Sherman whined.

And Darwin couldn't get the window open at all. It

wouldn't budge. He went back to help Sherman hold the handle. But Sherman let go of it and went stumbling around uselessly. Darwin cursed him. 'You're so fucking brave,' he shouted. 'Remember, this was *your* idea. Remember . . .'

The hammer banged on the door.

Darwin felt an angry tug on the handle.

He shouted for Sherman to help.

Sherman shouted back curses that he was looking for something to break the window out.

The door came open a foot as a wet and bloody hand gripped the edge. Sherman ran over and four hands pulling on the knob yanked it shut on the bloody fingers. They felt a tug, then a release, then a body falling to the floor; then they heard a cursing.

Suddenly, Darwin's grip on the metal knob was electrified with a stinging impact. Slime was pounding his hammer on the handle outside, then on the door panels, then on the wall, the handle, the door handle, door, handle.

Sherman cried out, sobbing and screaming at every impact of the hammer.

The door panels gave first, snapping and splintering. They could hear ragged breathing between the blows. Every once in a while another blow shattered against Darwin's grip on the doorknob. He screamed at the dazed, useless Sherman to hold the door.

Then he let go and ran to the window. He stood back and kicked at the glass, bashing it out, feeling cuts but no pain on his ankles. He refused to check himself for injury. Out that window lay freedom. If only they had time to climb down together, to help each other out.

He beckoned to Sherman. 'You first,' he shouted in a stage whisper. 'Come on.'

Sherman released the knob and ran at the window.

Darwin reached to take his friend's hand, to help him out.

But Sherman would not be helped.

He turned and ran at the window.

Shrieking for his mommy, he threw his shoulder at the glass shards and went flying into the night.

The stunned Darwin stood with his hand out, his mouth open. Incongruously, he felt funny about Sherman calling for his mother. Sherman hated his mom. That's what he always said, anyways. Why call for her now?

Sherman's call went out into the night with him and disappeared abruptly into the distance below.

Why?

Why the fuck?

The hammer struck another blow on the door, rattling Darwin from his frozen reflection.

He couldn't just run out the window like Sherman. He didn't have the guts. So he ran to the closet and opened that door. There was nothing inside but the powerful smell of urine. This, he knew, had been Slime's bathroom. Nothing inside but that smell and . . .

And a hole. There was a *hole* in the back of the closet as if somebody had thrown an angry fist through the fiberboard.

He ran and pulled at the edges of the hole. Great chunks came out. Maybe there *was* some hope, he thought, a hysterical giggle rising in his throat.

He widened the hole to the size of a basketball, tearing furiously like a dog burrowing. The dust and fibers gagged him, but he kept pulling away.

Until he heard the bedroom door slam open against the hallway wall. Then he froze.

As footsteps plodded across the floor.

As glass crunched under heavy boots.

As the smell of urine stung his eyes, as fibers tickled his nose. As he felt tears running down his cheeks. As he heard his heart clunking against his ribs.

Darwin was breathing through his wide-open mouth, taking quick, shallow, silent-as-he-could breaths, imagining Slime at the window looking out.

The glass squealed as it was ground under a pivoting boot. Maybe Slime would think they'd both gone out the window.

A sliver of light flashed under the closet door.

The boots plodded across the room again.

Darwin remained frozen in place, afraid even to breathe.

The closet door flew open, enlarging the sliver of light into a spotlight of the night.

The dark, glistening form raised the crisp, deadly outline of the hammer.

Darwin threw his arms up in front of his face and fell back against the rear of the closet. He expected to be smothered with blows, have his terror end quickly.

His butt hit the edge of the hole he'd torn through the wall, and he kept falling, squirting tail-first through the back of the closet. A blanket of insulation broke his fall gently before he'd even realized what had happened. Then the attic floor – the ceiling of the downstairs hallway – gave way, and he continued to fall.

The plunge took forever. It took his breath away, first by the sheer exhilaration of free-falling ten feet. Then as he smashed – hips, back, shoulders, head, all at once – onto the downstairs floor, his lungs were literally emptied with the impact.

The darkest of darknesses wrapped him like a blanket. It was a palpable blackness that came roughly as puffs of fibers and splinters of laths and chunks of plaster. The dust filled his nose and mouth, choking him softly as a creeping numbness came over his muscles that wanted to get up and run but couldn't. He knew he was choking on the insulation, that he would surely die from it. Not that it mattered because the fog in his battered head told him he'd die from brain injury anyhow, not that that mattered because he'd broken his back and probably his neck.

Momentarily, he wanted to scream in panic because he couldn't catch his breath. He was drowning out of water. But there was not breath enough to muster a scream.

Not that it mattered. Slime was going to kill him anyhow. He could feel the irregular vibrations, clunking footsteps, and in the distance through the white rushing noise inside his ears, he could even hear the steps in the hallway upstairs.

He felt a rush of panic, then anger as he couldn't breathe, let alone get up and run. But the hot panic and anger didn't last long.

It vanished the moment he realized he was going to die. Perhaps Sherman felt the same thing on the way from the second floor window to the ground, he thought.

He let himself go, easing himself into unconsciousness, hastening as best he could manage the trip toward death.

Darwin felt remarkably calm. Breathless and broken, he was going to die. He knew he'd be hung to dry and buried with the others in the basement. It didn't matter, wouldn't matter, because the pain was going to be over soon.

The footsteps drew near.

He felt a vicious kick in the side.

But there was little consciousness and no breath left, so the blow was wasted on his limp body.

Deep, deep inside his mind, he smiled and slipped away with a final thought, glad to be dying, pleased to be cheating Slime out of the pleasure of killing him.

Fuck you, Slime.

7

His hand clutched the neck of a half-empty bottle of whiskey wedged between his legs. Serious whiskey. Hundred-proof Kentucky Bourbon. Although he was asleep, the hand clutched it seriously too, as if it were his masculinity, as if liquor had become that.

Ted Dewey lay draped across his couch gripping that bottleneck in his dark, dumpy apartment.

Although he was asleep, it was the fitful, vague rest of the tormented. His body jerked, his clenched hand sloshing the amber. His temples knotted, his bottom molars ground against his top teeth, first ratcheting the enamel ridges, then grinding the flat surfaces like millstones.

Although he was asleep, tears leaked from the slits of his eyelids.

When his alarm clock brought down the curtain on his nightmare, he awoke, saw where he was. He felt relief, then sadness. He wiped the wetness from his eyes, then wiped the taste of strawberry from his lips.

Marguerite Smallwood, heavy sleeper, naked sleeper, lay on her belly, waiting deep in her subconscious for her own alarm to awaken her.

But it was not her alarm radio that awakened her. She felt her bed shake, but it was felt too deeply in her subconscious for that to awaken her. Then she felt the weight across her legs, then across her buttocks, and that did it. She started to push herself up, but weakly, too groggy to know what was happening. Another weight on her shoulders pushed her face down into the pillow. She felt hands on her neck. No, she felt hands working around her neck, then she felt the pull, the strangling, choking pull of something against her throat. And that awakened her fully. Finally. She struggled against the pull that drew her chin up, bowed her back. She tried to reach under her pillow, tried to clutch the sheets and pull herself down, reaching, grasping, stretching. But the strangling cord around her neck prevented that. She fought, wriggling, bucking, pushing. She felt the weight increase on her buttocks.

Rape.

She was going to be raped. Somebody had sneaked into her house and was now going to violate her body. The very thought of it made her all the more angry. She could barely breathe, and she knew it would not be long before she would be unconscious, unable to fight back, unable to prevent the ... violation. *Her body*. The body she had nurtured since she became aware of it in puberty.

Anger. Anger fueled her strength and made her fight back, bucking against the weight, struggling against the cord around her neck, barely able to hear or think or even be concerned about her safety. Worse even than the thought of death was the thought of rape.

But she was not strong enough. The room was already dark, and even though she had her eyes wide open, she could not see anything or anybody. Dark. And the darkness grew even darker as she began to lose her consciousness. She knew she had not yet been violated. But she would soon be unconscious. Then ... she heard the voice, a hoarse whisper, a whispering of a name in her ear as the owner of that voice drew his breath raggedly. He whispered the name.

86

'Laren,' he rasped at her.

Marguerite was too near unconsciousness to make any sense of it. The name. It was the wrong name. She was not . . .

Even as she sank toward a deeper unconsciousness than sleep, her habit of sleeping heavily saved her. For she always set her alarm radio to the hard-rock station at full volume. And the radio had always performed its duty, alarming her every workday, blasting her from her dreams as she slept usually uncovered, usually prone. Often it had alarmed her occasional lovers as well, electrifying them literally off the bed, leaving them cursing and her giggling.

Today the alarming music galvanized the figure sitting on her buttocks over her sprawled body and sent him recoiling in terror. With a heave, she threw herself up against the weight.

Marguerite felt the bed bounce. Felt a rush of the intruder's air at her feet. Caught the glimpse of a shadow framed in her doorway. She pulled at the cord around her neck and spun on the bed. Greedily, she sucked fresh breaths. But even as she breathed, she finally slid her hand beneath her pillow, grasping what she could not get to before because of the strangling cord. And came up with an A–90 double-action, semiautomatic pistol. She came up firing.

Down the length of her wall into the hallway toward her front door she spaced six holes two feet apart.

She was up, cursing herself hoarsely as the apartment door slammed open. If she had started the first hole toward the front instead of next to the bedroom door, she might have hit the bastard.

The bullet-shattered mirror, the holes in the apartment wall – they meant nothing to her. Even her life wasn't *that* important to her. All she had of value was sliding off that bed. Her body. She never let others use her body, but because of her looks, she'd gotten her job and her first promotion. After that, she advanced on ability, brains, cunning. If others felt obliged to give her things, to be awed by her God-given physique, then that was their problem. She gave nobody permission to enter her body without medical certification they were clean of AIDS and every other sexually transmitted disease.

And if anybody tried to violate her body against her will, God help him. She would kill him.

Outside she half-ran, half-staggered. She glanced both ways, but saw nothing among the parked cars down the line of apartments. Then as her vision cleared, across fifty yards of landscaped berms and geometrically placed trees, she saw the head and shoulders of a sprinting man.

She aimed and loosed four more rounds at the dodging figure as it ran up a slope and disappeared over the other side next to the street traffic. The figure bounced left and right like an arcade target, but Marguerite doubted she had a hit. She cursed after him. And she cursed herself for missing.

The salesman had been leaning into the trunk of his car when he heard the second set of shots fired. His mind was full of drab thoughts about the drive north as he arranged his sample cases. He peered over the trunk to see if they really were shots, those little pops that had gotten decidedly louder with this second fusillade.

He saw the gun and dropped to his knees. They *were* shots!

Then his stunned curiosity caught up with his instincts.

Slowly he rose to see if the vision would materialize as he thought he remembered it. There was way more than that gun, wasn't there?

Yes!

There was a woman. A naked woman. A gorgeous naked woman. A gorgeous naked woman with a pistol firing off toward the street.

He would have looked where she pointed, but his eyes would not be coaxed away from the vision of her.

He heard her curses and saw her take off, running across the grass. The low, long-shadowed sunlight confirmed what seemed so surreal in the shade of the apartment.

His wife came out robed to find out what all the commotion was.

But she couldn't get his attention. He was gawking toward the distant street.

She followed his gaze. She saw the woman, the nude woman, standing balanced atop the berm and pointing with both hands into the woods across the street.

She heard the shots. Five more of them. Then she heard a squeal of tires and crunching of cars in the street.

'C'mon, Herbert, let's get inside. That crazy woman is coming back this way. What do you suppose is wrong with her?'

Herbert gulped.

'Nothing,' he said.

She glared at him.

'Well,' he said as he reluctantly let himself be dragged back into the apartment, 'okay – so she's got tan lines on her butt.'

Theresa Dewey approached the door of her son's room as Jesse Lewis scratched himself on the way to the shower. He glanced down the hallway and saw her hand go to her mouth, heard her cry out.

He ran into the hallway as she rushed into the room.

He found her raising the limp body, precariously balanced at the edge of the bed. The boy snuggled down into his pillow with the smile of a sleep-drugged child being tucked with covers by a loving mother.

Theresa turned and smiled sheepishly.

Jesse yawned a smile and scratched his nuts.

'I thought Matt was going to fall out of bed,' she said defensively.

He made an impatient face.

'You use the hall bathroom,' she ordered by way of dismissal.

He did, muttering to himself about the kid and his nightmares, his propensity to disturb them at the most awkward of times, the kid's disgusting inability to remember to flush the toilet after himself, his raising such a big stink for such a tyke.

When the hallway bathroom door had gone shut, and she heard the toilet flush, Theresa slipped into Matt's room. She checked his closet and found it empty. With an obvious effort of will over incredulity, she also knelt and looked under her son's bed. Finding nothing, she was enormously relieved.

She never thought to check the hallway closet because Matt had never mentioned the boogeyman's staying in there. And even if he had mentioned it, she probably wouldn't have checked it, thinking now that it was, after all, a child's imaginary boogeyman.

And it never occurred to her to check under her own bed. If she had, she would have had her own fright, her own adult version of the boogeyman.

* * *

At the police station, the arresting officers stood in the center of the mob of brother cops, fielding questions like convicted politicians:

'Was she really naked? I mean totally buck-ass? And did you see her that way? Frontal and everything?'

'Damn right, until Sir Arthur Raleigh here had to go and drape a blanket over her.'

'How did you disarm her?'

'There she was, pointing three – not one, but three – .38s at us.'

'Yuk.'

"Course I only saw the two.'

'Yuk-yuk.'

'Yeah, and did you frisk her?'

'She have a permit for that gun?'

'Yep.'

'She have it on her?'

'Yuk-yuk-yuk.'

'And what about the fender bender she caused on the street?'

'Oh ... well, we had to turn that over to traffic division so we could ... take the ... suspect into custody.'

'And what about the marks on her?'

'Well, she would only let us look at her neck. And there wasn't much to see there.'

'Yuk.'

Hanover dispersed the mob when he took the pair of uniforms aside and heard their story told in the presence of Marguerite Smallwood, where the tone and demeanor of the briefing was less earthy, more factual and professional.

He then dismissed them, telling them their reports would go to him only, that he didn't see grounds for

91

any charges against a woman defending herself from an intruder.

'Or even a possible rapist,' he said for Marguerite's benefit. 'Who knows what that creep might have been up to?'

She smiled back at him, returning his condescendence, adjusting her jogging suit, pink and gray, satin and velour.

'Detective,' she said evenly, 'the man choked me. And I almost passed out. If I had . . .'

Hanover saw she had nothing beneath the pink and gray but her. He clenched his eyes shut for a moment, reminding himself who he was. And that *he* was not supposed to be the pervert here. Finally, he opened his eyes and spoke.

'Miss Smallwood, I'm . . . looking into a similar case of a prowler in that neighborhood.'

'Laren?'

'Oh. You know her. Why, yes, it is Miss Hodges,' he said with a tone of voice that hoped the two women hadn't compared notes on him. 'And in the time you've been down here, we've rounded up a number of vagrants and such in that area of the woods, and if you wouldn't mind, you could look at a lineup and help us.'

'I didn't get a clear look at the creep, and anyhow . . .'

'Well, that doesn't mean you shouldn't view the lineup, Miss Smallwood. There's always the chance something will jiggle your . . . memory.'

Hanover gave an order and a policewoman led Marguerite away as the detective grabbed for the phone and eagerly began punching buttons. Marguerite looked over her shoulder to try to get Hanover's attention to try to tell him something more. But she saw that he only had eyes for the pink velour back of her jogging suit. So she let herself be led out of his sight.

* * *

Laren was incredulous.

'You want to see me?' she wailed into the phone. 'Something obnoxious, disgusting, and perverted you forgot to say last night? Hell, no, I don't want to talk to you.'

'Oh, shucks,' said Hanover's phone voice in exaggerated sadness, 'and I thought you'd be interested if I was to give you a tip on . . . you know, the lurker perp.'

He paused, letting the burden of silence fall on her.

But she was a reporter and understood the use of silence. She knew the uninitiated interviewee would often blurt all sorts of information to fill a silence, as if feeling responsible for a lapse in conversation. True, her pulse had gotten a kick-start from his tantalizing hint. But she held the quiet.

'Or maybe it isn't the lurker,' he said. 'Maybe it's just a coincidence it happened just down the street from your old apartment . . . to a woman named Marguerite . . . Well, if I get a few more facts on this, I'll leave a message with your editor or with Dewey . . . yeah, Dewey. Like you said, he *is* the cop reporter. Maybe another time, Miss Hodges.'

'Wait.'

Hanover's silence was a smug one.

'Hanover,' she said. 'Marguerite Smallwood?'

'Why yes, ma'am.'

'Goddamn you, stop calling me that. Is she okay?'

'Why, yes . . . Laren. She's about to take in a lineup of suspects if you want to get in on it.'

'I do. When?'

'Now. But . . . well, I suppose I could hold . . .'

'I'll be there in five minutes,' she said.

Laren stood behind Marguerite's chair, massaging the shoulders of the gray-pink sweatshirt. The shoulders shrugged beneath her hands.

'I dunno,' said Marguerite. 'I told you, detective, I didn't see the guy. And none of these is even dressed like him, so I don't think you got him.'

After a moment's reflection, she said, 'But I am a pretty good shot, and I got off a full clip of fifteen at the creep. Maybe you should check the woods for a body.'

She stood up, shrugging off Laren's hands.

'Really, kid, I'm okay. I'm just mad that guy got in without me hearing him. Pissed off that I might have missed him fifteen times.'

'Let's get a cup of coffee and talk.'

'One cup. I'm already half a day late for work. But there is something very important I have to tell you, Laren.'

By late afternoon, Laren wore a tired, satisfied look as she leaned over the desk of Lou Albright, watching him read the dot matrix printout.

'Good shit, Laren,' he murmured as he read, his lips moving as he followed the dotted characters. 'Top drawer. First rate.'

He whistled and set the accordion of pages aside, then he picked it up again.

'I love that expression in the lead: "like some Lady Godiva gunslinger." That's good shit.'

She smiled broadly, unable to contain herself.

'And where'd you get this lurker tag?'

'It . . . uh, came to me.'

'We'll run it tomorrow morning,' he said, folding his fat-fingered hands across his belly, which bulged as if he were wearing the chest protector of an NFL quarterback – and the protector had slipped to his belt. 'Maybe a capsule for this evening's Blue Flash edition. Whet their appetites for the morning paper.'

94

She licked her lips.

'About twenty-six inches,' he said, glancing at the computer notation at the top of the first page, lifting his huge, grizzled head so the bottom slashes on his glasses would focus the dots for him.

'I suppose you could trim it to eighteen pretty easily.'

Her smile froze.

He continued, 'You know, so we can get some art on the page – a head shot of the lady and maybe a map of the area where this prowler has been operating.'

Her head lifted, then her chin tucked into a combative position.

'And we're going to have to know who this unidentified woman is . . . you know, the first woman who was . . . lurked.'

Her eyes softened and focused on the floor tiles.

'Who is this woman, Laren?'

'She has to remain anonymous.'

'I'll buy that. But I'm not letting any phantom Jimmies into this paper. You'll have to tell *me* at least.'

'Don't you trust me, Lou?'

'Not a question of trust, my dear. Question of my policy. And my policy is we don't use unidentified people unless the editor in charge of the story has the full name. And since you brought the story to me, I'm the guy who has to know.'

She brushed at something on the floor with the sole of her shoe.

'Is it you, Laren?'

In answer, she looked him defiantly in the eyes.

'Okay,' he said, 'now that that's settled, you have one of two choices. You take out the part about you . . .'

She drew back her lips in a snarl.

'Wait,' he said, holding up a traffic cop's palm. 'You

95

take it out and put it into a first-person sidebar or you leave this story as is, but we run it without a byline.'

She shifted her feet and drew a deep breath.

'Sorry,' he said. 'Those are the only two choices for running it. Only third choice is to kill it.'

The ball was back in her court. She interpreted his cold, blue, unyielding eyes, eyes staring expectantly at her beneath wiry, unruly, raised eyebrows, eyes she knew she could not charm with her looks – even the naked Marguerite wouldn't have been able to break his stare, she imagined – and said, 'Okay, Lou. Run it with no byline.'

'Good choice, Laren. I hate first-person shit except in a column. And I don't want to use the lurker tag just yet. Maybe later we'll call him lurker – if something more develops. Just call him a prowler. Say he *may* have been responsible for both incidents.'

Her face dropped. The longer she argued, the more she was losing here.

'But let *me* cut it down. I think I could shrink it four inches without hurting it. I don't want any dumbshit editor butchering . . .'

She remembered he was the editor.

He grinned sardonically.

'Eighteen inches. I said eighteen.'

'Twenty, Lou. Let me have twenty.'

'Okay. Twenty. Tops. And I want to see it before the desk sends it up to composing.'

She raised an eyebrow.

He raised her two.

'And no more cop shop stories. That's Dewey's turf.'

'Yeah,' she said, her tone adding: But this story didn't come from the cop shop.

He wouldn't let her have the last shot.

'And I want to be reading something about the state

fair board in the next couple months if you could find time. And how's that jazz piece coming?'

She surrendered and left without a further attempt at getting the last word.

Dewey had reduced himself to whining into the phone. Even as he heard his own voice, he hated himself for it.

'What do you mean no interesting stuff is coming out of the police beat, Lou?'

The voice at the other end was growling.

'Well I can't make up stories, for chrissake. I was out covering a semi overturned on the interstate, Lou.'

Growl.

'It was a fatal,' said Dewey weakly, not giving his lie the force it needed to be convincing.

The city editor's voice came across shoutingly clear. 'Fatal my ass, I had the desk check and the somebitch didn't die. You're covering fucking fender benders, Ted, while a woman is running around the north side buck-ass naked shooting off a pistol at a prowler. What the hell's wrong with your news judgment, pal?'

'Prowler?' – Dewey paused – 'Lou, does Laren have anything to do with this prowler thing?'

'Hodges has nothing to do with this, Ted. This is a story crying for space and where are you?'

'Come on, Lou, what'd you want? A frontal photo to go along with it? We're still a family paper, you know.'

'You listen to me, Dewey. It's not your job to maintain the reputation and readership of this paper. It's not your job to decide against a great story just because you're not able to get an erection over it. Laren said . . .'

'So it *was* Hodges. She on that prowler shit again?'

'Lurker or no lurker, Teddy my boy, a woman running around naked and shooting holes in the sky is a good story no matter what the reason.'

Albright's voice rose an octave as he launched into a string of obscenities.

Dewey sighed and apologized, his voice tinged with self-pity.

The editor's voice remembered, softened.

'We gotta cover those stories, Ted. We gotta sell papers.'

'Okay, Lou. I'll get the story. If I hurry, I can get something for a bulletin in the Blue Flash. Tomorrow . . .'

'Never mind, Ted. I . . . already let Laren write the story. But I won't let her take over the cop beat. I already told her to stay away from cop stuff.'

'Right.' Dewey sounded tired. No, more than that, he sounded defeated.

'All I want is for you to get off your butt and do the kind of job you're capable of, Ted.' He didn't even try to disguise the condescendence in his voice.

Instead of letting it go, Dewey lamely said, 'I can't be everywhere,' as if asking to be patronized even further.

Not even concerned about getting the last word, Albright hung up in disgust. He stared at the phone awhile, unconsciously shaking his head.

Dewey sniffed at his end of the phone and dropped the receiver into its cradle. He stopped by Hanover's desk on the way out, leaving the detective shaking his head, too.

The table was round, but the sides could easily be distinguished as the form of a triangle. At the apex were the two lawyers sitting side by side, ostensibly adversaries.

At one base angle sat Theresa. She had not been crying but gripped a fistful of tissue as if she knew she would be before all this was over.

At the other angle where the second leg of the triangle met the base sat Dewey, knotting and unknotting his jaw muscles, rippling his temples. He looked gray and sick.

The lawyers stared alternately at the Deweys as if the couple were playing Ping-Pong across the table. But the Deweys just stared blankly into the tabletop, one clenching tissues, the other facial muscles.

Finally the taller of the two lawyers stood up and pronounced: 'Why don't we just leave you two alone for a few minutes.' The shorter lawyer took the cue and followed his taller colleague from the room.

Outside the room, they compared golf scores and made a racquetball date.

'Think they'll reconcile?' asked tall.

'Whatzit matter?' said short. 'Long as we charge by the hour?'

Tall went for coffee. When he came back, he wanted to strike up a conversation on women, but short was pacing nervously before the door. Tall listened to the shouts emanating from the room.

'Forget reconciliation,' he said, shouldering the door aside, cradling his coffee so it wouldn't spill.

Theresa looked up from her wad of finally damp tissue. 'Go ahead with the divorce,' she sobbed at her lawyer, tall.

Tall looked at Dewey, who had resumed staring holes in the tabletop. He shrugged at short.

'He won't give in,' she said.

'Won't give *up*. I'll never give up,' said Dewey.

She broke down afresh.

Short tried to calm Dewey.

'Goddamn you. I don't want to calm down.'

Short gave him an exaggerated shrug. 'At least share this . . . concern, this last stickling point that you two are always fighting about . . . We can work it out.'

'No *we* can't,' Dewey said, including his contempt of all lawyers in sneering at the one he had hired. '*We* don't have the fucking problem here, do *we*? *Your* job is to file the divorce. Do *your* fucking job. Give *her* what *she* wants . . . Just go ahead with the fucking divorce.' Dewey rose and stormed through the door. 'Just tell *me* when the papers are ready to be signed. Then *we* will all be happy' came the final words from the receptionist area.

Tall held out a coffee.

Short reached for it.

Tall pulled it away in disgust and gave it to his tearful client.

'Theresa,' he said, 'give him a couple of days to cool off and we'll talk some sense into him.'

'No,' she said. 'You'll never change his mind. You just go ahead with the divorce papers. I'm not going to pursue him anymore. He thinks he's the only one who has problems to live with the rest of his life. Well, I have things to live with, too.'

She looked up at tall, narrowing her eyes in resolve, and said, 'But I *don't* have to live with him and his self-pity.'

Outside on the street, Dewey walked unsteadily out onto the sidewalk, into the glare of the sun. He pulled desperately at the knot of his necktie and staggered as if drunk to a toll phone on the corner. He picked up the receiver and slammed it back right away. He spun left, then right, looking up and down the street until he spied a liquor store. Fuck it, he muttered as he made toward the store. If he was going to feel it, he might as well be it.

At the *Post-Herald*, Laren was alternately yawning about and writing about the comeback of jazz in the city. Episodically, she was daydreaming about how her story might look in the morning paper, where it might be played, the point size of headline type.

Headline type.

All at once it hit her.

She signed off her terminal and strode down the hall toward the morgue. She ordered Sandra to direct her toward the clips on Dewey.

'Byline stuff?' asked the librarian.

'No. I want to see any news stories filed away under the Dewey name.'

'You mean the kidnapping stuff?'

Laren riveted the young woman with an icy glare. 'Kidnapping? You didn't tell me about kidnapping before.'

Sandra looked up into her head, searching for the answer to that one. She didn't find it. 'You never . . .'

'Never mind,' said Laren.

She snatched the folder proffered by Sandra, who slunk away to another row of files.

Laren opened the folder and felt the headline slap her eyes the instant she unfolded the fattest clipping: Cameron Hills girl fourth in string of disappearances.

The second-deck headline read: Five-Year-Old Vanishes After Leaving Kindergarten.

There was a school photo of the girl. Laren read the resemblance in the dark eyes before she even read the name line beneath the picture: Erica Dewey.

101

8

Sarah Thrasher's late afternoon screams brought her neighbor, a retired Navy officer, and he brought the police. The police drew the crowd, and the whole group moved to the backyard, where the screams had begun.

The Navy officer pointed to the hedge where he burst through after hearing bloody murder screamed at the Thrasher house. He swept his hand, palm upward, to Sarah.

Taking the cue, she told of kneeling in the garden tending tomatoes. As she spoke, more of the curious joined the back of the crowd, craning their necks to see, then fanning around the group, spreading into the garden until about a third of the forty or so people were smashing onions and carrots and beans, stepping on the creeping toes of squash vines.

Sarah told of looking up and seeing a movement out the corner of her eye. To demonstrate, she faced west and pointed toward the north, through the body of an onlooker toward the back of the Thrasher two-story brick colonial. The crowd looked where she pointed, saw nothing but more curious people joining their group of onlookers, then turned back to her.

'At first I thought it was a ghost, you know, one of those shadows you see from the corner of your eyes, but when you turn and try to catch a glimpse of it, it disappears. You know, an illusion?'

The policeman nodded, encouraging her to go on.

About half the crowd nodded, too.

'And sure enough, it did disappear. Then I began

102

thinking about the evening paper, that bulletin in it about the prowler. And I was sure I was just imagining things. And I was shaking my head like this to clear it . . .'

She demonstrated, then shivered.

'Then I saw him. In the shadows there beneath the crab apple. And my door was open and he must have come out of the back door. And that's when I started screaming, and, well, you know the rest.'

The policeman looked around at the heads in the crowd formed by the residents of the well-to-do neighborhood.

'Anybody else see any sign of a . . . prowler creeping around the Thrasher house?' he asked the group.

Seeing only shaking heads, he said, 'And, ma'am, did the suspect do anything?'

'He ran around the west end of the house.'

'And have you checked the house to see if anything's missing?'

'Why, no. I was hoping you'd . . . look around. I don't feel safe.'

'All right, Mrs Thrasher, why don't we go have a look. Fun's over, folks. Best you go on home.' Nobody moved. 'Best you go on home and see nothing's missing from *your* houses,' he added.

That got them dispersed.

At the back door, Sarah Thrasher stood aside and let the officers enter. Then she stepped up into the family room. The officer who'd done all the talking blocked the doorway, keeping out the young woman there.

'You a member of the family?'

She flashed a laminated ID. 'Laren Hodges. *Post-Herald.*'

'Crime scene, Miss Hodges. You can't come in.'

'Baloney. Mrs Thrasher, I'm the reporter who wrote

that bulletin you read in the evening paper. I've been covering this story, and I was hoping you could help. May I come into' – she looked defiantly at the cop – 'your house, Mrs Thrasher?' The cop looked away.

Sarah Thrasher said, 'Why, yes, I suppose.'

As Laren cockily stepped up into the family room, the smile dissolved from her face. Her head jerked and her shoulders bunched the instant she was inside, the moment she felt a cold chill ripple the skin at the back of her neck.

Hanover looked up and saw her coming. Again. Now he knew what it must have felt like to sailors during World War II when they could see the wake of a torpedo scratching a line of bubbled turbulence in the water toward their ship, helpless to do anything about it.

'Miss Hodges,' he said. 'Laren. Uh, what is it this time?'

She planted herself before his desk, her hands on her hips. Her eyes glittered.

'You said you were going to tip me off about the lurker investigation.'

He waited for her to finish, then realized she had.

'Yes?'

'Well, how come you didn't call me about the Thrasher family incident?'

A look of relief came across Hanover's face, relief that he didn't recognize the name. So Laren knew he was telling the truth before he told it.

'Thrasher? Honest, I didn't know there was a confirmed lurker incident there. Where is this Thrasher place?'

'Okay,' she said. 'I believe you. But we're going to have to get a better system of communications on this.'

'Wait a minute, Hodges. What do you mean system of communications? Your paper already has an office in this building and radios tuned to our freqs. It's your job to listen. Besides, I can't monitor every prowler call that comes into this place.'

'Hanover, I got news for you – a free tip from me to you. You may think this lurker thing is a big gas, a chance for you to talk to me, try to con me into bed with you . . . No, don't deny it . . . But that incident out at the Thrasher house, it's the real thing. That lurker was . . . or is . . . out there. And he's . . . the same guy who was in my apartment.'

His eyes narrowed. 'How can you be so sure?'

'Never mind that. I know.' She looked around quickly, letting him know she was changing subjects, letting herself off the hook of trying to explain something as vague as a *feeling*. 'Hey, speaking of jerks, where is Dewey? He should have called in to the city room with this bit of information – I had to get it from the chief photographer's radio. Good thing I was eavesdropping.'

He found something on his desk to busy himself about.

'Hanover, I'm asking you a question,' she said imperiously.

'I don't know. It's not my job to keep track of reporters, y'know?'

'You're covering for him. Where is he? Sleeping? Sleeping off a drunk? Sleeping off a drunk whore?'

He gave her a flat expression and snapped, 'Yes, I'm covering for him. He's with his lawyers finalizing his divorce papers. Why don't you go butt into that too?'

She knew she had almost gone too far. If he ever stopped believing he could get her into bed, he'd be a

105

hell of an enemy. He could sabotage her lurker stories. She backed off.

'I'm sorry,' she said sincerely and touched him briefly on the hand. 'I didn't know,' she said honestly. She turned sorrowfully and walked away slowly, her head bowed in honesty and sincerity.

Inside she was smiling, remembering the words of her first editor in Memphis: 'Listen, kiddo,' the old broad had said, 'the keys to getting ahead in journalism are honesty and sincerity. You learn to fake *them* and you've got it dicked.'

Inside the huge brick colonial, Sarah was checking the door locks for the tenth time. She was remembering the chiding the officer had given her for leaving open both the front and the back doors. She was just lucky, he had said, that half her belongings hadn't been carted out the front door while she was doing her gardening out back.

She had walked all around inside the ground floor looking out into the bright sunlight outside, looking for movement among the hedges, the garden.

Then she sat listening.

So many sounds she'd never heard before. Could an empty house be so noisy?

She tried to distinguish each sound.

The air-conditioner groaned outside, its noise diffused by the dense bushes around it. Inside the house the air whispered through the vents. One vent in the family room where she was sitting kept ticking like a tiny antique clock.

Somewhere nearby was a housefly banging its stupid head against a window, battering and buzzing like a dentist's slow drill trying to wear through enamel. Occasionally, one of the huge, green-bodied flies tried to bash its way in through a windowpane. They at least were sensible enough to give up after one attempt. She'd never realized how loud they could be.

A bird must be standing atop the chimney. She could hear it shrieking down into the fireplace. Then came a scratching on the roof. The little hairs on her neck waved like fields of grain in a breeze.

That scratching had to be a bird or a squirrel. Had to be.

Her breath was noisy as it rushed through her nostrils. She held her breath. But that didn't help her hear any better. So she opened her mouth and breathed slowly. Better.

A drip in the kitchen.

The tree outside swishing in a sudden afternoon breeze.

The house creaking, then cracking.

All this noise.

She'd never listened for it before.

Outside, a kid's scream. An impatient car horn.

Inside, the refrigerator's whirring – she could hear it all the way in here. And the clock . . . was it always so loud?

Inside her own body.

A gurgle in the bowel, a wheeze in the trachea, a crackle of wax in an ear.

You listen hard enough and you can hear them all, she thought. You hear them all individually and you hear them all blended into a rushing noise in your ears, white noise filtered through cotton. You listen and . . .

A body smashes into the front door.

She leapt from the couch, a scream rising in her chest.

She heard the voice shout in pained anger from the front porch.

'Maw-um. I'm ho-ome.'

She realized she was acting nutty. She ran to let in Buddy, the youngest, to greet him, happy for the company at last.

He was rubbing his shoulder.

'You locked the door,' he said petulantly. 'You made me run into a locked door.'

'Hi. I'm glad you're home,' she said, bending down to hug him.

'Maw-um, stop squishing me.'

Dewey lifted the bottle's mouth to his own. No point in using a glass, he thought. Already he was relaxed, numbed, the pain of the afternoon's meeting a vague memory. If only he didn't eventually have to sober up.

Now that he had anesthetized himself, he could traipse back through his mind and see the pictures there. There were the two years of anger growing between him and Theresa until she'd finally had enough of him. Before that was the mindbending grief of losing a daughter, a child. There was the emptiness – one morning you went to work after kissing the sticky lips of strawberry jam. You licked the sweetness off your smile as you drove to work. And when you came home she was not there to greet you. Ever again. There was no tragedy of an accident, no illness, long or short. Horrible as it sounded, there was not even a dead body in a grave you could point to and say: There lies an important part of my life that I can never recover.

There was simply nothing.

Dewey took a long pull at the lips of the bottle, felt

his breath taken away, waited for it to come back. He touched his fingertips to his own lips.

The worst part ended there – at his lips – with the kiss of strawberry jam. In his mind Erica was trapped in time, a smallish five-year-old who needed her face washed before she went off to kindergarten. She had never died. She lived in his mind, never aging, never changing, her only existence the short five years, most of which he'd missed out on because of the demands of his job. He hated himself for being a lousy father in those five years, although he hadn't been any better to Matt, given a second chance. No, he'd been worse. The thought that she was dead was unendurable to him. Yet he could not bring himself to hope she was alive, in the hands of who knows whom, suffering who knows what, wondering in that five-year-old – no, that seven-year-old mind . . .

The knock at the door ruined his scripted routine of anguish, self-inflicted misery, his own two-year march toward madness. He was to have begun crying at this point, letting the tears flow softly, letting the hand with the bottle lower it to the floor, letting himself drift into oblivion, his anger flowing out in helpless tears as he slept, licking strawberry jam from his lips.

But there was that knock. Again. Insistent. Even rude.

He ignored it.

But it would not be ignored.

'Dewey!' shouted the voice behind the knock. 'I know you're in there. Answer the door.'

It was Laren . . . that Hodges woman, damn her. No question – she would no easier be ignored than a case of flaming diarrhea.

He worked his mouth like a mime, trying to get some feeling back into it so he would not slur.

'Whaddya want?'

'I need to talk to you.'

'Go away.'

'No. I'll stay here all night screaming and pounding until you let me in. Now open the door.' She pounded some more. 'Hear that, all you neighbors?' she shouted.

He knew it was useless to argue. He doubted she would go away. But he could let her wonder. He went to the sink and splashed water into his face, rinsing the sweet taste from his lips. He let up the shade. It got no brighter in the room, so he knew it was already night.

He opened the door as she stood there, her chest refilled with air to shout, her fist poised to pound.

'What have I done to deserve this, Hodges?'

'I came by to apologize.'

He raised a corner of his mouth. 'For what? Pounding on the door? Waking me up?'

'That's good, Ted. Uh, you going to invite me in?'

He glanced back over his shoulder. She leaned one way, then the other to see inside. She wrinkled her nose.

'No,' he said.

'Why do we have to be enemies?'

He cocked his head. 'What do you want?'

'To be friends?' she said tentatively.

He shook his head. 'No, you don't. I don't think you're the type to make friends unless there's some advantage to it.'

'Such insight,' she said with forced sarcasm, 'and after only a couple of days.'

He raised an eyebrow and kept quiet, making no further accusation but giving her the chance to deny.

'Okay,' she sighed. 'Usually that's true. In your case, I got off on the wrong foot. I admit it. And I *do* want to have your help in pursuing the lurker story. But those are not the reasons I came over. I came over because I felt bad for the way I treated you. But it was only because I didn't know.'

'Know what?' he said in a tone that said he already knew what she was talking about.

'Tell me about her, Ted.'

'Who?'

'Your daughter. Tell me about Erica.'

His eyes looked to her throat. That's where he wanted to place his hands at the instant she said Erica's name. What right did she have?

But suddenly he was glad she wanted to talk about Erica. He realized he wanted to talk about her. Nobody else ever wanted to talk about her. Theresa was lavishing every ounce of love she was capable of on Matt. Whenever he tried to reminisce about Erica, she found a chore to do. They had argued. Finally, he left. Dewey's friends were so considerate they never brought up the subject, let alone the name, of the daughter he had loved so much he didn't know how much. Nobody ever wanted to be so insensitive as to talk about his missing daughter, who was all he ever wanted to think about. So all he had were these evenings – and mornings with dried tears and the tastes of whiskey and jam.

'You . . . would talk to me about my . . . Erica?'

'Yes. Of course.'

'Why? . . . Never mind why.' He looked over his shoulder again. 'I'll get my coat. We'll go for a ride.'

When he came back, Laren saw the neck of a bottle sticking out of his pocket. 'I'll drive,' she said.

111

She drove, he talked.

She knew how to listen, had found that the best interviewers are those who listen. For that matter, the best counselors, teachers, parents, coaches – the best everybodies seemed to have an extraordinary capacity to listen. Especially the best friends.

She wasn't going to be this guy's best friend, but there was no reason he had to know that. Besides, it wouldn't hurt to dispense a little kindness. It was clear to her that talking about his daughter was both a great joy and a great pain to him. He alternately smiled and frowned, laughed, and once even cried, perhaps the effect of the whiskey bottle he kept sucking on.

'It's all right,' she said when he apologized for crying. And she meant it.

Once he swigged, cradled the bottle between his thighs, and sniffed at her. When his breath returned, he said, 'You're conning me.'

She didn't deny it. She didn't even say a word. She just waited in the darkness behind the wheel of her car as the rural blackness swept by. And when he had licked his lips and started talking again, she resumed listening.

Outside, the evening was moonless, very dark.

Inside the Thrasher house was even darker, the walls and roof shutting out the feeble light of stars.

Sarah Thrasher lay at attention, heels together, toes pointed toward the ceiling, arms by her sides, fingers extended and joined, the left side of her body spot-welded to her husband's back and butt.

Marvin Thrasher had found the key to riches in used cars. He sold them by the hundreds every week, taking

112

the trade-ins that new-car dealers didn't want cluttering up their limited acreage, moving them to scores of used dealers all over the state. He never even had to touch the damned things – they were all paper transactions, a limitless supply of cars from people who wanted to move up vehicularly and an endless supply of teens looking for a good buy for their first set of wheels and those living on the edge of poverty who needed transportation for the new job or to get away from something. He never even had to turn back an odometer anymore. All he did was keep the paper flowing. It was up to the dealers to get the cars moving from one lot to another and until the new owner got out of sight. All Marvin had to do was siphon off his brokering fees, the road to wealth paved with clean, low-mileage, previously owned honeys that ran like tops.

He lay snoring, swallowing, smacking, snorting, probably counting junkers in his sleep.

She pressed closer to him.

She imagined the closing of five sets of eyes down the hall, the last mumblings of the day as her children, aged high school to first grade, drifted off to sleep.

For herself, she had no illusions about sleep. She knew she wouldn't be getting any tonight. She kept waiting for her eyes to adjust to the darkness so she could see enough to at least relax a little.

The darkness downstairs was suddenly shattered by an explosion of light in the kitchen, a nearly soundless explosion. The seal of the refrigerator door parted reluctantly from the food compartment like a good-bye kiss, and a slice of light flooded a pie-shaped piece of the room. A hand withdrew milk and eggs, then reached into the freezer compartment. One by one, three eggs disappeared into the black hole of a mouth, the only noise the muffled crunching of shells, a labored swallowing, the spitting of shell bits into a palm. Ice cream followed in great spoonfuls, the nutty bits washed down with gulps of milk from the pointed mouth of the carton.

Sarah's eyes opened wider, taking in more of the darkness.

'Marvin, do you hear something in the kitchen?' she murmured.

Marvin snorted his answer and twirled inside the cocoon of blankets he'd woven for himself. Suddenly, she was chilled, as much by her feeling of being alone as by the air in the room now that her covers were gone. She pulled at his cocoon and sidled as close to him as she could and lay in terror, her eyes open, searching the impenetrable darkness. She vowed she'd never sleep tonight.

Sarah Thrasher's eyes flew open as the terror renewed itself. Somehow, she had fallen asleep. But what she saw made her happy. She saw the bluish gray of morning seeping around the window shade. She snuggled up against her husband and drifted into oblivion, a smile on her face.

Within seconds – or was it minutes or hours? – she awakened, red-eyed as her husband flushed the toilet. She saw the light around the window shade had become hot white.

'Let's get breakfast,' he said, stepping back into the bedroom, 'before the Visigoths plunder the fridge.'

She would have protested, would have gone back to sleep, that delicious sleep, again. But not alone. So she got up. They looked in at the kids sleeping sweetly, the closest they would be to angels all day long.

Downstairs, they found the ice-cream carton empty, the milk left to warm on the counter.

'No,' moaned Marvin Thrasher, 'not the whole half gallon.'

He picked up the sticky carton.

She walked carefully over to it and looked in tentatively, as if some creature might jump out.

'It's gone. I knew it. Every time you buy that flavor, it disappears before I get a taste. I ought to go up there and kick all five asses out of bed, ruin their Saturday like they ruined mine. Shit. I got half a mind to go out and get a half gallon of black-cherry–black-rasp-berry–black-chocolate–black-walnut swirl crunch for each of them and cram it right up their blackhearted little asses.'

'Marvin, control yourself. My nerves are already on edge.'

He went to her and hugged her. 'I'm sorry. It's that stuff from yesterday, isn't it? I won't make a big deal of it, if it's going to upset you.'

They were lounging in the pool, feeling each other up through their bathing suits when the whole mob of kids came outside, dragging their battle with them.

When he found out what they were fighting about – the ice cream – Marvin threatened to drag them into the pool and drown every one of them. That settled them down – not the threat, but the anger they read in his voice, the anger he could not suppress over that black ice cream.

He demanded a confession.

They gave him one. They blamed it on Buddy, the

115

youngest. He denied it. But the evidence was condemning – he had a stomachache.

Putting on his best Solomon game face, Marvin, in his most rational voice asked, 'If you didn't eat the ice cream, Buddy, how come you have a stomachache.'

'I don't have a stomachache. I just feel sick to my stomach.'

When the cries of What's the difference? and See? and That proves it! had subsided, Marvin said, 'Why do you have a stomachache, Buddy?'

'Yeah, why? Huh, huh?'

Marvin held out his hands and pushed down on the air, silencing the jeers.

'Because it stinks in my room,' said the tiny voice.

'Shooo-WER,' came the rejoinders.

Dewey's first thought was that there was too much light. Then he opened his eyes a squint and saw a ceiling pattern he didn't recognize. He felt clean sheets against his body, and it smelled sweet in this room, so he knew it couldn't be his.

He jackknifed himself into a sitting position.

He saw he was in a woman's bedroom, saw he was naked in a woman's bedroom. A lump lay under the covers beside him. He looked around and didn't recognize the woman by anything he saw in the room. How could he? He never spent nights in women's rooms. Maybe this was a hotel. The room was nice enough.

His clothes lay draped over a chair beside the bed.

He jumped out of bed and was relieved to feel his wallet in his pants. But who did he stay with?

'Welcome back to the world, Dewey,' said a voice tinged with irony.

'Hodges,' he said between his teeth, both accusing

116

and remembering. He spun to face the lump in the bed, holding his pants before his nakedness.

She laughed as if to say, Don't bother – how do you suppose the clothes got off you in the first place?

'I'm sorry,' she said. 'I didn't realize until it was too late you didn't wear underwear.'

'What happened here?' he demanded.

She said, 'Well, I hate to crush your ego, but nothing happened here.'

'You undressed me.'

'You want coffee?' she said, refusing to be drawn into an argument about the obvious.

'No, I don't want coffee. I don't want anything from you but an explanation.'

'You got drunk, Dewey. You passed out in my car. We were closer to my house, and besides, you *do* have stairs at your place. So I dragged you in here. Did you know your nose whistles when you're asleep?'

'What's so damned funny?'

'You. Your nose. It whistles when you're awake and breathing hard, too. I can hear it from here. Put your pants on.'

Faced with that problem, he looked helpless.

'Your roommate . . .'

'She's in sales. She travels out of town.'

'I'm married, you know. My divorce isn't final.'

'But you *are* getting divorced, and you don't have to explain your whereabouts last night, and I'm quite certain you won't be bragging about last night, even if . . . *especially* if you could remember it. And I'm not going to say anything. So why the panic? Believe me . . . this was no more than an innocent sleep-over, no more than a slumber party. Put your pants on.'

She slid brazenly out of bed, making no attempt to

hide her own body, and walked into the adjacent bathroom.

He jumped to it, hopping about unsteadily on one leg, his other foot caught in the crotch of his pants. He crashed and lay on the floor groaning, more in embarrassment than in pain.

Still on his back, he slithered into his pants.

'You okay?' She was back, wearing a robe, suppressing a giggle with the palm of her hand as she watched him writhe.

For a moment, it seemed as if he'd calm down. Then he saw the clock.

'For chrissake, I have to get to work. I'm already late.'

'It's Saturday,' she said.

'Goddammit, I work on Saturdays. Crime doesn't . . . never mind. I'm late.'

'It doesn't matter,' she said as kindly as she could muster. 'Take your time. You leave work early sometimes – it wouldn't be all that terrible if you were a bit late. Give me a minute – give yourself a minute to sober up – and I'll come with you.'

He was poking his arms into his shirt.

'Didn't the city editor tell you this isn't your beat? Stay out of it. Didn't he tell you? Didn't I tell you?'

'I don't want your goddamned beat,' she retorted, her own thin stores of patience running out. 'I just want to do some more work on this lurker thing. Besides, I want to see how my story played in the paper this morning. Besides, I have to drive you to your place so you can pick up your own car. And you'd better not speed. I doubt if you could yet pass a sobriety test.'

'That's not your fucking problem, damn you.'

'Damn me? For what?'

'Sure. Play innocent. You'd use anybody for anything, won't you? You brought me here on purpose. You . . . made me spend the night so you could use me . . .'

She laughed harshly. 'You think you're a victim? Sure. You could file a complaint at City Hall. I'm sure your cop friends would bust a gut over a rape complaint from you.'

'I didn't mean it that way,' he snapped in answer to her savage grin. 'You think I should share with you because you're some kind of cheap bitch who'd do anything to get to a story that will move you on. Well, I don't owe you anything. Even if we'd fucked each other's eyes out, I wouldn't owe you anything . . . Jesus, you're ruthless. You'd fuck an AIDS patient to get a story, wouldn't you? No, don't shake your goddamned head. Goddamn, you're despicable. It'd almost be worth it to have AIDS if I could give it to you, you, you . . . *bitch.*'

'You're crazy, Dewey. You're so used to being a has-been, a . . . a failure, that it's gone to your goddamned head. You can't even think straight anymore. Well, I don't want anything from you, and if I did, you wouldn't be man enough to give it to me. If you *did* have AIDS, you couldn't get it up long enough to infect me. You proved that last night.'

'So you admit you tried it. You admit you used me.'

'I never used you, Dewey . . . you, you incorrigible loser. You're just like your namesake.'

'Goddammit, can't you tell the truth? You used me.'

'I couldn't use you. You couldn't even get it up, you dumb, ignorant, over-the-hill, drunken, impotent bastard.'

He paused.

She thought she had gone too far, that she had

finally stirred life in those dead eyes, but that she had stirred him to more, to kill.

'Maybe so,' he said evenly. 'Maybe I am impotent. But, by God, you're the first woman – the only woman – who could make me glad I was impotent.'

'Ouch,' she said. She started to laugh, but it came out a cry-laugh. She sniffed it away, refusing to show the slightest clue of vulnerability. 'That hurts, Dewey. I am selfish, I admit it. But I didn't have anything horrible in mind. I just felt . . .'

'Don't feel sorry for me. I don't want your fucking pity.' He tied the laces of his shoes in the ensuing silence.

Maybe she was telling the truth, he thought. Maybe he was the one who's feeling sorry for himself. He backed up for another run at trying to be civilized, but his anger didn't allow it to come out exactly civilized.

'Can't you just stop trying to play these fucking games with me? I don't even give a shit about this lurker bullshit. I don't care if you have it. Talk to Lou, and see if he'll give you another shot . . . hell, I'll talk to him for you. I don't want a byline. I just want . . . I just want you to stop treating me like one of your sources. Stop working me like a goddamned rainbow trout. Just for once, just with one person – me – be up-front. Be honest. Just for once, be sincere.'

Even as he spoke, he knew he was lying. But he was looking into her face and wanting to believe she would be sincere with him. He would lie to avoid hurting her feelings if she would just not manipulate him.

'I'll try to be up-front with you.' She brightened up, showing a most honest and sincere look.

Immediately, he knew she was lying, too.

He grunted in disgust. 'It's so easy for you, Miss

120

Facile. Isn't it? I don't like you, Hodges. I despise your type of reporter. You're a goddamned fake.'

She braced to defend herself.

'No,' he said, cutting her off. 'Let me finish. Even if you were a nun, I wouldn't like you. No, I'd like you even less. You're only looking out for yourself in everything you do.'

She was pissed. Her best look of sincerity, her best shot at the look of honesty had just been wasted. No more point in the pleasantries.

'Well, fuck you, Mister self-righteous. Maybe if I were a whore, I'd be earthy enough for you.'

He shook his head as he walked out. 'You already are a whore – at least a pretender to whoredom – but even that doesn't become you.'

She was left dazed and hurt, genuinely hurt. Either it hurt to be found out a liar or she really cared that she rated so low a spot in his esteem. What kind of loser *are* you, she mused, if a loser considers you a loser?

The thought of her lurker story in today's paper distracted her away from the gloom, though. The possibility of writing more stories grabbed her. Suddenly she was very eager to get to work on this, her day off. As she dressed, she considered how difficult it was to dismiss Dewey from her mind. That must mean she'd been hurt to be found out a liar. Thank goodness it was not the other possibility. Thank goodness she wasn't starting to like the tired old bastard.

Dewey made a phone call and bought a newspaper while waiting for the taxi. The lurker story made the front page. Below the fold, but on the page, nonetheless, with a picture and a map. He looked over the photograph longingly. Marguerite Smallwood. The halftone did her no justice.

He read the story.

She was good, that Hodges. An exciting writing style, conversational, lucid, free of the automatic writing, the clichés that were the staple shorthand of most newspaper writers. She was also an effective interviewer. In fact, he couldn't believe Marguerite would tell her so many intimate details about herself for a newspaper story, unless . . . unless Hodges had interviewed her without revealing the words would go into the paper for a third of the city to read.

At the Thrasher house, the great ice cream mystery had been forgotten, carried out with the trash.

The younger kids were running around screaming each discovery in a game of hide-and-seek. Marvin Thrasher looked up from juggling automobile inventory sheets, the shrieks too distracting, the boinging of an overfilled basketball – dribbling, pausing to fly, rattling the backboard, hitting the pavement – too inviting. He decided to quit working and join them on the court. He went out back with the high schoolers and their buddies to watch them shoot baskets. They had chalked a three-point arc on the driveway. He couldn't resist. They tried to resist, wouldn't let him into the game. He insisted. They desisted. He suggested it was time for chores. They let him into the game.

The exhausted Sarah sat in a cushioned patio chair. At first, she was amused at her husband's awkwardness among the lithe teen boys. But she closed her eyes. And although there were many grunts and shouts and a few curses, she was soon asleep.

Buddy Thrasher was a pretty lousy seeker, but a hider without equal. He could slip into some tight places. And he'd learned the thrill of lying still. He no longer gave himself away by giggling or calling to the seekers.

He ran into his room and sat down on the floor beside his bed. He lay back and slid himself beneath the springs. He watched the seeker's feet run down the hall past his room. He heard the seekers whispering, then calling his name, daring him to give himself away. He smelled the odor that had made him sick during the night. The smell was under the bed with him.

He turned his head to look deeper into the cubical cave of darkness.

A pale, gleaming, sickly hazel ring encircled a black dot. The hazel ring was itself encircled by red chicken scratching. Buddy realized it was an eye. It winked at him.

Marvin had crouched outside the three-point arc like a sideways Egyptian figure drawn inside a tomb, the ball ready to be launched from his obsolete set shot, when he heard the scream.

Marvin froze.

One of the neighbor kids blocked the ball right off the duck bill of his hands, driving it back into his face.

Even as Marvin started cursing through his hands, Sarah was up screaming for him to hurry inside and see what was the matter. Strong as her maternal instinct was, she'd seen enough terror in her sleep and lack of it in the last two days.

Wiping his teary eyes and checking for blood flow from his nose, Marvin shuffled toward the house.

Buddy was still shrieking, the sounds growing louder.

Sarah was still screaming, Marvin still cursing.

The gang of teens stopped shrugging at each other

and ran ahead into the house, intercepting panic-stricken Buddy as he came flying into the family room.

The teens burst into embarrassed laughter at his terror.

Marvin held Buddy in his arms and tried to calm him.

'There's a creepy bastard under my bed,' roared the child, eyes agape.

The teenagers laughed at the youngster's language.

'Stop it,' commanded Sarah, and they took her seriously. 'Buddy, what do you mean? Is there a real person under your bed?'

'Yes, and he stinks.'

'Let's go, boys,' said Marvin, pushing the basketball crowd ahead up the stairs. 'Sarah, you call the police.'

The police arrived in minutes. Later came Laren, having heard as promised from Hanover. Neither the professional search of the police or the haphazard one of the vigilantes had turned up anything but general agreement that the air beneath Buddy's bed smelled horrible.

'Hardly enough for a report,' said the police officer.

'Could be . . . you know, like a dead mouse or something,' said the other cop.

'Sir, ma'am, there is no sign of forced entry or anything. I'm sure the youngster saw something, but . . .'

'I saw a creep,' volunteered Buddy, recognizing that it was his credibility on the line. 'There was a creepy guy under that bed. He winked at me.'

The policeman smiled politely. To Marvin Thrasher, he said, 'Is there anything else, sir? You know, something for a report? As it is . . .' He left the statement hanging.

Marvin thought of the ice-cream carton. 'Nothing else, officer,' he said, deciding against bringing that up and removing all doubt that they were a clan of nuts. 'I'm sorry to have troubled you.'

Laren introduced herself to Marvin after the uniforms left. He put on his game face. He knew how to get rid of troublesome people, and all reporters were troublesome in his book. He'd read enough stories about the scams in used cars to know that.

'I'm sorry, Miss . . . Hodges, was it? But there's no story here.'

She looked straight past him to Sarah Thrasher holding the clinging boy.

'Mrs Thrasher, I was here yesterday . . .'

'Look here, young woman. Do you want me to call your editor and tell him . . .'

'It's all right, Marvin,' said Sarah.

'Sarah, I can handle this.'

'It's all right,' she said, leaving no doubt it was. 'I read the story this morning. Was that yours?'

'Yes.'

Thrasher was not through. 'Sarah, we don't need half the town thinking we're crazy because of what they read about us.'

Sarah handed off Buddy to him. 'Take care of him while I talk to Miss Hodges.' She looked at the curious crowd of teens and youngsters. 'The rest of you go about your business.'

They did.

'I don't think you're crazy,' said Laren. 'I believe you and your family about this . . . creep . . . this prowler . . . this . . .'

'Why do you believe me?'

'I was the unnamed woman in that story. I have felt this extra presence, the . . .'

'The extra eyes?' said Sarah. 'Like in the morning paper?'

'Yes.'

'I wish I could feel them – so I could know whether he left.'

'Well, you just had the entire house searched by a whole brigade of people. Even the police,' Laren said. 'Maybe he left.'

Sarah smiled a weak gas-pain smile. 'Tell me,' she said, 'do you feel him . . . the extra eyes now?'

'No, thank goodness,' said Laren through her most sincere smile.

On the way back to the paper with her notes, Laren kept asking herself why she had lied to Mrs Thrasher. Certainly, there was no evidence that this feeling was anything more than a product of her imagination. And what could the woman do if she had said, yes, I'm chilly right now because the sicko bastard is staring holes in me? It had been all she could do to avoid staring at the upstairs windows or ordering a search of the grounds. And if another search had turned up what the previous ones had, which was zilch, *then* who was the crazy?

She needed the status quo at the Thrasher house until this story could develop a bit further. If one more incident could establish the Thrashers were being victimized by this lurker, she would . . . what? Well, hell, she didn't know. She did know she couldn't have them moving out as if it were some kind of possessed house just on the basis of her case of the shudders. Could she? Hell, no. Then she'd be injecting herself into the story. Worse, she'd be driving it.

By the time Laren got back to the city room, she just had time to bang out an update bulletin to her morning story for the afternoon Blue Flash edition. Albright

126

was out for coffee, so she used the term, lurker, and her byline to see if he'd let them pass.

He did.

Dewey finished up his Saturday work more diligently than usual in penance for taking off a couple times this week. He covered a fatal fire and played up the heroics of a rookie firefighter who was going to get his scratch in the sands of immortality with a front-page picture of him bent over, puking.

He was on the way out when Hanover dropped by the press room with a rolled up Blue Flash. By the time he'd read the bulletin to the morning story, Hanover had disappeared to some refuge in the department.

In fact, Hanover was watching with glee from behind a crowd of traffic offenders paying tow charges so they could redeem their cars. He was delighted at the darkness in Dewey's face as he stormed out. The less Dewey and Hodges liked each other, Hanover figured, the greater the chance he could get into her undies. And if there was something he could do to engender a hatred between them, why, so much the better.

Dewey hit Lou Albright's door on the run and tossed the Blue Flash across the desk.

'This bulletin is a cop story, Lou.'

'So?'

'So you said you weren't going to give her this beat.'

'I didn't. I had her try to call you with the tip. She said you were out on the fire fatality. Hell of a job you did on that, by the way. I held the best of it for the Sunday front page to run with Laren's wrap-up on this lurker shit.'

'Don't soft-soap me, Lou. If you give her this story,

127

she'll just use it as her ticket out of here to LA or New York or wherever she thinks it will take her.'

'So? That's newspapering, Ted. In case you hadn't figured it out, most people are trying to make their way up the ladder. That's the way the system works. If she leaves, at least I'll have that story. And it will be covered well and enthusiastically. It'll sell some papers, make some noise at a few contests. If I put you on it, you'll ignore it because you think it's beneath you – shit, you think it's beneath both you and the paper – '

'It is.'

'You ain't the publisher, Ted. Even I ain't the publisher. But I am the city editor. And I want this lurker story covered, and I want it done right.'

'All right, Lou. I'll do it.'

'Too late, Ted. I'm putting Laren on it with you. I'm making you two a team. I expect you to use all your cop resources to help her when she needs it. You do a good job and I'll let you share the bylines.'

Dewey laughed bitterly.

Across the room, the eavesdropping Laren grimaced at the prospect of sharing the glory.

Dewey's voice boomed out of the office: 'Fuck it. I don't want a byline. I'm too old to worry about bylines and contests and bullshit from you . . .'

'This is it then, Ted? You're quitting?' Albright's face was cold, even. There was no trace of threat in his voice or tone. The threat was for the mind of the beholder.

Laren brightened.

Dewey paused, frozen.

A long, aching pause.

'No, I . . . I wouldn't give Hodges . . . and you the satisfaction . . .'

Lou opened his mouth.

'. . . and I know nobody ever gets fired from here. So keep your idle threats to yourself, Lou.'

'No threats. We used to be friends, Ted. What happened to you? Journalism used to be . . .'

'Fuck journalism. Fuck Hodges.' He paused, defiantly setting his mouth. 'Fuck you.' He waited for a reaction. There was none.

He spun and walked out. Seeing Laren trying not to be seen, realizing she had heard this exchange, he thought about laying into her, saying to her face what he had just told Albright. But he didn't. Much as he'd like to think it, she was not at fault for trying to get ahead at any cost. In an earlier time, he might have used the same tactics. No, she was not to blame.

He, Thomas E. Dewey, was the pathetic one to blame for his pathetic state of mind.

They looked a pair mismatched on a television dating game and forced to enjoy their prize.

Hanover was beaming, but awkward, as they walked into the lounge. He puffed out his chest as the sets of eyes from down the bar turned to look at his date, a stunner, as he would call her.

Laren was awkward too, knowing she had to be pleasant or she'd forfeit the detective's cooperation. She was a little nervous too, hopeful she wouldn't run into anybody from the paper who might think her guilty of a conflict of interest in dating a source – even though she'd already cleared that up in her own mind. This was work. She was seeing Hanover only for the purpose of vacuuming his mind for information. This was like a three-martini supper to her. Strictly business. Underhanded maybe – but business.

They'd barely been seated in a booth. Their eyes had

barely adjusted to the darkness when they saw him coming.

'Uh-oh,' she uttered, covering her eyes as if not seeing him would make her invisible to the staggering figure.

Hanover just moaned.

'Don't let him make a scene,' she said.

Hanover looked at her helplessly. 'What am I gonna do, arrest him?'

But Dewey surprised them both. He passed by, dragging his silent shadow across their table.

They sagged in relief, then stiffened as his shadow retraced its way back over them.

'Hi, guys,' he slurred. Then he smiled too broadly and left them to their individual guilts.

Laren found there wasn't much help to be pumped out of Hanover. The police weren't doing all that much. The lurker business, he said, was so far still just an unconnected string of prowler reports. And it looked like he among all those uncaring public servants was the only one who had devoted any attention to it at all. Why, he had even suggested a lurker task force.

And?

Well, 'they' just laughed at him. Course, he wasn't going to let that stop him, no sirree.

It was dark. She paid her half of the tab and left him sitting. He wanted to know where she was going, if they were going to meet again, if she was mad at him.

'Home. Yes. No,' she said, and walked away.

9

In the ensuing days, she realized there was a conspiracy afoot to drive her mad.

In the first place, she would have to work with *him*. Albright formally instructed her and Dewey on the ground rules for the lurker team. They would both be released from other duties. Dewey would get a general assignment reporter detailed to him to cover the routine of the cop shop. As soon as the GA could be familiarized with police contacts and procedures, Dewey was to be freed to head the team.

That was the second place. Dewey in charge of her? she demanded to know from Albright.

Of course, he told her. Dewey was senior, more familiar with the city, should have been an editor already, if he had wanted to move up the supervisory chain instead of being content to labor in the trenches. And what the hell did she expect?

But how the hell was the work going to be divided? she demanded.

Albright, who didn't particularly like being demanded at from below, told her to ask her team chief.

'This isn't going to work, you know,' she said, practically spitting the words into Dewey's face.

He answered pleasantly. 'Yes it is, Laren – we're professionals. We can make it work.'

That was the third place. He was being pleasant to her. One day he's going around yelling Fuck Journalism, Fuck Hodges, Fuck you, and the next he's smooth as an undertaker. And he wasn't even drunk, for chrissakes, and near as she could tell, he wasn't even hung over. For that matter, he seemed genuinely happy.

There could be no other explanation. They were trying to drive her nuts.

'And I suppose you'll want your byline to go first,' she said, uttering the words as if they were obscenities. 'You know, alphabetically.'

'Naw, you'll probably do most of the writing, so you'll get your own bylines. I'll just help you gather facts, do some editing, keep the brass off your ass – that kind of stuff.' He smiled and left her standing bewildered.

And tired.

That was the fourth place. She was exhausted from working overtime. Sitting for hours in the dark garden behind the Thrasher house the last two nights had started to cut into valuable beauty sleep.

Which led to the fifth, final, and worst place, that the goddamned lurker was staying away from the Thrasher house, keeping her from continuing this story, waiting for her to be committed to the madhouse before he started lurking again.

Dewey had his own set of problems.

His first place was that he was trying to back away from the booze. He'd gotten over the initial jitters when he went a whole day sober. Although the second and third day were tougher yet, he got past them too. Thereafter, there didn't seem to be quite the physical symptoms. All he had to do was stop thinking about that nightly drink – the half quart or so he was used to. But he couldn't get liquor from his mind. The more he tried not to think about drinking, the more it was

on his mind. He started noticing liquor ads more than
ever. Billboards he'd never seen before seemed to crop
up everywhere, every one touting drinks ten feet tall.
He started noticing how much he remembered it tasted
great and was less filling than the buttermilk he had
taken to drinking, up to half a gallon a day of the
awful stuff.

His second place was this story. Laren's lurker
stories had generated plenty of reports now. People
were beginning to discover signs of lurkers everywhere
in their homes. He and Laren split up, taking a few of
the most serious-sounding calls every day and visiting
homes alleged to have been lurked.

The effort turned up an obese zero.

The police were getting a hundred more calls a day
reporting lurkers who turned out to be anybody from
the paper carrier cutting through the yard, to squirrels
in the attic, to pranksters, to amateur burglars, to
plain harassing calls. Hanover was blaming Dewey. 'If
you'd stop calling this guy a lurker, like he was some
kinda Jack the Ripper, we'd stop getting half the calls
right away.'

Dewey wanted to say, Blame Laren – she's at the
bottom of this; all you want to do is get her into bed.

But he didn't. She was working for him now, unruly
as she was, and he couldn't lay blame off on a
subordinate.

That was his third place.

In the fourth, the story looked to be tailing off. No
matter how much life in Laren's writing, if there were
no confirmed lurker incidents, there could be no lurker
stories. And, as far as he was concerned, there might
not be such a thing as a lurker – except that specter
lurking in Laren's mind.

They had already wrapped up the history of these

133

incidents, even making a reluctant, strained tie to the past string of child kidnappings. They had already laid off a blame story on the police for not showing interest in the lurker incidents. They had done one too many wrap-ups on the lurker events they thought were related – though the public loved them, and every time the word *lurker* appeared in headline type, that edition sold out. And they had done a quick and dirty survey of police departments across the country that turned up no useful information, though it did yield twelve inches of copy about other forms of deviate crimes their city was lucky enough to not have to face.

'We ain't doing so good, Laren,' he said to her over coffees brought into the cafeteria from the composing room.

'What do you mean? Never mind, I know what you mean. Has Albright been bugging you?'

'No. He won't do that. He'll expect me to come to him and just tell him when we're at the end of the story possibilities.' He snorted into his coffee. 'My buddy Hanover is getting a bit upset, though. He's regretting he ever coined the term *lurker*.'

She hid her instant ire at that. She'd wanted credit for that term.

'And he's a little pissed at you for writing things as if the police were a bunch of incompetents, especially the detective named Hanover reported as being in charge of the lurker task force – when there's never been a task force formed.'

She returned his smile weakly. 'That's his tough luck. He bragged to me he was going to be in charge of such a thing. Let him explain it away. The cops aren't doing a damned thing about this lurker. They're not even taking it seriously. Somebody is going to have to be killed before they get off their asses.'

'You make it sound as if you wish . . . never mind, that was a cheap shot. What's wrong with you, Laren? You look a little tired lately.'

'And a little cranky? Maybe having my time of the month?'

'Don't mock me. I didn't say that.'

'Nothing is wrong.'

He didn't look as if he believed her. But he didn't press it.

'Heard anything from your friend Marguerite?' he asked.

It was an innocent question asked innocently enough. But she heard the tremble in his voice. Marguerite could do that to men.

'She's . . . uh, all right. I guess. I haven't heard from her in a while.'

She met his eyes. He wasn't buying it. Damn you, Dewey, where did you ever learn to read me? she thought.

'Okay. So she's mad as hell at me. But I never told her I wouldn't use her personal information in the story.' She turned her head and looked at him from the oblique, eager to change the subject. 'How are you and Hanover getting along? Didn't you used to be big buddies?'

'We'll be okay. Don't worry. I'll not cave in to him just because he let his alligator mouth overload his tweety bird ass. I'll support you.'

'As long as what?'

'No qualifications. Long as we're working together, I guess.'

She searched his face for the irony, the contradiction.

There was none. Goddamn you, she thought. Goddammit, Dewey, what the hell are you up to? What made her maddest of all was that, whereas he seemed to be able to see through her with X-ray vision, peering right into her soul, especially at moments when she was telling her best lies, she couldn't even penetrate his skin with a needle anymore. Why was he being so nice? What was he up to, dammit?

'What's he up to, do you suppose?' he asked.

'Huh?' She was shaken from her thoughts. My God, he *could* read her mind.

'This lurker. What the heck is the guy up to? Is he a sex offender? A burglar? What did he go into people's houses for, and in the case of the Thrashers, why does he go back? I'd like to be a fly on the wall out there.'

Dewey watched as some of the fatigue in her face was supplanted by a trace of color at the question. She would like to know, would go to great lengths to find out – probably already had. She was up to something, and he wondered what. One thing he did not wonder about: Even tired, she was beautiful, sensuous eyes and lips made even more attractive by her spirited, unrestrained behavior. Once you got past her self-defense shields of the reporter, which were selfishness and aggressiveness, you could really learn to like her. Well, somebody might – somebody else.

He wondered, What the hell was she up to?

'How much longer?' she asked.

'Huh?'

'How much longer are we going to give it?'

'I don't know. But something will turn up. If there is such a thing as a lurker out there, he'll probably make another move. And if there isn't such a thing, our stories are bound to create one, a copycat or something.' He grimaced at the prospect.

* * *

136

For the third night, Marvin Thrasher sat in his dark-ened den in a corner so he could watch the windows and the patio door. For the third straight night, he had fallen asleep, a blanket wrapped over his shoulders, a .22 caliber revolver in his lap.

And for the third night in a row, he awoke in a panic. He thought he heard a sound. But once awake he couldn't remember if the sound came from his dreams or from his house. Was it inside? Was it outside? Was it in his head? Was it something univer-sal, the feeling of waking up in dread of that sound and anger at being unable to identify the source? He strained his ears to hear, but the sound wouldn't oblige his frantic impatience and repeat itself. His adrenaline had his heart pumping. Then the rationalizations began as the adrenaline began to dissipate. There was no sound, he told himself. His eyes were itching – yes, there was such a thing as a sandman. He began to feel foolish for having a gun in his lap, a phallic symbol, a crazy idea.

What if his kids were to come down and find him like this? How would he explain it? Spooks? And why the blanket? It wasn't exactly cold in the house. Were you scared, Dad?

He shook it off. Feeling slightly embarrassed even though he was all alone and had only himself to be embarrassed with, he stood up, deciding to slide into bed for the third straight night without sex. Something mighty unhealthy about that for him and Sarah.

In her bedroom, Sarah lay on her belly. She felt the cover drawn back, the rush of cool air. She sidled over, making room until she felt the hand on her hip. Then she pressed back against it, rolling toward the warm body easing onto the mattress beside her.

137

But there was the creak of the floor outside the room. She was startled awake instantly, spinning in the darkness, whining for Marvin. But suddenly he was not there. She saw a shadow darken the hall light dripping through the slot under the door. She went for the lamp switch, all the while calling Marvin, Marvin ... MARvin ... MARVIN ... MARVIN! the last, a scream.

Before she could get to the switch, the door opened, silhouetting a draped figure in the doorway, a gun hanging from the end of the figure's arm.

She screamed Marvin's name again.

'Sarah, what the hell are you screaming about?'

In the doorway, her husband turned the ceiling light onto her hysteria. He stood there looking like Clint Eastwood in a spaghetti western, serape draped over his shoulders, pistol ready to sling lead. She sat there twirling on the bed looking for the figure she felt or dreamed under the covers, all the while shrieking. She was still screaming as he tried to calm her. She still was calling his name as the kids began stirring, wandering down the halls rubbing the sleep from their eyes, gawking at their naked, hysterical mother.

Marvin stepped into their lines of sight, shielding Sarah, the blanket spread like wings. He impatiently herded them back to bed and finally calmed her. A quick search of the upstairs revealed nothing. She insisted he take another look so she could be sure she was not dreaming that ... she couldn't say it again. It was too horrible to even think, let alone say. Was it possible to dream such a thing? Could some intruder have slipped into her dreams as well as her bed?

Marvin took her seriously. He vowed they would leave the house in the morning, go up to the lake cottage until this lurker bullshit was done.

He poked the revolver around in front of wherever he went. In the closet, he turned on the light, looked around, saw nothing, dropped to his knees, and looked all the way around.

'Nothing,' he said turning out the closet light, shutting the door, wrinkling his nose. 'Nothing,' he said. 'Nothing but that smell again. We must have mice.'

'This wasn't a damned mouse, Marvin.'

A thought struck him. 'I wonder if there are any mouse turds on the closet floor.'

He whirled on the closet door and hit the light.

He was on his knees among the shoes when the phone rang. So he didn't see the extra pair of shoes that didn't belong in their closet, hadn't gotten to the legs that began where the shoetops ended, didn't have time to see the hands wrapped around the closet pole. Didn't see the gleam of the eyes, red-rimmed and angry.

Marvin stood up and looked out from the walk-in closet. 'Was that the phone?' he asked.

The shoes and legs drew themselves up among Sarah's dresses, the longer, more formal gowns and other evening wear.

'It was only a half ring,' she said, 'just a tinkling like . . .'

'Like somebody cut the . . .'

There was another tinkling, of broken glass downstairs.

'Marvin,' she whispered.

He held his finger to his lips. But he didn't move.

'Somebody's breaking in,' she whispered.

He raised the revolver. But he didn't move. If anything, he leaned into the closet a millimeter or two, moving slightly closer to the angry eyes.

She picked up the phone. 'It's dead,' she whispered, hoarsely, desperately.

Their eyes widened at one another.

'You have to go down there,' she whispered.

Like hell, said his incredulous expression. Where the hell is it written? If it ain't in writing, it ain't no deal, said his face in the language of his business.

'The kids,' she hissed.

She leapt out of bed and grasped his gun hand, pulling him out of the closet, pushing him toward the bedroom door, shutting off the room light before pushing him into the dark hall.

He went down reluctantly. Looking back every other step. She leaned out the bedroom door, the darkness behind her, and watched him go.

Sarah, her head leaning down in the stairwell, ears perked at the disappearing back of her husband, could not have heard a sound behind her, even if there had been one.

Marvin was thinking that he should be stomping, not stalking. He should be cursing, muttering, singing, whistling his way to the door opening from the family room to the patio. A person could get killed surprising a burglar or whoever this bastard was.

He saw the hand.

It drew a shout from his throat, a shouted curse.

It was reaching through the broken pane of the French door, turning the knob, when he bellowed his obscenity and opened fire with the revolver.

Sarah screamed and ran down the stairs expecting to find the dead body of her husband on the floor.

Five shots.

Shrieking and a scream.

The rushing of footsteps across the lawn.

The noises jolted Laren awake, and she scratched her face on the wire staking up the tomato plants. But the outside floodlights and commotion kept her on her belly in the garden.

She was trapped. If she was discovered, she was in all kinds of trouble, even if she could get anybody to believe her excuse that she was just covering a story. You didn't find news stories lying on your belly in the tomato patch like Peter damned Rabbit or something. Her credibility. The ridicule of her peers – now she would have peers, where this afternoon she was peerless. The interrogation of her editors, the publisher. She'd be lucky to get Ruth Minton's job squawking at police dispatchers – forget about ever moving up to a major city paper. God, Laren, you know – whatshername, the one they found in the tomato patch, they would say.

In minutes the police arrived.

She did her best job of mimicking a tomato plant and tried to piece the events together from the jumbled stories the police were getting shouted at them.

The Thrashers had heard a prowler; searched the house; caught a burglar breaking in; shot him. The retired military neighbor had called police again. The would-be burglar lay shrieking and cursing all the way into the ambulance, yelling at the police to arrest the trigger-happy dude who shot him, threatening that he had a lawyer that would put an end to this other 'goddamnt subway vigilante.'

The police demanded to know, the red lights sweeping across their faces, if there were any others with him. He demanded his rights, wanted an attorney, a surgeon, an apology, lawsuit, damages, revenge.

So. The sounds of rushing feet had been accomplices. At least two. She was glad she'd been asleep. The sight of three men approaching the house would have been frightening as hell.

The police made a cursory inspection of the house, the grounds, spraying their flashlights around, forcing Laren's face into the tomato mounds again. Then the police dispersed the crowd from the neighborhood and asked Marvin Thrasher if they could come out tomorrow to look for footprints and such.

Go ahead, said Thrasher. We're moving up to our lake cottage. Tonight. He gave them the address and phone number.

Laren rehearsed it a couple of times.

We'll come back when this lurker thing is over, Thrasher said.

But you shot him, sir.

'No,' countered Thrasher, 'I only shot one of them. Another one ran away. I could hear him. There might have been more. Besides, Buddy said that man I shot was not the one who was under his bed.'

The incredulous cops asked for, and Thrasher repeated, that whole earlier story again. Laren lay shivering, achy, tired, wishing she didn't have to listen all over again. But, like the man who had been arrested, she was a captive audience.

Finally, the police left.

The Thrashers, kids complaining, parents insisting, tossed suitcases into the van. Then they left too. The house was dark, quiet, finally.

Laren waited until all the sounds of the night seemed normal. Then she ordered her body into motion. It did not respond so well, having lain on the cold ground stiffening for hours. She felt like a dirt ball. There was mud on her hands and on the side of her face from pressing into the tomato hill like a convict on the lam. She stood up and tried to dust her purple jogging suit. All she achieved was the smearing of mud. She needed to wash before getting into her car three blocks away.

She was at the pool kneeling, dipping her hands and feeling glad that the underwater lights were off, when she heard the squeal.

It froze her.

It was the distant cry of a dying animal, a bird maybe. No. It was the crunch and squeak of broken glass underfoot. She'd heard it when all those people were milling around the French door in back.

She ducked, then flattened at the pool's edge.

Her face pressing into the concrete, she looked back toward the house. At the French door stood a dark figure. A burglar?

She shuddered uncontrollably, the intake of her own breath sounding to her like a gasp. My God. Maybe it was *him. The lurker!*

The dark figure went stock-still in a crouch, one foot raised.

He had heard. Like a dancer or a martial arts expert, the foot still raised, the body began to turn toward her.

She slid a leg into the pool and pushed herself toward the water as quickly as she could without splashing.

All the while, the figure kept turning.

How like an animal he was. So stealthy, like a jungle cat on one of the animal shows public television was always showing.

Thank God, she thought. The water was warmer than the night air. Otherwise, she might have gasped again. Still she shuddered as the man faced her spot on the planet. But he was not merely a man. This was the lurker – The Lurker – something more or less than a man. She felt the shudder coming and controlled her breath as her eyes leveled off at the edge of the pool.

She stopped herself from sinking so she could watch. She heard the bubbles rising from her sweat suit, fizzing and gurgling, and she wondered if he would hear them, too.

The man was coming her way, a black shadow floating soundlessly across the darkness of the backyard. He drifted in and out of shadows, lit only by the sliver of the moon when he slithered out of the night shade.

She ducked below the level of the pool's edge. Now what? If he found her, he'd kill her, of that she was sure. She reasoned he hadn't seen her — otherwise he wouldn't be sneaking around. He'd walk right over, she'd scream, and he'd cut her, drown her, rape her . . . something. God, she should have run away down the back alley. She could have screamed. She might be ridiculed, but for dear God's sake, she'd not be dead. Not found floating . . .

She pushed herself sideways until she was beneath the diving board. Its flimsy shadow seemed to be the only cover possible. She wished she had done *any*thing but climbed into this pool to be drowned like a rat.

She heard nothing.

Slowly, ever so slowly, she raised her eyes and looked over the concrete edge.

And there he was, not six feet away — at least those were his dancer's legs padding silently toward her. My God, he was quiet. At knee-level was the blade of a knife catching a slice of the moonlight and flashing it into her eyes.

She drew the deepest breath she could.

As she went under, she heard the slightest crackle of fiberglass in the diving board, then a faint scratching sound. This scratching, she decided, must be from her own earwax crackling like cellophane.

Soon she heard nothing but the magnified pounding of her pulse underwater. She felt the sting of chlorine in the scrape on her face from the tomato plant's wire support frame.

She opened her eyes, although the chlorine burned. She wanted to see it coming if it came to death.

The blurry, distant, indistinct pincushion of light was the moon sliver.

Suddenly, a blurry shadow eclipsed the moon.

She shuddered under the water.

She readied herself to scream.

As if anybody could have heard that sort of thing underwater. God, she felt dumb.

Her lungs hurt. She whimpered, startling herself at how loud the sound came to her own ears.

The shadow gave back the light of the moon.

She decided to wait until he could be long gone.

She waited moments longer. Until her lungs would burst. She decided to wait longer, grunting to herself that she could. She waited, unable to stymie a whine in her chest. She grunted in determination, telling herself the wait would be fully worth her life even as her fingernails tried to dig into the side of the pool.

Again, she tried to see toward the sky, but only the dancing gleam of the moon came to her through the water, and even that seemed dimmer, as if she might be blacking out.

The whine in her chest rose to her throat and escaped as a stream of tickling bubbles through her nose.

She recognized it as a rising scream but felt too gripped by fear to dare rise to the surface yet. He might be there. Waiting.

With that knife.

She felt the surge of panic, the same feeling that the

drowning victim must know, she told herself. It was her last rational thought. For the panic gripped her simultaneously with the idea of drowning, with the realization that the very water seemed to be pressing in on her chest, trying to trickle into her nose.

She glanced toward the sky, the blackness above with the yellow gleam of moon . . . no, the gleam of two yellowed eyes coming for her from out of the darkness, from below the very level of the water . . .

He must be in here, she thought . . .

She let out a scream underwater, even as she felt something clawing at her legs, as two hands seemed to close on her throat, as her nightmare took possession of her reason. She scrambled toward the top, as if it were a dozen feet away, although it was hardly that many inches, her grunts and screams and squeals sounding like whales in a feeding frenzy.

The scream surfaced first as a mere sizzle of popping bubbles.

Then came Laren, launched from the water like a dolphin at a sea circus, clawing her way to the surface, hauling herself over the edge of the pool, rolling on the concrete, flopping around like a beached fish, gasping, grunting, whining.

She gulped the air and coughed on the trickles of water she inhaled with it. She spun around on her hands and knees like a madwoman, realizing that nobody had been underwater after all, that her imagination had conjured up those hands on her throat . . . just as in the dream. Instantly upon that thought came the feeling of vulnerability now that she'd given up her hiding place by climbing out and splattering her body – her moaning, whimpering body – around like a seal or a dying fish in the naked backyard.

But nobody attacked her, and she gradually began to get a grip on herself, giggling in hysterical relief.

She shuddered repeatedly. But she knew it was a different feeling. It was not from feeling his eyes on her, was not the extrasensory reception of his evil emanations. She shivered because of fear and the cold. The dream had almost come to life down there in the water. And the wetness . . . yes, the wetness, she told herself. Just the wetness of swimming at night.

She pulled herself together, felt her breathing leveling off.

She'd be all right now, she knew.

She knew she'd better get busy. For no longer was there any doubt, she thought as she squished across the Thrasher backyard in wet shoes and a crafty smile. Not a doubt in the world. This was going to be the story of a lifetime. It was going to be good-bye to this hicksville midwestern city in record time. It was going to be hello New York. Or at least, hiya LA.

10

Dewey found her draped over her keyboard, her face depressing a third of the keys, having written a message in Greek on the green screen. In one of her hands she clutched a printout.

He slipped it from her fingers and began to read.

Before he'd finished, Albright, the city editor, was at his shoulder blowing cigarette smoke and coffee breath.

'What's the deal?' growled Albright in his cigarette voice. 'Why does Hodges look like a bag lady? And why's she smell like a bottle of bleach?'

Dewey just shrugged and whistled. Then, 'God,' he said. 'Read this, Lou. This is great stuff.'

Albright's eyes took in the first page in a skim. 'Get your butt to editing, pal. This is top-drawer stuff – a little rough, but I want it in the earliest edition you can get it. And work in some depth so we can play it big for tomorrow. Get some reaction from the cops.'

'What if we get a shrink to comment on this character?'

'Yeah.'

Laren grunted and looked up, the impressions of rounded-off squares all over her right cheek, a trace of drool streaming down the corner of her mouth.

'And maybe we could get a police sketch,' she murmured.

'You saw this guy?' said Dewey.

'Saw him? I prackly went to a pool party with him.'

'Police sketch, my ass,' said Albright. 'We've got our

own artists. You get over there and tell him what kinda face to put down.'

'Lou . . .'

'Never mind, Dewey, we'll share it with the police the minute we put it in the papers. You want them damn TV glory hounds beating us on our own drawing?'

As the day wore on, Laren's reputation grew in the newsroom, although Albright had allowed nobody to read the story except himself, Dewey, Laren, the graphics editor – who was ordered to produce art and the front-page layout with the lurker material as the centerpiece – and the foreman in the composing room, who was ordered to personally escort the page layout to platemaking and then escort the finished plate to the pressroom. He ordered every proof page to be accounted for and he directed the story be copyrighted.

All of which fueled the rumors and speculation about and the reputation of one Laren Hodges. She was clearly exhausted from her ordeal, which, according to the story, began when she remained behind at the Thrasher house on a hunch after the police and family left for their lake cottage.

Dewey checked a near-final draft with her in the artist's cubicle. He saw that she was slightly disoriented and a bit giddy from all the excitement. She had trouble concentrating on the printout and kept ordering the artist to change the jawline on the tough-looking customer that glared out from his sketch pad.

But Dewey had no time for reflection on that. He was on deadline. He ran the final draft by her.

She griped that it was considerably shorter than she wanted. He told her he had to get it down to a manageable size for this edition, that they would have time to pump it back up with more details and a good sidebar for tomorrow – after she'd had some sleep.

He left her still fussing with the artist over the chin and went to send the final electronic copy to Lou Albright's computer queue.

Laren finally crashed, stretched out on a row of chairs in the conference room, thereby forcing a switch of the mid-morning news budget meeting to the cafeteria.

Albright said to let her sleep. She could go to the cops with her eyewitness report when the presses began to roll. And while she was being questioned, she could be interviewing the cops right back for tomorrow's story.

'God, what a first-rate opportunity,' said Albright, clapping Dewey on the back. 'We're right in the middle of this one, Ted, my boy. We're victim, observer, detective, reporter . . . the works all wrapped into one. Ever seen anything like it?'

No, admitted Dewey, he never had.

Dewey was troubled by something. He went to talk to Elliott Yates, the artist, who was worrying his lurker sketch with a gum eraser.

'What's wrong, Elliott?'

'I ain't sure. I can't seem to make this pitcher look like anybody, y'know? It looks more like one of them villains on the Saturday cartoons than anything, y'know?'

'I guess not,' said Dewey, who had not watched cartoons since his daughter . . .

'Oh, hell, I guess it's fine enough. Hell, I ain't no police artist. God willing, y'know?'

Yeah, said Dewey with a weak smile.

Albright woke Laren and sent her down to the police department as soon as the copy boy carried by the first papers from the mailing room after the state run. These, copies of the edition that would go to the outlying areas, went to editors and writers and executives, ad reps, production managers to check accuracy and production quality before later editions with updates went to the more important regions, the city and suburban homes.

Dewey studied the front page, its photograph of the Thrasher pool in the foreground and the house in the background. The pressmen had not adjusted the ink by the time this copy had run off, and the halftone was thin, washed out, with little contrast. As the press would be finely tuned, the picture would show up with crisp blacks and whites later in the run.

He studied the head he had written for it: Lurker Terrorizes Family Third Time. The subhead: Reporter Glimpses Suspect, Barely Escapes Stalker With Knife.

Elliott's line drawing did not have a credit line. He certainly wouldn't want his name on a sketch that couldn't be distinguished as either a white man or a black.

He read the story and marveled at the touch. She was such a storyteller, an accurate observer of detail – so accurate he could picture how her narrative was acted out in darkness just by looking at the photograph of the pool and house, taken in daylight. She had a sense of the dramatic so that a trivial detail was magnified – the shadow seen from underwater eclipsing the moon, for example – so as to extract the utmost in terror from it. Even the description of the knife blade catching a slice of moonlight was not as chilling. He found himself gasping for breath as if he'd been the one suffocating in that pool.

The emotions and feelings of the family and Laren were enlarged, perhaps even unnaturally enlarged in the first drafts – he had toned the emotions down – fulfilling more a dramatic purpose than a reporting purpose. Other facts, important facts even, were diminished, shrunk so they didn't get in the way of the drama.

For instance, one little detail that had shrunk to nothing was her explanation of how she came to be at the Thrasher house in the first place. She never said, and the narrative raced so fast, you never asked. You were too busy reliving the terror with the writer.

You read her stories and you were there. You had a man lurking through your own house, backing you into the pool. You almost drowned reading the damned story – hell, you'd rather drown than come up to the possibility, no, the certainty, of having your throat cut. Damn. That was the problem with this story. You felt the hot sting of a sharp blade – something like a paper cut across your throat – and for crying out loud, nobody had even been cut. Unless you count that scratch on Laren's face – which she likewise had never explained.

The terror, then, became larger than life, the lurker more mysterious, more terrible than any prowler had a right to be. Something bothered Dewey about these tendencies.

Was it jealousy at how well she wrote?

Or was it something else?

'The cops are pissed, Ted. Even Hanover is no longer being led around by his hormones. They're not going to help us anymore, and you can put that in the bank.'

He saw that she was still excited, as high on her story as if she had injected ink straight into her veins.

'Get this. What do you suppose they're so damned mad at me for? For reporting that bastard was around there all the time, even after they searched the place, that's what.'

'Laren, you need to calm down.'

'Hell, how can I? Look, I had my shower, a nap, changed clothes, a meal. Only thing that could settle me down now is a drink. What say?'

'No . . . yeah. We need to talk. Away from the office.'

They left the newsroom's quiet madness and her celebrity behind them. Maybe she could calm down if everybody from copy boy to managing editor wasn't coming by every ten minutes or so to pay her a compliment, he thought.

But even people on the street were talking about it.

The newspaper vending machines already had promotional cards tucked into their fronts: Read all the latest on The Lurker victimizing the city. Eyewitness Report.

Cripes, he thought, they were beginning to make this paper sound like the teasing, maddening promos for one of those stupid local television news programs.

Laren read the headline on every newsstand as if it were the first time she'd ever seen the story. Every time they passed an empty vending machine, she pointed it out.

He had to admit – she *was* selling papers.

He halfway expected a lurker drink special to be chalked up on the board in the entry of the restaurant. He was thankful the chalkboard featured a Bloody Mary instead of a bloody lurker.

He drank a spiced Bloody Mary, without the liquor. She took it with. He waited for the stimulation of her drink to pass, for the depressing effect to start taking hold of her. It came with the second basket of popped corn and third drink.

'You know what bothers me?' she asked, for the first time not grinning.

He shook his head.

'What bothers me,' she continued, 'is a thought I've been having all day long. This is it: We've been assuming the guy had somehow broken into the house and was creeping around to rape or steal or whatever.'

She waited for him to nod.

So he did.

She said, 'What if . . .' – a chill shook her shoulders – 'what if he was staying in the house all the time?'

Dewey knitted his brow. He had other things he wanted to bring up with her, but this idea struck him as a diversion well worth examining.

'Why would he do that?'

'I tried to think that through as a criminal would,' she said, 'but I came up with nothing. Then I just simplified my whole notion of what was going on inside those houses we think were being visited by this lurker. And I just asked myself, what do the really poor people do? What do the homeless do?'

She waved a beckoning hand at him.

'They go to shelters and missions, I guess.'

'Or?'

'They live on the streets, or in trash bins . . . whatever they can find.'

'Right. Now what if you had a very simple sort of person who just found his way into a person's house and hid in the basement or attic? What if the person never made a sound or a mess that could be identified as coming from an intruder?'

He gave her an incredulous look.

'Wait,' she said, 'what would you have if you were such a person lurking in somebody's house? Supposing you were never discovered?'

He shrugged. 'I'd go crazy . . . hell, I don't know.'

'You're already nuts – not you, but this lurker is already nuts. Only he's not so nuts, after all. He has a warm place to stay. At night he can get up and raid the cupboards. During the day, he can have the run of the house when everybody's out to school and work or whatever.'

Now Dewey took a turn with a case of the chills.

'Jeez, what an awful thought,' he said. 'And every time you locked the doors, you'd be locking the bastard in. You'd be worried about burglars, and all the time you'd be shutting yourself in with a crazy man. Gives me the creeps to think about it.'

'Right.' She was becoming animated again. 'And if things aren't working out, you just change houses. You never break in. You just walk in . . . walk out. Lord knows people go out into the backyard all the time without locking up. Or they shut the automatic garage door at night – never check for anybody – and then they leave the house door to the garage unlocked. So how hard would it be to get into half the houses in this country? And once inside, you never let yourself be seen. You never leave a mess . . . think of it . . . you could borrow clothes, watch television . . .'

'If the family had headphones.'

'Funny,' she said. 'And half the noises you made, if you did make any noise, would be blamed on the wind or other natural house noises. You just learn to creep around in the dark.'

'Interesting theory,' he said. 'I can believe it *might* work. But it doesn't explain our man very well. I mean, he was discovered at the Thrasher house, yet he kept coming back . . . or he hid out and stayed when he must have been in danger of being discovered again. Why didn't he leave?'

She gave him a helpless look.

'I don't know how he fits into this theory. I've got an

155

appointment with a shrink tomorrow. He deals with abnormals. Maybe he can give us some clues,' she said.

'What about ejaculating into your shoe? Why would he do that? And what about the knife? Why would he be carrying that knife you say you saw? And why would he advance on a sound . . .?'

'What do you mean "Say you saw"?'

'And why would he let himself be seen by that Thrasher kid and then not leave?'

'Dewey, what the hell do you mean, "say you saw"?'

'All right.' He didn't want a confrontation with her. He didn't want to ask. He was beginning to like her, and the answers she was going to give were either going to be combative and bitter or truthful and disappointing. If he was wrong about his suspicions, she would be pissed at him. If he were right, she'd be doubly so.

'All right,' he repeated. 'Something I have to know. First of all, your stories were beautifully written . . .'

'Cut the crap, Dewey. Get to the point.'

'But you left a couple big holes. I mean, the narrative was so smooth and suspenseful and quick-paced, nobody who read it cold would ask this question. But I'm your editor on this one.'

'For chrissake, no wonder you don't do any more writing. Get to the lead, Dewey. What's all this explanation about?'

Her aggressiveness did not reassure him. 'Just answer one question for starters.'

'Answer one question truthfully, don't you mean?'

He narrowed his eyes. 'You said that.'

They sat, stares locked, neither one willing to yield, to blink, to look away.

'Okay, Laren. Just tell me how you came to be in the Thrasher backyard in the first place.'

He saw she never flinched in any way. She was a good one, one of the best liars he'd ever seen – if she *was* a liar. Her answer would tell him.

'All right, I've had a deal going with Hanover. He promised to give me a tip anytime there was a possible police run on this lurker case.'

Their eyes were still locked like the antlers of bull elk in a battle to the death. Neat answer, he thought, but not the answer to his question.

'I know about the deal with Hanover.' There it was, a flicker of the eyelid. 'Now answer my question. How did you come to be in the backyard?'

The nerves in her upper lip caused a slight tug on the sneer muscle. But she held it.

'Hanover called me the night of the Thrasher business.'

Still not the answer.

'I know he called you. But you weren't home.'

'I got the message on my machine.'

'He didn't leave a message. He was as surprised as anyone to find out in the paper you were there.'

Her head snapped to the right as if she would spit on the floor. 'Goddamn you, Dewey, what right have you to check up on me?'

'This is my story too, Hodges. I'm the editor. My credibility is on the line, even if the stories don't carry my byline.'

'As if they could,' she said, now releasing her lip to sneer savagely. 'You couldn't write your way out of a wet paper bag. You're over the hill and a pretty goddamned small hill at that. Tomorrow I'm telling Albright I want another editor, one who's not washed-up.'

He choked it down. He knew this was merely another tactic.

'You're probably right,' he said. 'This was doomed to failure. Yep, somebody is going to have to be replaced on this story. And if you don't come clean about how you got into this Thrasher story, how you never took a single quote from anybody in the Thrasher backyard, how you had to haul your ass soaking wet all the way up to the lake to get your interviews hours after the incident, then I know who is going to get the sack.'

He left the answer unspoken.

Her anger was replaced by a blank expression, then an angry one again, then a defeated one.

'You know why I hate you, Dewey?'

'I can think of a dozen . . .'

'It was rhetorical, you bastard. I hate you because you can read me. And because you're so goddamned smug about it.'

'So. How is it that you came to be in the Thrasher backyard yet never conducted an interview there?'

The look of hatred on her face made him glad she didn't have a knife in her hand.

She told him about her stakeout, then retold the story of the terror in the pool, a quick, exciting narrative. But he wasn't seduced by the story again.

'You have this wonderful quality in your storytelling,' he said. 'You write and tell everything so factually. It just isn't always true.'

'For instance?'

'The face of this lurker. Our paper is running an artist's concept on a face you say you saw in the moonlight. Suppose we go out to one of the city parks a little later on and try to check out each other's faces. You think we could see enough to produce a useful sketch?'

'In your case,' she said, 'all we'd need was a drawing of a broken down horse's ass.'

He ignored the thrust. Waited. The seconds of waiting ticked by.

'Okay,' she muttered, 'so I didn't get the clearest view of his face.'

'You'd never know that by reading your story.'

'Okay, Dewey, my imagination was a little too vivid. You get that way when somebody comes after you with a knife . . . when you're in danger.' She spoke it as if to say, Something you couldn't identify with, jerk.

He ignored it, intent upon another train of thought.

'Let's suppose you did the best you could with the light that was available and that the artist's drawing is fair enough. Let's let that be a bygone. Then let's forget you trespassed to get your sighting of this lurker in the first place, because after all, the means *could* be said to justify. But let's ask ourselves another question.'

'Cut the Socrates shit, Dewey.' Still, she couldn't hide the relief in her voice that he wouldn't be going to Albright.

'What have you done?'

'I told a great story . . . make that *found* a great story and wrote it very well. I sold a few papers, some advertising. I got the police off their fat asses to check this guy out. I made the people in this city more aware of crime prevention . . .'

'Sold a few burglar alarms, security lights – hell, even the sale of light bulbs is up – as is the sale of guns and ammunition.'

'What's the point, Dewey? Conversation with you is as exasperating as stepping in dogshit, you know? Ever step in it? Ever notice how hard it is to get off? Get my point?'

'The point is, Laren . . . you have given this idiot the impression that you and Mrs Thrasher and the kid,

Buddy, and Marguerite can identify him. You may have given him reason to fear you and them. And what will a nut like that do if he's afraid? Maybe that's the reason he kept going back to – or staying at – the Thrasher place.'

She pondered a moment. In the chewing of the inside of her cheeks, he could see her mind working to rationalize her response.

Finally, she said, 'Bullshit, Dewey. If the sketch doesn't look like him, he won't worry. If it does, somebody will turn him in – he'll be afraid to show his face.'

'Bullshit yourself, Laren. We're not dealing with a rational person here. Why would he think like you? . . . Why would anybody for that matter? Besides, he doesn't show his face in the first place.'

'Well, it's not my fault,' she murmured. 'I was just doing my . . .'

She caught his half-amused smile. Once again, he wasn't buying it. Goddamn him.

'All right, Dewey. I'll tell you something I didn't want to bring up. Marguerite told me. When this guy tried to rape her, he used my name. He thought she was me, I was she, I don't know. He used my name.'

'What the hell are you talking about?' Dewey said, too struck now to be smug.

'My name: Laren. He was choking her and humping her and calling my name. She told me after she talked to the cops that she couldn't get an edgewise word with Hanover to tell them. She told me. I said I'd bring it up to Hanover. I never did.'

Dewey looked puzzled. 'How could he mix up you two' – he looked into her eyes – 'I mean . . .'

'I know what you mean,' she said. 'You mean she's way prettier . . . don't deny it. I know she is. I don't

160

know how or even if he did have us mixed up. I don't know anything except what she told me. And that I keep running across his path. So you see, it doesn't matter whether the others are named in the stories. It's me he's after.'

'And you're going to play this story for all it's worth, aren't you?'

'Whatever you think, Dewey, I can't control the news or this nut. He'll do what he wants. And we'll report it.' She raised her eyebrows at him, inviting an argument.

He gave her none.

Next day, she didn't have much time for reflection on the themes she didn't want to reflect on anyhow. Lurker news dominated the newsroom. A woman had accidentally shot a lurker suspect: her husband sneaking out of the house – to get cigarettes, he claimed. There were four incidents reported from hospital emergency rooms after people had gotten up in the dark to investigate strange sounds. A woman had fallen down her stairs. A man had shot himself in the crotch while trying to draw a pistol from the belt of his robe. Another man had tackled his own shadowy image in a full-length mirror. A teenager had jumped his father in the kitchen and dislocated a parental shoulder while spraining a youthful knee. A woman had sliced a fillet of thumb into the dinner salad when she jumped at the sound of the doorbell.

Employers were reporting people coming to work dazed by lack of sleep, staying up all night to ambush prowlers who never materialized.

Theater managers bawled that moviegoers were staying home in droves.

The chief of police just bawled.

The city editor called his lurker team in for a strategy meeting and expressed his concern over the paper's stirring up trouble rather than reporting it.

'Hogwash,' Laren retorted. She looked toward Dewey for a contradiction. He gave her none. 'Since when does the paper back away from the police department and the truth that it's not doing a decent job at bringing in this lurker?'

Albright said, 'We're not backing away from the cops. I'm asking whether we're starting a minor panic. I'm just asking, okay?'

'Look,' said Laren, grappling with herself for control, 'I've seen a town go nuts the first time we reported a blizzard is coming. People go on shopping frenzies, filling up their freezers, buying out the food stores – all the milk and bread. Does that mean we stop telling the poor, dumb jerks the blizzard is on the way?'

'No. Is this the same thing?'

'Not far from it.'

'People don't start packing guns and shooting each other at the weather reports, Hodges.'

'They shoot each other all year-round, Lou. And while you were entertaining the crybaby chief, I was checking his department's crime stats for the week since we began running the lurker stuff. Burglaries? Down. Breaking and entering? Down. Legitimate trespassing arrests? Down. I tell you, people are staying at home and being more crime conscious. Husbands are staying home with wifey instead of going out to carouse. And nine months from now, you'll be able to check birth records and see the rate is up. We're doing mankind a ser –'

'Listen, Laren, we aren't going to call this story off as long as it remains a legitimate one. What I'm telling you is, we're not going to create some kind of monster

162

psychopath out of a simple pathetic prowler. Or prowLERS, plural – we still aren't sure it's one guy, y'know. We're not going to get the whole populace upset over nothing.'

'You think this is nothing? A guy creeping around with a knife is nothing?'

'Laren . . .'

She looked to Dewey for help, although she was sure the jealous, incompetent jerk wasn't going to bail her out. But he did.

'Lou, Laren talked to a shrink this morning. When we do a story based on his remarks, the tensions will be diminished, I'm sure.'

'What's the shrink say?'

She gave Dewey a grateful smile and took the cue.

'He said this lurker really has no more potential for violence than an obscene caller. He said it's more likely he will continue to get bolder only because he's really calling out for help and wants to get caught. The shrink even downplayed the rape attempt on Marguerite as an "attempt". He says the guy will continue to escalate his risk taking until he's captured, but when he is, he won't even put up a fight. He'll be relieved the authorities have him.'

Albright growled, 'You don't have to sound so disappointed.'

'I'm not disappointed. When we print this, people will probably stop acting insane. I'm getting an entire profile together for tomorrow. We may even have enough so that somebody will recognize this guy and call in to police.'

She saw his eyes brighten.

'Do the police have a hot line?' Albright asked.

'No,' she said. 'I told Hanover it would be a public service.'

163

'What'd he say?'

'A lady can't repeat what he said.' She caught the sarcastic smile on Dewey's face, the smile that said, 'Lady?' but she ignored it. 'Lou, why can't *we* put in a hot line?'

'No way,' said Dewey.

Albright sat mulling, picking and biting industriously at a hangnail.

Laren, sensing a chance for a decisive victory here, said, 'We would only man it because the police aren't. Soon as we get something, we turn it over to the cops. As soon as they feel the pressure to start one of their own, we have the phone company transfer the line.'

Albright spit out a fragment of fingernail and said, 'Ted?'

'My opinion is, it's police business. And we don't have the manpower, either.'

'Manpower is my problem, not yours. I'd use Ruthey – sort of a nasty little irony there, a crank of our own to keep the crank calls down to a minimum. There's something to be said about using it as a tip line. You know, not an investigative line but just as a tip line. We'd sort things out, send the most valuable tips or recordings of all calls or something over to the cop shop.' As he talked, it was becoming a reality. Laren saw it taking shape.

So did Dewey. 'I don't like it, Lou,' he said.

'Well, it could be our way of reducing tensions, give people an outlet. If it will do that, I like it.' Albright squinted at the ceiling. 'I like it,' he repeated.

Dewey scowled at the fait accompli.

Laren gloated.

By evening, Laren was drunk. Although she hadn't had a drop of liquor, she was unnaturally high. The

164

stimuli coursing through her veins were the thrill of her victory, the agony of Dewey's defeat, the power of gloat. She had neutralized Dewey this morning in the meeting with Albright. Having lost the little battle over the hot line, he could never bring up the little indiscretions in the tomato patch and the swimming pool. It would look like petty jealousy. Besides, she had decided, it *was* petty. The more she thought about it, the more that sketch, which had been run in edition after edition, *did* look like the person she thought she had seen.

And now she had begun planning a counterthrust against Dewey, a virtual coup d'état. She had asked the librarian to photocopy a handful of his clips. She wanted Dewey's best stuff, the prekidnapping clips, for background, she had said. She wanted to build a little dossier of her own on the guy. The SOB had trapped her the other day, and she was going to get even somehow. She knew the place to start. That was with his writing – not the laboring, boring junk he had been writing from the cop shop lately, now out of ennui, but the supposedly passionate writing he'd done in the olden days – if it ever had been passionate. You want to know somebody, you study what they write, she decided. There is no such thing as objective writing. Every word is an exposé.

Besides, she might get a few laughs comparing his junk to her own work. And once she learned what made him tick internally, maybe she could slip a blade into the chink in his armor. Sure as hell hadn't done her any good to insult his manhood or his drinking or even his Dumbo ears. What would do it would probably come out of studying his writing. And once she had set him back upon his heels, maybe he wouldn't be so eager to bare *her* vulnerabilities, something only her father, the bastard, had been able to do.

She mixed a weak drink, a light whiskey to quench her thirst while not making her dizzy. She set a bag of popcorn to popping in the microwave – as long as she was in a festive mood anyhow . . .

But once she started reading, her sweet humor soured.

As the pile of newspaper clippings to her left continued to shrink and the pile on her right stacked up higher, the dampness of tears began to form around her eyes. The dampness wasn't really the emotion of sadness. More like anger and frustration.

Finally, she gave up, threw both piles of photocopied clips into the trash, and emptied her unfinished drink into the sink.

'Goddamn you, Dewey,' she muttered as she threw herself across the bed into the beam of light cast from the bathroom, the light she left on every night since moving in with her traveling friend. 'Goddamn you sonofabitch.' Now she'd have to play a different game. The scenario had changed. She knew she could no longer underestimate him.

Next day she tracked down Hanover, who refused to return her calls. She caught him in the department's coffee shop.

Hanover's buddies saw her first. They scattered like roaches under the kitchen light. He looked after them in dismay. 'Hey, what'd I do? I forget to shower? My deodorant let me . . . oh . . . You.'

'Detective, have you got a minute?'

'Nuh-uh. Not for you.'

'This is off the record.'

'Shee-it. As if ground rules mean anything to you.

Nope, not on the record and not off. You feel better if I would turn my back? Or would you rather stab me in the face?'

'C'mon, Hanover, cut the hysterics. You're not a victim here. Sit back down. I'll buy you a cup of coffee.'

'I won't drink it.'

'I want to talk about Dewey.' She sat looking pleadingly up into his face.

'Kee-rist, you are something, Hodges. You rip me up in the papers and then you want to tear up your partner. After what he's done for you.' Despite his protestations, he sat down.

She saw he was interested enough in looking down her silk blouse to hear her out. It was the reason she wore it. Reason alone wasn't going to appeal to this bullheaded cop.

'So. What's Dewey done for me, anyhow?'

'You don't know, do you? Well, he's given up friends down here on the force that he's had for years. He got into one hell of an argument with some of the boys when they was — mind you, I wasn't one of them — when they was cutting you down. Though I don't know why he'd rather have you for a friend than us.'

The way he was eyeing her cleavage belied his last statement. In another set of circumstances, she would have nailed him for the roving eyes. But her purpose today was to get information.

'Well, I'm flattered that he would stick up for me with his . . . cronies. But I'm not doing so well with him, hard as I try.'

He gave her a look that said he didn't believe that. Then it switched to not caring.

'It's true,' she answered the looks. 'I can't figure what makes him the way he is. And lately, today for instance, I can't even talk to him.'

'Well, that part's easy, the today part. I heard his divorce papers have come through. He didn't want a divorce.'

She perked up. This tidbit alone made her silk blouse manipulation, cheap and dirty as it was, worthwhile.

She probed. 'His wife didn't want the divorce?'

'I doubt it. It's just that he can't put the death of his little girl to rest. Well, there, I just said it – if she was only dead, he probably could put it behind him. He doesn't know if she's dead or not.'

'Well, what does he do about it?'

'I'm not exactly sure. He's not doing nothing, yet he never stops doing something. It's like a news story he's been working on for two years since it happened. He keeps tapping me for information about similar cases over the national crime wire. He keeps digging into the case, keeps tabs on our old list of suspects ... things like that. He never writes anything, though. He never tries to dump his leads on us or the courts. He just keeps digging into the most useless details about the death ... disappearance of his daughter. It's like a part of his brain snapped and he won't let her go.'

'Why?'

'Just wants to bury her, I guess. Her body was never found, naturally. Hell, who knows what makes people snap? He keeps on researching that story ... He just never writes it.'

'He was a good writer. I mean, before.'

'Oh, hell yes. You just now finding that out? He was always going to quit the paper and write books, like novels and shit ... stuff. I seen part of one he showed me when we was out drunk once. Good stuff.'

'And he just gave up on his dream?'

'Just let it die. He was the paper's top writer ... had an offer to New York and another to Washington. But he turned them down to stay here because he was going to quit newspapering and write books. Then he just got himself on covering cops after . . .'

'Erica?'

'Erica.'

'Erica,' said Dewey. 'What right have you to speak her name?'

She had found him in a watering hole long after work. He was drunk but well under control, as she knew the heavy drinkers could be even when they fell off the wagon.

'Ted,' she said, 'I'm not here to stir you up. I want to . . . apologize for my bad form in the past. I want to start fresh with you.'

He narrowed his eyes. 'Why? You see a chance for a Pulitzer? Something I can do to get you moved out to LA?'

She knew it was useless to lie to him. To protest his suggestions would simply intensify his scorn. 'If this story will get those kinds of opportunities for me, I will take them, yes. And in an earlier day, even you might have grasped for the ring of LA or a prize or even the luxury of being able to retire from the paper to . . . oh, I don't know . . . write books or something.'

He warily searched her face for a clue to this new tactic.

She remained impassive, hoping she could carry this off.

His eyes shifted, gazed into his headless beer.

She knew he was puzzled, off guard. Now to press her advantage. Carefully.

'I heard about your divorce papers. No wonder you got so angry with me. It seems as if I've been so insensitive, Ted. I'm sorry. If I had known . . .'

169

'Ya know?' he said, drawing out the words. 'You're absolutely right. I would've done those things at one time or another. And you should, too.'

For a moment she was happy with her victory, at least his concession. Then he just sat staring into his beer glass. And she had nowhere to go with the discussion. She'd been prepared to argue, to stamp out angrily, to apologize if necessary – that is, if it would have gained her anything – but to have him agree with her and sit in silence was a twist. This SOB was always getting away with something, always pulling one over.

'I read some of your clips,' she said. 'From before. Your writing was . . . wonderful. I thought I was pretty good. But I could learn a lot from you. I read about the father of the soldier missing in action, and it brought tears to my eyes.'

'I cried when I wrote it,' he said matter-of-factly. 'He doesn't know whether his son is dead or alive. If he's alive, he's still in a prison-of-war camp in Vietnam. So what's the choice for that father? To wish his son was alive and suffering? Or to wish he was dead? In his mind, his kid is still nineteen, still standing in the door of that plane. Waving.'

She was at a dead end again. What could she do? Ask him how come his talent had gone to dog cables on the lawn? She was so engrossed in wondering what to say, she forgot to observe as tears welled up in his eyes. Dewey had almost cried just now. She had seen but not observed. Until he spoke again, drawing attention to his emotional condition.

'I don't cry anymore.' He looked at her helplessly. 'Except in my sleep – I think I cry in my sleep.'

Then he seemed to remember who he was, who she was. He cocked his head and said, 'God, why do I tell you such things? I know why you're such a good reporter, Laren. People will tell you anything, even things you don't ask about. They used to do that with me. I tried to be the guy sitting next to people on the plane, the guy people never expected to ever see again. I just sat there and nodded and talked like we were flying to Cleveland or something. And they just spilled their guts for me so I could lay them out to dry in print the next day.'

To Laren, he seemed to be saying he knew the game and wouldn't be spilling his guts to her anymore. She just sat. Bit her lip. Stayed quiet.

'But I've changed,' he said. 'I just ask a lot of impatient questions like some goddamned rookie so I can get the who, what, when, where, why, how – slam, bam, thank you, ma'am.'

'It's the beat,' she said. 'You have to be quick with cop news. Not much chance for embellishment.'

'Naw. It's a great beat. Full of drama. Heroes. Villains. Salts and scums of the earth. Life. Death. All the great issues.'

She had absolutely no idea where this conversation was going. He was beginning to mumble, to slur, to show signs of intoxication. And she began to look for a chance to exit gracefully. There was no talking to a drunk. She could finish her snow job on him tomorrow, she thought. No, that wasn't true – she didn't really want to snow him. She wanted to make him feel better, to cheer him up. She was beginning to feel sorry for him.

'Don't you wanna ask me about my wife?' he asked, a tinge of belligerence in his voice.

'No,' she lied.

'Liar. She loves me. Loves my kid. Loved my daughter.'

She sat waiting.

'You thought I was going to say she's a bitch or something. She isn't. She's an angel.'

'She must have suffered a lot, too.'

'Suffered. There's the word. Loved. Past tense. She loved Erica. Now she wants to forget her. Well, having one child is no excuse to forget about another one.'

He ordered another beer with the flick of his hand. She refused, grappling with the relevance of seemingly aimless conversation.

But wait . . .

Maybe it wasn't so aimless, after all.

Finally, it began dawning on her. God, she'd been thick. He hadn't been telling her about a father and an MIA son. He'd been talking about himself and his daughter.

'That father of the MIA?' she said, concentrating on suppressing her excitement.

'Hmmmmm?'

'What could he do?' she asked.

'Nothing. Write letters. Talk to a newspaper reporter – me. He sure as hell couldn't take on the Hanoi government and get diddly out of them. He couldn't travel over there and find out for himself if the bastards had buried his son.'

'But you could.'

'Go to Hanoi? You crazy, Laren?'

'No. And neither are you. Jesus, you're clever. Crazy like a fox. A damned rabid fox.'

'What's with the Aesop's fables, Hodges?' He was growing angry.

'You know damn well what I'm talking about, Dewey. I had you pegged completely wrong. Talk about falling for a snow job. You've got everybody snowed. Me too. I fell right into it. You're not just some slob

172

wandering around in self-pity and grief. You're not just some over-the-hill bastard kicked downstairs to write the cop beat. You're a goddamned conniver, a manipulator, a fucking con man.'

'You learn that kind of talk in finishing school?'

'And you gave me that lecture on integrity, credibility. What bullshit. You haven't lost your writing touch. You're a good – ' she bit her lip and reluctantly corrected herself, 'no, you're a wonderful writer. You didn't lose that ability overnight. Your dogshit writing nowadays is no accident. Right? Am I right? Don't shake your head at me. Don't give me those downcast, godforsaken, bullshit doe eyes, you bastard.' She pounded on the table for emphasis.

'You *could* do it this very minute. And you're *not* destroyed by grief. You *want* people to tiptoe around you. You *want* people to ignore you, to feel sorry for you – just so they leave you alone. Just so you can stay close to the cops and their investigations. Just so you can be near them when they bring in the suspected murderer . . . or, or . . . kidnapper of your daughter. Just so you can get your revenge.'

He shifted on his barstool as if to get in position to throw a punch. His face darkened.

'You ignorant bitch. You don't know what you're talking about.'

She slapped her forehead. 'God, it's so clear now. You're willing to be a shitty run-of-the-mill reporter so you never have to be promoted. You're just consumed by hatred, by your passion for vengeance. Fact is, you've gone over the edge, haven't you? You've been plotting a murder for the past two years. Haven't you? Come on, admit it.'

'You're full of shit, Hodges. You ought to be writing sci-fi fairy tales with such an active imagination.'

173

She grinned into his face, called his bluff. 'My imagination? Just my imagination? Well, let us just see. You're carrying a gun, aren't you?'

His face went blank.

'C'mon,' she taunted. 'Deny you're carrying a gun and let me pat you down. Then I'll own up to being the crazy one. I'll admit this whole thing is just my imagination if you're clean. C'mon. Prove you're not packing a pistol.'

He didn't deny it. He kept a blank expression, but she knew she had him. She knew well enough to offer him the ultimate prize.

'If you're not packing,' she said, pausing to sniff noisily, arrogantly, 'I'll resign from the paper tomorrow.'

The heat left his complexion. She pounded a fist on the table in triumph.

'You sonofabitch. You poor, pathetic sonofabitch.'

He smirked and laughed. 'I underestimated you, Laren. You are one hell of a judge of character. You have instincts. I thought you were a one-way mirror, that I could read you at will and stay impervious to you. Guess the lurker isn't the only presence you can feel.'

She snickered. Now that she had him by the gonads, she decided to put the squeeze on some more.

'You bastard. It isn't funny what you did to me. You've been acting the righteous one, making me feel the bitch. All along . . . don't smile so smugly, you bloody creep . . . all along you've been the sonofabitch – worse than the rest of us. At least we didn't spend *all* our time arrogantly looking down our noses at the world.'

'All right,' he said to her back as she walked away. 'So we're both sonsabitches.'

'Not exactly,' she shot back over her shoulder. 'I'm a sonofabitch, but you're an insane sonofabitch.'

11

The *Post-Herald* hot line, the Lurker Line, as it was dubbed, produced immediate results.

As predicted, the police became outraged because the paper was meddling in an investigation. After much shouting by the chief in the office of the publisher, it was agreed the paper would drop the project, turning it over to police in a week. Which was the aim of the exercise in the first place. And the transaction provided a few column inches for another news story, the object of newspapering.

The *Post-Herald* happily gave up the line. Even though it was open for only two days, it had generated more than 250 calls, keeping Ruthey Minton shrieking and complaining into the line continually. And the city room didn't have the resources or experts to sift the crank calls from the useful tips.

Laren could go nowhere in the building without being ambushed by somebody about the latest scoop on the lurker. She told only news that had been culled by Dewey, bits that didn't make it into the paper. Her newest leads were never revealed to anybody, she told them.

Fact was, she didn't have a lot of new leads. She was beginning to wonder if the momentum of this story could be sustained.

She did overhear a fragment of conversation between Lou Albright and the managing editor. 'All we need is to capture the somebitch and get a few police heads to roll for incompetence,' said Albright.

The ME clucked his tongue and murmured, 'Wouldn't hurt if somebody *did* get hurt . . .'

They grimaced at each other, each's expression telling the other he didn't *really* want the lurker to hurt somebody to increase the importance of this story. Honest. Not *really*.

Laren knew what they were talking about. They were talking about news contests, maybe even the Pulitzer, she imagined. No, that sort of thing didn't happen, except in cases of national importance – or at least local stories with national interest. Still, the thought of a prize . . . even a nomination . . . Sure she didn't want anybody to get hurt either – though it was nice to have her every story scarfed up by the wires lately. The exposure wasn't hurting her career choices.

Well, no, she didn't want anybody to get hurt. But she could sure use a break to keep the lurker interest rolling.

An apparent break came very late in the day – in the form of a caterwauling shriek across the city room from Ruthey Minton.

'Laa-REN, pho-own.'

Laren saw she was holding up the new phone, the Lurker Line. Could it be? She fluffed her hair through her fingers, as if primping for the caller. But today's fine sprinkling mist of rain had flattened her curl.

Could this be *the* lurker?

It was.

'Laren Hodges.'

Her name was growled back to her.

She grabbed a notebook from Ruthey, getting a scowl as well. But Minton held her squawks and leaned in closer to eavesdrop.

She saw Laren's notes being scrawled on the pad:

Going to kill you.

176

Cut you from ass to Adam's apple.

Spill your guts.

Eat your heart.

In your house right now.

'What's the address, sir?' asked Laren politely, '. . . I mean, what's the address of my house? Or my phone number there. If you're there, you must have that information. Or is this just a crank call. You see, we have to sort out the cranks from the real lurker calls . . . Well, yes, I understand you want to kill me, sir, and I can go along with that all right. But if you want to get your story into the paper, you have to have some proof you're who you say you are . . . Well, if you can't prove it, I'm afraid we're just going to have to conclude this is a prank call . . . Well, same to you, buddy.'

She looked at the phone and hung it up.

She looked around and found she'd gathered a crowd of eavesdroppers.

Albright took her by the elbow and led her to his office. He beckoned for Dewey to follow.

'Laren, you stay off the phone to these lurker cranks,' the city editor said.

'What? Lou, come *on*. You think I've never handled an obscene call before?'

'Probably *made* a few,' offered Dewey.

Laren was amused. She actually laughed.

Albright was not amused, did not laugh.

'I want to think this out, sans the black humor, if you please. What do we do?'

Laren shrugged. 'We keep on doing what we're doing. I can write a wrap-up of the calls Ruth has logged. I can lead with the crank threats.'

'Naw, that will just generate more weirdos,' said Dewey.

'So what?' said Laren. 'We're turning the line over

177

to the cops anyhow. Wouldn't hurt to juice it up first, would it?'

Albright grimaced. 'I don't like it. We're getting into a briar patch with this damned Lurker Line. We created it . . . We virtually invited the cranks to call. Then we write about them calling . . . No, this is too much like making news. We've not yet sunk to the level of those pretty boys on TV . . . at least not yet.'

'Come *on*,' Laren protested.

'Well,' said Albright, 'have we had any useful tips to check out ourselves or to pass along to the PD? Answer me that.'

Dewey and Laren wagged their heads.

'I rest my case. Ted, what's your suggestion for getting out of this pickle?'

Laren slumped visibly.

'Oh, I'm not too worried about wrapping up the hotline results – long as we don't overplay it.'

Laren straightened up in surprise that he would be supportive in the slightest.

'But,' he continued, 'there's one thing I can't get off my mind. This lurker guy might have been just a simpleton prowler, a guy who creeps into houses for some perverted pleasure or who stays in houses for a living. Now we're giving him celebrity status. We're suggesting he's possibly dangerous. We've given him a kind of omnipresence – the majority of those 250 calls were from people who sincerely thought the SOB was in their houses or apartments or garages.'

Albright slumped into his chair, troubled.

Laren stamped her foot impatiently. She didn't grasp the point Albright seemed to have gotten.

'So?'

'So we may be driving the guy to do more daring things. He may find it necessary to live up to a

178

reputation we're giving him or to nourish it. We may be bringing on a confrontation.'

'Oh, bull . . . loney. That's paranoid thinking. It's like saying we cause hijackings just because we cover them.'

Dewey raised his eyebrows.

Albright said, 'One thing we can't deny – we are bringing out the perverts to make threats. You'd better be careful, Laren. You might become a target.'

'What should I do, Lou? Hire an armed bodyguard? Start carrying a gun?' She shot a meaningful look at Dewey, whose jaw muscles tightened in response.

As she walked across the city room, she could see eyes watching her while trying not to. She knew she was the current celebrity, though newspeople bestow such honors reluctantly, usually waiting a dozen or two years before granting competence to peers. She'd learned that the greatest praise among reporters was envy, and she knew there were plenty of envious eyes on her as she went to the wall of sliding doors that was the coatrack to retrieve her raincoat and umbrella.

Well, if they must grant their adulation so circumspectly, she must bear it so.

She reached for her coat.

As a growling figure leapt from behind the closet at her.

'LURRRKERRRRR!' the figure roared.

She shrieked.

And the city room's chaotically ordered silence disintegrated into disordered laughter.

There was nothing else to do. She laughed with them, unable to help it that she grew very hot and red with embarrassment, first for being so smug about why they were looking at her surreptitiously, second for being so absolutely frightened by the office prankster.

She hadn't been that scared since . . . well, since feeling the lurker in her apartment and seeing him at the Thrasher pool . . . and hearing Marguerite tell the details of being choked and nearly raped by a weirdo whispering, 'Laren.'

All the way home, she could not shake the rattled feeling. Damn that jerk for jumping out at her. Lately, her mind had been full of stories, leads, clues, stratagems, prizes, offers, the works. She'd had no time for fear, had healed over. But now that prankster had jumped out of the closet and scraped off the scab. Her fears had begun seeping, even bleeding again.

For instance, she could not shake the feeling of being followed. There seemed to be one set of lights behind her at every turn. Sure, it was a common route for most late downtown workers to slide back to the north and home. But there were four lanes in most places and plenty of chance for the car to pass, to race ahead to supper or *Star Trek* reruns or whatever the working slob entertained himself with.

She slowed. So did the headlights. Their brightness was magnified, nearly doubled by the reflection off the water in the streets. She approached a traffic signal as it turned from green to yellow and dashed through. The headlights behind her ran the red.

A few blocks from her apartment, she whipped into a shopping mall and took the drive-through lane at a fast-food place. The lights went by.

She slumped into the car seat, embarrassed at her behavior. She ordered a soda for appearances and drove home. The lights did not materialize behind her again.

180

She parked her car and lifted her collar against the mist and the chill at the back of her neck. She ran, happy for the excuse of the rain. She was about to skip over a puddle at the curb when she saw him lurking.

He was just a shadow sitting in a car. For an instant he looked like one of those high-backed seats with the roll on top. But there was the high-backed seat *and* the roll that was a man's head.

In the middle of her leap, she flinched, landed wrong and fell, her ankle giving way, burning white-hot in her shoe. She went down, hitting her shoulder on the sidewalk. She kept pitching forward, her legs coming up awkwardly. She felt the mist wetting her high up on the thighs, even as she struggled to breathe, to catch another glimpse of the shadow inside the car.

The interior light came on. The car door opened.

She lurched to her feet and hobbled toward the door, all the time fumbling in her purse, feeling the icy water soaking through her clothes, feeling prickly cold creep up her spine, feeling a block of ice weigh down her belly.

She grasped her purse against her body, her right hand still inside. With her left, she juggled her keys until the right one came up. Then, as she aimed the key, it slipped from her wet fingers and the entire ring dropped and clanked unmusically on the sidewalk.

She glanced toward the car, cursing under her breath as she knelt to pat the wet concrete, feeling a whining groan ushering involuntarily from her throat.

He was standing in the shadows in front of the car. He was watching her. But at least he was not advancing.

Even if he had advanced, she found the key in time and stood up briskly. She plunged it into the lock, turned, shook her right hand from her purse, and threw a sore shoulder into the door.

She went inside. She glanced out the peephole.

He was still standing there by his car. She had half a mind to storm out and confront the bastard. But her ankle stung her, sending a twinge to remind her what she had done.

If she confronted the guy, he'd probably die laughing at the dive she took. She'd be better off to get on the phone and call the police. But then, what would she tell them? That the sight of a guy made her take a swim in a puddle? Shit.

She giggled, began laughing at herself.

God, what was her sanity coming to?

Her back to the door, she stood slumped, laughing half in humor, half in hysteria. Her hair was wet, dipped like a mop into the water on the sidewalk. Her coat sleeve suffered an abrasion from the fall. Her ankle hurt, and she was dampened up to her butt. God, who was the jerk now?

She dropped her purse to the floor with a heavy clunking sound, shucked her raincoat, and slid the closet door across its track. She took a deep breath with which to sigh in relief.

She had only enough breath for half a scream before two dirty, grappling, grabbing hands closed on her throat, cutting off the scream in mid-shriek.

If she hadn't had the deep sigh prepared, she might not have been able to muster any sound at all.

Before the wild eyes materialized from the depth of the closet. Before the pair of hands went for her. This was more frightening than even the prankster jumping from a closet at the office. This was living the dream, feeling the nightmare.

Her ankle turned again.

Her left shoulder hit the wall, and she went down, her head cracking against the front door. She landed with her ribs on her purse.

She would have grunted in pain, but no air could be forced past that sphincter grip of the two rough hands. Not at all like that prankster. No. This was no office prank, no joke. It was much worse, worse even than the nightmare.

The wild eyes came out of the closet after the hands, and she could see they were enclosed inside the woolen circles of a ski mask. She'd read enough stories – she'd written enough – to know what came next. She'd be raped and killed. Or killed and raped, depending on whether the particular perversion of this lurker creep was to feel his victim squirm or not when he penetrated her.

The crack on her head dulled the pain of the hands. Or else she was already blacking out from the throttling. Why wasn't he whispering her name? she wondered.

And another oddity, she thought: Why had this harmless lurker suddenly become violent? The words of the shrink rose from her subconscious. There was no chance of violence from this guy, he'd said. He was as harmless as an obscene caller.

Right.

She'd be the dead contradiction of that.

One hand released her throat and began tearing her skirt hem, pulling it up.

She heard him kick against the door.

No.

Somebody hit the front door.

The doorbell sounded, electrifying her assailant.

Then all went silent.

She flinched.

It was all the encouragement he needed. The lurker went back to choking her.

Then he called her name after all.

No.

Her name was being called through the door – by a familiar voice.

The doorbell sounded urgently.

The door thumped against its frame again.

The lurker pushed off her and knelt beside her.

She gasped for air.

He looked at her.

His eyes through the circles of the mask were wild still, but now with fear. Clearly panicked. Maybe he would run, she thought.

The door bashed inward again. 'Laren!' shouted the voice from outside.

The lurker looked at the door, released her, and started to his feet.

She reached beneath her for the purse, grasped it, swung it with what breathless force she could muster.

It was enough. The lurker took the blow in the mouth and sat down hard on the floor holding his grubby hands to the cracked lips protruding from the oval of wool, catching the blood.

She lurched toward the door.

He jumped for her.

He hit her in the back, and she went down, her face crashing into the door again.

But not before she had turned the knob, snapping the lock.

Dewey was already beside himself with worry when he heard the snap of the lock. Although his shoulder throbbed, he was prickling with embarrassment. If he should be caught throwing himself at the apartment door . . . if that was *not* a scream he thought he heard just before getting back into his car. If she just called the police or fired a shotgun through the door. He wouldn't have a prayer of an excuse for bashing into her apartment door.

But there was that scream, wasn't there?

Then there was the snap and the sound of a body hitting the door from the inside.

He turned the knob and threw his weight once more.

It came open, pinching somebody – no, two somebodies – behind it. Then he saw the ski mask.

It triggered a madness in him.

For two years the madness had been incubating, at first glowing fiercely hot – with senseless anger at everything and everybody, including God. Then he'd cooled. But, like a volcano whose hot magma seethes unseen beneath a cold, rough crust before erupting, Dewey exploded. His rage blew all at once, taking the cap off two years of pent-up ferocity. When it happened, even Dewey could not have anticipated the quickness and strength and depth of his passions.

The mask touched it off. The mask, the very picture of the murderous bastard he had imagined his daughter's assailant to be. But it also ended with the mask. For Dewey did not recognize what he had become, did not realize how quickly his mind had snapped. For he had become the killer now.

Two killers, really.

One killer was the empassioned Dervish who began beating on this lurker. The other killer was the calculating Accomplice who oversaw the assault, who coldly observed and supervised the execution of the Dervish's every blow, the lurker's route to death.

There was the lump of the pistol at the small of

185

Dewey's back. But the Accomplice didn't want it done with a pistol.

He wanted it done with his bare hands, bald knuckles.

The Dervish part of Dewey gladly obliged. He renewed his attack of the fists. At first, he felt a couple of return blows. They merely stung him, stoking a fresh onslaught.

The Dervish had the advantage of the attack, the ferocity of that two years' pent-up rage, the Accomplice reasoned. So attack, he ordered. The Dervish obeyed.

The lurker was on his back shielding his face from the onslaught of blows, when the Dervish began throwing intermittent kicks in with the rain of punches, finally landing the telling punt toe – first, deep and sharply hard into the groin, bringing an agonized moan to the bloody, bluing lips encircled by the mouth opening in the mask.

The Accomplice laughed, and the Dervish growled.

Dewey straddled the helpless attacker, barely hearing the laughing growl that came from his own lips amid his grunting and puffing.

He dropped down on the man's chest, driving air from his lungs, spattering the floor with a fountain of red speckles.

Then another laugh. Another growl.

Then the Dervish in Dewey went to work in earnest. He sat on the lurker's chest, pinning his arms. So the lurker was helpless. Then he was senseless.

As Dewey bashed one blow after another, distributing them over the eyes, the cheeks, the nose, the mouth, a few blows grown slippery by the blood of the two men, ricocheted down against the neck.

The neck, observed the Accomplice. Nice touch.

That's it, beat on his fucking neck. So the Dervish pounded the man's Adam's apple.

Dewey felt no pain in his own hands.

He barely heard the feeble shrieking of Laren, she croaking through her own damaged throat.

He never even felt it when she took to slapping his head and pulling his hair. If there was any feeling at all, it came as a tousling of the white-hot turbulence already in his head, stoking his fury all the more.

He slung an arm back, tossing Laren aside.

Then he went back to smashing this lurker, this attacker, this coward, this would-be killer, this symbol that had become reality. He growled. And he laughed. Laughed and growled.

Laren shrieked for him to stop.

'Dewey, you sonofabitch, you're killing him. Stop it before you kill him. Stop. STOPPPPP!'

He threw her a savage glance, a tortured, inhuman grin.

Kill the bastard, ordered the Accomplice.

'Stop killing the bastard,' Laren shouted.

Dewey the Dervish raised one battered fist then the other and returned to pummeling the lurker's face.

Then he was slapped hard, his ears smacked by the report of a gun, his mind snatched back to conscience.

He looked over his shoulder.

Laren stood there in the open door shaking, one hand holding her bruised neck, the other pointing a smoking pistol into the base of the shrubbery outside.

Dewey swallowed. His hands throbbed. He gasped for air. He looked around for the being, the owner of the voice who had been commanding his violence, for the maniac who had been executing it. He gazed at his bleeding fists. And he realized the owners of the voices

187

were in fact him. They were him. And he was them. Suddenly he knew how close he had come.

'Thanks, Laren,' he sobbed in relief. 'Thanks for stopping me from killing him.'

'Ted,' she whispered, holding her neck. 'Your mind . . . it took a hike. I didn't recognize you.'

He shrugged and gave her a weak smile. 'The guy pissed me off,' he said.

She didn't laugh at his attempt at a wisecrack.

And neither did he.

After the police had accompanied the swollen-faced assailant in the ambulance and Hanover had finished asking his questions, Laren and Dewey just looked at each other tiredly, sighed, and went to his car, she limping, he flexing his fingers cautiously.

'Ted . . . except for the crazy part . . . you were magnificent. You saved my life. I didn't realize you were so . . . why did you follow me?' she rasped through her raw throat.

'I was worried about you. I've been following you home most every night. You turned off at the ice-cream place. I just came up here ahead of you.'

She smiled a thanks, reached out a hand, touched his shoulder.

'One question,' he said. 'Where did you get that gun?'

Finding her voice suddenly became even more difficult for her.

'Come on, Laren, where'd you get the gun?'

'In my purse,' she said sheepishly.

'Did you have it in there when you gave me the tongue-lashing about reporters carrying guns?'

'One question. You said one question.'

They sat with half grins the rest of the way to the *Post-Herald* parking garage, each putting the half grin to the side that couldn't be seen by the other.

When he set the parking brake, he said, 'Too bad we're going to have to break up the team.'

'Why?'

'You know, the lurker team. With him arrested and passing through the hospital to jail, we'll be out of the lurker business pretty soon.'

'Hardly.'

'What do you mean, Laren?'

'That wasn't the lurker. The lurker is more than a rapist, an assailant, more than a man. He's a presence . . . a presence I can feel when he's looking at me. He gives me the creeps, the chills. I can feel his eyes. That guy didn't do it for me.'

'Gimme a break,' he said sarcastically.

But the look in her eyes, the eyes that *he* could read so well, told him she wasn't kidding.

It was after midnight before they finished. He drove her home. She invited him in. Her throat was tender, her head sore. His hands were swollen and sensitive.

Inside, they kissed, stealing each other's breath.

Their lovemaking was done very gingerly – so as not to hurt each other.

BOOK III
Murderous Lurkings

12

Darwin awoke with dirt in his eyes and mouth and
nose. He could barely breathe for the dirt. No, that
wasn't correct – he could barely breathe for the constriction of his throat. He couldn't even work his
Adam's apple past the tightness around his neck. He
pulled at it, desperately.

Painfully, he realized a rope was knotted around his
throat. Frantically, he struggled for breath. But it
would not come except as a leakage of air, and the
more he struggled the tighter that constriction
became, allowing barely as much as a squeak of air to
pass.

He tried to force a finger between the rope and his
neck so he could pull and make space for breathing.

His temples itched, his face felt bloated by the
pulsing of blood building up above the rope.

He finally got a finger through, but he could not pull
any slack. The finger simply put more pressure on the
neck, reducing the flow of air and blood.

He remembered his pocketknife and dug into his
pocket. He felt the blade hotly against his neck. Either
it pinched a flap of skin or it cut him. He did not know
and he did not care. He had to have the air. The knife
was dull, but he pulled on it desperately. It parted a
strand – he felt it whip lightly back across his collarbone. Flushed with that fragment of success he put the
last of his energy to it.

The blade came through and scratched him on the
jawline.

He didn't care.

He had the air.

He sucked it in. The itching, the pain of returning circulation did not diminish his gratitude for the return of his breath.

When his breathing became normal, his recollection went to work. He remembered what had happened. He remembered Slime. He remembered the grave . . .

He gasped aloud and sat up.

He was in a grave – *the* grave.

The arm.

It had been pushed to the side.

It beckoned him to lie down again.

He would have shrieked, but no sound came from his damaged throat as he scrabbled at the walls of earth. The half-filled grave was willing to let him out, but his frantic efforts just kept tearing away every toe- and handhold. He was no longer a rational boy, no longer normal, no longer thinking or sensitive or practical. The fall, the choking lack of oxygen, the fright, the knowledge that he was left to die in a grave with others might have snapped his hold on sanity. But whatever damage those things did not do was done by that child's hand beckoning him to lie down in the grave and surrender his life.

Only when he became too tired to tear away the dirt did he keep a foothold. Then he pushed up a knee. His hands pawed at the earthen floor, throwing loose dirt down, and he finally rolled over the small mound and lay panting, agonizing at the pain of every breath sucked past the swelling in his throat.

His body wanted to give up. It wanted to drift out of consciousness so it could forget this horror.

But his mind could not surrender. He could not simply fall asleep. Not in this house.

He started for the basement window in the small room.

Then he remembered its being blocked.

So he headed in the dark toward the stairs.

But before he could even get there, he was met by light and sound from above.

He ran back to the smaller room.

The thumping that accompanied the footsteps on the steps encouraged him to at least take a peek.

At last he saw Sherman.

The Slime carelessly and awkwardly dragged his friend's body over every step.

The only light came from the top of the stairs.

At the end, on the last bump, when Sherman rolled to the packed earth of the floor, he moaned.

Alive.

Sherman was alive.

Darwin's tears dripped from his eyes in simple joy.

Sherman was alive. They both were.

Maybe.

. . . Just maybe they could get by Slime.

Maybe they could gang up on the bastard.

Maybe they could hide out.

If he would just leave them alone for a minute . . . maybe they'd be recipients of a miracle.

And miraculously Slime did leave.

He stepped over Sherman and took the trip back upstairs, his footfalls heavy. Maybe he'd be going to bed.

Maybe this was all over.

The door closed.

Darwin heard the progress of the heavy footsteps.

They were going up . . . no, not up the stairs to the second floor. They were going to the back of the house.

Darwin stumbled through the blackness, amazed at

195

how well he could make things out. He ducked beneath the swinging body of the girl, not wanting to touch her brittle skin again. He gave wide berth to the open pit in the floor. He found the limp body at the bottom of the stairs.

He shook it and called its name.

Sherman did not respond, except his breath gargled from a hole in his neck.

Darwin felt all over his friend, especially the head.

Sherman responded to the probe of hands on his head with a groan. He responded only to pain. Darwin's hands found the jagged tear in the Adam's apple, and he even nicked a finger on the glass embedded in his friend's throat.

But that was not important now. Only escape was important. If only Darwin could carry him up and out the front.

He struggled with the arms, trying to throw his friend over his shoulder. All he could manage was to drop him again and bring another pathetic moan from the darkness.

This was stupid.

He could sneak up the stairs and run out the front to get help . . .

The plodding bootsteps were returning.

Darwin started up.

At halfway, he stopped.

He'd never make it. He should have left immediately for help. Now he was trapped again. Still.

And he could never overpower . . . he patted his pockets for his knife. He'd left it in the grave. It was in there with that arm. It would stay there. He would not go back.

He stepped down the stairs carefully and avoided treading on Sherman. Then silently he retraced his steps back to the small room. Before he got there, the door opened above and a bright light shone on Sherman. The shaft of light let him miss the swinging legs of the girl again. And he ducked around the corner before he could be seen.

Slime came crashing down into the basement a step at a time.

Darwin peeked and saw he was carrying a folding table this time.

Again Slime returned to the top of the stairs. But this time, he left the door open on himself and the others, the children, dead and alive. And he carried a battery-powered lantern back down. The lantern hung on a nail.

From his belt he pulled a boning knife, stuck it into a wooden step and began setting up the folding table.

Darwin looked around frantically for an escape route.

Then he saw the two-by-four with the bloodied, splintered end, the end that he had thrust into Slime's face. A weapon that had drawn blood once could be used to do it again.

He picked it up.

His heel crumpled a dirt clod, and he whirled to see if Slime had heard, had discovered him. He had not.

Darwin leaned around the wall again.

The table had been set up.

Slime grappled with Sherman's limp body and finally carried it to the table. He threw it across the top. The table creaked but it was a sturdy one.

Darwin wondered if he might cover the ground quickly with the board before the bloodied man could get to the knife.

As if in answer, Slime reached out a hand, worked his knife back and forth, and plucked it from the wood.

197

Darwin decided he would have to attack to save his friend from being cut to pieces.

But when Slime began slashing, it was at a length of rope, not Sherman's body.

So Darwin watched for his moment to present itself.

The scene transfixed him.

Four lengths of rope. Sherman lay on his belly across the table. Slime tied a limb to each leg of the table. No sound came from Sherman. The only sound was the ragged breathing of the madman at work, a hulking, dirty, bloody figure busying himself with the body of a boy.

He brandished the knife again.

Darwin crouched, bracing his body and his courage for a dashing attack across the basement floor.

But the man was not cutting the boy.

He was cutting the clothes off the boy.

Darwin was naïve. He was young. And inexperienced. A virgin. But he knew what was going to happen. This Slime was going to rape his best friend.

13

Laren was in a deep-blue funk. Her throat had healed through the stages of deep scarlet to purple to black to blue to green to yellow. Dewey's hands had shrunk to normal size. He could resume typing at the keyboard, something he all but gave up for the three days after bashing his knuckles all over the facial bones of Laren's attacker.

Laren's reputation had soared again with the report on the possible lurker arrest – they decided it would be too hokey to print anything about her intuitions that the attacker was not the real lurker. And Dewey was something of a hero too, for saving The Damsel, as the office wags – the jealous wags – now called Laren behind her back.

But all glory at the newspaper was fleeting. Nobody was better than their last story in print – and only if that was in today's paper.

There were no more instances of lurker sightings to speak of, and the police reported the phone traffic had died off with the arrest. The citizens, feeling sure this arrest was the right one, wanting to believe, believed. So they went back to leaving their doors unlocked, stopped trading in alarms and high-dollar security systems, and began putting their firearms away to rust, the ammunition to corrode.

Laren called the Thrasher cottage at the lake, but they had moved back to their home. The pool, the school – they were too far away from the lake cabin if this lurker stuff were really over.

So there was nothing to write about once the attacker was brought up on assault charges.

The attacker turned out to be Jimmy Odum, a small-time burglar who once found a naked woman asleep in her house and raped her. Then he turned out to be Jimmy Odum, small-time burglar and rapist, casing houses to be sure women were home before going in rather than entering only unoccupied houses as before. Currently, he was on probation.

Laren was Jimmy's fourth rape attempt. He'd gotten his knowledge of the lurker from rumors on the street, the legend he decided he would emulate. He figured he could lurk with the best of them. He told the judge through swollen lips and tooth fragments that if he had read the paper he would have known the lurker didn't jump out from closets. If he had known Laren Hodges was going to bring her boyfriend home, he never would have bothered her. The judge, a woman, wasn't impressed with any of Jimmy's arguments. She vacated his five years and gave him five more to be served consecutively.

Speaking through wired jaws, Jimmy asked, 'Mutt muh fuh im at comfeckifee?' as the bailiffs grasped his arms. 'What the fuck is consecutively?' one of the deputies translated to the lawyer.

His lawyer held up both hands, all fingers splayed.

'Ten years, Jimmy.'

They hauled him off, his eyes, what could be seen of them through the black, swollen slits, were wild as ever.

It turned out Jimmy had found a picture of her in the paper. He'd gone to the paper's public service counter and asked to see all the lurker issues. Assuming he wanted to buy back copies, somebody had lined up a stack for him. He walked out without buying, and

200

when the papers were being put away in their drawers, the clerks noticed the mug shot of Laren had been torn out.

Then all he had to do was follow her home from the paper once and start casing the apartment. All of which disturbed Laren.

'The SOB didn't even buy a paper to see what a lurker is supposed to do,' she said. 'Didn't even read my stories.'

'Just be glad most of the dregs don't read,' said Dewey.

They were reclining nude on her bed after love-making. It was just another reason for her to be blue. She enjoyed their sex – he was unselfish, practiced, courteous, and never kinky. But she wasn't supposed to be bedding with men fourteen years her senior. Oh, she could if she wanted to, but what kind of entanglement was that?

At least Dewey had the decency never to say he loved her, even at the most passionate of moments. And he never seemed to expect her to say it either. Thank God for that.

He blew a stream of cool air on her breast. It reacted immediately, the nipple hardening, tugging the nerve that ran directly from the tip of the breast to the spot between her legs.

She rolled over to him.

What the hell. Give the poor, senile bugger one more moment of happiness before he dies of old age. And if she were to get some satisfaction from it, too, what was the harm? She could always ditch him tomorrow or next week – whenever the mother lode of this lurker thing ran out. The lurker. Why didn't the lurker, the inconsiderate bastard, show himself, put a little excitement back into her life? For the moment, it did arouse her, and she dispensed a charitable bit of her passion to Dewey, all the while wondering whether the lurker would show himself again.

She was nineteen.

He was twenty-two.

She had left home in a huff, left town to make it in the big city.

He worked in the city, knew the night scene, bought a handful of self-improvement books where she was stocking and clerking at minimum wage. He took her for drinks, then to her apartment. He asked her about her sex history.

She resisted telling, saying it was none of his business.

He asked her if she'd ever heard of AIDS.

She said, oh.

He produced a condom.

She said she was on the pill.

He wondered aloud if maybe she wasn't a virgin.

I am *not*, she said, and if you're going to be insulting . . .

He apologized. God, you're not kidding, are you?

They fell into her bed — in the dark because she was shy.

Their bodies began slapping together wetly, eagerly, then desperately.

She shrieked.

He moaned.

She giggled and tossed about violently.

He moaned all the more.

'How'd you do that?' she asked.

'Superior breeding,' he answered.

'Not *that* . . . how did you manage to tickle my feet right in the middle of . . . you know, orgasm?'

He lunged at the lamp base, one of those that need only be touched to be turned on. He jammed his fingertips into the brass and studied her face to see if she was crazy or kidding.

He saw her eyes widen. She was not looking at him but over his shoulder.

The scream that ushered from her throat paralyzed him with the shock of it, coming as it did so close to his ear.

He rolled away and saw the face leering back as the figure left the bedroom as soundlessly as a shadow.

The sight electrified him. The thought that he'd been watched, that the woman had been tickled. He was frozen.

Then too, the leering face seemed to be daring him to the chase. Now, *that* was scary.

'Aren't you going to do anything?' she asked weakly.

'Sure. Yeah. I'm . . .' he shouted out the doorway, '. . . I'm going out there and kick some ass.'

There was the sound of the apartment door opening.

Finally, he jumped off the bed and struggled into his pants, cursing as he zipped into his penis, agonizing as he unzipped it. Then he ran out. He was relieved to find the front door open. He closed and locked it.

She was up too. She locked the bedroom door, then went to the telephone. Even as she spoke, she heard a crash and a moan. She babbled into the phone.

Her bedroom doorknob rattled.

She screamed into the phone, unaware whether it was her boyfriend who was at the door.

The hysteria in her voice must have seemed to be convincing enough to police. In minutes, officers pounded on the front door, announcing their presence, demanding to be let in. She slid a window up and shrieked at them.

Then silence.

Then her bedroom doorknob rattled again.

She screamed, moving toward the window – she'd read about that lurker, and she'd dive out the window before she'd let him . . . do whatever lurkers did.

She heard a police radio squawk outside the door.

The police officer's voice was solemn.

'Ma'am, it's all right. I'm Officer Wilson. You can open the door now.'

She cried in relief. She thought of her lover. In her hysteria, she couldn't remember his name.

She didn't need the name, though, and neither did he.

When she opened the door, she saw him sitting on her couch.

The couch was ruined.

He sat there, his head thrown back, his mouth open in a silent scream at the ceiling, his eyes bulging but sightless.

His throat was a second opening, a crooked, bloody hole sliced diagonally from jawbone on one side to collarbone on the other.

His chest was scarlet and wet where the opened throat had gushed.

His hands were folded, palms up in his lap, trying to hold in the avalanche of bowels poured from the enormous Caesarean section incision across his belly.

He died trying to pack his guts in.

In her living room.

And she couldn't even remember his name to tell police.

Laren found her at the hospital. She and Dewey had gone to the apartment, arriving with Hanover, who let them walk in, glance around, and run out. Ordinarily,

204

the only way to enter a crime scene was to arrive there in the confusion before police got control of things. This time, judging by the sly smiles, Hanover was only too happy to let Laren in, to make her sick, and get his jollies at the sight of her vomiting.

She gave him his money's worth.

Hardass as she liked to appear, this was too much even for her. She ran outside and puked.

Dewey stayed at the scene to keep in touch with the investigation, to discover whether this would be a bloody lovers' quarrel or whether a jealous lover would be turning up in the questioning of curious neighbors and passersby.

Laren went to the hospital to confirm the snatch of conversation she'd overheard about a creepy figure sneaking around the bedroom just before the young man was killed.

Dewey hadn't run out gagging at the sight of the butchered body in the room. It made him queasy, yes, but something much deeper struck him. He took Hanover aside and pumped him earnestly for information.

Hanover was callous and flippant.

'Hope it was a good piece of ass,' he muttered. 'Hope it was worth it.'

Dewey recognized the wall of indifference as the self-protective device cops and surgeons and ambulance drivers and combat soldiers must put up to safeguard their emotions from being crushed by everyday horrors in their work.

'Hanover, is this the MO of the lurker?'

Hanover grimaced.

'He never killed anybody before, Ted. This ain't the lurker, so don't start with it in the paper tomorrow. You'll have this town digging in for a siege worse'n Atlanta during the child killings.'

205

'I understand your concern, Bret. I have the same concern, believe me.'

Hanover searched his eyes. He did believe.

'Bret, what happened before the killing? Was *that* the same MO?'

Hanover gulped.

'It is, isn't it? He was lurking this house and was discovered and had to kill.' Dewey was not asking. He was asserting.

Hanover didn't deny it. 'This whole pissant thing has taken a turn, Ted. Either we have a homicidal copycat who has decided he can outlurk and outattention the real lurker . . .'

'Or?'

'Or the real lurker has gone over the edge, turned a corner. Now that he's a killer, he can't go back. There will be more killings . . . goddamn, Ted, don't print what I just said.'

'I won't.'

'With you I forget I'm talking to a reporter. Ted, we been friends a long time . . .'

'Hanover, I won't print your speculation that there will be more killings.'

'Thanks. My head would roll.'

'Bret, I think we'd better put a little distance between us, I mean our friendship, until this lurker case is closed. I'm going to have to play a little hardball. So don't tell me any more things as a friend. I'll find them out on my own, and you won't have to take them personally when you read them in the paper.'

Hanover looked at him quizzically. 'You seem to be getting back some of the old fire. That Hodges woman seems to be injecting you with a little enthusiasm for your work. She must be one great piece . . .'

'Hanover, I get your point. I, uh ... hell yes, I'm worried about her. She's reckless and headstrong and she's made herself a target.'

'You're falling in love. Well, kiss my ass. Dewey in love.'

Dewey grimaced at the inappropriateness of such talk in a room where a white-sheeted corpse was still sitting up, staining the sheet and the furniture with the last of his seeping gore.

'Okay, if that's what you want to believe, I admit I do have a ... certain fondness for her. And I think she's in danger. You can't blame me for being concerned over that.'

'What danger?'

'Let me ask you this: Suppose, just suppose, you were right with your theory that this was the real lurker, who's finally snapped, turned a corner, and can't go back. Now he's a killer.'

'Okay. Suppose so. So what?'

'Why the hell didn't he kill the girl? I mean, he could have finished them both, couldn't he? He was in that bedroom, wasn't he?'

Reluctant to give up details, Hanover grunted his assent.

'Well, if he was there while they were in the middle of sex, and if he had a knife, how hard would it have been to stab them both or him and rape the girl or whatever the hell he wanted?'

'Well, maybe . . .'

'No. I said to *assume* that this *was* our lurker, and not just a jealous third side of a love triangle. If this *was* our lurker, why did he do this horrible crime, yet not put the finishing touches on it? Hell, a double murder is always more spectacular than a single. It would have made a hell of a bloody splash in the papers.'

Hanover nodded in agreement, though his face showed he still hadn't divined the direction this reasoning was going. His eyes were roving, though, as if he could find some clue, some answer on the floors or walls. He was interested. He seemed to know Dewey was onto *some*thing.

'Get on with this Agatha Christie routine, will ya?'

'And then he could have left a note, right? If it was a copycat, he probably would have. He would have gone right for the obvious – Hey, look here, I'm a real serious lurker, not that other two-bit jerk you been writing about.'

Hanover set his jaw and talked through his teeth.

'Come on, Ted, out with it before the TV assholes get here. If they see you inside, they're gonna want to come in and shoot too, take back blood samples, and the whole shootin' match.'

'Hanover, this guy did leave a message.'

Hanover glanced at the walls as if to find it scrawled in blood.

'Not that kind. He left the girl alive so she could tell about whatever happened in that bedroom, that the guy revealed himself . . . what *did* go on?'

Hanover blurted it: 'The bastard tickled her feet. Then he faked like he was slipping out. They locked the door . . . locked him in. Then . . . We've got an artist at the hospital working with the girl now.' He hesitated. 'You're not gonna use this, are you?'

'Laren is down there already. She's already gotten the details out of the girl, believe me. You won't be quoted.'

'So what's the point of this so-called message?'

'He's sucking us in, Hanover? Maybe he truly does

208

want to be caught? I don't know. Maybe it's a game of hide-and-seek, you know, catch me if you can.'

'Dewey, you asshole.'

'What do you mean "asshole"?'

'You don't have no theory about this lurker. You just set me up to get some shit out of me, you bastard.'

'Bret, no.'

'Get your ass out of here, Dewey. This is a crime scene.'

Hanover was right about a couple of things, Dewey conceded to himself as he drove to the hospital to see how Laren had made out with the girl.

He was right that he cared a lot for Laren. He sure as hell didn't love her – that's why he could never moan it to her in the middle of lovemaking. And he was worried about her. If the young man just killed had met his end at the blade of a knife unrelated to the lurker, no problem. If it was a copycat, which he doubted, the maniac was simply after attention. But if it was the lurker, Laren might be in danger. And Hanover was right that he had been pumped for information.

He, Dewey, had much to thank Laren for. He now cared, for instance, about how he looked. He'd taken up jogging. He'd taken to downing salads and high fibers. He sent his clothes out more regularly. More important to him, he cared that she cared about his writing. He didn't jump into any major essays of his own, but he began hammering her words into more precisely shaped sentences and paragraphs, improving her writing. The few sidebar paragraphs he wrote had a touch of wonder to them. They weren't literary gems exactly. More like Cape May diamonds, pretty quartz

209

gravel washed smooth on the beach and well worth fondling.

Most important, his anger had banked up like overnight coals. He no longer felt the need either to lash out with his feelings or to suppress them in a bath of alcohol.

Maybe he was getting over this vengeance idea she had thrown up in his face. Well, he still carried a pistol at the small of his back. But that was because of lurkers and copycat lurkers, he told himself.

Wasn't it?

He found them at admissions and discharges.

Laren had an arm on the girl's shoulder, supporting her as a mother or a big sister would.

Dewey led them to a row of chairs and took Laren aside near the water fountain.

'What the hell do you mean you're helping her out? She should be staying here overnight. Her family . . .'

'She doesn't have family, Ted.'

'Friends, then.'

'She's new in town. She has nobody and she sure as hell can't go back to that apartment – not tonight, and probably not ever. I'll have to get her things for her after the police are through.'

He shook his head as if clearing water from his ears after swimming.

'Since when did you get so compassionate?' he asked suspiciously. 'Laren, what are you up to?'

'Goddammit, Dewey, I'm not up to anything,' she whispered hoarsely through her teeth. 'I'm taking care of this kid, that's all. I'm doing something decent for her.'

The word formed on his lips.

'Don't ask me why. Because it's the right thing to do, that's why,' she said, daring him to contradict her.

He shrugged.

She went on the attack. 'You can't believe it, can you? You don't think I can be nice to somebody.'

'No. I'm sure of it. Laren, I don't want to be insulting, but the fact is, you never did a selfless thing in your life.'

'Till now, Ted. And look who's talking. The only reason you're concerned is you think you'll be missing out on some of the . . . sex you've been getting.'

His look was one of disgust.

'You have a way of taking the romance out of everything, Laren. God. Sometimes . . . sometimes . . .'

'Oh, go on, Ted. Insult me. I can take it.'

'No. I was going to say that . . . sometimes I care about you so much . . . sometimes I even think I might be starting to . . . really like you, you know? Then you come across with something so brutal, so throat-cutting' – the irony of that gave him momentary pause – 'I feel like spitting on you. It's as if you were some kind of emotional Nazi. I wonder how you can be so cold and so cruel. How could anybody with your talent and looks and potential and . . . how could anybody be so externally gifted and so internally . . . depraved?'

Momentarily, she was speechless. By the time she had formed a sarcastic enough comeback, he was gone, impatiently stopping for the automatic doors, which didn't slide apart fast enough for his storming pace. He turned back to her.

She looked at him expectantly, hopeful of a better parting than this.

'I'll be at the paper putting this together. Give me a call if you uncover something new.'

The doors parted, paused for him to pass, closed.

211

Laren shook herself when he had gone, putting her thoughts, her strategy, back into place. Dammit, she wouldn't let him unsettle her. Not when she'd gotten onto something really new in this story.

She went to the desk nurse and told her something.

Then she went to the girl.

'Janisse,' she said, 'let's go.'

'Where?' murmured the girl, whose calmness was induced by sedatives. She stood up, but her feet were glued to the tiles. 'I'm not going back there.'

'I gave the nurse my old address. I have an apartment there.'

'I'm not staying alone.' Janisse's feet were still stuck to the white, gleaming squares.

'You're coming to my place. With me. I only gave my old address in case somebody tries to track you down.'

Janisse hugged her.

'Thank God, I have you, Laren. I mean, I don't know what I'd do if it weren't for you. That guy touched me and then he . . .'

'Janisse,' said Laren, squeezing her so she would not go through the gruesome, chilling story again, holding her over her shoulder so she would not betray her own reservations about what she would be doing next, pressing her close so she would not have to look into the girl's trusting eyes.

Back at her apartment, Laren shucked another capsule from Janisse's prescription.

'This will help you sleep,' she said, tucking the girl into her own bed.

'You'll be here?' The question came with wide eyes.

'Yes, dear. I'll be in my roommate's bed. She's out of town.'

'What if she comes back?'

'That's why I'm using it. She won't find a stranger in her bed.'

The girl accepted that.

When Laren looked in twenty minutes later, the girl had pulled the blankets tightly around her throat. And she would not answer to her name, even when Laren spoke it gruffly loud.

In minutes, she was at Janisse's apartment, now decorated with yellow police streamers.

Hanover met her at the door.

'Fun's over. And you still can't go in.'

'I don't particularly want to go in. I'd like to pick up some of her things. She's staying at my old apartment.'

'Not tonight, Hodges. We gotta sweep it one more time in the daylight. Then we can release the property for cleanup.'

'When then?'

'Bring her down tomorrow when she's a little more coherent. We'll finish questioning downtown. By then, this place should be picked clean.'

'Did you search the apartment?'

He sneered at her. 'Why yes, commissioner, we did. You gonna write us up nice and pretty in the papers tomorrow? We collected all kinds of evidence, including a cigarette box full of joints and a roller for homemades.'

'You can't use that against her,' she snapped.

'If you don't print it, Lois Lane, I won't prosecute her with it.' His sneer evolved into a nasty smile.

'Listen,' she said, 'let me walk around for a minute. I have a feeling about this lurker every time he's near. Maybe if I felt his presence . . .'

'You mean like a psychic? You going into the crystal ball business, Hodges?'

'You going to let me walk through?'

213

'You already were in there once. Member? You puked your guts out.'

She thought about that, remembering, feeling her stomach lurch again.

She braced herself for another lie. 'If you need her tonight, she'll be at my old place, 608 Carmen Drive.'

'We won't need her. And you don't have to shout — I'm not harda hearing.'

It took all of her courage to put the key into the lock. This was so damned dumb. And yes, unprofessional. She'd been reading too many detective novels, watching too much television.

Her purse was slung over her shoulder so her hand would be free to grip the pistol in her jacket pocket.

The door hit the stop and rattled on its hinges.

Gingerly, she stepped in, her fist and the pistol leading the way. It was the Astra A-90, the model that tough, vigilant, knowledgeable Marguerite used and recommended. Maybe the .38 didn't have the knockdown power, she had said. But anybody who could withstand fifteen shots from the clip wasn't going to be intimidated by the .357 or .44 anyhow. So she had bought the semiautomatic and fired a clip through it, at a target range, scattering holes all over the paper silhouette of a man. Already it had saved her from at least a rape, when she had used it as a mace, bashing it and her purse into the face of Jimmy Odum. Two and a half pounds of steel. No wonder he'd lost a tooth or two even before Dewey started beating on him.

But now the pistol didn't give her much comfort as she stepped into the stale, warm air of her vacated apartment. She pushed the door shut behind her. To lock it or not? Locks didn't seem to stop this lurker

214

creep. And did she really want to lock him out? Or would she be locking him in?

She shuddered. Goddamn.

No, that was not the shudder of his presence, she decided. She was merely scaring the hell out of herself.

She took a deep breath and decided to leave the door unlocked. She would put the safety chain in place, though. So she might be warned if he came in the front.

She let the pistol lead her through the living room, around the circle into the kitchen. It peeked into the bathroom. She flicked on lights as she went.

She looked into the refrigerator. There never had been much food, but now there seemed to be even less than before. But she couldn't be sure if that were fact or fancy.

She checked the wall phone. The dial tone hummed at her. For once, her inattention to things like getting phones and utilities disconnected had paid off. The phone would be there if she needed it.

So far, so good.

Another deep breath.

Time for the closet and the bathroom.

She jumped aside as the closet door came round and hit the stop. She jabbed at the coats with the pistol.

Nothing.

Good.

Now.

The bedroom.

She stood a long time gathering her nerve. She looked around for a string. Maybe she could tie it around the knob and . . .

Hell with it.

Boldly she stepped up and jerked the door, bashing it into her knee.

She cursed, her kneecap numb, but her adrenaline too high to linger on the pain.

She felt no chills.

She strode into the bedroom, checked the bathroom and closet.

Nothing.

She sighed in relief.

Now she could set her ambush.

The lights were at a minimum throughout the apartment – on the stove, in the bathrooms – enough to act as nightlights. As if somebody scared were sleeping here. She'd decided to lock the front door after all. The lock wouldn't stop the lurker, but the obviousness of a frightened girl leaving the front door open after her boyfriend was killed was an absurd idea. If he thought she was there, he'd get in. He'd try to kill her, all right. Janisse had seen his face. She could identify the lurker. And she recoiled in horror at the sketch Laren produced from her purse, the one that had been in the paper, the one she'd helped the *Post-Herald* artist produce. So there, Dewey, she thought. Up yours. The sketch *did* look like the lurker after all.

Laren sat in a corner of her former bedroom, her knees up, the Astra propped in her hands.

She was in a position to see the doors to the closet, the bathroom, the bedroom. There wasn't a window close enough for somebody to reach through, and she was out of line if somebody were to scale the building and cling to the bricks and shoot through. Yep, she'd seen all the damned cut-and-slash movie clichés. No lurker was going to jump her through the glass because she was stupid enough to back up to a window.

A string ran from the bedroom doorknob down to a nail she pounded into the drywall. The string took a bend at the nail and went up to the dresser where it was looped around a can of hairspray. A bottle of cologne sat atop the spray. Above that was the teeter-totter of an emery board with a lipstick on one end balanced against a bottle of nail polish on the other end.

If the door moved half an inch, the Rube Goldberg affair would topple, alarming her so she could fill the door with lead. And the wall. Laren had already tested it, made the string even more taut, more sensitive. Marguerite had told her about shooting through walls. Dumb cop shows, she'd commented. People were always bracing against walls and bad guys were always shooting through doors. Shoot the damned door up if you're making a movie, she advised. But if you want to draw blood, aim for the walls next to the door.

Soon, the excitement of lying in ambush had worn off.

Her mind played across her last conversation with Dewey. The bastard was right again. She was doing something despicable and stupid, something self-serving, seeking the glory. God, if she did kill the lurker – and she hadn't a doubt that she could pull the trigger – she'd have to confess to setting up this charade instead of doing the responsible thing, going to the police.

She hoped like hell he wouldn't come, after all.

An hour after that hope, she knew he wouldn't be coming. It was past three. Only a couple of hours till daylight.

She sighed in relief.

Her head fell forward onto her forearms, which were crossed on her knees.

The pistol had begun to feel like a dumbbell.

She was feeling it slip from her sweaty hand.

She was debating whether it was such a good idea to

have her eyes closed, whether she might as well set the pistol aside. Maybe she could slide under the bed. She was thinking that was an ironically good idea . . .

. . . when the alarm went off.

She jerked upright, banging the back of her head against the wall, pointing the pistol at the door, clutching the trigger, whining to herself because it didn't fire.

Then the phone rang again.

It wasn't her alarm after all. It was the phone.

And the cosmetics stack still stood as precariously as ever on the dresser.

She cursed herself for falling asleep.

And she thanked God, she had left the safety on her pistol or she might have emptied it into the door and walls.

Imagine the damage deposit argument that would make.

And if the television people ever got hold of a police report showing she was so nutty she shot holes in her apartment . . . And if Hanover had the chance, he would have given the story to the damned hairspray crew of the *Eyewitness News* – or he would have extorted a piece of her body.

The phone rang a third time.

She picked it up, her heart pounding.

God, she was stupid. She made a promise to repent this brand of stupidity if she could just get through the night without being exposed as a dope.

She didn't speak into the phone, merely cleared her throat to let the caller know she was there.

'Janisse?' came the hoarse whisper hissing the name.

Her heart stopped.

'Uh . . . yes. Speaking. Who is this?' Her heart kicked off like a jackhammer inside her chest.

218

'Liar,' the voice exhaled.

Laren's pulse leaped to a gallop, making her dizzy with the sheer flutter of it.

'What is this?' she asked. 'What do you want?'

'Wrong number,' the voice whispered.

'Oh,' said Laren. No, that couldn't be right. 'But . . . how did you know my name was Janisse?'

'Wrong number for Janisse, liar.' The voice was wheezing, laughing in its whisper.

'Who . . .'

'Wrong name, Laren.'

She shuddered violently at the sound of her name.

'Wrong number, Laren.' Then he gave her the address and number of the apartment Laren shared with Cindy Lee.

Laren shrieked and dropped the phone before she could hear the 'bitch' part. She tossed the instrument away from her ear the instant she heard the address, her new address, the apartment where she'd left Janisse sleeping in her bed.

Janisse awoke startled, sitting up naked.

She'd heard the noise of something crashing to the floor. A crash and a ring. As if the phone had fallen off a table.

The room swam before her doped vision. She remembered where she was.

'Laren,' she whimpered. 'Laren, is that you?'

She struggled to her feet and staggered to the bedroom door.

She held her breath, trying to listen through the bedroom door over the sound of her heart beating in her ears. She leaned down to hear, pressing an ear close to the doorknob.

She heard the click of the springs in the knob.

219

But that was all.

The door flew into her drugged head, and she sprawled backward, her last vision a blazing white light, either inside her head or from the overhead light. She never even caught a glimpse of her own blood speckling the plastered ceiling.

Dewey finished his crime story in time for the last deadline of the morning's first edition. He'd decided to play it safe, a straight news report on the murder of Greg Spivey, whose name finally turned up in his wallet identification.

Dewey's connection of this murder to the lurker was a weak one, some denials by police, the details from Janisse about the man running from the room. His own conjecture in the form of questions.

But he knew he could get more facts into later editions, and if he put the right headline on the first, people would buy up a second paper because they'd want to follow the story all day. And so his head was a question: Stabbing Death Work of Lurker? He'd taken to capitalizing *lurker*. When he discovered he was doing it, he realized he was beginning to take this thing much more seriously.

Soon after midnight, he began trying new versions of the story. He wrote it once in full, graphic detail, something he knew could never go into the paper. But it got the story's gruesome impressions out of his mind where they were scurrying around like troublesome little rats in a maze.

Once done with that, he sent the whole piece to the spike queue, the electronic wastebasket, which systems people would erase periodically.

Then, with a clear mind, he started a dramatic feature piece, something with suspense, something that used quotes like dialogue, something that got more from a telling detail – such as the silent scream on Greg Spivey's lips – than from sex, blood, and guts, plentiful in this story.

He borrowed from the fiction writer's tools of the craft to tell the facts of the Spivey murder.

He remembered his feelings, the gut-wrenching sight of the hysterical Janisse, the pathetic attempt of the dead man to hold his intestines together until he might get aid, the fearful look on the face of Spivey, who must have known he could not have walked to the phone without treading on his entrails.

He didn't write those details, but he wrote the agony he felt into the less graphic specifics.

And he knew many potbellied readers would reach down with both hands and lovingly cradle their own guts in sympathetic reaction to his words.

He paced his story deliberately, opening with the woman screaming out a window, the police bursting in to find the dead man and the hysterical woman. Then he painted the scene the police found. The explanation for the placement of things came from the mouths of Janisse and the police. Then background of the Lurker showing similarities between this crime and previous reports, establishing enough of a connection to Marguerite's experience to make it seem an MO without actually saying so. He reminded readers of the knife Laren had seen at the Thrasher house. He painted a large stroke with the point that the murder – if it was the Lurker's – was a signal departure from his previous method of operation. He wakened Laren's psychiatrist source and hit him cold with the murder, asking if the shrink still thought the Lurker could be so harmless after all. The shrink mumbled and stammered, saying that it was a remote chance but that after all, psychiatry was not such an exact science.

The shrink's babbling was eminently quotable, thought Dewey, tinged with only a little guilt for doing what he despised in other reporters — making a source, an expert at that, eat his words. But here was a case of an arrogant, self-styled expert who'd said the Lurker was harmless. Justice, Dewey thought. God, he wondered, what was becoming of him? Why was he getting so sadistic? Is this the way Nixon hatemongers had felt when they went for his throat?

He shook off the guilt and went on writing.

Dewey left hanging the question of whether this was a Lurker crime. Let the reader answer that with his or her own opinion based on the facts. A little reader participation. They'd love it.

He loved it.

He hadn't written so professionally since before . . .

It was after three when he quit, sending all thirty inches and a message electronically to Lou to read in the morning. He was betting all thirty inches would stay in the paper.

He wished Laren had been there to help him admire the story. But then, she was taking in that poor girl. That was something to admire in her. He felt a tinge of embarrassment for having said the cruel things to her earlier.

From force of habit he found himself on autopilot driving toward Laren's apartment. When he realized he'd missed taking himself to his own place, he was only a block away. He gave himself a bemused smile in the rearview as he looked back to clear himself for a turn.

He had already begun his illegal U-turn when a green-and-white city squad car blasted by him on the right at a stoplight just half a block from her apartment complex. He'd been day-dreaming, hadn't seen it coming, hadn't heard it until the car's siren yelped in his ear.

He'd about shaken it off when a second car shot past on the left around him on the green. They both careened right and turned left into the complex.

His heart skipped, then began pounding.

He hit the accelerator and followed them.

It couldn't be.

But it was.

They jerked to a stop in front of her apartment building, and three men and a woman dashed to the door, knocked, held pistols up by their ears, and finally kicked at the door. One by one they hopped into the room, guns first.

He simply ran up to the door and went inside.

He found himself stared down by twelve eyes, eight human, four pistol bores. Automatically, his hands went up. His lips formed the words 'Don't shoot,' which came out a whisper.

But that was not the shock. For the sergeant knew him as the police reporter and instantly ordered the others to train their pistols elsewhere. Then he told Dewey to leave.

But Dewey couldn't. He could not move. He could not even uproot his eyes from the bloody vision they beheld.

He was gagging, trying to catch his breath and hold down the rising, bitter taste of the dozen cups of coffee he'd had at work.

The woman officer jerked on his arm.

'Laren,' he choked on her name.

His breath came fast as his panic grew.

Then his breath came in panting whines.

'No God, it can't be Laren.'

If he had had breath enough, he would have

screamed her name, but he was breathing so fast, a blackness was closing in on the edges of his vision.

'Sir . . . Sir . . . SIR . . .' the policewoman was saying.

'Dewey, wake the fuck up,' shouted the sergeant. 'You know this woman?'

The woman was not a woman at all but a butchered body.

'Is this Laren-somebody, a person you can ID?'

She was hanging naked from the ceiling fan.

Her back had been carved.

Blood was still dripping from her body, her opened abdomen, the mess from her insides.

'Laren,' he squeaked.

And Laren was the name scrawled in blood on the wall. 'By Laren Hodges' was the crudely written name. Her byline. In blood.

Both officers grabbed him as his knees buckled. They held him up as a third cop touched an unbloodied spot with the tip of a finger.

The body slowly began to swirl.

So Dewey could look into the contorted, choked face. Of Janisse.

He found some strength in his knees, a spark of life. 'Is there another . . . woman around?'

The fourth cop shook his head, then corrected himself as his eyes flicked at the entry to the apartment.

As Laren stepped into the doorway, saw her byline, and screamed.

After the stories had been told and retold, Hanover cursed one final time in disgust and released the pair of them.

They went to his apartment.

She would not be comforted.

She insisted Janisse's death was her fault.

224

He scoffed at the idea – to console her more than anything else.

'Well, Hanover seemed to think it was my fault for that stupid detective trick of mine,' she said.

'You're getting hysterical again. Let me fix you a hot whiskey to take the edge off your nerves.'

He did.

She sat quaking at the table.

It was the first time he'd seen her come close to crying.

'You can't blame yourself.'

'If I'd been there, I'd have had the gun,' she wailed.

'Right. You ever kill anybody?'

'No, course not, Dewey. But I could kill *him*.'

He shook his head. 'You don't know that.'

'Oh, and I suppose you're some kind of cold-blooded killer right out of the movies. How many people you ever kill?'

'I don't know. I never cut notches into my M-16.'

She sobbed, almost bursting into tears. 'I'm sorry, Ted. I didn't know. I shouldn't say things like that to you. This is all *my* fault, goddammit, not yours, not anybody else's but *mine*. I killed that girl.'

He dropped the whiskey with a rap on the table.

'You don't know that, Laren. If you had been there, he might have killed you . . . or he might not have. It seems to me, he has told you today that he could have killed you anytime he wanted to.'

'Ted . . .'

'No, listen. He could have killed Janisse when he cut Greg, but he didn't. And he could have gotten you at your old apartment when you came out – he knew you were there. He could have probably killed you before you left Janisse alone. I'd even be willing to bet he could have killed you that night at the pool.'

'Ted, don't say that.' She shivered, sloshing the hot drink from the glass in her cupped hands. The look on her face showed she knew he was right, though.

'Laren, listen. This guy is not chasing you.'

'Ted, you're scaring me with this crazy talk. I'm already feeling bad enough. What the hell are you talking about?'

'He has you figured out. He knows you – maybe even better than you know yourself.'

He saw the question forming on her mouth and answered it before it was spoken. 'I'm not sure how. Maybe he knows you from reading your stories. Whatever the reason, he's playing a game. But he's not chasing you. He's . . .'

'What, Ted?'

'He's . . . letting you chase him. He understands your ego, that you have latched onto this story and will not let him go. You have to have this story to make something of your career, and he's letting you try to destroy him. But all the while, you're destroying yourself. He's just helping you do it, just messing with your mind.'

She jumped up from the table, nearly knocking over her chair.

'I don't have to listen to this . . . this crap, Dewey. Where'd you get your shrinking license, anyhow? K-Mart?'

'What if I could prove it?'

'Come on, Dewey, how are you going to do that? Get him to call in on a talk show?'

'That I'm not sure. Maybe in the morning . . .' He looked to the window shade and the light leaking in around the edges. 'Maybe we could go out this morning to the Thrashers and look around the pool for a clue or something.'

226

'Listen to you, Sherlock Holmes. I've had all the detective work I want to do for a lifetime. After that stunt I pulled last night, I . . . Ted, what's wrong?'

'Goddamn. The Thrashers.'

'Shit. We reported the Thrasher boy and Sarah saw him. If he murdered Janisse for it . . .'

He was already at the phone directory, swiping at pages, then punching out tones. He cursed and hung up and punched out more tones. He talked to the police, and when he hung up, his face was even more gray and drawn than from the night's horrors.

'What is it?' she asked, not wanting to hear the answer.

'The cops,' he said grimly. 'They're already out at the Thrasher house.'

'Oh, my *God*,' she murmured. 'What have I done?'

He pulled his car up behind the squad car in the street and walked toward the driveway. It was past seven.

A blond, crew-cut cop was sitting on a retaining wall pointing his face at the sky, worshiping the warmth of the morning sun. He was startled when Dewey spoke to him.

'Sir?' said the sun worshiper.

'Where's the tape? Who's the chief investigator?'

'Tape?'

'Restraint line, yellow tape, crime scene, you know?' Dewey didn't recognize the officer.

'Sir, this isn't a crime scene. Me and my partner are on security here.' Suddenly, his expression hardened. 'And you, sir, do you have a reason to be here? Identification? Ma'am?'

Dewey hung his head sheepishly as he turned to Laren.

227

'Sorry. I never asked *why* the police were out here. I just assumed . . .'

'Hah.' It was Hanover's triumphant jeer. He spoke from the window of his unmarked sedan in the street, grinning all the while. 'If we waited for you guys in the press to think of protecting the public, the public would all be dead. I had a patrol out here since after three – ten minutes after we found that girl.'

'All night,' said a relieved Laren. The crisp light of the morning sun showed every tired chink in her face. There were lines of fatigue streaking from the corners of her eyes, lines of sadness slanting down from the corners of her mouth. The whites of her eyes were hatched with tributaries of red.

'But I called . . .'

'And . . .' Hanover said conspiratorially, 'I had a cop follow you two to Dewey's place.'

Laren blinked.

Dewey said, 'But I called here this morning . . .'

'Looka there,' said Hanover, pointing up the driveway.

Dewey and Laren turned and saw Buddy Thrasher at the end of Hanover's point, materializing as if to prove all was well.

He was lugging a sleeping bag rolled under one arm.

'Probably slept over at the neighbors,' Hanover said smugly.

Laren touched Dewey's elbow.

'Come on. We'd better get down to the paper and write . . . about Janisse. Then we have to get some sleep.'

Hanover leered at Dewey behind Laren's back.

Dewey wagged his head in disgust and led her to his car.

He pulled out ahead of Hanover as the detective gave instructions to his officer in the driveway.

Halfway down the block, he slammed on the brakes. Hanover, who had caught up, nearly rear-ended him.

'What?' asked Laren, startled from some daydream.

'Stay in the car.'

He ran back to the detective – the cursing detective.

'Hanover, I, uh ... called out here this morning. I called the Thrashers and there was no answer.'

Laren was at his shoulder. 'Maybe they were sleeping in,' she said hopelessly, utterly without conviction.

'So what?' snapped Hanover.

Laren was holding her arms, shivering as if it were mid-winter instead of a humid spring morning. She was staring fearfully back at the house.

Dewey said, 'Families with young kids don't sleep in.'

Hanover put his car in reverse.

Dewey said, 'Did you sweep the house after you put security on? Did you tell them to watch for a prowler to come out of the house as well as to look for somebody trying to get in?'

Hanover's answer was the squealing of tires as his sedan flew backward up the street. The pair of reporters ran after.

The blond sun worshiper stepped nervously to the street at the end of the drive. Hanover threw open his door and bolted toward the house, the blond uniform following in the waddling run of officers with ten pounds of slapping gear strapped to their hips.

They found Buddy cowering in the corner of the family room hugging his sleeping bag.

In the cedar timber that was the fireplace mantel, they found seven spikes.

Seven ropes hung from the seven spikes like Christmas stockings.

Six of the ropes were taut from the weight of their grisly burdens. One rope – Buddy's – hung limp.

On the wall in blood, the crude, familiar byline of Laren Hodges was scrawled.

When he saw, Dewey recoiled, stepping back into Laren. He turned to shield it from her view, but she had seen already. Her eyes reflected the horror, and though her open mouth uttered no sound but a hiss, the silent scream was as piercing as if it were amplified a thousandfold.

Averting his own eyes and choking down the heaving in his own stomach, Dewey pushed past the horrified blond cop and grabbed the child, Buddy, who had yet to make a sound.

He hugged him hard and carried him out.

Laren was still backing across the yard, the fingers of one hand pulling at her lower teeth, dragging open her mouth.

The ugliness of what she saw and the revulsion that she might have caused it were reflected in her face.

She wheeled and threw up into the garden.

The blond cop, too young to have seen much of this in his career, burst from the house and puked into the shrubbery.

Hanover came out talking angrily into his radio. He was cursing at the nincompoop at the receiving end of his report. Although he was shouting fiercely, his complexion was not red, but as pale as all the others.

Dewey took the child to the poolside, into the bright, open sun. Somehow that seemed the safest place.

The six-year-old had nothing to say. He did not seem stunned or afraid. He was simply confused, incapable of understanding what was going on.

230

Dewey knelt and began splashing chlorinated water into his own face, trying to refresh himself, to fight his stomach still. He shook his head, but the vision of that family room would not be shaken. He kept seeing the faces, strangled and stricken. The bodies, slashed and mutilated. The byline painted on the wall.

Laren was on her knees, supporting herself by a staked tomato bush, vomiting still, and gasping and sobbing in between.

Dewey called to her, but she did not seem to hear.

And he would not leave the boy, sitting at arm's length on the diving board still hugging his rolled sleeping bag.

Ambulance after ambulance came to take the dead bodies away. And police car after car brought live bodies. Hanover's superiors came, and their superiors came, the press, the television vans, the passersby.

Hanover hotly answered the question repeated dozens of times in half a dozen ways: How could this have happened with a police guard on the scene?

Hanover asked it of the blond cop.

Hanover's superiors asked it of him and the cop.

Their superiors asked it of everybody below in the pecking order.

The television reporters asked it.

Dewey asked it of himself.

An enraged Hanover demanded a virtual wrecking crew be brought in to search the house, to tear it apart if necessary to find where somebody might have hidden out.

As the morning edged into afternoon, an exhausted Hanover called another ambulance for Laren, who still knelt in the garden soil, her forehead in the dirt.

Dewey was embarrassed he had not called a doctor

231

for her earlier when clearly she had suffered some kind of breakdown.

But he wasn't so sound upstairs himself. And he had that boy on his lap and on his mind.

Finally, Hanover pried the child away.

'But I want to keep him ... you know, keep him safe.'

'No, Ted. He belongs to the courts until his relatives come. They've been called. Somebody's on the way.'

'But ...'

'No. You have your own family.'

Dewey looked up in fear.

'I had a guard out there, too. I didn't tell you, but since you were starting to show your by-line in the paper, too, I thought it would be a good idea.'

Dewey's eyes widened.

'I know,' said Hanover. 'Don't rub it in. I know I had a guard here, too. At your place I had somebody inside. And I called your wife. Everything's all right. She's probably putting Matt down for a nap this very minute.'

Hanover took the child and turned him over to a social worker. Dewey took Buddy's place on the diving board. He felt so grimy and dirty, hot and useless. Now his job would be to go down to the paper and spill his guts through his fingertips into the keyboard, mentally and emotionally regurgitating what he had worked so hard physically to keep down. He hated the very idea.

Bracing himself with a hand on the diving board, he knelt and drew up a couple of cupped palms full of water to splash onto his face again.

The surface of the board was covered with a nonslip grit except at the edge, where it was smooth blue – except that beneath his fingers, the smooth edge was rough.

Dewey paid no attention to it.

Until he pushed himself up to his feet and saw somebody had carved a name into the board.

Some vandal had defaced . . .

The name was not that of a vandal or a Thrasher family member.

The name was scratched with a sharp instrument, perhaps the point of a knife.

The name was a byline:

By Laren Hodges.

14

The young, black eyes had grown used to seeing the boogeyman day and night. Boogeyman lived in the closet, sometimes under the bed, sometimes in the empty bedroom. Sometimes he went out of Matt's room and didn't come back for a long time. The boogeyman tucked him in at night and for afternoon naps – usually right after his mother had tucked him in, sometimes later, when he was nearly asleep. He did this when his mother stayed upstairs cleaning the bathroom or making beds or if she read late or if Uncle Jesse stayed over.

He told her about the boogeyman. And he told Jesse.

They didn't like talking about the boogeyman. At first, they didn't like him talking about him either.

But they had stopped arguing about the man.

They let Matt talk about him all he wanted.

They called him an imaginary friend.

But he was not a friend.

Friends didn't make you afraid like the boogeyman. Do they, Mom? he would ask.

No, she would say.

Then he's not my friend, he would say.

And she would leave the room, sadly looking back from the hallway.

He would never hurt me, Matt would say, right, Mom?

Right, she would answer.

And she would leave, sadly shaking her head, believing all she'd ever read in the women's magazines about the variety of ways children agonized over the divorce of their parents.

He lay waiting.

His mother had tucked him in.

The boogeyman would come and tuck him in too.

He was nearly asleep when he felt his bedroom door opening. He never heard the boogeyman speak – only felt him as a whirled vortex of disturbed air or a pair of hands, and he saw him, of course, usually through squinted eyes. And, yes, he smelled him. The boogeyman stunk.

He tried to lie still, but couldn't help tightening up, closing his eyes a little harder, pulling the covers against his chin.

The bed jiggled as a knee brushed the mattress.

Next would come the hands.

They patted his small shoulders and bunched the covers even tighter against his neck.

Matt was sure the boogeyman was just checking to see if he could choke him – that's why he always kept his covers and his fists bunched against his throat.

He held his breath against the stench of the boogeyman's breath.

Next, the closet door would open.

And the boogeyman would go in and take a nap too.

But this time when the closet door opened it was loud as an explosion.

'Freeze, mister.'

Matt opened his eyes in terror.

From his closet jumped a police officer, a woman. 'Freeze, you creep,' she shouted.

She was tearing at the strap on her holster.

The boogeyman bolted toward the door.

235

She leaped, tackling him, dragging him to the floor.

He squealed like a child, and Matt joined him in a real child's scream.

Then Theresa Dewey shrieked from the bottom of the stairs.

'Call my backup, Miz Dewey,' shouted the struggling cop. 'Call the cops.'

She had found the door jamb to her liking, a sort of immobile nightstick. She grabbed the collar of the man and repeatedly bashed his head into it until he went limp and she could finally snatch her service revolver.

She was huffing with the exertion and excitement.

'Don't move, you bastard, or I'll blow your fucking brains all over the wall.' She inhaled and shouted, 'Mrs Dewey, did you call for my backup?'

Theresa was running up the stairs, affirming she had, asking the policewoman if Matt was all right.

The cop laughed a guttural laugh.

'Yes. Fine. Matt, we got your booger man, all right. You weren't making it up, were you?'

'My God,' said Theresa, halting at the door, wanting to leap to her son, afraid to go near the battered form on the floor.

The cop impatiently waved her to go behind, so she would not step between the revolver and the panting figure huddled on the carpet.

'Mrs Dewey, we got us a booger man here,' she said, the medal of commendation virtually flashing in her eyes. 'And I think maybe we got us a Lurker.'

The city room had mobilized as if for Pearl Harbor. Too much had begun happening for the two-reporter Lurker team to handle, especially with half the team in the hospital.

A general assignment reporter had been dispatched

to interview Laren. The GA was to get facts to phone in to add to the main story. For that, Laren was to be interviewed as a victim, not a reporter. Once that report was called in, the GA was to cover the ground all over again with Laren and write a first-person horror story about what had happened the last twenty-four hours. Laren would, in effect, be dictating it to the reporter, and her byline would go on it – this was important, Albright said, shoving the GA out of the room.

'Fuckin' critical,' he shouted down the hallway after her. 'Even if she's doped up, get enough for a first-person piece. We need to show some of that personal fright under a byline.'

Somebody from the state desk was pulled to go out and get reactions from the man on the street about the latest murders.

The reporter at the cop shop was put on an open line to feed every scrap from police directly to somebody sitting at a keyboard.

Dewey was too weary and had too few hands to get everything he knew typed into the text processing system. He was ordered to sit in a chair as a bevy of reporters and a stenographer surrounded him, firing questions, drawing out answers. Two would be responsible for the lead story, tying all the murders and background together – a librarian was pulled from behind her counter to gather clips and follow orders of the lead story reporters.

One reporter was to dig into the background of Janisse and Greg Spivey, whose murders had already begun to grow old. Another reporter was to pull together the Thrasher family murders, the really hot crime, the big breaking crime. Another would track down the kid, Buddy Thrasher, and if he never even uttered a word, get a description of his fearful silence. And if the people who were taking care of him wouldn't permit reporters in, that was a story anyhow – just don't come back empty-handed.

Dewey, when he was pumped dry of information, sensations, observations, and feelings, was to rewrite his 'dynamite feature' that went into the second edition, a story that would include something from everybody.

Around noon, Albright was smelling a prize story.

'All we need is for the fucking cops to capture that fucking Lurker and for somebody's fucking cop head to roll for incompetence,' he muttered aloud, making it sound more like a command or a wish than a statement.

A thought occurred to him, and he ordered an assistant city editor to assign somebody to write an incompetence story.

The assistant editor shrugged, telling him nobody was left.

'Then you do it,' he ordered. 'And call and see if the fucking deadheads upstairs are planning an incompetence editorial – or maybe they're waiting till next month. Have them demand some action, some heads, some asses.

'Goddammit,' he wished, 'all they need to do is nail that fucking Lurker and it's cigar time for us . . . no, make that champagne time.'

'Lou,' shouted the reporter whose fingers were poised at the keyboard and whose ear was rooted to the open line to the cop shop. 'Lou, they got the somebitch.'

'Who?' said Lou, unable to comprehend that he could have ordered the capture in time for the Blue Flash deadline.

'The Lurker. They caught the fucking Lurker.'

Albright was stunned for only a second – until his news judgment caught up with his astonishment.

'Dewey, get your tail down to the cop shop and see what you can do with this . . . God, this is a dynamite development. Maybe they'll let you in to view the lineup.'

But Dewey was already up.

'Lou,' said the man with poised fingers, 'they want Dewey and Laren down there for a lineup.'

Albright's astonishment enlarged a fraction along with his eyes. 'How'd they know I ordered that up?' he muttered. 'Where the fuck is Hodges when you need her?'

'Here, Lou,' said Laren. 'What do you need? I couldn't stay at the hospital.'

Albright flopped into a chair. 'What's happening here? Am I a psychic or something? I always wanted to . . . God, maybe I should take the day off and see my bookie.'

Dewey grabbed Laren by the arm and led her off down the hallway toward the elevator.

She looked drawn and pale, but he marveled that she could have recovered at all from the horror of the night and morning.

'The wonder of modern drugs,' she said. 'And a little sleep, even drug-induced, did wonders – at least I didn't dream.'

In the elevator he told her about the capture news.

'How?' she asked. 'Where?'

He shook his head. 'Call just came in. I don't know a thing but that they've picked up a suspect. We're on the way to the cop shop to observe a lineup – you will probably have to help ID the suspect.'

For a second, she looked as if her knees might

239

buckle, and she went a shade paler. But she stiffened, shaking her brunette mop of hair.

'It'll give you a chance to show how good your artist's sketch was,' he said lightly.

She smiled at him, relieved for the slightest of breaks in her dammed-up tensions.

'Then it will be over,' she sighed. 'Thank God. I couldn't have taken much more of this.'

'I don't know how you got over the . . . shock of this morning.'

'You,' she said. 'You were right. He *was* drawing me in. A moth to a flame. He *is* drawing me in. Still. I'm going down there, aren't I? I'm everything you say I am, and if he's been drawing me to him rather than chasing after me, then I decided to play it out. I couldn't run away. I couldn't lie there in the hospital snoozing on drugs. If the bastard ever was to be caught, I felt it would only be if I kept going after him – only if he let me catch up. Am I making sense to you?'

'I think so,' he answered reluctantly, 'which is what bothers me.'

He decided he could not heap another straw onto her back. He wouldn't tell her about her byline scratched into the edge of the Thrasher diving board. The thought of her pushing herself underwater, thinking she had outsmarted the Lurker while he sat above the surface, smirking, carving her name into the board three feet away, might just be too much. Hell, he didn't know if he was so tough he could take it much more himself. He'd seen bodies, war casualties, crime victims, accident fatalities. But in the last hours, he thought he'd been yanked to the very edge of his own sanity by the emotional as well as the physical terror unleashed by this Lurker madman.

Dewey was concerned about Laren's well-being. So

240

he was totally unprepared for the staggering blow to his own when Hanover told him the Lurker had been apprehended in Matt's bedroom. Like a suppressed acidic belch, a fury inside him lurched up hotly, burning his chest, firing up inside his head. And at the same time a voice ordered him to kill. The voice came cold and calculating. He had felt these feelings before. He had heard the voice. He knew he had to fight them both down even as he wanted to succumb to them.

The agitated detective tried to cushion it by leading with the news that Dewey's family was all right. He forced Dewey to sit before he spilled the story about the Lurker's capture.

Dewey sat stunned and listened, all the while shaking his head to shake the thoughts and words in there.

Laren, whose emotional condition had seemed in jeopardy all day, was now stiffened as she helped brace up Dewey. She seemed to know and to appreciate – for once, Hanover noted, she seemed to empathize with somebody else with no motive for self-advancement involved. She seemed to appreciate that the memory of his daughter's loss was coupled with the jolt of learning how the Lurker had been struck down even as his hands closed on the covers at Matt's neck.

Although he at first was shaken, Dewey seemed to recover his composure. Repeated assurances that Matt and Theresa had not been harmed brought some color back into his complexion.

'At least not *physically*,' he shot back at them.

Nobody had an answer for that.

Dewey finally stood up. He said he was going to Theresa's to hug his child. Hanover wanted him to stay with Laren for the lineup.

'We need to try to connect him to the other crimes,

the murders, the lurking at the Thrasher house the night Laren went . . . into the pool.'

'Well, I never saw the bastard,' Dewey muttered.

Hanover's jaw tightened. He jerked Dewey aside so he could mutter in his face.

'You fuckin' reporters are the most selfish bastards I ever run into. I don't expect anything from you as a witness. I'm thinking of the woman – Laren. I don't want her coming apart again when she sees this creep. You could give her a little support, you know.'

Dewey nodded. His eyes narrowed. Suddenly, he seemed to remember something. A mask of sullenness came down over his face. 'My family . . . my wife and son.'

Hanover said, 'You can see your . . . ex and your kid right away after the lineup. Now 'spose we take a look.'

'You question him?' asked Dewey coldly.

'Course,' Hanover snarled. 'You think we're idiots? – never mind answering – I withdraw the question.'

Dewey inhaled deeply, exhaled slowly. 'Did he confess to anything? Any crime at all?'

'Come on,' said Hanover evasively. 'You can interview me later. After the lineup.'

Laren was as confused as Buddy Thrasher.

When they brought in the child, Buddy pressed into the bosom of the social worker. He would not look out the glass at the five men paraded out before them. They could not force his head around by cajoling him or even by gently holding it and trying to turn it. He just clung to the social worker as if he had adopted her as a mother. Finally, Hanover directed the woman to stand with her back to the one-way glass. Then two officers pried the child away, his arms and legs held toward her as if by static electricity. Hanover waved her aside, leaving the window and five men to Buddy's eyes.

He shrieked and immediately began sobbing.

But he would not speak or look again.

He simply curled up into a fetal position and would not be comforted, not even by the social worker who had betrayed him so.

Hanover was as shaken as anybody in the room. He patted Buddy and nodded first to the woman, then at the door.

'I knew we shouldn'ta done that,' he growled. Then he looked combatively around the room, daring anybody to ask him why he had ordered it done.

Nobody asked.

Next came Marguerite, also holding her elbows as if the dark viewing room were chilly.

She was confused too.

Hanover ordered each man to step up, then back.

Each time, Marguerite shrugged.

Laren watched.

Hanover was serious. He barely gave the black-maned beauty a glance except to check her reaction to each man in the lineup. His eyes did not roam her body at all. Serious.

Laren saw Dewey standing off to the side, checking each of the men in the lineup meticulously, checking the reaction of each witness.

When Marguerite had left the room shrugging, Hanover cursed.

'My wife and son coming in to ID the bastard?'

Hanover grimaced impatiently. 'What the hell for? We got their ID at your house. And we got an officer who made the collar, Ted. We're looking for connections to the other crimes now.'

Dewey cleared his throat. 'Sorry. Which one is he?'

'Come *on*, Dewey, you know better than that. You know I can't poison this whole exercise by saying so in front of a potential witness.' He swept an open palm from Laren to the window. 'Laren, do you see the man out there?'

She was confused all the more. She was sure the moment of truth would be much more dramatic, much more emotional. She had braced herself for gut-wrenching emotions. And this was nothing.

She looked to Dewey for eye contact, for moral support.

But Dewey had sidled to the side door that opened to the stage area behind the lights. His hands were on his hips.

Suddenly she felt a jolt of adrenaline.

'Hanover, I know what's wrong. I can't feel him looking at me. You know, in the past, I could feel his presence, as if there were extra eyes staring at me. Once I even thought I smelled him.'

Hanover's head tilted back. 'Are you shittin' me? Well, he can't see you with the lights in his face and the one-way glass.' He looked toward the window and sighed. 'And I sure as hell ain't takin' you out there so you can lift their armpits and sniff or so they can see you. You want him to feel you up or . . . what the hell?'

Laren barely beat Dewey out the door to the stage where the five men in the lineup dropped their gazes to see what the commotion was there behind the lights.

Hanover shouted a curse.

Four of the men began cursing.

A fifth cringed away, shrieking the chilling shriek of a wounded rabbit. As Laren pushed Dewey aside and approached the stage, one man laughed at the chaos and one – obviously a cop – stepped forward with a hand up.

The fifth man shrieked and lunged at her like a cornered animal that had been pushed too far.

Hanover came out and shoved Dewey aside again.

The cop in the lineup grabbed the shrieking rabbit of a man.

Hanover threw Laren away from the stage and put himself in the way to protect her. He threw one punch, a blow that struck on the nose of the shrieking rabbit with the sound of a wet towel slapping concrete, and the man went down.

Hanover turned, cursing at Dewey and Laren.

Laren was hugging Dewey, pinning his arms behind him.

The agitated Dewey shouted, 'That was *him*, wasn't it? The bastard who lurked my house, my son . . .'

Hanover had had enough insanity for one day.

'Get the *fuck* out of here!' he bellowed. 'The *both* of you. Before I throw both your asses in the pokey for disorderly conduct or obstruction or some fuckin' thing.'

Laren loosened her grip on Dewey's arms when she was sure the man had been dragged out, two officers pulling him along by the armpits.

Outside in the hallway, she whirled on him.

'I know what you were going to do,' she said.

'You're crazy,' he snarled. 'I wasn't going to do anything.' He trembled in rage.

She quaked as well. 'You're a liar, Dewey, a lying bastard. You were going to kill him . . . You were going to sacrifice yourself blindly . . . stupidly . . .' She glared at him, trying to fight back tears. 'Mistakenly,' she sobbed.

For the second time in only a day, she nearly began to cry, hugging herself.

He stepped up to hold her gently.

But she didn't want to be held. She wanted to vent

245

her own fierce anger at him. 'Get your goddamned hands off me.'

He held her anyhow, letting her bawl, curse him, beat her arms against his chest until she tired. Finally, when her tired arms hung down to her sides and she leaned on him, he spoke.

'Laren. I'm sorry. You're right – I was going to . . . he might have done something to my son. I don't know what came over me . . . something snapped . . .'

'You stupid son of a bitch,' she howled, showering him with tears blown off her lips. 'It wasn't him.'

'He was there, Laren. He was arrested at my house, for chrissake.'

'But he wasn't the Lurker. He wasn't him. I didn't feel him. . . . I didn't feel the extra eyes. You were going to kill the wrong man. And he's still out there. The Lurker is. And he . . . I . . . he . . .'

She couldn't finish.

He tried to hug her, to comfort her.

She wouldn't be comforted anymore. She pushed him away and stalked away, leaving him ill at the thought of what he'd nearly done, what he would have done.

'Where . . .'

'To the city room, damn you. And don't follow me there because I'm not going to share the byline with you.'

'Who cares about the goddamned byline – ' He cut himself off. He realized the byline wasn't the point. What she meant to say was she wanted nothing to do with him – not at work and not at his apartment. Of course, she couldn't say it in those words because that would mean she felt something for him in the first place. So the easiest thing had simply been to drop into character, her old character, the uncaring, selfish Laren who would never willingly share a byline with anybody. And what about himself? he wondered. What had he become?

He realized something new all at once. She *did* care. She had to. Because just now was the first time he'd ever seen her cry . . . *really* shed tears. That she cared for him merely made him feel sicker.

He found Hanover and apologized.

Hanover had his own apology to make. It had been a big mistake – a long shot at the very least – to have a lineup at all, let alone to bring in Buddy Thrasher, Hanover muttered. This suspect, this mute half-wit, could not have committed any of the other crimes.

'Mute? Half-wit?' said the astonished Dewey.

Hanover told him about the guy arrested.

'If Matt's story is true, and it probably is, this kid's been in your . . . Theresa's house a long while. He would of had plenty of chances to harm the boy, to grab Theresa . . . do God knows what. But he ain't done a thing but creep around and eat some food and stink up the place, near as we're able to put your youngster's story together.'

Dewey tried to talk but could only gulp back his words.

'Ted, this guy probably ain't the Lurker. I had a strong notion he wasn't even before the lineup, so I shoulda gone with my instincts and avoided putting him up. His face has been battered up a long time ago, and he's had his head busted up. He's demented, the docs say. His vocal cords has been cut, so the pathetic little shit can't even talk. He's been making a living by lurking around people's houses, keeping quiet as a mouse. He's got no fingerprint records on file. No family's come forward to claim him. He couldn't or wouldn't read or write even one letter of the affabet.'

Hanover shrugged helplessly. 'Ted, he's useless as a

247

suspect or a witness. I had him tested out by the shrinks. They say he's at the mental age of less than a eight-year-old.'

'But he *was* a lurker – you said that he must have made his way by creeping around houses.'

'But he's not our man, Ted. He's not *the* Lurker. The real Lurker called Laren, remember? Last night with the murder of Janisse? He could talk.'

'A fake?'

Hanover shook his head. 'Had a doctor check. The kid's vocal cords are long gone. He was cut in the neck – look like he was stabbed with a broken beer bottle or something. I had him sent out to the state mental home. Ted, this kid ain't getting out and he ain't getting any better. He'll be in that home all his life.'

'But what was he doing to Matt?' Dewey nearly choked on the question.

'Better talk to Theresa on that. Like I said, Matt says he was there a long time ... He's been calling him a booger man for weeks. When Theresa and ... and ...'

'Jesse Lewis. His name is Jesse Lewis,' Dewey interjected impatiently.

'Yeah, uh, Lewis first heard Matt tell of this booger man, but nobody believed it ... I mean, who would of? Would you of? The guy we arrested is more of a child than Matt, you know. Like I said, if he'd wanted to hurt somebody, he could of.'

Dewey released a steamy puff of breath.

'Ted, I'm sorry we ain't got nothing. But at least he's not in your house anymore.'

His apology was wasted on Dewey's back. Rather than making Dewey feel better, it made him even more depressed for the way he'd acted.

He called the city editor and pleaded exhaustion.

Truthfully. He was whipped physically and emotionally. Albright told him he wasn't needed anyhow, good work, get some sleep, get your ass in here tomorrow.

Dewey went to Theresa's home to see if he could give comfort. But Matt preferred to cling to his mother for comfort. And Jesse was there to give comfort to her. So he wasn't needed. It exhausted him all the more.

The glances between Dewey and Theresa were pained ones.

But he declined her invitation to come in.

He headed toward his apartment. To be alone with his depression, his desperation, his defeats.

Along the way, he stopped for a tall, long-necked quart of Kentucky Bourbon, the only enemy he could rely on.

He awoke to a different morning. His eyes were damp; that was no different. And there was the taste of strawberry jam on his lips again. And there was that bottle, his hand clutched around the neck.

But the seal had not been broken on the bottle.

So he broke the seal.

And poured the whole thing into the toilet – even before he peed.

Before he lost his nerve and took a first drink. He felt proud of himself. He even felt semi-happy. Maybe he could make things right with Laren – if she'd give him the chance. He decided he would try. It was time he got on with the rest of his life. Apparently, fate did not intend for him to spend his life with Theresa and Matt. So he'd damn well better make amends with Laren, he told himself. He would try. He would tell her how he felt. At least how he thought he felt. Today, dammit.

15

Laren was in the city room when he arrived. Still. He saw she had on the same dress as yesterday.

But rather than being a total rag of exhaustion, she was bright and busy and friendly – even to him.

He smiled, exhaling a huge sigh of relief.

'Jeez, Laren, I'm glad you're still not furious. I thought I'd have to go through a whole rigamarole to get you to listen to my apology – '

'Ted – '

'No. Laren, I'm sorry. I must have been crazy to cling to this whole idea of revenge for all these years. Yesterday ... God, in that lineup room, I thought about Erica and Matt and that somehow this guy could have been responsible for harming them ... or trying to – '

'Dewey, don't do this ...' She was tossing her arms about nervously, shifting her weight from one foot to another.

'I have to. You saved my life there. If I had pulled that gun, if you hadn't burst through to raise that diversion, hadn't held my arms, hadn't talked some sense into me ... hell, I could be in jail.'

'Ted, listen, I'm starting vacation today.'

He looked puzzled. 'Well ... sure. That's a great idea. Why don't we take a trip together, take a look around the country, maybe even give up newspapering? I've had enough. We should wait until this Lurker business is finished, I suppose, but no longer. I could start my novel again, this time on a personal computer.

250

We wouldn't have to get married or anything . . . just . . . you know, spend some time together, give it time . . .'

She was on the verge of tears. Again. She stamped a foot.

'Goddammit, Dewey, shut up and listen. You're tearing me up. Can't you see what I'm doing? What the fuck does it look like I'm doing?' She waved her hands, palms up in front of her waist. 'Huh? What the *fuck* am I doing?' The last was shouted.

Reporters and editors were looking on, listening uncomfortably – except for Ruthey Minton, whose bustling took her closer, the better to eavesdrop. The clicking of keyboards, the usual barely audible tap dancing of cockroaches on plastic, had slowed to a kind of soft-shoe tempo.

He looked at the mess on her desk, the box, the stacks of tear sheets, the clippings, her treasure trove of hate mail.

'It looks . . . you're cleaning out your desk. I . . . don't understand.'

She blurted, barely controlling the tears, 'That's because you're not listening, goddamn you. I'm cleaning my desk because I'm quitting the paper. I got a job offer in LA. I'm taking it. I'm not finishing this Lurker shit. I'm using my vacation as my two weeks notice.'

She was beginning to shout again.

About half the editors and reporters decided it was time for coffee break and left the city room. The other half, on deadline, were trapped uncomfortably at their terminals.

Ruthey Minton flitted even closer to the scene, the better to hear.

'What about finishing out the Lurker thing? Are you just going to run away?'

'The Lurker . . . a suspect has been arrested. That's enough for me. I got the job offer.'

'I don't believe this.'

'Why wouldn't you believe it? You're always accusing me of looking out for myself. Why is it so hard to believe I'm bailing out to take a chance in a lifetime?'

'What are you going to do in LA?' he asked aimlessly, not caring for the answer but simply filling the empty air.

Her response was as aimless as his question. 'Some rewrite. I'll get a few feature assignments at first. If it works out and a front-line vacancy opens up, I'll start features full-time, maybe some investigative stuff.'

Ruthey was practically shuffling the papers in Laren's departure box. Laren looked at her in disbelief.

'What about us?' Dewey asked weakly.

Ruthey looked up for the answer – as if it were exactly the question on her own mind.

Laren looked up at him, then at Ruthey.

'Fuck off, will you – not you, Ted – Ruthey, do you mind? Why don't you go occupy yourself in a bag of potato chips or something.'

Ruthey went scurrying off indignantly.

'Us?' said Laren.

He choked a couple of swallows down his dry throat.

'I . . . I'm sorry,' he said. 'I don't know what's gotten into me lately. I . . . thought we had something . . . that we had helped each other through some pretty tough times.'

'Ted . . . we were a couple of emotional crutches to each other.'

'Jeeesuzkeeerrist, can't you two take this soap opera somewhere else where people don't have to work?' shouted the wire editor into his cathode-ray tube.

'Shut up, asshole,' said Laren.

252

Dewey collapsed into a chair.

'This isn't happening,' he said. 'I thought I . . . loved you. I . . .'

She interrupted. 'What we had wasn't love . . .'

'F-U-U-U-U-C-K,' screamed the wire editor. 'I give up, let me know when you two announce the wedding. I'll be in the goddamn press room where the only whining they have to listen to is in the presses.' He stood up and stormed out, gesticulating wildly all the way. 'Fucking soap opera,' he shouted back from down the hallway.

'Stick your . . . arm into one of the presses, why don't you?' Laren shouted after him. 'No, stick your . . .'

Ruthey was edging closer again.

Laren picked up her box of belongings.

Ruthey cringed, ducking away.

'Ted,' she said.

'Never mind, Laren. I get the point. I'm sorry. I must have been out of my goddamned mind to think we . . . *we* of *all* people . . .' He laughed harshly at the irony.

She smiled a smile that threatened to evolve into a sob. She grabbed her box and ran from the city room.

Dewey felt like crying. He looked up through watery eyes at Ruthey peeking at him from around a terminal. He felt the pistol pushing between the small of his back and the chair's. He blinked away the wetness. Ruthey. He wondered what it would be like to pump about six slugs into the four-eyed bitch. Better yet, how could he get word to the Lurker that Ruthey Minton had revealed her true identity was Laren Hodges?

Nuts. He felt he was going goddamned nuts.

He wished he had his bottle of Bourbon back. It was a mistake to have poured it out.

* * *

Either a minute or an hour later, he realized the phone was ringing nearby and that nobody was answering.

He looked around the city room. It was full again, so it must have been nearer an hour. But people were avoiding him. He looked at the clock. Nearly time for another deadline to pass. It had been two hours since he'd lapsed into his vegetable state.

The phone kept ringing.

He saw it was the Lurker hot line.

He leaned forward to punch the buttons that would transfer the call to him.

Ruthey Minton pounced and picked it up before he could hit the right buttons.

She gave him a dirty look.

He returned it, thought about those six slugs.

Then she stared into the phone and squawked, giving the caller a caterwauling lesson in phone manners. Then she slammed the phone down.

'Nice, Ruthey.'

'What's with you, buster?' she croaked.

'Nice way to deal with the public. No wonder they think we're a bunch of pricks.'

'Well, I don't have to take any shit off a whispering caller and don't give me any lectures about manners, Mister Potato Head. I've heard the way you talk to ladies, but you're – '

'What?'

'I said don't give me any lectures . . .'

'Not that, Ruthey. The whispering guy. What'd he say.'

'He wanted Laren.'

'And you hung up on him?'

'Nooooo,' she squealed, 'he hung up on me. Sounded like he dropped the phone or threw it on the floor. *Then* I hung up on him.'

254

She started to squawk the whole story at him, all over again, but he was not listening.

He was pounding his finger into the button panel of the telephone. There was no answer at his apartment, where she had a few things. He tried the apartment she'd been sharing. No answer there, either. He didn't know the number to her original apartment. And he didn't know Marguerite's number. Hell, he didn't even know Marguerite's last name yet.

He headed for the parking garage.

Albright called after him, asking what the Lurker story today might be. He got no answer.

By the time Dewey hit the stairs, he was running.

Laren burst into her musty old apartment. There wasn't much she wanted, but she'd carry out what she could. Marguerite promised to come over and help as soon as she finished loading her own car down at the curb. She left the front door open – for Marguerite and for her own peace of mind.

She had cleaned her small cache of clothing and toiletries from Dewey's. She would go out to the shared apartment, and if the police seal hadn't been taken off yet, she would just have to make a trip back later. Today was the day. She was getting the hell out of this town.

She had marched all the way into her old bedroom before she realized what had hit her.

It was a chill.

A shudder.

She threw her purse on the bed and withdrew the pistol, pointing it around threateningly.

Nothing.

She checked the stupid safety and slipped it off. God, don't do anything dumb, girl, she told herself.

255

She sat on the bed and pulled the phone to her.

She put the receiver on her thigh.

The gun swept the room.

Another chill swept over her body like a cold breeze.

She punched numbers into the phone.

Looked up.

Swept the room with her gun again.

Held the phone to her ear.

Heard the silence of a dead line.

Punched madly at the buttons.

The tones beeped back at her.

But the line was dead.

She saw why.

In the kitchen.

About a mile away.

The wall receiver lay on the floor.

Belly up.

And she knew. He was here.

Finally.

She had come to him.

Alone.

'You son of a bitch,' she said into the eerie, musty silence. 'You make a move at me, and I'll shoot. I've got a gun here . . . but you know that, don't you, you bastard?'

She was whistling in the dark, and she knew it.

Should somebody come along now and see this, they'd testify that she should be committed.

She didn't care.

She was sure of the feeling.

To confirm it, another shudder shook her shoulders.

She had to relax her finger a bit, fearful a shudder might cause her to jerk the trigger accidentally.

Maybe she should.

Fire a couple of rounds to make him duck his head so she could run.

But where?

She couldn't shoot into the floor – there were apartments below. Maybe into the bed.

Maybe just make the run for it.

Wait for Marguerite?

Damn.

Marguerite.

She might burst in any second and be jumped by the guy with the knife.

No, she wouldn't be responsible for another person being hurt by the Lurker on her account.

God. Dewey was right.

She realized she had done it.

She had walked right into his snare.

She had come to him.

Right to the very place this whole thing had started with her.

He hadn't had to chase her at all. She had raced to his embrace.

Now he would try to carve her byline into her belly. As he had carved it into the back of Janisse. And every member of the Thrasher family except Buddy.

Over her dead body.

No.

This was not happening.

This Lurker didn't really exist.

This terror was not happening to her physically.

It was only the terror of the mind. He was not really here.

She shuddered.

Yes. He was. He was HERE!!

She pointed her gun at the closet door.

And took off running.

Half a step.

That's as far as she got.

When a filthy hand swept from beneath the bed and flipped her to a one-point landing on her chin.

The clenched pistol grip hit the hardwood floor and exploded in her fist.

The phone receiver on the floor in the kitchen blew apart.

The pistol leapt from her sweaty hand.

The blow to her chin stunned her. But she knew enough to kick and roll and scream, so she did all three. On one revolution she saw the pistol and rolled toward it.

While momentarily on her back in the middle of a roll, she saw the bed blow like a whale, from the sea, humping up toward the ceiling and rolling toward the wall.

Somewhere back in her mind she marveled at that feat. The bed was heavy. She moved it around a couple of times, and it seemed to weigh a ton. Yet this Lurker bastard was shrugging it off like a cape.

And there he was.

She almost had the pistol.

He leaped over her, landing a heel on the back of her hand.

She screamed in pain.

But somehow, she was not shuddering.

In the flesh. In the daylight. He was not so terrifying.

She held her hand and shuffled away toward the wall.

'Don't hurt me,' she said.

She looked into his face.

My God, she thought.

He was a boy – well, a young man, but a very young one. Something was wrong here.

'Who are you?' she said.

'You call me Lurker,' he said in a perfectly normal tone of voice, no croak, no whisper. He said it in a young man's voice. 'But my name is Darwin.'

There was an awkward silence – but a normal one – as there is when an adult woman finds herself face-to-face with a young man who is unsure of his masculinity, intimidated by her womanhood.

She looked him over.

He was muscular, tall. Dirty, but so . . . normal. Yes, he needed a shower, a shave, a haircut. And there was a long, jagged scar on his jaw. But when he cleaned himself up, he would be . . . God, he would actually be . . . almost handsome.

'Do you have a knife?' she asked.

He shrugged.

'Sometimes. Not now.'

She felt herself taking control. She was the reporter asking the questions.

'Are you really the Lurker?'

'My name is Darwin.'

She looked into the eyes and shuddered. No, she was not in control at all. Those eyes *were* the extra eyes.

'Did you kill all those people?'

'It was Slime done it.'

She narrowed her eyes. No, this kid was not normal, after all.

'They were all decent people.'

'Slime.'

She shuddered.

'Are you going to kill me?'

He didn't answer. He just stood staring at her sitting there rubbing her hand, shuddering now and then. His eyes were narrowed, thoughtful. His breathing began to get deeper. It came more rapidly as it grew deeper.

She thought about asking him some more questions, but then again, if he wasn't already killing her, why hasten his decision?

But his breathing pace could not continue to increase like this indefinitely. He was now panting. Something had to give.

'Are you by any chance hungry? You know, like for pizza?' she said.

It sounded so stupid, she began to laugh.

It did not touch his funny bone in the least. He was filling with rage with each inhalation.

The smile slid off her face.

'No,' she said.

Yes, she thought.

He was the Lurker.

And he was going to kill her.

'Tell me,' she said desperately, 'was it something in my news stories?'

'I could of lived my way forever . . . forfucking EVER . . . if YOU . . .'

His face had gone red, had puffed up to half again its size. She looked past his heel at the pistol. She could lunge. And she knew she'd take a foot in the face.

Maybe under the bed.

No.

The bathroom?

She'd never make it.

She looked at her nails.

They would have to do. She would tear his dirty face off, goddammit. She started inhaling a bit of rage herself. Damn right. When they found her body, when they uncurled her goddamned fingers and peeled out the flesh and pieced it together, they would find the face of this fucking bastard.

She kicked her pumps off and coiled, her knees on the floor, her feet pressing against the baseboard. Maybe the others had tried to run. Not her. She was going to uncoil, go right for the eyes. Her hands were two sets of claws poised at shoulder level.

She heard a growl.

It surprised her that it rumbled past her own lips. Goddammit, she liked herself at this moment. After so much self-condemnation in her life, she was going to die at peace with herself.

He, the madman, crouched.

She curled her lips back so they would not get in the way when she tore his throat out with her teeth.

He leaned toward her.

She braced against the wall and let the growl tighten into a scream of a banshee.

He reached for her.

She slashed at those eyes, those extra eyes she had felt so often. God, if she could just bury her thumbs in them, it would almost be worth dying.

He ducked back, feigned with a left slap, and bounced a right fist off her head.

She was not going to be able to spar with him. He'd tear her apart.

So she cringed – feigning the paralysis of fear, her forearms over her head, thinking how deceptions had always gotten her by in the past – her whole life, in fact. Faking it had always been her best subject.

She felt rather than saw as he leaned in closer.

Then she bunched and sprang.

Leading with her claws.

She heard her name as her left hand closed on stubbly flesh.

Just before her head lit up inside and she went unconscious.

* * *

261

Dewey had found Marguerite at the curb, packing her car for the interstate flight from the Lurker madness sweeping the city.

She told him where Laren was, and she said she was just going over to the apartment herself.

But Dewey wasn't waiting.

He dashed into the apartment hoping he'd find her packing a suitcase, wishing she'd curse him out for being the fool. He put his hand to the small of his back. He didn't draw the pistol – that was too much melodrama for even him – but he was ready to.

He hardly broke stride.

Into the bedroom.

And saw:

The back of a crouching man.

Laren cringing against the wall.

As he dived, he pulled the gun and called her name.

Before he hit the back, he saw her uncoil, springing at the front of the man.

It was a brilliant sandwich tackle, something for the football highlight films. Laren hit her forehead on his knee, coldcocking herself, but pinning herself to him as a fulcrum. Dewey's tackle was a spearing one, leading with his head to the back of the man's neck, driving him forward.

The man's head flipped into the wall, rebounded an inch, then crashed again as Dewey's weight came driving into his back.

He was out cold before he hit the floor.

Dewey had the pistol out, a light-framed semiautomatic thing, small and flat. It held ten rounds of .22 caliber hollow points. This was not a gun for accuracy or target shooting or sporting of any kind. It was a Saturday night special, a gun for committing crimes –

stickups and assassinations. Assassinations for revenge, for example.

Dewey was slightly stunned himself. A trickle of blood ran from his hairline to his eyebrows and split into two tributaries that ran on either side of his nose.

He knelt and grabbed Laren by the face and shook her. Nothing. He felt for a pulse in her neck and found it.

His relief came as a burst of anger.

This bastard was going to harm her. And at that moment, he realized he cared for her very much, that much of that drivel he'd uttered at the office this morning when he'd been saying he loved her was not drivel at all.

And thus, he'd almost lost yet another loved one to a perverted weirdo sick creep.

He raised his pistol and puffed, blowing blood from the creases in his lips.

He stuck it under the dirty nose, judging the angle that would take the bullet toward the base of this so-called Lurker's skull. Then he lowered his wrist, deciding it'd be better to shoot toward the direct center of the head. The bullet would never exit the head anyhow. It would hit nothing but soft matter and a thin wall of bone at the bottom of the cranial cavity. The hole in the nose of the bullet went down into the slug where it opened into a cavity, a tiny cul de sac in the lead. As the bullet drove into the soft matter, the compacted gore would be forced down into that cavity, fill it, and cause the slug to fly apart with the pressure. The expanding lead slug and brass jacket – about the time it reached the center of the skull – would separate, sending flattened chunks into two or three parts of the brain. There'd be no comeback from the wound of this tiny, unassuming bullet. He'd shot a couple of small animals after he'd bought the gun, which was after Erica. So he knew.

Kill him, ordered a cool voice inside his own head. His grip tightened on the pistol.

The picture of a squirrel inside this creep's head, literally popping like a balloon, splitting down the sides, the idea of a sparrow exploding into a burst of feathers and two separate body parts right inside this pervert's head . . .

Kill him . . .

Marguerite's scream brought him back, his pulse racing, his head clearing of the visions of small, dead animals.

'Call the police,' he ordered calmly, as if he had not had murder on his mind, 'and tell them to send an ambulance.'

'Ted,' murmured Marguerite, who had not moved from the doorway. 'You're not going to kill him, are you?'

He rotated his head, pulling the tightness from his neck.

'No, I'm not going to kill him.'

As if to prove it, he took the barrel away from the dirty nose. Then he bent and tenderly kissed Laren, tasting her sweet breath, leaving the lipstick of his blood on her mouth.

She stirred, and he found a grin at the thought of the prince kissing Snow White. Some Snow White – she'd looked like a rattlesnake a few minutes ago.

And some prince.

Marguerite came in carrying the receiver Laren had blown apart with her errant shot. 'Gotta use the bedroom phone,' she explained, never taking her eyes from Dewey. Clearly, she was afraid by what she saw in his eyes.

'Marguerite, what's your last name?'

'Smallwood. Why?' The incongruity of the question reassured her, though. She picked up the phone and pushed the buttons, her nails ticking on the plastic.

'I'm not going to kill him,' he said to nobody in particular, perhaps to the very voice inside him.

That wasn't the question, though. The question was: Would he have done it? And how about this: Would he have been glad? And: Would he have lied, saying it was self-defense, or would he have just done it, confessed it, and let the shit fall where it would?

Once again, he didn't know exactly how near the edge of insanity, how close to brink of murder, he had come.

Thanks to Marguerite Smallwood.

16

Hanover was proving difficult.

He wouldn't let Dewey and Laren near the suspect who called himself Darwin.

So Laren refused to give a statement. She even blurted that she wouldn't press charges unless she could interview him.

'Hodges, you can't get away with this hardass routine – it's called extortion.'

'Watch me.'

'Ted, talk some sense into her,' Hanover said helplessly.

'Right,' said Dewey. 'I'm going to take your side over hers.'

'Look, I read the papers this morning. You printed your testimony in the damned stories. Any judge worth a pinch of pepper will throw your asses in the lockup for contempt if you hold back.'

'Perhaps,' said Dewey. 'But why would you be in court in the first place? Do you have any evidence linking this fellow Darwin to any of the murders?'

'He'll be out of the hospital lockup tomorrow and . . . damn.' He watched Laren scribble the leaked detail about the release into her notebook.

'So you'll have a lineup.' Dewey scratched his head and read the script thoughtfully off the ceiling. 'You'll bring in Buddy Thrasher. He'll whine and shrink away from the whole mob on the stage, and the defense lawyer – chrissakes, even if it's a second-year law student – will put a nail in your coffin. Lessee . . .

yeah, then you'll bring in Marguerite. Maybe she'll be more certain than she was yesterday in the apartment. Maybe she'll come right out and identify the guy she shot at for lurking her apartment weeks ago so you can hold him. Then Laren and I can say, well, maybe he was threatening harm or maybe he was just looting the bedroom when he got caught, but she doesn't want to press charges, anyhow. You know, nothing of value in there anyhow. So the lawyer argues for cheap release.'

'Bullshit. There's holes all in that scenario.'

'For instance?'

'First of all, you two wouldn't be so irresponsible to let that bastard go just to spite me. Second, you would be saying your own newspaper stories were as much as made up or at least overdramatized if you said this guy was a common thief instead of the devil himself, the Lurker, *the* Lurker you been peddling papers over.'

Laren made a move to argue, but Dewey sent her a glance telling her he'd rather handle it his way.

'You have a point, Bret . . .'

Hanover's eyes rolled up.

'Shit, he's using my first name. Here it comes.'

'Why don't we just treat each other with a little common decency. You know, professional courtesies exchanged. You give us a little something . . . we give you everything we know.'

Laren interjected impatiently, 'Ted, Albright would have our asses if – '

He held up a hand. She shut up. Dewey loved it. Her response could not have been more persuasive. If Hanover thought they were risking something, he'd be more likely to bite.

Hanover narrowed his eyes and cleared his throat.

Dewey knew he had him.

'What . . . what the hell do you two want? I can't be funneling information to you without the TV people throwing a fit about giving exclusives. We're starting to get correspondents in from New York and Chicago, too. The brass upstairs are spilling their guts to the outsiders.'

'Well. There you go. If the brass are letting outsiders scoop the hometown boys, what's the harm of us being a little closer to the trenches?'

'Dammit, I just said I can't give you exclusives. The others would be on me like stink on shit.'

'No, you don't have to give exclusives.'

'What then?'

Laren chimed in. 'Yeah, what?'

Hanover was pleased at her apparent lack of collusion with Dewey.

Dewey made it sound as reasonable as he could.

'We've not been just reporters on this. We've been victims. We've been witnesses.' He left out detectives, not wanting to inflame Hanover. 'We are part of your investigation resources. There would be no harm in our observing your interrogation of the suspect – '

'Are you crazy? Even if the public defender didn't tear my ass up, the other reporters would see you in there and – '

'Hear me out, Bret.'

'Okay, but the answer is already no.'

'Maybe not. We wouldn't be anywhere near the interrogation. You tape them with video, don't you? Well, then, why couldn't Laren and I sit in a remote office – somewhere completely out of sight and sound of the interrogation and way away from the other reporters, just somewhere where there's a television monitor. While the taping is going on, we sit watching a closed-circuit shot. If he ends up telling you lies,

268

things we know contradict our observations, we tell you. If we can corroborate his statement, we tell you.'

Hanover chewed on his lower lip.

And Dewey knew the negative answer was no longer automatic.

'But what do you write? People aren't dumb, you know. I mean, even the television morons are going to figger out you have insider's info.'

'You put up a middle man. You have your technician tell us where the monitor is, but you don't know yourself. Then when they ask, you say you don't know where Dewey and Hodges are getting their information. You tell the same thing to the press and your bosses.

'And you don't give any details away yourself because they are relevant to the ongoing investigation. On the surface, you're treating everybody fairly.'

Hanover laughed harshly. He enjoyed the idea of screwing some people in the press, even if it meant cooperating with other members of their kind.

'One thing. What do I get in return?'

'Full cooperation. We tell you the essence of our stories before we print them – '

'Ted – '

'Laren, for chrissakes, we have to give him something of equal value in return. Look, Bret, we give you the good news and the bad. You won't have any power of prior restraint . . .'

'Prior what?'

'You won't have any power to censor in advance or to change what we write, but at least you have a head start at preparing a public response. And if we tell you something you know to be inaccurate, you can tell us the genuine facts – or you could even sit back and

269

watch us print the wrong scoop and get your jollies that way.'

Hanover obviously liked the sound of that part of the proposition. He smiled and even allowed himself to lick his lips.

Laren did not. But she had never before let an excess of scruples stand in the way of a story. So although she complained bitterly, she finally acquiesced.

Dewey for once liked listening to her bitch and moan. It served to cement the deal with Hanover, who delighted in their strained relationship.

But it was not in the least strained.

Later, they lay in his bed laughing at what they had pulled on the detective. Last night, in this very place, they had cooked up the scheme – after loving each other gratefully and gently.

She had called LA and told the managing editor out there of the new Lurker developments. He was impressed that she would be staying to continue covering the story. He tried to get her to do it as stringer for his paper. But she said she owed it to the *Post-Herald* to finish what had been begun.

Albright, of course, was delighted that she'd declined the ambulance ride to the hospital and instead had come in to write another piece with an ice bag taped to her forehead.

'What a bonanza,' he crowed. 'The Lurker team confronts the Lurker in a climactic capture.'

Dewey had cringed at that. What if that hollow point had done what it was manufactured to do? The last word on the Lurker would be the self-destruction of the Lurker team chief.

When they stopped laughing at the gullible Hanover, they rolled to each other. When they finally rolled

270

apart, he asked her if she thought she could handle what they would be seeing and hearing in the morning.

'What about you?' she asked.

'Not fair answering with a question.'

'I'll be okay. He's behind bars. How are you going to handle it?'

'So what's to handle?'

On the television monitor, it looked like one of those phony courtroom dramas, the supposedly real cases acted out by second-class actors who can't read their lines off the teleprompters and cue cards without stumbling.

The public defender was nervous. He knew he'd been handed a bag of snakes. He could play it safe and stay out of trouble. Or he could take a few risks and make himself a name. Or he could blow the ass end out of his career.

He told his client he didn't have to say a word.

But his client wanted to talk. He felt so relieved to be free of the burden of all those years. He would hold nothing back, he said.

He'd been cleaned up at the hospital. He'd even had a haircut while doctors monitored the progress of his concussion. He looked perfectly normal on the screen.

And he wanted to talk.

Hanover interrupted to read Miranda rights directly from a card, pausing to peer into the camera and to smile for the defense attorney, who later might view the tape looking for holes in procedure.

'Look,' said Laren, moving the tape recorder closer to the set. 'He's winking at *us*, I'll bet.'

Then Hanover became earnest.

'Listen, kid, I'm gonna be straight with you right up front. Just so's you'll know I'm on the up-and-up. And you can be straight with me. I talked to the shrinks, the psychiatrists who interviewed you in the hospital. I know all what they said about you, and your lawyer knows I know. You know?'

The young man nodded and spoke: 'And if you think I'm lying, let me know. Because sometimes I don't know the difference between truth and lies – you know, like in my own mind? – and if you could help me straighten out the spots that don't seem just right, I'd be thankful to you . . . officer.'

Hanover threw a confused expression at the lawyer, as if to say, you gonna let him talk like this?

The lawyer shrugged.

'Okay, kid, I'll try to keep you honest. You just tell me as much of the story as you can. Then we'll sort out truth and lies later.'

'That's fair, detective. Where do you want me to start, sir?'

'Start with your name, kid. Tell me everything you know about yourself.'

'My name is Darwin Robbins. I'm seventeen or eighteen . . . I'm not sure which . . . I lose track of time sometimes. Unless I'm at a house where they get the paper. On Halloween about two years ago . . .'

Dewey sat up erect.

'My God,' he said. 'He's sitting there talking like he's a regular high school senior or something. He looks absolutely, positively harmless.'

Laren was riveted to the set. She held up a hand. 'Listen,' she said, shuddering with the memory. 'You never saw his face yesterday just before he came for me. For a minute I thought he was normal, too. But then he changed into another person right before my eyes.'

272

Dewey checked her face to see if she was exaggerating. He decided she was not. He leaned back in his chair, letting himself be riveted as well.

'So. Darwin. Where is this house?'

'I don't know, officer.'

Hanover shifted menacingly. The kid looked up with a new idea.

'But I could take you there.'

Hanover relaxed, but cocked his head, unwilling to set aside his natural suspicion too far from his immediate grasp. 'Okay. Later. How did you get into the house?'

'Me and Sherman.'

'Sherman?'

'My buddy. There were two of us.'

Another idea lit up the young face.

'How is Sherman? I haven't seen him for nearly a year.'

'Sherman?' Hanover sat up at the name. He squinted, trying to place it in his recollection.

'Jesus,' whispered Dewey in the television room. He slid to the edge of his chair.

'What?' asked a confused Laren as she saw every muscle in Dewey's face begin to tighten.

'Sherman England,' said Dewey through a tight throat, just as the name came across from the television speaker as well. 'He's a kid. Was a kid. He disappeared along with that string of young children two-three years ago. He . . . the cops didn't connect it . . . wouldn't connect a teen disappearance with the youngsters. They told his parents he'd probably run away. That lurker . . . suspect they nailed in my house

273

. . . the one with the cut vocal cords . . . he might be
Sherman England.'

He said it just as the television speaker confirmed it,
as Darwin told of the mental incompetence and damaged throat of his friend.

Hanover beckoned an officer, whispered in an ear. The
officer left in haste.

'Darwin. Are you saying Sherman was with you
when you went to the house?'

Darwin was feeling – at least he was showing –
powerful emotions. His face screwed up to cry. He
fought it off.

'I'm sorry,' he said. 'Yes, he was my best friend,
Sherman was. His mother didn't love him. She drank.'

'Where is your mother, Darwin?'

The young face went flat.

'I don't have a mother.'

'Well, where *was* she?'

'I never had a mother.' He never flinched.

Hanover cleared his throat. He'd had plenty of cra-
zies before. But this interrogation was more bizarre
than usual.

'We're not getting anywhere, son. Maybe I should
just let you talk. You tell us about that house. Then
I'll ask questions to . . . you know . . . to fill in the
blanks and such.'

'Yes, sir.'

There was a pause.

'Go on, Darwin.'

'Sir?'

'Yes?'

'Before I do, I'd like to thank you.'

Hanover flinched.

'Why?'

274

'For saving my life. And Miss Hodges and that other man. They saved me. Was he a detective too?'

Hanover sighed.

'Darwin, they were under the impression you were trying to hurt Miss Hodges, that you were going to harm her.'

'Oh, no, sir. I wasn't going to do that. I was just laying in . . . you know . . . sleeping under the bed in a empty apartment when she busted in – she . . . Miss Hodges called me names. She hollered she had a gun. She said she was going to shoot me. I didn't even know how she could see me, but she said she was going to hurt me with the gun. Sir, I'm very quiet. I been living in houses all over this town for two years, and I never had nobody see me. And I never, *never* hurt nobody.'

Hanover's head snapped erect.

'What about the Thrashers, son?' he said argumentatively.

Darwin's response was a pained question mark of an expression, an absentminded look of innocent confusion.

'Never mind, son. We'll get to the Thrashers later. And what's this about living in homes all over . . . never mind, we'll talk about that later, too. Back to the apartment two days ago. Didn't you take the gun away from her?'

'Well, I had to knock her down. And then she came after me with her nails. They were like claws. I think she would of clawed my eyes out.'

Hanover looked up accusingly into the video eye, right into Laren's eyes.

It was Laren's turn to whisper an oath. 'My God, he's so convincing. I almost believe it myself.'

275

'Was that the way it was?' Dewey demanded in despair.

'No, dammit, no. Hell no. I don't think so ... Ted, I'm getting scared again.'

Dewey was no help. He was engaged in trying to work down another dry swallow again. Something horrible was happening here right before their eyes and ears. He fought back the other connections that kept trying to establish themselves.

Hanover turned his stare from Laren back to the youth.

'Son, why are you thanking us?'

'For saving my life.'

'From what?'

'From him.'

'From *who*, son?' Hanover intoned through a taut throat.

The boy looked into Hanover's eyes and cocked his head, giving him the look that asked how everybody could be so stupid, so dense.

'From the Lurker, sir.'

The four words electrified everybody who heard them. Hanover jumped to his feet, knocking his chair over.

Laren stood up too, dropping her pad and pen from her lap to the floor.

Dewey was no longer sitting at the edge of his chair, his haunches having come up as if he would leap at the television monitor, driving his bandaged hairline into the tube.

Darwin's lawyer scooted his chair away.

The cops in the interrogation room gripped their only weapons, the nightsticks.

276

Hanover leaned across the table, his palms splayed out.

'Son,' he uttered in a half-growl. 'There are those who would say you're the Lurker, that you're the one who's done those murders.'

Darwin took his turn at being alarmed.

'What murders? Sir, I never done no murders.'

'You telling me Sherman did them?'

'No, sir. Sherman is barely more than a baby . . . I mean mentally, he ain't been right since that night out at the house. He wouldn't kill nobody . . . he couldn't. He just knows how to creep around a house and feed himself and so on. He's real good at that. But murder? Never, sir.'

'Goddammit, then who done them?"

Darwin shrugged. 'It could have been anybody – '

Hanover bellowed, 'Damn you, don't you start playing games with me, you little – '

'Officer – ' said the defense attorney, his first word of the proceedings.

'Sir,' said the cowering Darwin. 'I didn't get to finish my sentence. It could have been anybody who's been doing the creeping around for the Lurker. Or it could have been the Lurker himself.'

Hanover found his chair and set it right. He needed to sit.

'You mean there are more . . . boys like you . . . creeping and crawling in houses and such?'

'Yessir. Dozens of us. All over town. But we don't do no harm. We just live in. When we get tired of a place or if people seem to be close to finding us out, we leave. It's easy – anybody could do it. Once in a while we report in to Slime . . .'

'Slime?'

'Yes, sir. That's what we call him, all of us. I don't know his real name. You call him the Lurker.'

Another new idea struck Darwin.

'I'll bet he's the one who did the killings you've been talking about.'

Hanover inhaled very deeply, his eyes closed.

'Break time,' he finally said. He stormed out of the interrogation room.

Laren was still talking low, as if they were in church instead of a remote conference room.

'Where do you suppose Hanover is going?'

Dewey pointed to the door.

'Five . . . four . . . three . . .'

Hanover burst in.

'Deal's off, you two.' He marched across the room and stabbed the television button with a finger, as if poking it into somebody's eye.

Laren said, 'Hanover – '

'No amount of bitching is going to make me change my mind, Hodges, so don't even bother. There is *nothing . . .*'

'Hanover, he might be telling the truth,' she said.

'That's why I'm ending this deal right where it is. If you were to print this shit, we'd have the city in a goddamned uproar. Can you imagine the panic if we told people there are dozens of these creepy little bastards all over this town?'

'What's to stop us from printing it?' Dewey said.

'No. Hold it,' Laren said before Hanover could counter. 'What's more important than this deal is whether the Lurker is still out there. I'm telling you, he's telling part of the truth, but not all of it.'

'Well, which part is which, Miss Mind Reader?' Hanover said.

'Oh, don't be so goddamned sarcastic, Hanover. I'm telling you something right now: I don't know whether there is such a person as this Slime or not. But I *do* know that boy was going to kill me yesterday. He had me disarmed and helpless. I was on the floor talking coherently to him, and he was answering. Then something came over him and he changed into a ... a monster. He was not threatened by me, but he sure as hell was going to kill me.'

'So? What's that got to do with this deal?'

'We hold back what we got from the paper ... yes, Ted, hear me out. We'll promise to hold back this multiple lurkers and creepers stuff, the stuff that would cause panic. You let him continue to talk, with us monitoring from here. I have a feeling he's about to tell you something very, very horrible – very evil.'

'What are you? A clairvoyeur or something?'

'No, but the more innocent he becomes – the more harmless he seems – the more terrible I believe he is. However, this guy Darwin is the Lurker. I *know* that. You let him talk and you'll find out.'

'You're not making sense, Hodges.'

Dewey thought the same thing. But he held his tongue.

'Go back down there, Hanover. Let us listen in. We'll hold this stuff back because I'm betting you're going to hear a hell of a lot more – stuff you're not going to be able to keep under your hat anyhow.'

Hanover seemed too confused to argue. He sidled to the door and left, as if he were glad he still had the shirt on his back.

When he had gone, Dewey turned the television on.

'Laren, I didn't understand a damn thing that just went on. But you're one hell of a conniver, I'll give you

279

that. How can you be so sure of the things you just said?'

She was staring into the set.

'Ted, move your chair closer to mine ... That's better. We need to be close.'

'Laren, this is a side of you –'

She whirled on him. 'Don't make light of me, mister. You know how I could always feel the presence of this guy? The extra eyes?'

He nodded.

'It's in his eyes. I can read his eyes – even better than you can read me. I can feel his eyes, even when I can't see him. And when I look into his eyes – at certain times I can sense the evil in them. He's a horrible person ... or he knows of horrible evil ... one or the other – or both. I realize now what I was feeling and when,' she said.

Dewey shuddered.

'And?'

'And he got that look when he talked about the murders, the Thrashers. His face showed innocence. But his eyes gave away his guilt. He killed the Thrashers ... I'm sure of it. And that house he's talking about –'

'Yes?'

'Something is there ... something evil.'

'The Lurker? Another Lurker?'

'Maybe. But I think something even worse. It's in his eyes.'

He sighed.

'You don't believe me, do you?'

'Laren, you must admit, this is pretty speculative.'

'You believe that little sonofabitch then?'

'Yes ... no ... I don't know. He's pretty persuasive. I'm pretty good at judging people myself, you know.

280

Okay, yes, I do believe him about halfway. You said yourself, he had you believing the circumstances in the bedroom were as he described them.'

She wouldn't answer. She focused on the television.

Hanover took his seat. He plunked down a can of soda in front of the boy, who drank it greedily, but silently, not stopping until he was done. When he belched, there was no sound. When he set the can on the table, there was not the faintest noise, although it could not have been more than two inches from a microphone that picked up Hanover's breathing from two feet away.

'Did you hear that?' said Dewey. 'I mean, of course you didn't hear it . . . but did you see it? The kid is like an animal . . . a jungle cat or something.'

Laren closed her eyes momentarily.

'Or something,' she said.

The boy waited.

Hanover folded his hands on the table prayerfully.

'Son, now we're gonna take a fresh run at this thing the way I said. You're gonna talk, and we're gonna listen. You start at Halloween. At the house. You and Sherman were sneaking up to the house through the weeds. What happened then?'

The boy told them. It could have been yesterday, so vividly did he tell it. He held his shoulder in pain when he described falling through the window. He shivered at the shadow shutting off the faint light into the basement window. He blocked his nose when he talked of the stench in the basement – the stink of death, he called it.

Laren watched his face intently. She began to doubt

her theory about the eyes. God, she was glad she'd told only Dewey. She was going to be as nutty as everybody else before this was over. She wondered if she shouldn't have gone on to LA after all.

She watched the others, too.

Hanover, who had heard hundreds of gruesome stories, was entranced by this one.

When Darwin talked of the stink of death, she put a hand on Dewey's forearm.

Darwin told of finding the dead body of a girl hanging at the end of a rope, another body in a grave.

Dewey groaned. He sagged in his chair, squirming as if he wanted to leave. But he could not. 'No,' he whispered to himself.

Laren tightened her grip on the arm.

Softly, she began to weep.

She wanted to suggest they leave.

But she knew he could not. Not now.

He was biting a knuckle. Near crying. Near vomiting. Near the edge of sanity.

Hanover was looking ghastly pained as he stared into the video's eye, into Dewey's eyes through the screen.

Everybody was transfixed as the story unfolded, the terrible, terrifying story poured out in even tones from the mouth of this boy who had seen and smelled the dead bodies of children, had heard their decomposing skin crackle, had seen his best friend throw himself through a second-story window, had been pursued by a man called Slime wielding a ball peen hammer, had fallen through the ceiling of this house of horror.

The boy choked as if truly dying when the foot of Slime kicked him in the ribs.

He seemed unable to go on.

Laren hugged Dewey.

282

Now he was crying softly.

He was leaning forward, begging with his body language for Hanover to go on asking questions, to keep the story going, although nobody wanted to hear the ending, inevitable as it was.

The boy had his hands to his neck, choking himself. No, he was pulling something from his neck.

'What's wrong, boy? What happened next?' Hanover asked.

'He buried me.'

'Alive?' whispered Hanover.

'I guess so . . . yes. I woke up with a rope around my neck and dirt all over me. I was in a grave. Slime was . . . Sherman wasn't dead. Slime was . . . using him.'

Hanover, the tough cop, gulped for the breath to ask, 'Using him?'

Darwin's eyes changed, narrowed, shot a ray of evil that everybody, not just Laren, could see.

When he spoke, his voice was even, flat, emotionless. 'He . . . raped him in . . . from the back,' he said. 'He was almost dead, but he did that to him anyhow.'

Hanover waited, his silence was the question.

'I crawled out of the grave. I tried to help Sherman.'

Hanover gulped another breath. He didn't have to ask.

Then Darwin broke down. He cried out in a long, drawn, moaning cry. Indeed, it *was* the cry of an animal.

'Then he fucked me tooooooo,' came the agonized words.

The boy gasped, writhing in pain on the chair, fighting for breath, pulling at his neck and fighting the imaginary bonds. At last he screamed, setting everybody on edge, and he fell sweating and exhausted on the tabletop. His sobbing was for everybody to feel.

Laren was still crying. As was Dewey. The public defender blew his nose. The cops wiped sleeves across their mouths, as if they needed a drink. Hanover ordered another break and bolted for the door.

But he did not come to the monitoring room where Dewey and Laren sat unmoving and silent. The video eye kept its vigil on the figure of the broken boy. And Laren and Dewey could not look away from him.

Hanover returned to the camera's field of view with another soda, his face shiny from being freshly washed.

The boy recovered his composure better and more quietly than his questioners.

Uneasily, Hanover asked him to continue.

Darwin returned to his flat tone of speech. The rest of his story was brief, quickly summarized, coldly told. He told of being made slaves to Slime. He told of being made to bury the other children. Then they were instructed on the art of creeping about, lurking, as the papers called it. That's how they made their way in the world. They lived in other people's houses without their knowledge, let alone their consent. When they left a house, having learned where the valuables were kept, they stole the most valuable things and turned them over to Slime at the haunted house. To the obvious question that Hanover never had to ask, Darwin said they could not escape. Besides, they had no families to go back to – when they told him that, Slime seemed to accept it as a reason to spare them. Slime had another hold over them. They were his slaves. They were part of the buryings and thus the murders. And now they were homosexuals, and he threatened to tell on them. He had powers, did this Slime. He could lurk better than any of them. He had legions of lurkers all over the city. And they could track down anybody who turned on Slime. And they would kill if necessary. It was Slime's standing threat. And everybody believed him. He had the proof hanging right there in the basement.

And Darwin knew he'd be killed if he ever got released from custody. That's why he never wanted to leave jail. He begged Hanover to keep him behind bars, to protect him from Slime.

Hanover promised.

'Darwin, can you take us to this house where the children are buried?'

'Yes. If you take plenty of men to protect me in case Slime is there.'

'I promise.'

'And you'll need men with shovels.'

Laren hugged the quaking shoulders of Thomas E. Dewey.

17

Laren knew it would be useless. But she tried anyhow.

'Ted, why don't you go back to the paper and start putting together a story. I'll phone with details in time for the last . . .'

His look silenced her.

It was a look of deep sadness, fierce anger, utter defeat, bottomless depression. It was despair and hatred. It was fear. It was a look that said he'd rather be dead than go out to that house with a battalion of gravediggers, but that he would die – or kill, if necessary – before he could be kept away.

As she saw herself coming into focus in his eyes, as she recognized a glimpse of affection that disintegrated into that fear again as he remembered his circumstance, she heard him speak in a low, calm voice.

'Maybe you should go in to the paper instead. I'll call you.'

'No,' she said. 'You need somebody . . . you need me.'

'What about the story?' he asked, somehow finding a wry half grin left to wear for a second on his drawn face.

'It'll keep.'

Even in his pain, he recognized the immensity of her words. Diverting from a story for even a short time was a hell of a gesture for her. But this . . .

'Thanks,' he said and hugged her back.

When she withdrew her arms, he jerked away and patted his beltline in back. She dropped his .22 into her purse.

'I'll keep this for you,' she said, 'in case they find this ... Slime. I don't want to lose you to a murder charge before this story is over.'

He studied her face – she felt his gaze as she turned off the television set whose remote eye still kept watch on an empty interrogation room. He was, she knew, trying to fathom whether she meant what she said about caring for him more than the story – or whether she was merely trying to pick him clean of the pistol. And if she merely meant to get the gun, was it because she cared for him or because she needed him to finish this story?

She kept a blank expression, unwilling to give away her feelings.

Because she wasn't herself sure.

They were trailing close behind a convoy of police cars heading north through town. Dewey drove. He started to lag behind, and Laren began to toss him nervous glances. She grunted as the last green-and-white slithered through a yellow, and her foot crammed down an imaginary accelerator on her side of the car. But he braked for the red.

When he looked at her, she was biting her lips, holding back an obscenity, fighting off a scornful look. She was trying to be considerate of his feelings, and consideration for anybody but herself was unfamiliar territory for her.

'Don't worry, Laren. I know where we're going.'

She looked at him.

His breathing had become rapid, anxious.

'I know where this house is.' He gripped the steering wheel until the car behind him honked to urge him through the green.

Laren said nothing.

She was watching the word spoken soundlessly in the back of his throat.

'Erica.'

The house was the grayed clapboard remnant left over from the time these streets were meadows, then fields. It was the house sitting at the edge of Cameron Hills development, about a mile and a half from the house Theresa and Thomas Dewey had built, fulfilling their chapter in the Great American Dream. Two years ago it was a mile from the edge of the development. Now, as the development had oozed outward, it lay less than a quarter mile away. Next year it would be burned for firefighting practice by the volunteer department. Then the ashes would be scraped into the basement and filled over. Then it would become somebody's backyard.

But the basement would be explored, emptied of its contents.

Since no radio calls had been made, there was no press at the house when Laren and Dewey arrived.

There were nearly a dozen cars, though, and more arrived every minute or so, using flashing lights but no sirens.

Darwin sat buckled and handcuffed in a sedan surrounded by officers with guns drawn.

Cars and men swarmed the scraped, barren earth surrounding the weedy, trashy lot. When they had secured the moonscape, a team closest to the front assembled on the porch and burst in.

Then more teams followed.

Soon, there was a platoon of flak-vested light infantry inside.

Dewey and Laren stayed across a dirt street freshly scraped, watching as Hanover spoke and listened into a tactical handset intended to be used only in dire emergencies, supposed to be secure from eavesdropping by criminals and those other vultures, the press.

Dewey was watching Darwin. He seemed nervous and afraid until Hanover relaxed. Then he seemed to relax as well.

Two or three officers stepped from the house and tugged at the zippers on their vests. Their baseball caps sat cocked back on their heads. When cops pulled their hats down, Dewey knew they were serious. When they pushed them back, they relaxed.

So. No Slime.

Dewey was surprised to find himself relaxing, too.

Shovels were brought up. Among the cars, now at least two dozen official ones and half a dozen of the curious, were the coroner's, a mobile forensics lab, two ambulances, and a fire wagon.

Dewey knew the television crews would not be too far behind now. There were too many radios around for an inadvertent call not to be made. And he knew police officers were among the most curious, most rumor-inspired, gossip-driven people alive – they would be calling their buddies at home, and the off-duty cops would be the next wave of snoopers.

Like a presidential candidate surrounded by Secret Service agents, Darwin was brought up and taken inside.

Laren followed, but a rank of uniforms with rifles opened for the guest lurker and closed in front of the reporter.

Dewey hung back. He heard her questioning and being questioned. Naturally, she wanted to know what was found inside. Naturally, and probably truthfully – so far – they said nothing. They wanted to know how the goddamned press could get out there so fast when a radio hadn't even been used, when everything had been done by telephone.

Their yammering voices drifted off somewhere to the back of Dewey's consciousness and hung there like a cloud on the horizon. He was feeling something else besides the urgency of the newsworthy moment.

He was feeling déjà vu.

He had been here before.

Of course.

He had come – not physically – but metaphysically. In the words of Darwin Robbins. This morning he had visited this haunted house in the vivid description the boy had given.

The only difference was that the first visit had been at night. And this was day.

A hot day. He wished he could remove his jacket.

Then he remembered he could.

He no longer had to hide the pistol. Laren had taken it because . . . because she liked him and felt sorry for him and didn't want him to get into trouble by leaping out like some Jack Ruby after Lee Harvey Oswald to kill the captured Slime. So he told himself.

The baking effect of the sun cleansed away some of the grief. It was difficult to bask in depression and fear on a day like this. The bright sun, crisp breeze, unnaturally blue sky – they didn't tolerate gloom. Gloom was much better suited to an apartment room with the shades drawn and a bottle of Bourbon for company.

He walked to the west side and found the picket fence. There were several pickets off, so he couldn't be sure which was the hole described by Darwin. He stepped over a section of fence that had fallen, that had been stitched to the ground by a mat of weeds growing up through the boards.

Picking his way through the waist-high growth, he found the junk pile and knelt.

Yes, at a very low level, you could see trails of rabbits and maybe dogs and cats, tunnels through the undergrowth. And, since acres and acres of land had been scraped off and sold elsewhere – or was waiting to be sold back to new residents who needed topsoil for lawns and gardens – all the rabbits, rats, and other varmints for miles had probably found this place as their last refuge in a vanishing habitat.

He walked around the trash pile, which seemed much smaller and flatter than he'd imagined from Darwin's description. Perhaps time and weather had hastened its settling in on itself.

He pressed his back against the house and found it very hot, although the afternoon sun had not yet found this side. Maybe heat had been built up inside and was now radiating outward. Or maybe he was just crazy. He closed his eyes and tried to imagine this at night. Hot, red light strained through his eyelids, preventing an effective image.

He stepped around the corner and found an oil drum and a box against the house.

He knew what was behind them. A window. A basement.

He had been there this morning – living the story as Darwin told it to the police.

He looked behind the drum and saw where Slime must have squeezed his head in to look before the two-by-four was thrust through the glass into his face. He planted his feet wide and hugged the drum. The stenciling on top said fifty-five gallons. It was heavy. Not full, but not empty.

He hugged it to his chest. He leaned back. The barrel came along, at first sticking to the ground, then easing

291

over, then – as the liquid center of gravity met the side against his chest – it tried to push him over. He balanced it. He twisted his body, rolling the barrel along its bottom rim. He let it thump down and heard the sloshing.

He leaned over the top to see.

There was the dark crescent of earth where no vegetation had grown for years, where bugs and mice had burrowed.

And behind that was the window, just as Darwin had said it would be. One of the panes was smashed. Dingy gray glass lay on the ground. The irregular star of the hole was black.

From the hole, he could hear faint voices.

He dropped to his knees.

He knew it was impossible.

But it was almost as if he could smell the stench of decaying bodies, the stink of death.

He lay flat and moved his face closer to the black star of emptiness the glass shards had formed. Inside, lights were dancing. Soon his eyes adjusted, and he could see there were so many flashlights, it had become very bright in the far room.

The angle allowed him to see only the beams of flashlights, which collected in a pool on one part of the earthen floor. Then, arms and hands pointed at the pool of light. A pair of legs moved into the spotlight, and a pair of handcuffed hands motioned downward and tossed a scoop of imaginary dirt to the side.

One tentative shovel followed, then another, and immediately there was a flurry of legs, shovels, and tossed dirt. The dust began to billow from the room, even reaching the star in the window twenty feet away, where its earthy fragrance and the rising anxiety made Dewey swoon.

It could not have been a depth of two feet when the first remains were found.

Dewey could not see for the forest of legs.

But he knew, because the sounds of digging had stopped and because soft curses began to emanate with the dust. Then a thin, curved bone was held up to the light. A clavicle bone. A small one. The collarbone of a child.

The sun was nearly down when Laren found him lying at the window, his forehead buried in his arms. It took her a long time to persuade him to move, that the police were leaving, that it was time for him to go, that it had been hours.

An officer was making a final sweep of the yard.

'You people will do anything to get a story, won't you?' he clucked sarcastically.

Laren cursed him bitterly, savagely.

Dewey came to his senses as he saw her reaching into her purse. He clasped the bag, trapping her hand inside.

She looked surprised, then understood.

She smiled.

'Welcome back,' she said. 'I was getting out my notebook to write down this clod's badge number.'

He returned the sardonic smile weakly.

'Forget it.'

She drove to Theresa's house.

'You sure?' she asked. 'I mean, don't you want to wait for the I.D.?'

'No. I want her to start bracing for the news. I . . . We'll know soon enough. I have to do this before . . . before the damn newspeople start calling . . . start flocking to the front door . . . asking her how she'll feel if the grave actually produced . . . Erica.'

She waited in the car as he walked reluctantly to the door.

From the car, she could see Theresa's surprise, then her question and tentative smile. Then, even before Dewey spoke, Laren saw Theresa's face grow tense. She had seen what was in her ex-husband's face.

Dewey went in.

When he came out half an hour later, Laren could see he'd been crying again.

She kept her silence.

'I'm moving Theresa out of town. Tonight. Until this Slime or Lurker . . . or whatever the hell you want to call the monster . . . is put away.' To the question on her face, he said, 'Her parents are in Florida. She can stay with them awhile.'

Still she said nothing.

'I want you to move in with me,' he said, 'until this is over.'

She saw he was waiting for an argument. She did not oblige.

'Hanover may want us to have protection. It'd be easier for him and us if we stayed together. Marguerite left town, didn't she? Who else is a potential victim of this . . . what's wrong?'

'I just never heard that one before.'

'What?'

'The move-in-with-me-so-we-can-save-on-the-police-department-budget line.'

He returned her weak smile.

18

Time wore on. And time wore out. Nothing happened. And everything happened.

As the Lurker story wore on, nothing new happened beyond the first sensational days after Darwin's revelations. No other lurking boys materialized, and no speculation about them had been printed in the *Post-Herald*. There was no sign of Slime. The skeletons were identified as the children who'd disappeared.

Erica Dewey was among those buried in services so saturated with news coverage that the whole community was wrenched from the clutches of everyday humdrum into a couple days of sadness. Then the citizens began to forget, and they expected families to put the tragedies behind them, too.

For a while, the reports of lurkings increased, but these were laid to common burglars and copycats.

One such copycat was shot, and two other highly publicized shootings – one of a paperboy in the early morning and another of a drunk trying to fit his house key into the wrong locked house – were enough to discourage further copycatting.

So the incidents dwindled, and the Lurker stories moved off the front pages of the paper.

Police distributed sketches of Slime nationwide, theorizing the end to incidents two years ago could only mean he had left town.

Against her ex-husband's advice, Theresa Dewey moved back from Florida and into her house.

Fingerprints could not tie Darwin to any crime

except the assault charge against Laren, which was enough to hold him.

But he said he didn't want to be released anyhow. Not while Slime was still free.

Sherman, the demented man-child captured in Matt Dewey's bedroom and sent to the state mental home, was positively identified by Darwin. Police located Sherman's mother and told her of the boy's condition. She swore she wouldn't have cared if he had *not* been brain damaged and told the investigators she didn't want to be bothered anymore. She didn't even call him by his name. She called him a dumbass. She had enough problems, she said. Indeed. For she was dying from cirrhosis.

No family of Darwin could be found. He was not surprised, of course, because he never relinquished the contention he had no mother.

Darwin was examined and questioned and probed, threatened, cajoled, bribed, and tested by a legion of cops and doctors and lawyers and shrinks.

He was proving to be difficult.

Not personally. For he was entirely personable. He was polite to everybody. He cooperated fully with police, admitting to dozens of lurkings, most of which could be confirmed by families who had reported burglaries or had been victimized by burglars but didn't make reports. Most of them would not believe they'd been visited – it would have been too much to accept that somebody had crept about their houses for weeks at a time, looking into every private part of their lives. But they all had a common experience. What had been stolen was usually the most valuable, best-hidden thing in the house, as if somebody knew exactly where to look. And the police used a few intimate details gleaned from Darwin's testimony to test reactions.

Many were impressed that police knew their family's favorite foods and hiding places of valuables. Some were deeply embarrassed at graphic reports of their sexual behavior and family fights. A couple felt threatened that the police knew the hiding places of drugs. Two cheating wives and one homosexual husband grew terrified when the police told them of Darwin's detailed observations.

Darwin could not be trapped in a lie.

Everything found at the clapboard farmhouse supported his story.

Of the families he said he lurked, every one – intentionally or unintentionally – corroborated his reports.

Even when the questions were being asked of him for the twentieth or thirtieth time, he answered the same way – and in the case of the most frequently asked questions, in the same words. He was always even-tempered.

Except he always broke down when asked to repeat the story of crawling out of the grave. And he became agitated at any suggestion he be released where Slime could get to him.

When the police could think of no new questions to ask, they asked the district attorney to ask the courts to commit him to the mental hospital. After all, the diagnosis was psychosis, a paranoid personality, who'd undergone severe abuse and trauma. Grounds enough to hold him behind padded doors. There he would be warehoused until evidence could be found to bring him to trial – although his insanity would probably stand in the way of that. Perhaps forever.

Dewey and Laren moved into her original apartment. She never again felt unease from the feeling of extra eyes.

Instead, her unease came from uncertainty, something she'd never experienced before. Always she'd been decisive enough, knowing what she wanted, what stood in the way, how to get around obstacles in her climb to the top. Now she had that job in LA. But the managing editor out there had begun to grow impatient. All she had to do was go. Nothing at the *Post-Herald* could keep her – the Lurker story had run its course. Either Slime would be captured or he wouldn't. In any case, the story was done. So she was ready to leave for California after dispensing with one obstacle: Dewey. Him, she didn't know how to deal with.

At first, Dewey struggled with his grief. And once the remains of his daughter had been put back into the ground properly, he felt only partly exorcized of the demons that had possessed him for years.

He tried to stoke his anger, knowing that Slime, who had killed Erica, was still out there free. But if there was no Slime – if Darwin was lying – then he could try to generate fresh hatred for the man confined in the state hospital.

But having two possibilities for hatred, two objects of his vengeance, was worse than having none at all. He simply could not keep up the intensity of the hatred that had driven him these past years.

So the job in the cop shop held no interest for him once he no longer needed it to give him a position to commit his revenge killing. The Lurker team ran out of work for two people, and Dewey recommended to Albright that Laren be given sole responsibility.

'Fine,' the city editor said, relieved he didn't have to bring it up himself and deal with the argument he expected to get. 'Since Laren is leaving anyway, the

298

whole effort will be left to die when she's gone – unless this Slime creep shows up.'

Albright had already begun interviewing candidates to fill Laren's vacancy. He tentatively asked Dewey if he'd like to leave the cop shop and take her position.

'Yes and no,' said Dewey.

'Yes, you'll leave the cop shop?'

Dewey nodded.

'And no, you don't want to be a GA reporter?'

Dewey nodded.

'So. You holding out for an editor's spot finally? After all these years I been – '

Dewey shook his head.

'What, then?'

'Lou, I'm quitting the paper. I'm going to finish the Great American Novel.'

Albright grimaced.

'I heard that story a million times, dammit. Ted . . . goddammit, you're not just quitting so you can go play detective after this Slime guy, are you? I've noticed you've been out a lot in the last couple of weeks. You can only get so much background at a place like that, Ted.'

'I know. No, I'm not playing detective. I'm really going to write my book.'

'About this?' Albright looked skeptical.

'No. It's my war story. From Vietnam. Everybody has one, Lou.'

'Yeah, but they're all the same fucking thing – what I did in the war – aw . . . never mind, Ted. I can see you aren't going to be talked out of this. And hell, if you write the way you have been lately, you'll sell the thing too. And . . . look . . . if you need to have a job to tide you over until the royalties start pouring in, you don't have to be too proud to come back here. I'd take you in a minute.'

Dewey thanked him and left, knowing he'd never be back.

Later, Laren stormed into the apartment.

'Damn you, Ted, don't you even have the decency to talk over something like this with me? You just quit. Do I mean so little to you?'

'Laren, I –'

'Forget it. Why don't you pack your bags and move back to that damned cave you inhabited before coming over here.'

Then she saw that he already was packing.

'I kinda figured you wouldn't want me around. And you're leaving for the Coast soon. So –'

'Shit.' She glared at him. 'The thing I always hated about my dad was he could always read me. That's the thing I hate about you too, smart guy . . . and . . .'

'And now you're going to say I reminded you so much of your dad that you thought you could try some kind of seduction to get even or to at least seek a sexual reconciliation in place of an understanding that you could never achieve before he died.'

She guffawed at him. 'He's not dead. You're some shade-tree psychiatrist, Sigmund Freud.'

With his glare, he dared her to deny the rest.

She didn't.

He was disappointed she didn't deny the part about his being a father figure.

'Laren, you're leaving for LA and a new job. I've gotten over my difficulty – and I'm grateful for the help you've given me in the past weeks. I've been an emotional cripple. But the convalescence is going to have to be in my own hands the rest of the way. I want to be friends. But working at the paper has no use for me anymore. I'm going to write for myself, to expunge all that's been pent up. Once that's let out, maybe I can write something useful.'

She didn't fight him.

He knew she'd been withdrawing from him, too. They'd been thrown together – on the job, emotionally, physically, sexually – by the perversion of the Lurker, more correctly the lurkers, Sherman, Darwin, Slime. Once the perverse glue had been dissolved, the natural bond between two people – commonly known as love and its synonyms – was revealed to be as adhesive as spit. Theirs had been merely a situational love, he decided.

They knew they were on opposite poles in so many ways: age, aims, adaptability.

Best they parted now. Friends and one-time lovers.

19

He'd actually rolled paper into the typewriter. He'd actually begun to write. The words came easily – even automatically. Perhaps that was the trouble he saw after he stopped to check over his war story. Four pages of automatic writing, the stuff every journalist can churn out, he realized. Most do it because it's all they know to do, because they think automatic words are the domain of the journalist. Bureaucrats and the military use jargon. The reporter scorns them, using the automatic language of journalism to do so.

Dewey had spent most of his career learning to recognize slop in his own prose, editing the junk phrases out. Now he'd just written four pages of it – slop, junk, shit.

He decided it was because of the distraction.

No, it was the lack of distractions.

He no longer had the attentions of Laren, the demands of Albright, the kidding of Hanover, the caterwauling of Ruthey Minton.

He had only himself.

Lousy company.

And his thoughts.

Little solace.

Erica.

The hurt of Erica.

First the terrifying gloom of thinking she might be alive. Now the devastating realization she wasn't. Now the gremlins of the mind asking: How? Why?

Maybe if he could answer the question he could exterminate the gremlins.

Maybe if he went out there one last time.

No.

He wouldn't do what he'd done the last two nights.

He would stay home and write automatic, shitty words first.

If only he weren't so distracted.

His mind went on automatic.

He'd heard the story. He'd stepped it off. He'd walked the yard during the day. By himself and with Laren. He knew every single detail that Darwin had told. He knew how – at least he could fill in the gruesome blanks.

So why was he dressed in black and blue? Jogging pants, dress socks, blue sneakers? And why was he wearing a black turtleneck pullover and stocking cap?

Why was he tossing his wallet and identification beneath the seat of his car?

So why was he driving out there again?

Laren came by to say good-bye. She'd barely shut off the engine when she saw the figure leave his apartment. If it hadn't been for the white temple hair contrasted against the stocking cap, she'd have rushed somewhere to call the police. But Dewey wasn't being burglarized. He was leaving, dressed as a burglar himself.

She thought of all the possible explanations for a man to dress like that. One was that he'd be going out to a lighted track to run. That was certainly possible.

The other possibility was too terrifying to think about.

She wouldn't follow.

303

She'd wait.

Then she'd drive out past that house of horrors.

If she saw nothing, then Ted had gone to a track — or anywhere else. As long as it wasn't to that house.

She could call him later. She'd go home. Catch her early westbound plane tomorrow. A telephone good-bye would be better anyhow. She could say what she wanted without regard for the truth he might read in her eyes.

She might — for the first time — even tell him she loved him. What harm could it do the old guy? It might kick-start his hormones again for his wife or somebody else his own age. God, it embarrassed her. Going to bed with a guy nearly forty-two.

Hell with driving by the house.

She'd go home, she decided.

But home was the opposite way. And she was driving through Cameron Hills when she saw his Ford at the edge of the development nearest the clapboard house. She pulled up behind and stopped. Well, maybe not *his* Ford. Just *a* Ford. A Ford with an expired *Post-Herald* parking sticker on the rear bumper? Not likely.

She was in the purple jogging suit, the one Dewey liked because it accented her eyes. God, she'd actually fallen for that one with him once, actually fallen into bed, but . . .

What was she stalling for?

She could call the police.

Or she could drive home and let him go insane solo, without any assistance or hindrance from her.

There was that job safe and sound in LA, possibly the last one she'd need to strive for.

All she had to do was start her car, turn on the lights, and leave.

So why was she stepping out into the embrace of the darkness?

Why was she padding down the streetbed scraped into the dirt?

Toward that geometric black form etched against the night sky?

He knelt at the picket fence, choosing the middle gap. Last night, it had been the hole on the right. The night before, it had been the left-most hole. Neither one felt right. The center one was right, he decided, because it caught a piece of his hair and tugged at him.

The trip through the weeds and around the trash pile were as before. Then he pressed against the house.

Listening.

He had discovered how much in life there was to listen to. In two nights, he had learned to focus his hearing outside his body, to select a sound and savor it, turn it over in the ears, catalogue it.

And he had begun to learn how to walk soundlessly.

All it took was patience.

At first you simply had to stand, weight on one foot until it ached as you found a place to put down the other. Then you had to transfer the weight slowly, ears turned to the night, listening for any change – from your own sources of sound or somebody else's.

The first night he'd worn, then abandoned, a windbreaker. The whistling it made against the weeds might as well have been a rhythm band.

By the time you'd begun to master your own sounds, you'd already begun learning to walk soundlessly, he discovered. You did it in reverse of a normal walk. Instead of striking the ground with the point of your heel and rolling forward, unleashing sound ahead of the stride like a lawn roller crushing leaves, you

pointed your toe like a dancer's. The toe touched first.
Then the foot went down flat, all at once. If a twig
began to crackle beneath the foot, you could stop and
place the toe again because the weight was completely
on the rear foot. This was opposed to the momentum of
normal walking, which threw the weight forward continually. In normal walking, even if you wanted to
stop, you had to plant the front foot, wait for the
weight to transfer, and push back. That necessity
would break off a twig like a firecracker.

But Dewey had begun to walk leading with his toes,
and he went silently along, not touching the house,
barely crackling even the dried grass, until he reached
the fifty-five-gallon barrel.

On his knees, he slid the broken window frame
aside.

Gingerly, he checked for fragments of broken glass,
which he had crackled both previous nights.

He lay on his belly and went in feet-first. It gave
him great satisfaction not to have snapped a piece of
glass this time.

His toes touched. His fingertips let go of the ledge of
the window as he let his weight down. He sat, back to
the wall, to let his pupils adjust to the furry blackness
before him.

He had a penlight in the elastic band of one stocking.
But unlike the previous nights, he would not use it.
He had already vowed not to. He decided he would do
it his way – in total darkness.

The Lurker's way.

And he had the .22 strapped to the other ankle.

Stupid move, that.

If he were caught, even Hanover might not have
enough influence to get anybody to believe he had not
taken up some form of crime. The really upstanding

306

citizens didn't go around dressed like cat burglars – hell, *acting* like cat burglars. And they didn't carry Saturday night specials tied to their legs like assassins.

And even if he were not arrested as a criminal, he most certainly would be thought a nut.

Thought?

Hell, he knew he was crazy.

How would he persuade them he had not become a lurker himself? And while he was at it, what proof did they have that he was *not* the Lurker in the first place? Well, even in the very first of the investigations, all the fathers and uncles of children who had disappeared were among the suspects. Especially when there seemed to be no other leads in the cases.

He thought about that a moment.

Was he a lurker now? Well, if a lurker was somebody who sneaked into houses – even unoccupied ones – and lurked about most of the night in the dark, padding as silently as possible . . . then he most certainly was. He certainly had adapted to the silent walking technique quickly.

And was he the Lurker all along? *The* Lurker?

Damn, he thought, the mind could play one hell of a trick if it wanted. It was letting him ask himself the question, wasn't it? And he didn't exactly have an answer.

Could he be Slime?

Could he have killed those children, then discovered Sherman and Darwin and used them in that way?

Was the reason Slime had disappeared that he, Dewey, was Slime part of the time and Dewey the rest?

He and God knew he'd had enough drunken stupors and blackout episodes.

Maybe . . . but could he have possibly killed his own

daughter and hung her from the rafters in this awful basement? What about his feeling of déjà vu? Was he the man called Slime? He patted the .22 pistol. If he ever arrived at an affirmative answer to that one, he'd be found French-kissing the tiny bore of the gun – that much he knew.

Dewey had felt himself slipping into a realm of a hundred unasked, let alone unanswered, questions. And he hadn't even tried to fight off the feelings of slipping away. It was a turbulent realm, this, with its dark, heavy seas at night – mentally and emotionally foreboding. Yet, inexorably, he let himself be drawn into the storm inside him.

But he never got past the thought of sucking lead from the bore of the .22.

Because at that point in his reflective struggle, a shadow fell across the window.

And tossed him overboard, off the frail skiff of his sanity.

Into the roiling seas of his living nightmare.

His eyes had begun to adjust, and the patch of darkness had lightened in the long, skewed rectangle across the floor. When that rectangle suddenly redarkened, he lurched away from the wall and scrabbled around on his hands and knees so he could look.

But there was nothing to see.

Perhaps a fleeting cloud passing its shadow darkly.

Then the shade of night seemed to be jerked aside for an instant, passing from left to right.

He saw its edge was too sharp to be a cloud.

And it came back from right to left. Clouds didn't reverse their courses across the sky. It was a figure. Of a man. My God, Darwin's own story . . .

With a thud against the side of the house, the light

was blocked from the hole for good. Dewey knew about clouds. He knew they didn't make noises crashing into houses – with the sloshing sounds of a fifty-five-gallon drum. He had heard about that drum in Darwin's story and he had rolled it aside himself in the daylight. He couldn't turn drums into clouds.

Now he was suddenly adrift, the actor in the drama of his mind. He was Darwin in Darwin's story. What came next was the hammer. The chase. The trip to the closet. The fall. The grave. The sex slavery.

Dewey knew the sequence of events. He didn't want to live them. Didn't want to be part of them. Yet what could he do? he asked himself. Did he have a choice?

A little whine started growing in his chest and worked its way up his trachea into his throat. He choked it back. Now, inside his chest again, it began to balloon into a scream.

He was breathing hard, but he couldn't catch his breath.

His mind was racing, but he wasn't thinking of anything – he was seeing Sherman and Darwin, two terrified kids huddled in the basement whimpering. The movie in his mind was going to go on without his consent, and he was going to be dragged into it.

Unless he got out of this house.

Was he dreaming this? Or was he living it? Was the source of this nightmare the same as that of that voice? And that rage? Inside his head? Was he finally going nuts?

He got to his feet and began backing away from the window.

No, he couldn't go into the upstairs of the house – he wouldn't.

He went back to the window and jumped up to the ledge. Hauling himself up just off his toes, he could feel the barrel. He pushed with one hand. All it gained him was to push his body away from the ledge. A stroke of panic hit him, and he threw his weight back against the barrel.

Nothing gained but a throb in his wrist as his palm rebounded.

He dropped to his feet and looked around the darkness. But he'd been looking down into this room the day they were digging bodies from the basement. If there'd been a box or ladder or chair to stand on, he would have seen it then. And even if there was one, that didn't mean he'd gain enough to get a purchase on that half-full drum.

His wrist began to stiffen. He felt as if he'd rasped some skin off the palm of his left hand as he hung to the concrete ledge. And now his kneecap was beginning to ache as if a local anesthetic were taking effect. He must have barked his knee against the wall when he spun around. Yet he hadn't felt it. But these pains helped ease the panic. With the reality of the pains came a tenuous grip on his sanity.

He sat down on the floor below the window and clutched his knees, wrapping his arms around and pulling hard, exerting himself until the cords standing out on his neck made the skin prickle with heat. A voice . . . the cool voice that always accompanied the heat in his head . . . it spoke to him. He shook it off. It came back. He cleared his throat noisily, hard and long, drowning out the voice, recapturing his sanity for the moment.

Then he breathed deeply and forced himself to exhale completely. With his returning breath control came his reasoning. The voice went away.

He reasoned he could not sit down here crying.

And he could not get out the basement window.

He would have to go upstairs and out the front – no, he remembered, that had been sealed off by police, a heavy hasp and lock installed.

He would have to go out a window on the main floor – break one if necessary.

And he would not have to go in the dark like some goddamned lurker. He was not a lurker. He had a penlight and a pistol. He would use them, and damn the soul of anyone who got in his way on a night like this . . . when he was in such a state.

He held the flashlight in his left hand and the pistol in his right. They were his rod and staff. They comforted him.

He was back in control of himself as he stepped from the small room. He saw the stairs across the larger room. At the head of those stairs was the front door. To the right of that were windows he might break out – he remembered Darwin's words about the windows being stuck shut, at least the upstairs ones.

He had started toward the stairs when he heard the noise, the unmistakable noise of creaking footsteps and a heavy crash.

He had jumped back, when he was hit on the neck.

He whirled away from his gentle assailant, backpedaling, throwing his light, tightening his pistol grip.

He saw it.

A heavy rope knotted at the end, forming a loop, a noose – a swinging noose.

It had not struck him, he realized. He had backed into it when he recoiled from the sound from above.

He stumbled backward and fell over a mound of loose dirt.

Falling took a long time.

For he had reached the level of his feet and still he fell.

311

Down, down, down. Into a grave. Into *the* grave, he realized. The open grave of his own daughter.

He lay freezing, stunned, choking. His neck and shoulders were forced forward and down toward his belt, cutting off his breath. What breath he could manage was poisoned with the dust dry for decades in this basement. The dirt kept sliding down from above, tiny avalanches falling in his face, clods bouncing off his body, burying him slowly, almost perfunctorily.

Buried.

Buried alive.

He remembered.

Darwin was strangled, left for dead, and buried alive.

You are no longer Ted Dewey, said a voice. You have become Darwin, have begun living Darwin's dream. Next comes the rape, the slavery, and then the conversion to lurking.

'No,' Dewey shouted in protest. The voice in his head did not answer. But then again, it didn't need to. Dewey knew. He'd become Darwin. No, in truth, he'd made himself into Darwin. Willingly. He'd made himself voluntarily into a lurker. He heard a sardonic laugh, realized the sound had come from his own throat.

He found his feet, but not the flashlight. The pistol was gone too. But that no longer mattered. Darwin had had neither when he crawled from the grave.

He staggered on his feet, his kneecap numb again. Still.

The ground level was only to his chest, but the sides of the grave angled outward rather than being vertical. And those mounds were up top.

So he could start his climb but fell back in.

He wiped the mud from his eyes and spat mud from his mouth.

He tried climbing out again.

Again he slid back in, snorting with the exertion, clearing his nose. He found the smell to be all-powerful. There was the smell of death in this dust. God, he was literally breathing the death of his daughter.

And he slipped a bit deeper into panic.

He stepped to one end of the grave and ran at the other. He hit it, scratching and clawing with hands and feet, and this time he made it out.

When he peered back into the dark hole he could see a sliver of light coming from where the flashlight had been buried and probably uncovered as he scratched his way out. But he would not go back for it.

His chest heaving, his breath coming fast, he started up the stairs as silently as he could.

Now the madness is nearly complete, the voice said to him. 'Yes,' said Dewey in answer. He began to wish he would encounter this Slime, this Lurker. He wanted to kill him barehanded. He wanted to throttle him and slash his abdomen with his teeth. He wanted to plunge his hands into the evil chest cavity and tear out the beating heart. He wanted to bury it in that grave below. Yes, said the voice. Maybe then and in that way he could bury his own sanity. Of course. 'Of course.'

Laren had waited in the dirt street for a long time. It was in the same spot they had stood watching the police storm the empty house before digging into the basement.

She thought she might stand here until she saw a light or Dewey's figure. Then she might call to him.

But there was no light or figure or even a sound but

for the low, level chatter of insects. It must have been a quarter hour she waited, though she couldn't be sure.

She decided she should go back to her car, and she did.

She decided she would drive away, leave him to his madness, but she didn't. She couldn't. She cursed herself, feeling something she didn't want to feel. She cursed herself because she suspected she might care about this middle-aged loser who might not be a loser after all. Well, she thought sardonically, if *she* liked him, he couldn't *be* a loser.

She drove the car back to the clapboard house and made half a U-turn in the street, pointing the lights at the front door.

She fished in her purse and drew out the .38. She flicked the safety off. She swallowed hard, and walked downstream in the current of her headlights to the porch of the abandoned house.

She mounted the first step, and it bent beneath her weight. Softly, she called his name.

'Ted,' she whispered, then realized he'd never hear that.

Better to be bold, she told herself. So she stepped up to the porch and marched across it to the front door. The boards creaked, but she wished they were even noisier. She thought about knocking and even brandished her knuckles. But that was stupid, she decided.

Besides, the front door was decorated with an official-looking police poster warning that this was a crime scene sealed by order of the chief of police. And a heavy steel lock enforced the order.

'Hell with it,' she muttered and whirled on her heel. She cursed Dewey and the house as she stamped her way upstream through the beams of her headlights toward her car. Back inside her car, she let out another snatch of invective. But she didn't move the shifting lever. And the cursing was at herself for what she knew she was about to do. She reached into the glove compartment and pressed the button to open the trunk.

In another minute she stood on the front porch again, her tire tool in one hand, her pistol in the other.

'Damn you, Dewey,' she said, squishing the words between her front teeth. Even so, she wondered if she'd have the strength to twist the lock off the hasp.

The tire tool was iron, twenty inches long. One end had been formed into a sharp tip for prying off wheel covers. The other end was formed into a gooseneck and tipped with a socket for removing lug nuts.

She touched the lock with the pointed end, a gesture of futility because the lock was so heavy, one of those she'd seen shot through in television commercials – shot through and still effective.

But even as she touched the tip of the tool to the lock, the hasp fell off the door and landed at her feet with a crash.

She leaped back, startled. Then she cursed at herself. It was a wonder she hadn't clenched her grip on the pistol and fired off a bullet who knows where.

'Damn you, Ted Dewey,' she said, more to help her regain her composure than anything else. What the hell was he doing breaking into this creepy place? For that matter, what was she doing standing out here on the porch, basking in the headlights of her car, a pistol in her hand, a police lock lying at her feet? The predicament gave her an enormous sense of urgency.

She decided to rap on the door and call to Dewey. If he didn't come out in a minute, hell with him. She'd leave him to explain this situation himself.

She drew a deep breath and raised the tire tool.

But one rap was all she got. It sent the door open,

315

pivoting on rusty hinges back into the house. Her second knock landed on emptiness, surprising her and stopping Dewey's name behind her teeth.

An ordinary citizen might have turned and run. Her first instinct, was, in fact, to bolt, to go back to her car, lock herself in, and lay on the horn until Dewey showed himself or until she tired of the game and left him to his madness or whatever it was that would cause him to break into the scene of so gruesome a crime.

But she was also a reporter. She had covered this story from the beginning. Yet she'd never seen the inside of the house where it began. The curiosity that drives reporters held her now. After all, the whole scene was bathed in light, wasn't it?

She reached inside with her left hand and pushed the door back against the wall. Her crouching shadow was cast against a door in the entry foyer. That would be the basement.

Pistol first, she leaned inside for a look.

There was nothing to see. The trash had been picked through and carried out by police in huge, tagged garbage bags. So except for small litter and dirt from hundreds of tramping footsteps, the room was empty.

Another step inside and she could look to the left where the stairway began and went up, climbing above the basement door.

She took the step.

Was Dewey up or down?

She was going no farther to find out.

She pointed the pistol at the basement door and took a breath to call toward the upstairs.

Her breath came out a scream.

As the basement door burst open, it smashed into her hand, setting off a brilliant flash of light and deafening blast of the pistol fired indoors. The gun went spinning from her hand, and her fingers stung from the blow of the door.

But she never felt that.

She was too horrified by the dirty, muddy monster that leaped from the basement.

He was literally a dirt ball in the light, with wetness around his eyes, nose, and mouth forming a mask of mud.

And he roared at her and came for her.

'Slime bastard!' the man roared.

She screamed and turned toward the lights of her car, but he was there first and spun on her, enveloping himself in a momentary cloud of dust. A halo of light shined around his head in the dust. But the halo of his hair was even whiter than the dust. She recognized him.

'Ted, goddamn you . . .'

But this was not Dewey advancing on her. This was a heaving, trembling monster.

'Ted,' she shouted.

The figure hesitated, shook his head, then advanced again.

'My God,' she murmured, the thought coming to her that this was indeed Slime, that Dewey was a lurker, *The* Lurker. Dewey was Slime.

She backed away, saying his name softly, as to an aggressive dog.

He reached out a hand.

She sidestepped and swung the tire iron. It spanged unmusically as it banged off the side of his head.

'Goddamn, Laren. What the fuck? You trying to kill me or something?'

He was holding his head. He took another step toward her.

317

She backed off another step and raised the tool.

'Dewey, I'll break your damned skull if you don't back off.'

His knees buckled, and he crouched, steadying himself with one hand on the floor.

'My God,' she said, 'are you all right?'

Dewey came to his senses slowly.

The last thing he remembered was falling into the grave. No, there had been Laren bashing his brains into jelly a few seconds ago. He remembered that. But what happened between the two events. Had he gone nuts?

The fingers touching his head felt wet. He pulled them away and looked at the blood.

'Dewey,' she gasped, 'are you all right, Ted? Please, you're not going to hurt me are you?'

To him it was such a relief to hear his name. He was not Dewey, not Darwin. Not Slime. He was Thomas E. Dewey, no relation, variously known as Ted to his friends, Thomas or Tom to presumptuous people who read his signature. And to the frightened woman whose ankles he was now admiring, he was once known as Dumbo ears.

He craned his neck back, smiled at her, making the side of his head throb.

'Know what the nice thing is about having you bash me on the head with a tire iron . . .?'

She gaped down at him.

'Feels so damned good when you stop.'

He touched his fingertips to his skull and felt the hard knot there. The bleeding was slight.

He reached out to her, but she cringed from him.

She was not smiling. She still brandished the tire iron.

'What happened, Laren? How did you come to be here?'

'Dewey, you jerk. What the hell are *you* doing here?' she rasped, an incredulous look still in her wide eyes.

He shook his head, then winced at the pain of the action.

He stood up unsteadily. 'I'm sorry, Laren. I guess I just went a little crazy. I thought you were the Lurker.'

'Me the Lurker? You scared me to death,' she said.

He shrugged, waving two open palms at her as if to demonstrate that he hadn't actually killed her.

Tears suddenly welled up in her eyes. 'I had a gun. I was ready to shoot. I could have . . . I almost . . .'

'No,' he whispered. 'My fault, not yours.'

She nodded.

He smirked. 'I'm sorry, Laren. God, I'm sorry. I don't know what happened, honest to God.'

'What the hell are you doing out here, anyhow, damn you?' she demanded, recovering her usual acidic balance.

He gave her a that's-more-like-the-Laren-I-know look.

'I . . . came out here to try to put the pieces together, to try to understand how such a thing could have happened.'

'I guess you damned well found out. You were nuts a couple of minutes ago. Dammit, Ted, you . . . you . . .'

She burst into tears at the thought.

He tried to hug her again, and she let him this time. The tire tool slipped from her grip finally and clanged on the floor.

'I'm sorry,' he said. Over and over.

Finally, she composed herself.

'What were you doing in the basement?' she asked.

'All I remember . . .' His expression hardened.

319

She shrank away.

'No,' he said. 'I'm all right. Something odd happened to me though. I sneaked into the basement window. I was letting my eyes adjust – '

'The basement *window?*'

He shushed her.

'And the barrel, the fifty-five-gallon drum, was rolled up against it behind me.' He studied her face. 'No kidding now . . . was that you?'

'Ted, you *must* be dreaming. Maybe I hit you too hard or something. Maybe you *are* crazy. I never moved a barrel. I've been out front.' She pointed in the direction of the headlights.

'You came in the basement window?' she said. 'You really didn't break the lock on the front door?'

He nodded, then shook his head. 'I didn't break the lock. I went in the window. The last thing I remember' – he shivered – 'was the rope, the grave . . . That's *it*. . . . I fell into the open grave down there in the basement. Then' – he looked at her helplessly – 'I can't remember getting out of the grave or anything else until I heard your voice, then felt this awful pain in the side of the head, and the next thing was waking up with you standing in front of me with that' – he pointed at the floor – 'thing.'

'Well, who broke the lock?' she asked, turning toward it. It was her turn to shiver.

'You didn't?' he asked.

She shuddered.

He pointed at the front door. She moved in close behind him as he limped painfully toward the headlights.

On the porch, he picked up her pistol. 'How many rounds?'

'Fourteen now,' she said.

320

'You have a flashlight?'

'In the car.'

He remembered where his own was, shook his head. 'Get your flashlight,' he said.

They went through the entire house, starting in the basement. He carried the powerful flashlight in his left hand, her pistol in his right.

Downstairs, he found his .22 lying on the dirt mound. The penlight beam was dying yellow in the grave. But he would not go in after it.

They checked out the upstairs as well, stepping over the hole where the bottom step board had been. Back downstairs in the living room, he shrugged at her.

'Well, I've lived the whole thing practically,' he said. 'I've been upstairs and I've been partly buried in the basement. All I need is to throw myself out the upstairs window and damage my head permanently.'

'Well, you haven't been totally made into a lurker,' she said. 'Yet. Let's get out of here.'

'Yeah.'

'And,' she said, 'you haven't dived through the ceiling.'

He gawked at the white patch of wallboard nailed up there.

'Why?'

'Why what?' she asked.

'Why would the cops patch that ceiling?'

She shrugged. 'They wouldn't.'

'Why would anybody?'

'I don't know . . . just to clean up the mess?'

He narrowed his eyes to a tight squint. 'But nothing else was ever cleaned up in here. The cops hauled out tons of junk to test for clues. I mean this guy, Slime, never even cut down the ends of the ropes. He just

buried the . . . kids with the nooses around their . . .'
He went silent.

'What's wrong, Ted?'

'Holy shit.'

'Ted, you're scaring me again.'

'I'm sorry, Laren. I'm okay. It's just . . . you remember anything spooky down in the basement?'

Her shoulders jerked. 'The grave.'

'What else?'

'That rope, the noose.'

'The police took down all the rope ends that were spiked into the beams – well, they said they took down four of them.'

'For the four bodies . . . Ted . . . you don't think that's a new rope?'

He looked around the living room, waving her pistol into the dark corners threateningly.

She sidled closer to him. 'You think . . . Slime?'

'He's around. He rolled that drum against the house. He had that rope placed for another victim. I didn't roll that drum back into place tonight. And I didn't put that noose up. And I'm *not* the goddamned Lurker – '

'The police,' she said. 'We have to get the hell out of here . . . and, you know, get the police to stake this place out.'

But he was already on the way out.

She ran to keep up, as much from fear of the darkness behind her as urgency to be with him.

BOOK IV
Terminal Lurkings

20

Darwin had watched as Slime began raping his friend. Watched in horror.

But horror at what? he wondered.

Perhaps even the beckoning hand in the grave had not tipped the balance, sliding Darwin's stability to one extreme of the spectrum, to the extremity of horror.

Perhaps the child's hand in the grave was only the penultimate horror.

Darwin started across the basement, again bending low, again skirting the grave. He had figured out how to walk silently, touching his toe first to the ground, then lowering the heel, then transferring weight soundlessly.

He never looked to the floor once.

His eyes were transfixed on what he saw.

At first he thought he might race across the twenty feet and lash out with the board.

But he knew he might not make it without being detected. And Slime was bigger. And he did have that knife. Even if he didn't cut Darwin, he could certainly stab – or threaten to stab – Sherman.

As he shortened the distance between the board and Slime's head, Darwin moved more slowly.

He told himself it was because he needed to be quiet.

But he knew silence or lack of it wasn't the problem.

He knew the source of his horror.

Darwin stopped creeping in toward Slime when he was but six feet away.

The horror was not that his friend was being raped. Not that he lay limp and broken, naked, helpless, moaning with ragged, gurgling breath. Not that this subhuman creature was pounding his hips against the body on the table. Not the savage sounds and scents of this macabre room where some bodies swung like effigies of themselves on taut ropes and others lay half-buried in a grave.

No, the horror was not in this room.

The terror that rooted Darwin to this spot was in his mind and in his body.

Adrenaline dripped into his bloodstream, setting his pulse off rapid and hard, sending blood racing through his bruised neck to his aching head.

And sending blood to engorge his genitals.

Darwin was horrified at the pleasure he was finding by the utter fascination of seeing Sherman raped.

Slime's frenzy was his own horrible frenzy.

Slime's breathing was his horrible breathing.

Slime's ecstasy was his own.

He felt horrible and sick and guilty and repulsed by Slime and Sherman and himself — most of all himself. But he did not make another move until he felt the horribly fevered rush of his own horrible orgasm nearing its explosive end.

The man called Slime was truly insane.

He was insane with the pain of having been bashed in the face by that board through the window. He was insanely angry that his little pets kept dying when he strung them up on ropes. And he was insane with the ecstasy of this boy on the table.

Even in the midst of his animal passion, though, he felt the presence. It was the presence that drew him to check the basement in the first place. Then it made him look into the closet upstairs. Why, he even thought he'd felt the presence from that hole over there – the pit, he called it.

It was an awful presence.

The presence of extra eyes.

Extra eyes were boring into the back of his head.

Extra eyes were causing him to lose his passion – some things couldn't be done while watched.

He started to turn from the table.

He heard the groan of an orgasm not his own.

And came face to face with Darwin.

21

When Dewey was yet half-bashing down, half-unlocking his apartment door, he heard the phone ringing. He ran to it and answered out of breath.

A small, distant, wheezing laugh answered his hello.

'Who is this?' demanded Dewey, though by the raising of hair on the back of his neck, he thought he might know.

'So,' said the hoarse whisper, 'you got out of the basement all right, did you?'

'Slime, you bastard.'

Laren's intake of breath was almost a scream.

The phone filled with laughter.

'We just missed each other,' whispered the voice. 'Maybe another time, eh?'

'What about now, you damned –'

'Fine. Come see me. Come get me.'

'Where are you, you bastard?'

Laren inched to the phone, and Dewey tipped it so she could hear the phone number spoken. She fumbled in her purse for a pencil and paper. The whisper laughed again, but his wheeze was cut off by a click.

Laren repeated the number to herself.

'Never mind,' said Dewey, his face contorted in pain.

'I've got it,' she insisted.

'Never mind,' he said numbly. 'It's my house . . . Theresa's . . . Matt.'

She went speechless.

He punched out the number.

A sleepy woman's voice answered.

'Theresa, for God's sake, this is Ted. For crying out loud, grab Matt and get the hell out of the house. Theresa, do you hear me?'

There was a wheeze. The voice of the Lurker said, 'First your daughter, and now your son, eh, Dewey?'

Then Theresa's scream.

And the line went dead.

He punched another number. Miraculously, Hanover answered his own phone, although it should have been too late for him to be at work still.

'I been trying to call you for an hour, Ted –'

'Listen, Bret, get out to my house . . . get a car out there right away. Slime –'

'Ted, I will, for Pete's sake, but you oughta know . . . Darwin has walked away from the state hospital.'

'Forget him,' Dewey shouted. 'Forget fucking Darwin . . . Slime is at my house, goddammit . . . he's got –' His voice broke, and he slammed the phone down, missing the hook, and ran off leaving it to dangle.

The car was careening north.

'I should have driven,' said Laren.

He shot her a murderous glance.

'Watch the road, Ted. I mean, you have too much on your mind . . . hey, where are you going?'

'Not to my house.'

'What? Ted are you –'

'Mad? Don't say it. I *was* mad – back there at that house of horrors. Now I'm rational. If you can call thinking like that sick bastard a rational state.'

'Ted, please say something that makes sense. You *must* go . . . you must *want* to go to your house.'

'Of course I do, Laren. That's the problem.'

She found she couldn't swallow as she studied his

329

face for signs of insanity encroaching again. 'Ted, you're scaring me.'

'It's exactly what *he* expects – that we go to Theresa's. Look – every other time we sent the police racing somewhere, what did we find? Okay, dead people, but did anybody ever run across the Lurker in a place he called from?'

She shook her head.

'No. And the police will go to my house. If everybody is dead, there won't be anything they or I can do about it. Even if everybody is alive, *he* won't be there.'

She gazed blankly into the distance beyond the beams of the headlights hurtling through the night. Her eyes suddenly snapped into focus.

'You're right . . . he'll be at the old house where – '

'Where the noose is. He's planning . . . he was planning all along to take . . . Matt back there to that noose.'

She gasped.

The car careened around a corner.

She studied his grim expression in the green reflection of the dashboard lighting. She couldn't be sure he had not gone over the edge again.

'Ted, tell me you're not . . . crazy again, are you? I mean, you haven't snapped or something, have you?'

His smile, reflected green in the lights of the dash, did nothing to reassure her.

'Got a hammer on you?' he asked, eyes wide open in exaggeration.

'No, but I left my tire tool in the living . . .'

She caught his smile and knew he was all right.

Half a mile away, he turned off the car's lights.

A quarter mile away, he coasted to a stop and stopped with the parking brake.

330

'Don't get out.'

'I'm going,' she said. The set in her jaw indicated she would be firm about it.

He put a hand on her shoulder. 'I actually want you to,' he said. 'You have those antennae about this guy. You'll feel his presence before we ever see him.'

He handed her the .22. He took the .38.

'Only use it if you're attacked,' he warned. 'Don't shoot at shadows, only at somebody – somebody with extra eyes – somebody who is after you.'

He rolled his window down and slithered out into the darkness. He beckoned her to do the same. She balked.

'Come on, dammit, Laren. You'll have to be cooperative for once in your life. We don't want to light ourselves up with the interior lights.'

She watched him slither out the window, then followed suit.

Outside the car, he asked in a whisper, 'Laren, do you feel anything?'

She shrugged and raised her eyebrows.

'Good,' he said. He turned to walk toward the house.

'Ted. Are you sure you want to do this? Wouldn't you rather be with your family, I mean . . . at least know about your family?' she whispered urgently.

He answered in a low, determined voice.

'Laren, I know . . . I went a little crazy earlier this evening. It's been coming. But what happened was I began to think like this bastard. I have a very strong feeling that he will have tried to trick us into going to Theresa's. But he won't be there. He'll be gone. With Matt. He'll be going to that basement. And then by the time we would have figured it out, we'd have the police storm this place and find that noose . . . full of my son's neck . . .'

She shuddered.

'You feel him?' he whispered.

'No. I'm just afraid. For you. For your boy. For all of us.'

'He's been drawing us toward him all the while, playing his perverted little mind game. But this time we're not going to chase him. We're going to let him come to us. Then we're going to burn his ass.'

They were outside the house by the basement window. The trip across the yard had been a hasty one and not too silent because Laren had no innate sense for creeping around. But Dewey decided haste was more an essential than silence. They had to be sure the Lurker had not beaten them to the basement.

He rolled the drum aside yet again.

Then he whispered in her ear for the tenth time: 'You feel anything?'

She shook her head.

He whispered again, 'Get down and look inside into the darkness and tell me if you feel anything.'

She did, then stood up and shook her head again.

He relaxed. He had no doubt about this sense of hers. He slithered inside, dropped down, and turned to receive her weight. He helped her down.

When her feet stood on the floor, he whispered again, 'You stand just inside here and keep an eye on the sky. If you see a figure lean over and start to roll that barrel, start shooting at his head. No matter what, don't go into that other room.'

He couldn't see her face, but he knew she was grimacing at his coldness. He knew though. Nobody but the Lurker would be moving that barrel in the dark of night. Only Slime or Darwin or whoever he

332

was would do that in yet another attempt to trap their prey.

He went across the smaller room to the doorway. He looked back toward her and could see the faintest of outlines – of her head, the hair giving off a little sheen. She was pretty . . . no, make that beautiful. She was the kind of woman a man could love easily. Maybe she could love a man like him, too. He prayed he would not be seeing her hurt tonight. And he prayed he would be right about the intuition his last days of madness had given him about the madman he had been emulating. He prayed the sun would not come up on them still waiting in this house. And that he would never receive another braying phone call from that hoarse whisper.

He decided to reach around the corner with the flashlight and cast a beam quickly to the four walls so he could memorize the layout. So he could avoid falling into that grave again.

Laren had been staring into the fuzzy blackness of the basement, then looking at the distant rectangle of the heavens the window hole permitted.

She was grateful for the momentary sweep of the flashlight so she could fix on Dewey's position.

This was awful.

This was frightening. But, on the other hand . . . No, she told herself . . . Yes, she contradicted.

This was . . . okay, so it was one hell of a story. If this guy materialized . . . she had a story, a series, a book, for chrissake.

But this was the first time she could remember that she cared more about the people in the story than in recording their story. She was horrified every time she thought of Matt Dewey. And Theresa, poor Theresa. If she was still alive, how must it be to have her second

333

child threatened, perhaps stolen? If it happened, she would surely wish herself dead. Or she might make herself that way.

And poor Ted. He seemed to be possessed by his demon still. Even the burial of his daughter had not rid him of it after all. Now he was lying in wait to ambush evil personified, perhaps Satan himself – the Lurker.

How feckless he must feel – to try to ambush the devil.

Ted Dewey crouched into an even tighter ball.

His memory had played a savage trick on him.

He wanted to flash his light around the room again to prove it.

But he didn't have the guts to find out it was not a trick of the memory at all.

He didn't want to see the empty air.

It had come to him a full minute after he'd turned off the flashlight. He'd looked into the corners, under the stairs, beyond the mounds of the grave. And there was nothing.

And that's what terrified him.

He didn't remember seeing that noose that was there earlier in the evening, the noose that had slapped him on the back of the neck.

Finally, he screwed up his courage enough to stand and wave his arm around the corner. He carved wider and more frantic arcs into the blackness . . . the empty blackness.

Wider and wider, emptier and emptier, until he realized the noose had been taken down.

The Lurker had been here after they had left.

The goddamned Lurker could have taken it before he went out to the Dewey house, of course.

But if the bastard had come back from Theresa's and *then* taken it down, it could only mean one thing.

Matt. The name rolled off his lips and silently into the darkness as he mouthed the word breathlessly.

In answer, a clunk came from far away in the house.

Dewey crouched back deeper into the smaller room.

Was it from the porch?

No.

Upstairs. That sound had come from up there.

There. He heard it again.

The Lurker had gone upstairs. Dewey knew he had him now. He would go up. Surprise him. Then . . . then what? He didn't know.

Dewey rose silently and began moving across the basement. Silently.

22

They had come.

As he had known they would.

The Lurker had been nearly surprised by the pair of
them, and if one of them hadn't been tramping so
loudly through the weeds, he might have been discovered setting up his snare.

But now he was back in control.

He'd almost always been in control. And soon he
would be back in control again.

He had drawn in Hodges and Dewey again.

They were the iron filings to his own magnetism.

This time he would kill them.

Like the others, their bodies would rot.

Then he could return to his invisible life.

Again he would become a man with no visible
existence, more a spiritual phenomenon than a physical presence.

All he had to do was wait.

They would walk to their deaths.

Wait.

They would volunteer to die.

Wait.

He was a man who had trained himself to become as
crafty, sensitive, and patient as a stalking animal. A
jungle beast with the skills of the jaguar applied in the
environment of the forest that was a house – anybody's
house.

He closed his eyes, the more to concentrate on
sounds. His eyes had begun to adapt extremely well to

darkness in his two years of lurking. He could see in almost total darkness. He could hear the ragged breathing of Dewey. The Lurker could identify people by the sounds they made, the individual grunts and manners of drawing breath and exhaling. The noises were as distinctive as voices. And years of listening intently had given him the special skill to identify patterns in minutes. This was Dewey who had come.

Dewey had flashed the light for a few seconds and then had turned it off, giving him back his advantage of the darkness. Then suddenly his breath had been drawn quickly and had gone on unevenly, through the nose – it was the nose whistle as much as anything that fingerprinted Dewey's breathing. Perhaps Dewey had somehow sensed that the rope was gone from the beams, the Lurker surmised. That meant he would be on the move soon.

The other person was too far away to hear well enough. But he could smell her. It was Laren Hodges. Her fragrance was not strong, but it was as distinctive as if she had announced herself by name through a megaphone after crawling through the window. She had a fine, pleasant musk that made the sterile fragrance of perfume into a sensual, tantalizing scent.

Perhaps he would rape her – not the regular way, but as Sherman had been raped, over and over in the intervening years. Maybe he would string her up – use her writhing body.

He heard the clumping noise of the boy from the second floor.

He had expected it earlier and more continuously.

But now was fine. And random was all right.

His ears picked up a movement, a change in the breathing, then the gentle sounds of dirt softly crumbling beneath the muffling soles.

He adjusted the knife in his belt and opened his eyes.

The sound moved closer.

He saw the vaguest of forms vaguely lit from the distant stars reflected into the basement.

It was Dewey.

He went by.

The Lurker marveled that Dewey had become quite good at walking silently. His breathing was still quite out of control. But the walking had progressed well. Perhaps – with the right training – he could become a lurker as well.

Dewey's nose whistle climbed the stairs, the weight as usual creaking the fourth step and making the seventh seem to sigh. Next the door handle would rattle.

It did.

The Lurker drew his own silent breath, held it, and stood up in the grave to look around and see why Laren's scent had not grown stronger, why she had not moved with Dewey.

She felt it at once.

It was the stare of the extra eyes.

It chilled her, instantly and thoroughly.

It was not a random shudder one feels whimsically run through the body.

It was the same frisson of fear she'd felt in her apartment when he was under the bed. It was that feeling distinguished by the presence of *him* ... the Lurker.

She whirled on the rectangle of midnight blue above her head. She pointed the pistol at the sky. Suddenly, the tiny pistol seemed as if it would fly from her sweaty grasp like a bar of soap in the shower.

She whirled back to the darkness and sat frozen.

Nothing.

Nothing but blackness could she see.

She whispered to Dewey.

He did not respond.

She took a tentative step toward the last place she saw him, the spot she'd fixed in her memory when Ted Dewey, crouching, had swept his flashlight beam around the room.

In half a dozen scraping steps, she was completely disoriented. She had to look back to the window to reorient herself. And she had to tell Ted about the extra eyes, to ask him whether the squeaking, the distant knocking, the metallic rattle could be the Lurker she felt.

She found the middle of the opposite wall and started feeling to her left.

Finally she came to the edge of the doorway.

She knelt, feeling with her empty hand for Dewey.

But he was not there.

The Lurker hoisted himself from the back corner of the grave. He heard the padded squeaks upstairs going across the parlor floor toward the stairway to the second level.

Then he slipped silently and casually around the hole. He moved toward the wall by the doorway – where the cringing, shuffling Laren would come when she stepped from the relatively well-lit small room into the inky larger room of the basement. He heard her feeling along the opposite side of this wall. She was patting her way toward the opening. Soon . . .

Laren cursed.

'Damn you, Dewey.'

Then she flattened against the wall.

She'd never intended for the words to be spoken aloud. But what the hell? The bastard had left her alone – well, he had moved. And that other bastard, the Lurker, was around. She knew it. And he knew it. So why bother?

'Dewey?' she half-whispered, half-moaned.

She reached out her hand and swept the darkness.

Then she turned and stood in the doorway.

She swept both hands into the blackness.

Then two gentle hands closed on her fist with the dampened pistol.

'Thank heaven . . . Dewey, you sonofa – '

The shudder and the blow arrived at the same time.

And she knew she was in the hands of the Lurker.

Even though a fist crashed into the side of her face . . .

Even though she felt nails clawing at her pistol hand . . .

Even though she felt herself propelled across the dark, uneven floor of the basement . . .

Even though she felt the grip slipping away from the pistol . . .

Even though she was falling . . .

She tried to squeeze off a shot from the .22 – and she tried to scream.

The pistol slurped as it left her slimy palm.

But she did manage a yelp before her head cracked into the wall of the grave, finishing the job of stunning her, knocking her out.

Dewey was halfway up the flight of stairs to the second floor when he heard her call. For a second, he was paralyzed. Upstairs was that knocking about, that almost random clunking. It might be the damned Lurker daring him to come.

Or it might be a diversion.

Below was Laren.

She would not call out unless . . .

Silence was no longer the imperative it had been.

He ran down the stairs and hopped over the hole left by the misplaced board. He spun like one of the cops he'd seen on television, in fact, as he'd seen them trained at the academy while he was doing stories in the cop shop. His flashlight was now on, held out far to the left side and in front so anybody shooting at the light would get an arm at worst — 'Unless the fucker's aim was shit,' as the academy instructors would tell the trainees.

But nothing showed itself in the light's beam, nothing he might blast away at with the .38.

Next was the stairway to the basement, the door still open as he left it.

He called out to Laren as he ran, spinning, leading with the pistol, pointing into the darkness with the gun first, then bringing the light around.

Nothing.

He called out again.

Nothing.

He was down there.

He had her.

Erica.

Then Matt.

Now Laren.

He felt the rage coming back, the hot spot in his head, the cold spot in his chest. A voice murmured unintelligibly to him. He ignored it.

Pointing his toe toward the downstairs, he leaned as

if to sneak. He would beat this Lurker at his own game.

But he was hit before he could even snap off the light.

The Lurker's attack was brutal, violent, slashing, aggressive.

For he too was filled with rage. His own revenge was as hot as Dewey's — hotter. For it was fueled by the insane passion and resultant guilt of sexual perversion. For it was a sexual rage, a frustrated rage, a rage of hatred of himself whether he achieved his sexual aims or not.

After hearing the slap of Laren's body into the bottom of the pit, he had dashed up the basement stairs to the first floor. He had waited between the door and the wall.

Once again, he knew Dewey would come. Just as he knew he would go upstairs to investigate the noises he'd planted there.

Through the space between the door and the jamb, he saw the flashlight beam casting irregularly into the basement. He heard Dewey call uncertainly for Laren. When the light settled down, he knew a decision had been made. He knew his quarry's attention was all focused down the stairs, following that narrow beam of light into the basement.

With all his might, he pushed off against the wall, launching the door and himself at Dewey.

Dewey had dropped his left hand to his thigh to flick off the flashlight button. His right still pointed into the darkness.

He never felt or saw the assault coming.

For the second time in hours, the basement door set off the semiautomatic pistol.

Dewey was smashed hard on the right arm, shoulder, hip. Then his head was whipped violently right, and it smashed into wood as well.

The momentum tossed Dewey left, but the door crashed on his forearm. The snapping was both of wood and of the two forearm bones, the radius and the ulna.

The pistol fell away, bouncing down a couple of stairs.

It was not as if Dewey had dropped it. His hand was so numb, so stung, he could neither open nor close the fingers. The pistol just slipped from his grasp as the arm whiplashed unnaturally where there had not been a joint before.

Dewey's scream, bellowed involuntarily, stung his throat.

The flashlight bounced, then rolled, carving a lighted arc of nearly 360 degrees before coming to rest pointed at the front wall, bathing the room in indirect light.

Dewey would have been slung across the room with the light. But his broken arm had been trapped in the door. It was the pain of the violent pull as much as the actual breaking that hurt so much.

The Lurker released the door, and Dewey's arm fell out, bringing a gasp.

Dewey tried to clear his head, to lift his arms to fight, to brace himself for the continuation of the attack.

So stupid.

He thought he'd been so smart.

But he'd been a regular dumbass, he knew.

This was a lurker who'd been at his perverted craft for going on two years. And he, Dewey, had spent a couple of nights creeping around a vacant house and thought he could take him on. Something akin to an urban cowboy slipping out onto the savanna to rob the lion of its kill.

Dewey heard himself laugh at the bitter irony as he staggered away. But it sounded more like a cry.

He shook his head again. He had to keep his attacker off like a fighter stung on the jaw. He had to get his legs back – the arm was gone, hanging limp, swinging at the elbow joint, which he could control, and the new joint, which he could not. He had to fight till saved by the bell, whenever that was in a situation like this.

He backpedaled, trying to get a look at his attacker in the dim light. He could not.

The Lurker did not press the attack right away.

His fury at the first onslaught had been enough.

He saw the damage. He'd heard the bones go. He watched his quarry stagger away, the pain too much to even cradle the broken arm in the sound hand.

He dropped Laren's .22 into his pants pocket and drew the boning knife. His sharp boning knife. He'd kept only the sharpest knives around. Sharp enough to carve words into human flesh without dragging or tearing, sharp enough to part flesh at a touch as if by some magic.

The knife was for up-close and personal killing. There was the slapping of the fist against flesh as the blade vanished to the wood grip. There was the warmth, the fragrance of gore. There was the magic of steel slicing effortlessly through muscle, sliding across bone.

Dewey he would slash, dragging as much blade as possible through as much flesh as possible.

The woman – Laren – he would stab. With steel and with his own turgid flesh.

* * *

344

Dewey had made it across the room, nearly to the bottom of the stairs to the second floor. The only clearing of his head had come from the intensity of the pain in his arm. Every time he moved, he could feel broken ends of bone grinding together. Before long, the pain alone would take him out. Already, his stomach had begun to press against his diaphragm. It was only a short time before he would vomit or faint, whichever would come first.

He saw the feet moving catlike toward him.

There was not a sound.

The Lurker uttered not a word.

His clothes did not rustle.

His feet did not scrape or shuffle.

Even the floor seemed not to respond to his weight as it did Dewey's. It did not creak at all.

Dewey, mesmerized, then saw why. This Lurker *extraordinaire* was walking in an irregular pattern. He must have known where the loose spots were, where the squeaks could be found.

Dewey was up against the banister. He couldn't see his attacker's face.

He never saw the blade until it hit him.

His downcast eyes saw only the shadow looming toward him – and the ghostly, silent feet. When the feet seemed to brace and the shadow jerked toward him, Dewey ducked.

He felt a hot slash of pain across his forehead. If he hadn't ducked, it might have been his throat. As it was, the wound stung as if he'd been whipped with a wire. But it was not a minor wound, for almost instantly, warm drops fell away to the floor, and he saw the drops were blood.

The sight of the torrent gushing from his head made him recoil again.

Another swipe of the knife missed him.

His heel caught and he fell.

Painfully.

His right arm slapped around like a fish just landed in the bottom of a boat. His left arm pulled him back. He was wincing in agony, was nearly blinded by the blood.

It hurt. God, it hurt. But Dewey decided he would not die crying. He would die with a sarcastic sneer on his face.

He braced his back against the wall and waited.

But the advancing feet stopped.

Dewey looked up and snarled, barely able to see through his own blood coursing down his face steadily enough for him to feel the current.

But he saw. He saw the Lurker recoil, as if in fear.

Why in hell this killer should show any sign of fear, he didn't know.

Dewey decided he did not want to die after all.

With his left hand, he pushed up. His legs did the rest, allowing him to slide his back up the wall. Why the hesitation? he wondered.

The Lurker took a quick step and lunged.

Dewey, like a sandlot Sunday football player, gave him a hip to the left and dodged right.

It was enough.

The knife jab missed.

Dewey noticed.

This was a stab, not a slash like before.

The games were over. The fun had ended. Now he would be killed.

If only he could make one more fake and get by. If only he could dash down that basement to wherever the pistol lay – maybe he could even get outside – no, he would not leave Laren in here, dead or alive. He would not run from this nightmare. He would live it out – or he would not, and die.

He doubted he could pull the same fake twice. This personification of evil was too well schooled in craftiness.

So, as the Lurker closed in again, he gave the hip left, went right, then back left.

It almost worked.

If it were not for that useless arm that would not even serve to balance him, it might have.

Dewey leaped into the space between the Lurker and the banister, his broken arm following like a streamer.

The Lurker hit only the arm – not even with the blade but with the fist that clutched the knife.

It was enough.

The arm slung behind Dewey's back. The excruciating pain and the shift in balance caused him to stumble. He went down screaming. And it was almost his end. He nearly fainted with the agony. He nearly gave up, nearly decided a knife drawing deep lines into his throat or poking slits into his heart would be a welcome end to this horrible dream.

But because his sprawled arm, the good arm, hit a heavy object, he did not quit, did not succumb like a helpless newborn.

He reached out and grasped the object, recognizing it by its heft and feel, remembering how he'd felt it earlier this very evening.

He scrambled awkwardly to his feet and spun.

Uttering an angry half-screaming curse . . .

. . . the ghostly light to his back . . .

. . . he raised Laren's tire tool over his head . . . his wet face glistening . . .

. . . and instead of backing away . . .

347

. . . he advanced a step . . .

. . . toward the figure with the knife.

The Lurker's reaction answered every question Dewey
had harbored about this whole mess.

The Lurker dropped the knife and recoiled against
the wall with a gasp.

And Dewey finally understood.

He knew this Lurker was Darwin.

He knew the blood pouring wetly down his face
moments ago had reminded Darwin of Slime's face
those years ago.

He knew that raising the tire tool had raised a
horrifying specter for Darwin – the vision of that
hammer.

Now Darwin was reliving the terror he'd suffered as
barely more than an innocent child. The fear that had
snapped him in the first place had snapped him again.

Now, to Darwin, Dewey had become Slime.

And Darwin was no longer the Lurker.

He was Darwin.

Just a helpless kid.

Darwin felt all the turbulent emotions. Again. He
couldn't believe Slime could have survived the first
killing. But he *must* have. Because here he was again,
his face bloody, his weapon raised to strike.

Again.

Why didn't he die?

The first blow should have done it. Darwin had
swung the board fiercely, full of fury at the assault on
his friend and at the guilt for the gratification the
attack gave him.

When the two-by-four struck Slime, Darwin felt the
crunch of bone relayed from the skull back up the wood

348

into his grip. But one blow had not been enough for him. He turned the wood in his hands and brought the splintered end down into the exposed neck. Then he started pounding from the back of the head down the neck and across the back and back up into the face, even though it was clear no life remained in the beast they had called Slime.

Still Darwin kept killing what was already dead.

It was not merely that he would ensure this death before tending to his wounded, battered, abused friend.

It was that he had not yet fully expended his first orgasm. And only when he was exhausted sexually did he collapse and begin to cry.

Dewey watched the frozen boy. He remembered the story and knew what to do if he wanted.

But should he?

Should he play it out?

He took another threatening step.

Darwin launched himself up the stairs.

Dewey thought of Matt. Erica. Laren.

And he took off staggering, the tire tool still raised, his footsteps clumping on the stairs.

23

Laren had heard the rumbling of bodies, the pounding of feet, the cries of pain upstairs. She could not hoist herself out of the grave, so she began raking dirt down. Greedily, she pulled the loose, putrid dirt down, raising dust, choking herself, blinding herself. But still she pulled it down, first by the handfuls and then, as the mound at her feet grew, she scooped it in with her arms.

Until she could stand tall enough to raise a knee and roll away from the hole.

The reflected light from upstairs lit her way. She climbed slowly, then, as feet clomped directly over her head on the way upstairs, she realized she could go on without stealth. The pistol lay on a step halfway down. She picked it up and ran up to the parlor.

Upstairs on the second floor, the footsteps were still moving. One set was running, a second set was tramping unsteadily.

Dewey must still be alive.

She grabbed the flashlight and ran up after him, stepping around pools of blood, following a trail of blood spatters.

But the second floor hallway was empty too.

From hearing the story, she knew where the bedroom was, the one where Sherman and Darwin had gone. The light beam pointed the way, the pistol prepared to send bullets down the beam, and she began advancing on the bedroom door, hoping Dewey would not burst out and get shot.

She heard the bashing inside the room at the end of the hall. Her heart stopped momentarily. Somebody must be getting killed. There were instant tears.

'Ted,' she whined and broke into a run.

Before she'd gotten a few strides down the hall, a door opened in front of her, blocking her path.

She stopped. Thought about bolting. Then poked a pistol at the closet. Then, in the dim light, she saw.

Her reactions were rapid: horror, grief, relief.

A rope hung from the closet pole, and at the end of the rope was a noose.

In the noose was the neck of the Dewey boy, Matt.

But his eyes were open, and his feet were on the floor.

His hands had been tied behind his back, and he had been tethered here to wait, to bait, to make noise that would draw them past the Lurker in the basement to the upstairs.

Laren's decision was no decision at all.

If there were only to be one survivor to this satanic scenario, it was going to be the wide-eyed, black-eyed frightened boy.

She put down the pistol and loosened the noose, slipping the rope over his ears.

He winced in pain.

But she knew he'd survive that.

She scooped him up and ran back down the stairs, kicked open the front door and continued running across the porch, down the yard to the dirt street.

24

Dewey bashed at the closet door handle and at the wood panels, sending flakes of paint like snow.

The more he bashed, the greater his rage became. The greater his rage, the less he felt the pain in his disabled arm. The less he felt the pain, the less sure he was that he had control of himself. Kill him, said the cool voice inside him, stoking the fire in his head.

If Darwin had suffered a flashback to the terrible moments of that night years ago, what had he, Dewey, become?

Was he now Slime?

Was he the demented beast?

Would he kill this boy? He was, after all, still a kid.

Would he go on and be the depraved one?

Could he stop what he was doing?

Did he want to stop?

Instead of pausing to answer the questions racing through his pain-racked mind, he delivered a stinging, crushing blow to the doorknob.

He saw it give. Part of the door panel and the knob fell into the closet and a body slumped into the back of the enclosure – he heard it.

He stuck the socket of the tire tool into the splintered hole where the knob had been and yanked the door open.

Darwin was at the back of the closet.

His back was to Dewey.

He was tearing his way into the wall, into the patched hole Dewey knew was there.

He yanked out a piece of the patch and turned.

Kill him, said the voice.

'No,' said Dewey.

He relaxed.

He could not do it, could not kill.

He laughed in relief that he could not murder this pathetic, demented boy, could not blame him for the murder of Erica.

He lowered the tire tool.

But Darwin shrank away. For him the dream was not over.

Dewey reached in with the tire tool. He had intended to grab a piece of the shirt front and tug the terrified kid out of the closet – he had no good hand free to do it, and he didn't trust the boy enough to drop the tire tool.

But Darwin took the move as a threatening one.

He grabbed the tire tool and the hand.

Dewey pulled back.

There followed a frantic tug of war.

Darwin clamped down on the tire tool and Dewey's wrist and yanked.

Dewey went along, his broken arm flapping again, unable to give him any purchase or balance.

He went into the closet with the boy.

And he went through the back of the closet.

Through the hole.

Into the dank, musty, stuffy darkness of the attic.

Screaming as his broken arm caught on the edge of the hole.

Then through the patched ceiling.

Through the empty air of the parlor.

To the floor below.

25

Dewey realized he was still screaming, half in agony, half in rage and surprise.

He jerked on the tire tool.

But Darwin was no longer holding it.

Darwin had been knocked unconscious by the fall, by Dewey landing on him.

He lay limp, relaxed, finally at peace.

Dewey remembered.

Darwin had recollected being at peace two years ago. He had wanted to die, to cheat Slime of the pleasure of killing him. They had gone the distance, gone full circle.

And they had ended up where it began.

Dewey shook his head.

Then he saw it.

The skull.

Then the skeleton – the skeleton with dried jerky stretched across the bone. In places, the jerky was stretched so tight the bones could be seen in the gaps of dried skin. Almost everywhere the bones were broken. The facial bones of the skull had been battered into an enormous, splintered, toothless smile.

Dewey knew it was the skeleton of Slime, the man who'd had no name. The man who'd killed his daughter.

And lying limp, barely breathing beneath him, was the Lurker. Darwin. Darwin, the killer of those other people.

Dewey raised the tire tool.

It would make no difference now.

Another bash in the skull would end it all.

There would be no more terror, no more lurking.

There would be no more demons to haunt Dewey.

He started down with the blow.

Laren screamed for him to stop. 'Ted . . . No!'

She was in the doorway.

'Darling, PLEASE NO!'

But she could not stop the downward fall of the tire tool.

The skull gave.

It flew apart into dried crackling pieces like a china vase, teeth and concave bones rattling across the parlor floor.

'I thought . . .' she murmured, 'I thought you were going to kill the boy. I found Matt.'

'Matt?'

'He's safe. I locked him in your car. I had to come back . . . for you.'

Dewey pointed to the skeleton. 'Free at last,' he said. 'This was Slime.' He said it as he would an introduction. She seemed to understand.

He was freed of his demons. He knew Slime, not Darwin, had killed Erica. Now Erica had been properly buried. And Slime had been served his revenge.

She went to him and touched him.

He recoiled.

There was a mask of drying blood on his face, the parted lips of the gash on his forehead. He knew it must be repulsive.

There was the filth from below and the stuffing from the attic insulation sticking in the glue of his blood.

And there was the battered arm that would probably never heal right, hanging unnaturally askew.

She put her hands to her mouth.

'Can I help you? I'm afraid to touch –'

'Matt,' he said. 'Bring Matt to me.'

He struggled to his feet, leaving the tire tool on the floor.

'Yes.'

'Now . . . please, Laren.'

'Ted . . . I *do* love you.'

'Laren –'

'I know. I don't have to say it. But I realize I do, I do.'

She turned and ran out onto the porch.

He walked to the door.

'Come back,' he whispered tearfully. He wanted her back. He wanted to start again. Maybe it wasn't such a good idea for his son to see him like this. And he must tell her he . . . well, he probably did love her, but not like Matt. Not like Theresa. Now that he had freed himself from his vengeance, maybe he could become a whole man again. Maybe he could put his family back together. Or maybe he couldn't. Maybe Theresa wouldn't have him. But he wanted to try. He wanted to tell Laren he loved her but he didn't love her enough. Not enough to give up Theresa and Matt. Not now. Not now that he had been emancipated.

'Come back,' he said. But his voice was weak, and she was already at the street, watching the police cars come roaring up the dirt road.

26

Laren got to the street, saw the cars, and realized she could never bring that child back up here. Dewey would have to be cleaned up, too. Otherwise, he'd scare the boy to death.

She started back up the walk.

There he stood, braced against the doorway.

Ted Dewey, middle-aged crazy man. The man she said she loved. The *only* man. She'd never told her father. She'd never moaned it to a lover. She'd always loved herself more.

But she had told him.

And now she wished she hadn't.

Already.

She felt so ... vulnerable. Did the admission of loving do that? If so, could she stand the vulnerable nakedness of her emotions?

She wanted to change her mind, to bring up the emotion of the moment as an excuse for her utterance.

He was smiling, she could see, as she approached.

Poor man. He had been hurt so. And the smile through the blood mask looked more like pain and surprise.

Perhaps it was surprise. After all, she *had* told him she loved him. And now she would be telling him worse. The desperate words were meant only to keep him from killing that boy, for ... what? What had she done?

She searched for the proper words to weasel out of the commitment her words had trapped her into.

But she didn't need the words.

At the porch she opened her mouth.

Dewey opened his mouth.

Probably to tell her he loved her, she thought.

But it wasn't that.

'Theresa,' he said. 'I didn't kill him.' Strangely garbled. 'He killed me.'

'Ted, you're talking nonsense.'

'I love you . . .'

She shuddered violently.

'Theresa, I love you.'

And he toppled forward, an emancipated, painful smile painted onto his death mask, an exhalation of relief sounding from his mouth.

When he hit the boards – that was when she saw the tire tool sticking from the hollow where the neck meets the base of the skull, the pointed end buried somewhere up into the brain.

From the back, his oversized ears looked ridiculous to her. It was an awful last thought to have of the only man in the world who'd ever heard her say she loved him.

She screamed. It was as much in desperate anger at her own coldness as in horror of what had happened.

And shuddering continually – as if she would never be able to stop – she backed away, then ran away from the presence she felt inside the house.

The police found her cringing in the yard, her blouse caught on a rusted nail in the fence. By then she'd screamed herself hoarse.

They searched the house. Found nothing but Ted's body on the porch and a pile of bones on the floor. No Lurker. No Darwin.

The ambulance took her away.

Still screaming. In hoarse whispers.

'Ted,' she shrilled, 'I love you, Ted . . . Goddamn, Ted . . . I love you, I really do.'

Over and over.

One ambulance attendant looked at the other and twirled a finger beside his ear.

'I love you, Ted.'

Over and over.

Epilogue

The wind was hot and damp, barely enough to blow the sweat off her body.

She could have driven with the glass up and the air on. But she wanted to feel, to taste, to smell Arkansas.

She wanted back to nature, her nature, her beginnings.

Perhaps, she thought, if she started again, took another run at life – maybe in another line of work, maybe with another group of people . . .

No, that was not the problem.

The problem was her. The problem was Laren. She had to rehab Laren . . . that was the mission. The stay at the . . . resort had helped her deal with her guilt. Now she was on her own to begin dealing with herself.

Maybe she could try her second run with a different personality, a different outlook. Maybe she could begin to consider others before herself. Maybe if she started all over she could learn to love.

Maybe she could even learn to stop the shuddering that had accompanied her back to Arkansas.

Probably not.

But she could try.

The trunk of her car was packed tightly.

But her load had not completely settled.

And when she got off the interstate, the patches in the asphalt made it a rougher ride for the shifting contents of the back seat. So the contents moved about.

As if trying to get comfortable.